Stories of Enchantment from Nineteenth-Century Spain

Other Bucknell University Press Books
Translated from the Spanish by Robert M. Fedorchek

- Palacio Valdés, Armando. *Alone and Other Stories*. 1993.
- Pardo Bazán, Emilia. *The White Horse and Other Stories*. 1993.
- Picón, Jacinto Octavio. *Moral Divorce and Other Stories*. 1995. In collaboration with Pedro S. Rivas Díaz. Introduction by Gonzalo Sobejano.
- Bécquer, Gustavo Adolfo. *Legends and Letters*. 1995. Introduction by Rubén Benítez. Drawings by Jane Sutherland.
- Alarcón, Pedro Antonio de. *The Nail and Other Stories*. 1997. Introduction by Cyrus C. DeCoster.
- Caballero, Fernán, Antonio de Trueba, and Pedro Antonio de Alarcón. *Death and the Doctor: Three Nineteenth-Century Spanish Tales*. A Bilingual Edition. 1997. Introduction by Lou Charnon-Deutsch.
- Alarcón, Pedro Antonio de. *The Nun and Other Stories*. 1999. Introduction by Stephen Miller.
- Alas, Leopoldo, Clarín. *Ten Tales*. 2000. Introduction by John W. Kronik.
- Picón, Jacinto Octavio. *Sweet and Delectable*. 2000. Introduction by Noël Valis.

Stories of Enchantment from Nineteenth-Century Spain

Translated from the Spanish by
Robert M. Fedorchek

Introduction by
Alan E. Smith

Lewisburg
Bucknell University Press
London: Associated University Presses

Associated University Presses
2010 Eastpark Boulevard
Cranbury, NJ 08512

Associated University Presses
16 Barter Street
London WC1A 2AH, England

Associated University Presses
P.O. Box 338, Port Credit
Mississauga, Ontario
Canada L5G 4L8

The paper used in this publication meets the requirements of the American National Standard for Permanence of Paper for Printed Library Materials Z39.48-1984.

Library of Congress Cataloging-in-Publication Data

Stories of enchantment from nineteenth-century Spain / translated from the Spanish by Robert M. Fedorchek.
    p, cm.
    Includes bibliographical references.
    ISBN 0-8387-5533-X (alk. paper)
    1. Fantasy fiction, Spanish. 2. Spanish fiction—19th century. 3. Short stories, Spanish. I. Fedorchek, Robert M., 1938–

PQ6256.F35 S76 2002
863'.087660805—dc21

              2002021541

PRINTED IN THE UNITED STATES OF AMERICA

In memoriam

Ruth Pierson Fedorchek
1942–1979

Contents

Translator's Preface   9
Introduction: Word Stories
        Alan E. Smith   11

Fernán Caballero   35
• "The Wishes"   36
• "The Girl with Three Husbands"   39
• "Lovely-Flower"   42

Antonio de Trueba   47
• "The Adventures of a Tailor"   48
• "The King's Son-in-Law"   59

Juan Eugenio Hartzenbusch   73
• "Beauty as Punishment"   74

Luis Coloma, SJ   83
• "Green Bird"   84
• "Pérez the Mouse"   96

Gustavo Adolfo Bécquer   107
• "Believe in God"   108
• "The Devil's Cross"   119

Pedro Antonio de Alarcón   133
• "Death's Friend"   134

Juan Valera   189
• "The Green Bird"   190
• "The Wizard"   212

Benito Pérez Galdós   235
• "The Mule and the Ox"   236
• "The Princess and the Street Urchin"   248

Leopoldo Alas, Clarín   265
- "My Funeral"   266
- "Socrates' Rooster"   274

Notes   279
Select Bibliography   281

Translator's Preface

THERE WERE NO BROTHERS GRIMM IN NINETEENTH-CENTURY SPAIN, NO CHARLES
Perrault, no Hans Christian Andersen, no latter-day Angela Carter, but
fairy tales and folktales and wonder tales there were. Stories of
Enchantment. And in the broadest sense of enchantment—that which
tells of a marvel, that which goes beyond the extrasensory, that which
upends our sense of reality—this book contains tales after the manner
of the brothers Grimm, Charles Perrault, Hans Christian Andersen,
and the latter-day Angela Carter.

Their magic, or their appeal to the supernatural, exerted pull on
authors as dissimilar as Fernán Caballero and Antonio de Trueba, on
the one hand, and Benito Pérez Galdós and Leopoldo Alas, Clarín, on
the other. As a vehicle—whether as a morality tale, a story for children,
or a stylistic technique—stories of enchantment served different ends.
Fernán Caballero and Antonio de Trueba culled their stories from the
oral tradition, and some of them are, properly speaking, morality tales,
while others are fairy tales, like those of the Grimms and Perrault,
whereas much of what Luis Coloma wrote was specifically intended
for children, patterned either after the Grimms or after stories with
a didactic twist and a religious end. Juan Eugenio Hartzenbusch also
looked to the popular tradition for his stories and tales, a number
of which, like those of Coloma, are intended to edify and instruct.
Virtually all of Gustavo Adolfo Bécquer's legends are tales of enchantment and wonder that sweep the reader along the path of fantasy and
chimerical—that is, marvelous—occurrences, and the aerial journey
made through time by Death and his "friend" in Alarcón's "Death's
Friend" can be seen as another marvelous occurrence, one that represents the culmination of the Godfather-Death theme. Juan Valera,
with mystery and history, reminds us of *The Arabian Nights*; Galdós,
with flights of fancy, draws us into the magic world of children's
fantasies; and Clarín, with his suspension of reality, parades a talking

dead man and then comes close to a fable, albeit a mordant one, with a talking rooster.

A number of the original texts used for the translations that comprise this volume, as well as some of the secondary sources, are difficult to come by, and I am pleased to acknowledge the generous assistance of my friend and colleague Bob Webster, who procured them for me.

And I am very grateful to Alan Smith of Boston University, a noted scholar of nineteenth-century Spanish literature, for writing the introduction to these stories of enchantment from nineteenth-century Spain.

Words and passages marked with an asterisk (*) in the text are explained in the notes section at the back of the book.

Antonio de Trueba's "The Adventures of a Tailor" and Juan Valera's "The Green Bird" first appeared in *Marvels & Tales: Journal of Fairy-Tale Studies* (12, no. 2 [1998]: 351–63 and 13, no. 2 [1999]: 211–33, respectively) published by Wayne State University Press in Detroit, Michigan.

Alan E. Smith

Introduction:
Word Stories

This collection is representative of the evolution in nineteenth-century Spain of the story of unnatural events, from the transcribed oral tale (Fernán Caballero) to the modern fantastic short story (Alarcón, Clarín), though even these, as we will see, are not entirely free of the oral accent. Mariano Baquero Goyanes reminds us: "[T]he story, initially part of myth, with ancient beliefs and centuries-old traditions, became a literary expression in the nineteenth century, and is thus the strangest and most paradoxical of genres: perhaps, the most ancient and at once the one that took the longest to reach literary form" (1992, 3).[1] And he adds, "one thing was to *tell* tales, and another to *write* them, as personally and originally as the novel" (3), a dialectic that will condition the story in the century of the novel.

Andrew Lang noted in Grimms' *Fairy Tales* that "everything yields to the spell of magical rhymes or incantations" (1962, 904). These Spanish stories, which the English-language reader now has in hand, thanks to Professor Fedorchek's fine translations, all partake—though in varying degrees—of that power of incantation, and are therefore quite appropriately named in this collection, *Stories of Enchantment*, for it is not just a curiosity of etymology that links enchantment to incantation and both to chant. These nineteenth-century Spanish stories share the same genealogy, the folktale, born from the same rhythms of meaning in the collective imagination of humanity. "Enchantment," then, has to do with being in or suffering the effects of a chant, which is a song, often of public character, and even of religious nature. The folktale, moving to ancient rhythms, takes one back (as Miguel de Unamuno says) from the sea to the fountain, the birthplace not only of the individual, but also of the collective, spirit. Though not generally religious, folktales do serve to bind us together, even as the original associations of the word "religion" suggests (*religare*, to tie).

11

The Spanish word *cuento* may be translated both as story and as tale, and it shares with the latter a remarkable characteristic. Both words, *cuento* and "tale" (like the French *conte-compte* and the German *erzählen-zählen*), have etymological links to "tally," to counting numbers (*contar* and *compter-conter* are derived from the Latin *computare*), like the English verb "recount," with its two meanings, or the noun "teller" (one behind the bank window, the other telling a story). This bivalence seems to point to the strict sequence of events in the folktale, akin to counting, in which one event necessarily follows another. This characteristic, already observed by Vladimir Propp, in his foundational *Morphology of the Folk Tale* (1923),[2] is so universal that it must give us pause: it is as if part of the magic spell of these tales, part of their incantational and enchanting power, is not only the characters and their specific adventures, but the consistent fulfillment of expectation, as strictly as 3 follows 2 and precedes 4. In short, these stories take us where we have already been, and where we return as we hear or read these primordial sequences: a common place, a place of origin and recognition. Perhaps that is why children love to hear these stories, and why they very justly protest mightily if the story sequence is changed by as much as a hair on the head of a fairy. But the English work "tale" points to another essential aspect of the folktale: it is or was originally "told," that is, spoken.

TELLING, WOMEN, AND THE HEARTH

It is fitting that the first Spanish author to strive to record the folktale, with modern criteria (that is, since, and including, romanticism) of rescuing a vanishing cultural treasure, was a woman who published her work under a man's name: Cecilia Böhl de Faber, Fernán Caballero. If, until recently, publishing one's writing was mostly the activity of men, telling marvelous stories was done often, characteristically, by women. So much was this the case that women gave the name of their gender to a genre: "old wives' tales" in English, *cuentos de viejas tras el fuego* in Spanish ("old women's tales told by the fire"). This association, centuries old in the written record of Spanish, was referred to in the important seventeenth-century dictionary of Corominas: "[O]ld women, when they entertain the children, telling them tales, say that a nymph with a gold band in her hand, does marvelous things . . ." (quoted in Chevalier 1978, 29). And Cervantes, in the "False Marriage," avers: "And what you think are prophecies are only old wives' tales, like the one of the headless horse and the magic wand, with which they pass the time by the fire on long winter nights" (quoted in Chevalier 1978, 29–30).

Many of the fundamental collections of folktales of the nineteenth century avow the womanly origin of their stories. None other than the brothers Grimm attest to their indebtedness to women's speech, specifically to "Wilhelm's wife, who had heard many of them from her old nurse, and to the wife of a cattle farmer whose memory for details was exact and whose repertoire was unlimited" (Untermeyer 1962, vii). The reader will notice references to this origin in women's speech in some of the stories in this collection. Gertrudis Gómez de Avellaneda, another prominent woman author of the first half of the nineteenth century, actually puts herself in the role of the old wife by the fire: "Upon taking pen in hand in order to write this simple legend of old," she says, "it's impossible to preserve all the magic of its simplicity, and to give it that vivid interest with which my benevolent readers would welcome it . . . if, instead of offering it in the common form of a novel [she was actually referring to a short story], I could tell it to you by the fireplace on a cold, long, December night" (quoted in Baquero Goyanes 1992, 7). Antonio de Trueba, one of the authors included in this anthology, makes the following representative attribution, in his collection *Tales of Several Colors* [Cuentos de varios colores] (1866):

> More than thirty years ago my mother told me the story I call "The Beam of the Scaffold," almost as I have told it, and she probably heard it from her mother, toward the last third of the eighteenth century. The one titled "The Adventures of a Tailor" was told to me two years ago by a girl from Biscay, who told me she had heard it from her grandmother. . . . (quoted in Baquero Goyanes 1992, 70)

Pedro Antonio de Alarcón, author of the remarkable story included in this collection, noted, in a review of Poe's tales, that such narrative discourse "is a child of the Middle Ages, and forms part of *catholic mythology* [*sic*], understood as all that is purely imaginative, which sanctimonious women during hundreds of years told by the light of the fire, during December nights" (quoted in Amores 1997, 101).

The documentary evidence that attributes an important role to women in the oral transmission of folktales is abundant, and, as is manifest in the Spanish phrase *cuentos de viejas tras el fuego*, suggests certain analogies among the three basic elements: women, fire, story. First, the story is not infrequently associated with a long December night. The fire, during this symbolically dangerous solstice, draws the group together, fulfilling a physical need for banding together against the cold and the dark, which symbolically suggests the other need, to come together emotionally in this time of natural retrenchment, which intimates death. Women's proximity to fire, in that age-old phrase, points to her relation to the hearth, and thus to the heat and nourishment that all human beings associate with their first home, the womb; if a dream is a private myth, and a myth a public dream, as Joseph Campbell expresses it,[3] then the marvelous tale, which shares the same stories and sequences with myth, is likewise a publicly shared collective dream, at once a matrix of the imagination, and of memory.

These stories are an astonishing collective act of remembering, and their frequent association with women seems to resonate in the words of Catherine Clément: "Both [Freud and Michelet] thought that the repressed past survives in woman . . . woman, more than anyone else, is dedicated to reminiscence. The sorceress, who in the end is able to dream Nature and therefore to conceive it, incarnates the reinscription of the traces of paganism that triumphant Christianity repressed" (Clément and Cixous 1986, 5). Akin to the sorceress is the old wife telling tales by the flame of the hearth. Not coincidentally, the figure of the old woman and the hearth appears not only as the medium of the tales, the teller, but also as subject of the tales: the wise or dreadful old woman in the forest, one of whom appears in Trueba's version of the Little Tailor. Both the dreadful and the benevolent Yaga, to use Propp's term for that old woman (1983, 63), fulfill the same function of making possible the hero's survival. It is the function also of these old wives through their telling, for they have made possible the survival of that heroic archetype's journey through the space and time of the collective imagination itself. Because these stories were uttered from outside the sphere of political power—and this seems to me to be one of the important points of their historical association with women— their identity has maintained a primordial quality, in the face of changing ideologies and fashions of discourse. Upon emerging into the world of print, this oral stream was soaked up by the plains of convention, but it fertilized them, and undercut as well many a shaky monument.

The Amphibian Nineteenth Century

Folktales had been put into writing for centuries, of course. One only need remember such collections as the *Thousand and One Nights*, or, in Spain, *The Conde Lucanor*, so richly leavened by the popular imagination, as well as some very interesting sixteenth-century compilations, such as *El sobremesa*, by Juan Timoneda, or the *Floresta española*, by Melchor de Santa Cruze (Chevalier 1978, 14). The difference between all previous written and published collections, and those of the nineteenth century in Europe and in Spain is that the latter had a specific, scientific, self-conscious purpose: to come to a deeper understanding of the "authentic" identity of the various European peoples. The surprise, of course, was that when, owing to publication, these stories began to be compared, they were all essentially the same: the *Volkgeist* really was the *Menschengeist*. But there was another distinguishing characteristic of the publication of tales of the supernatural, beginning with the romantic movement: they appeared after the scientific and reasonable eighteenth century, and continued to be published during the scientific and reasonable nineteenth century, as part of the fundamental *other discourse* of the unreasonable and the mythopoetic, which, to a degree, filled the lack left by a chilling loss of faith. The French romantic Charles Nodier, himself an author of fantastic stories, documents for us that hunger for food for the soul that the marvelous discourse satisfied:

> The fantastic . . . demands a virginity of imagination and beliefs that derived literatures lack, and that are not reproduced in it [literature] except after revolutions whose passing renews everything; but then, and when religions themselves, shocked to their foundations no longer speak to the imagination, or offer it but confused notions more and more blurred by a restless skepticism, it is necessary that this faculty for producing the marvelous with which nature has endowed it, should exercise itself on a more common creative genre, and more appropriate for the needs of a materially inclined intelligence. (1972, 209)

From a conservative perspective as well, the spiritual value of these tales was recognized. Fernán Caballero, daughter of J. N. Böhl de Faber, an early theorist of romanticism in Spain, was, like her revered father, an extremely conservative writer, who could say in a letter that a certain French writer, "a ridiculous caricature of Voltaire," makes "all noble souls break out in divine religious fire" (1912, 31). In another letter, she reports that, working on her father's papers, she "stayed up till ten, copying the magnificent passage of genuine and lofty orthodoxy, so necessary in our times of confusion . . . of ideas and things" (10). It was, therefore, in order to counteract the pernicious influence of modern literature that she puts the stories to paper, as she writes in a letter as late as 1866: ". . . I am working on the second volume of folk stories and poems [*cuentos y poesía populares*] so that these things, which are so quickly replaced by translated novels and imitations of penny dreadfuls, . . . may not be lost for ever" (170).

Folktales began to appear in print, and, specifically, in newspapers, with increasing frequency in nineteenth-century Spain. In Madrid alone, in 1843 there were approximately eighty-five newspapers and magazines (Baquero Goyanes 1992, 4 n. 5), and as María Montserrat Trancón Lagunas informs us, in that city "between 1818 and 1868, more than three hundred stories are to be found disseminated in the pages of numerous magazines and newspapers" (1997, 21). Fernán Caballero, Alarcón, Bécquer, Galdós, Valera, Pardo Bazán—all published their stories in newspapers. The practice was then to publish them later in collections in book form, as Galdós did, for example, with both of the stories in this anthology. As the century closed, Clarín notes, in an article of 1892, titled "The Press," "the fashion of the story extended to all the Madrid press" (quoted in Baquero Goyanes 1992, 5).

What can we make of this change of medium, and how does it affect the "message"? The oral tale has countless midwives, but no recognized parent; countless tellers, but no individual creator. The fact of its survival bespeaks its universal appeal: or to put it another way, it survives as a communal story, because it tells the story of all of us, giving voice to the stuff of our unconscious being and elaborating a public consciousness (and conscience).

The modern authored story, on the other hand, does not have to run the gauntlet of long time in order to reach a broad audience. Whether it is then forgotten or not is another, if related, question. In other words, it does not rely on collective recognition for its publication. It does not have to bear within it a collectively recognized sequence of events, or even characters. Within certain constraints, it only has to appeal to an individual publisher or editor. On the surface, therefore, it is obviously a more personal statement, the relatively less mediated statement of an individual. Even Hans Christian Andersen, though "he delighted in recasting myths" (Conroy 1980, xxxiii), has stated, "most of what I have written is a reflection of myself" (quoted in Rossel 1980, xxvi). On the other hand, as we shall see, the authored fantastic story could become a vehicle for dissent in the public sphere.

THE MARVELOUS, THE FANTASTIC

One would expect that stories written for publication manifest, therefore, a tension between tradition and originality, and between the expression of the author's personal, individual concerns and the collective imagination, which not only informs the genre of the story but is also part and parcel of any individual imagination. The marvelous has already been partially characterized in the beginning of these observations, when we considered enchantment. It, like enchantment, is a collectively sympathetic worldview, instead of an individual, or original, utterance. Further, the marvelous is in storytelling, the representation of a world that breaks the laws of nature, as we know, but whose unnatural physical laws are the same for all the characters: for the hero and for all the other characters and things. The hero is part of the invented nature, and accepts and has a place in its continuum.

On the other hand, the fantastic discourse, as has often been noticed, is the expression of a system that is divided, rent asunder. Not only, as Todorov has seen (1970, 29–30), is there an ambiguity in interpreting events on the part of the hero and the reader (is the creaking door pushed by the wind, or . . . ?), but we see in that ambiguity and breaking of the system a related and fundamental characteristic of the fantastic: the isolation of the hero, bordering on the radical solitude of the madman. The fantastic, therefore, is characterized by two conditions: ambiguity and isolation. The marvelous is just the opposite: it is characterized by community and an unambiguous, consistent system of nature, which is supernatural only from the point of view of the reader, or listener, but not from that of the characters, as quite at home with talking crows as we are with talking parrots.

STORIES OF COMMUNITY

In view of these considerations, therefore, we shall address first the works of Fernán Caballero, Antonio de Trueba, Juan Eugenio Hartzenbush, and Luis Coloma, which form a group of tales close to the folktale and are, generally, conservative in ideology, as well as the much more individualistic example of literary fictions of Juan Eugenio Hartzenbush and Juan Valera, which, while further removed from the oral tradition—but not, of course, free of its heritage—are nonetheless stories of resolution and community.

Cecilia Böhl de Faber (1796–1877), who published and intermittently signed letters as Fernán Caballero, is considered the most important precursor of the realist novel in Spain, a reputation particularly maintained on the merits of her still-romantic novel of rural manners,

The Seagull [La gaviota] (1849). But she has greater claim to our attention here as a pioneer, in Spanish letters, in collecting oral tales, and publishing them, in an idiom relatively unmediated by literary retouching.

All three of her stories published in this collection are examples of the folk tradition, alloyed to the conservative ideology of its "scribe." "The Three Wishes" is a barely modified folktale, with an explicit moral. But when we realize that what the old peasant couple have wished for is material advancement (a larger house, a better animal of burden), one can understand not only its anticapitalist vision but also its message favoring the status quo for the peasant class; as its ending sentence maintains: "People who possess things are rich, but people who wish for nothing are happy." "The Girl with Three Husbands" is a story based on that magic number. Not only are the suitors three, but three are the gifts that make the happy ending possible. However, all three gifts are proffered by one and the same donor, a "little old man," a typical folk character, who aids the plural hero with his gift. This situation leads to the interesting conundrum of a girl with three husbands, an impasse left unresolved by the truncated ending. "Lovely-Flower" also has many folk elements: the tasks imposed upon the hero, which he fulfills and (though without realizing it at the time) which will help him gain the hand of the lovely heroine; the good deeds done to humans and animals, which eventually result in their help; and the wise giver, again—in this case, of a remarkable horse. In this story as well, harmony is restored as a community is upheld by a joyous marriage.

Antonio de Trueba (1819–89) also collected and published many a tale, but, unlike Fernán Caballero, did not aspire to transcribe the oral tradition so faithfully; rather, he wished to give it the proper literary form. In the prologue to his collection *Tales of Several Colors* (1866), which included "The Adventures of a Tailor," and from which we have already cited, he remarks, a bit painfully: "The stories that roll about in the countryside are pebbles, that are worth very little, if not dressed with a good sauce" (quoted in Baquero Goyanes 1992, 71).

"The Adventures of a Tailor" is, according to Trueba himself in the aforementioned prologue, very similar to the Grimms' famous story, "The Brave Little Tailor," though there are also important differences. Perhaps the most notable is in its style and tenor, its "polishing" of the rustic pebble by the litterateur, as was his expressed purpose. These stylistic flourishes may be divided in two groups: the addition of a psychological touch in the (romantic) love interest, and the folding-in of a sociopolitical commentary, which is shared implicitly by Fernán and Coloma.

There is no mention in *Grimms'* of the little hero's amorous interest that we see in Trueba's story: "The little tailor arrived at court and, while visiting the palace gardens, saw the princess leaning out the window. 'Good Lord!' he exclaimed. 'What a lovely girl.' And he gazed at her as if fascinated until the princess withdrew." And then in Trueba we have the innocent spice (one would have to choose cinnamon) of a "romantic" flirtation: "As he spoke the little tailor did not take his eyes off the princess, a fact that was not lost on the king." She looks back. There is, in fact, in *Grimms'* no mention of the princess until the king imposes the three tasks on our tailor, nor does he see her until after the trials are surpassed. Far from making eyes at the tailor, Grimms' princess, once married, tries to get rid of her plebeian husband, but fails. The addition of the more detailed amorous interest in Trueba's rewriting is characteristic of the romantic interest in personality, which is not as important in the folktale.

Nor can Trueba resist interjecting political commentaries in his story. After the first trial, for example, Trueba's king makes mention of a very nineteenth-century institution indeed: "The secret police have informed me that the people are grumbling." When the king uses the same pretext again for not granting his promise, the little tailor blurts out: "Not the people again! There's nothing that irks me more than these shamefaced kings who don't dare to be absolute or constitutional. All this concern about the people! The people approve of what's fair."

These stories reflect the political situation in Spain just two years before the convulsion of the revolution of September 1868, which dethroned Isabel II and set off a historical shuddering that would lead to a constitutional monarchy and a republic, before the fateful restoration of 1874. It is within this context that we hear the warning tone in the narrator's comments: "The rascal of a king still tried to avoid keeping his sacred promise, but the people rebelled in view of such villainy. . . ." And the final words ring with an injunction that the reckless queen might have done well to heed: "*nowadays* [emphasis mine] to take a crown it is not enough to have a right to it: it is also necessary to make oneself worthy of taking it by dint of ingenuity and effort." This sort of not too subtle political reference is in keeping with Trueba's general moral and ideological purpose: in "Tragaldabas," a story with the same folktale origins as Alarcón's "Death's Friend," also in this collection, the hero says to the monarch, whose life he has just saved: "Does your highness think that I don't know what ails the kings? What ails the kings are all those hangers-on they carry with them." To which the king answers, "And the darndest thing is that we the kings and the people are limping while those ones are skipping right along" (quoted in Amores 1997, 96).

"The King's Son-in-Law," a story full of folk and mythic motifs (the lost baby, who is put in a small vessel in the river; the hero who helps various people, who in turn help him, and who marries a princess), also evidences political concerns, as is already clear in the beginning paragraph: "There once lived a king who was so avaricious that, instead of spending his life engaged in making his vassals happy, he spent it crisscrossing his kingdom in search of gold and silver mines, leaving the devil at the rudder of the ship of state. A curse on such kings!" Actually, this initial paragraph also contains two motifs that recur throughout the story: gold (with the echo of the Midas myth), and a sometimes felicitous, or ferocious, punning on the devil, a character in the story.

Closer to Trueba in tone than to his avowed model, Fernán Caballero, Father Luis Coloma (1851–1914) is best known for his novel *Trifles* [Pequeñeces] (1890), a conservative thesis novel, which became a best-seller immediately. However, his short stories had already begun to appear in the early 1880s in a Jesuit journal, *El mensajero del corazón de Jesús*. Compared to Fernán Caballero, there are in his stories at times a rougher, almost naturalistic, edge, in addition to a certain mundane humor (or *boutades*, as Trueba might have called them sympathetically).

Of the two stories included in this collection, "Green Bird" is clearly closer to the folktales that, as the author informs his readers, he had heard from his housekeeper (quoted in Baquero Goyanes, 1992, 82). In it we see a combination of the Cinderella motif, with an adventure story of the hero's voyage of initiation, and a victorious outcome. "Pérez the Mouse" is a more original foray into the medium of print, though it, too, is firmly within the integrity and communal world of the marvelous tale. Nonetheless, there are various references to contemporary Madrid, including the mention of specific shops and celebrities, which are a reminder of the story's applicability of the message of Christian charity as a remedy for contemporary ills.

The ideological thrust of this story, written for the boy king, Alfonso XIII, is easily discernible. At first, already turned into a mouse, the young king, led by Pérez the Mouse, sees a mother and child living in misery in a freezing garret: "[N]ever had he seen such a sight! How was it possible that he had not known that there were poor children who were hungry and cold and dying from want and grief in a horrible garret? He no longer wanted to have blankets on his own bed so long as there was even one little boy or girl in his kingdom who did not have at least one complete outfit of clothes!"

When, back in human form, awakened from his "dream," the young king complains to his mother about the suffering he has seen—"And why am I king and have everything and they're poor and have nothing?"—the queen mother answers: "Because you're the older brother, that's what being a king is. . . . God has given you everything so that, as far as possible, you can see that your younger brothers and sisters do not want for anything." God is responsible for the king's privilege, and the poor's plight is to be remedied "as far as possible" by the king's charity.

This story of ingratiating rodents, however, has a more than literal *subterranean* quality. Obviously the little creatures live in their own little world, in the cellar, and their trip begins thus: "Their run was wild and their way dark, dank, and sticky, and at every turn they came across bands of tiny vermin that haphazardly pricked and bit them." The dangerous voyage of fables, then, is an underground voyage in Coloma's story. If Pérez the Mouse is the Spanish version of the tooth fairy, who brings a little treasure to little children who put their milk tooth under their pillow, this particular mouse gives the king another treasure: a trip through the world that society's conscience wishes to ignore, its underconscience, subconscious, or, better, "Subconscience." This treasure, however, seems to be allowed to languish, as waking life in the adult voice of his mother softens the harsh relief of the scenes the boy king saw.

Quite different are the stories of Juan Valera (1824–1906), the elegant, urbane writer of some of Spain's most famous novels of his time, particularly his love story, *Pepita Jiménez* (1874). "The Green Bird," tinged with orientalism, is a story of marvelous events, spells, transformations, and love, while "The Wizard" is unique in this collection for its lack of supernatural events. The Hellenic grace of Valera's eroticism is felt in some of the passages of "The Green Bird," while "The Wizard," one of the masterpieces of this fine collection, is also a love story, so clearly and delicately told that it bespeaks the profound wisdom of the author's mature heart. In it, one can only marvel at the deft exploitation of elements and situations that are typical in supernatural folktales, but here placed totally within a verisimilitude that is heightened by a poetic and profoundly loving vision, but not breached. The forbidding castle on the mountain, the magic cave, and the wise old man all contribute to the atmosphere of the marvelous, but instead of establishing the stage for the supernatural or magic, contribute to the magic of human love, thanks to the effective characterization of the protagonists. It is this characterization which shows the master's hand, and which I will forebear from discussing as one does from touching butterfly wings: may the readers enjoy these stories with the same open, clear eyes and heart with which Silveria discovers that Juan's wizard is also hers.

If these stories be a mixture of folk elements and genial individual art, then "Beauty as Punishment," by the great romantic playwright Juan Eugenio Hartzenbush (1806–80), may serve as well as our transition from a discussion of the more folkloric and marvelous tales, informed by harmony and the choral community, toward the tales in this collection characterized by fantastic solitude.

"Beauty as Punishment," a touching story of a beautiful girl's isolation by means of a secret only she knows, is a didactic tale of clear moral intent, which considers the true nature of beauty in the context of physical blindness and nobility of spirit. In spite of its hybrid nature, for the story does end in spiritual integration, true to its proximity to the romantic fantastic discourse, it is the protagonist's isolation that seems most salient, and that serves as the real punishment of the heroine. Pulqueria gains her eyesight, but she can see all except herself, a secret she cannot divulge: "Pulqueria wanted to explain to those present the terrible wonder and relate the conversation with Flaccila [her deceased mother], but against her will her tongue refused to reveal her secret, which by divine order was to be kept hidden for many years." She tried to express her secret in other ways: "So as to unburden herself in some way, she once wrote a letter to her husband recounting Flaccila's appearance and the harsh rule to which her eyes were subject, but the moment she finished the missive it disappeared from her hands." How she finally achieves communication and simultaneous integration with herself and with the world, the reader will discover. Suffice it to say that not only does it mean the end of her fantastic isolation, but also the erasure of the fantastic mode in the story, which then climaxes within the marvelous in a supernatural event seen by all those from whom she had been somehow separated.

FANTASTIC ONES

Gustavo Adolfo Bécquer (1836–70) is often acclaimed as the greatest lyricist of nineteenth-century Spain. His *Rimas*, published posthumously in 1871, is a collection of poems characterized by a speaking tone, rather than the more emphatic voice of his romantic precursors in Spain. His stories, deeply poetical, closer to that romantic full-throated song or cry, are a testimony to the generic closeness between poem and story. Often haunting, they verge on the border between cultural memory and personal longing.

"Believe in God" and "The Devil's Cross" both contain allusions to the oral tradition. In the first, the narrator informs us: "This tradition has come down to me by word of mouth . . . perhaps I'll embellish the bare skeleton of this simple and terrible story with some poetic finery, but I'll never knowingly depart one whit from the truth." And in the second, the following passage insists on that connection: "The elderwood cup, drained and then replenished . . . had been passed three times around the group that sat together in a circle next to the fire. All of us were waiting impatiently to hear the story of the Devil's Cross." Nor is the association with women's voices absent in this tale: "The story of the *Evil Noble* . . . was beginning to be the exclusive property of old women, who, on endless winter evenings, would tell astonished children his fiendish deeds. . . ."

Both tales rush into fantastic terror. Both are about nobles who ravage their people and are avatars of the satanic archetype. Carried off by a runaway horse, Teobaldo "felt himself descending and descending without even falling—burned, blinded, and deafened, as the rebellious angel must have plunged when God knocked over the pedestal of his pride with one puff from His lips." The dreadful lord of "The Devil's Cross" is branded with satanic nature from the very title of his story.

The satanic archetype as fashioned by Milton was to be recovered by the romantics as the great transgressor, but also as the loneliest of creatures, separated from his throngs by his excellence, from God by his insubordination, and from man, because that dark general could not experience the essential human act of love. His radical uniqueness was cried out in his "me miserable," which was to echo in many an outcast romantic hero, including these terrible nobles of Bécquer's imagination. After his dreadful gallop, Teobaldo can only knock at the door of a monastery and beg admittance, and thus, enter the human community, even in his extraordinary condition. One final note: if rhythm be the soul of poetry, so it is of the short story, and the hoofbeats of Teobaldo's "nightmare" resonate also in the unbridled will of the "The Devil's Cross."

"Death's Friend," by Pedro Antonio de Alarcón (1833–91), author of the delightful short novel *The Three-Cornered Hat* [El sombrero de tres picos] (1874), and other, perhaps less successful, late romantic novels, seems to me to be the most extraordinary of these fascinating stories, and, in some ways, the very heart of this collection. I say that not only because of its high art, but because in it we see the most intense struggle between the oral tradition and individual voice, which is one of the most significant lessons of this book. Let us, therefore, linger in its landscape and accompany its hero for a while.

The story was first published in 1852, at a moment not too distant in time from Spain's relatively late romantic period, which extended well into the 1840s. It then underwent modification and elaboration before its definitive and final version appeared in Alarcón's *Complete Works* in 1882 (Amores 1997, 90 n. 2). It is a highly original and extensive development of a traditional tale, a version of which is included in Grimms' collection, titled "Godfather Death" in the English translation. The story has had a rich life in Spanish folklore, and it has been published in twenty-two versions in modern compilations of stories still told in the twentieth century (Amores 1997, 90). Faithfully transcribed by Fernán Caballero in 1850, Trueba had published a slightly more altered form, though still closer to the original than Alarcón's, in 1867 (Amores 1997, 90). According to Montserrat Amores in her study of this story and the versions of Fernán Caballero and Trueba, Alarcón "takes only the essential elements of the ethnopoetic tale as a pretext for the composition of a completely personal story (91). Judging from the fact that the tale occupies 4 pages in the Heritage Press edition of Grimms' fairy tales, and 109 pages of the typed manuscript in Alarcón's *Complete Works*, it is clear that a far-reaching transformation has taken place.

As Amores points out, Alarcón's version, as opposed to the folktale, and to Fernán Caballero's and Trueba's versions, is "fantastic, not marvelous" (98). She explains that the other stories take place in a world unrelated to ours, while Alarcón's takes place in a historically specific time and place, eighteenth-century Spain. Therefore, the unnatural events are charged with a tension characteristic of the fantastic "rupture." This rupture, as we have mentioned, places the fantastic hero in a world of his own, of at times dreadful uniqueness—in fact, of a solitude as close-fitting as a grave.

Solitude is not surprisingly, therefore, a constant motif in Alarcón's masterpiece, starting with the hero's dispossession and going out, a variation of the folk motif of the hero's initiation of his journey: "[A]nd so he abandoned the stand (refuge of his ancestors and already the property of another shoemaker) and headed along the first street he came across, without knowing where he was going, what to do, to whom to turn, how to work, or for what reason to live." As Death tells him, he, like Pulqueria in Hartzenbusch's story, enjoys a dreadful privilege: "Your advantage over the rest of men consists only of the fact that I am visible to you, so good-bye and don't forget me."

But solitude is most apparent at the moment of his marriage to his beloved, a tragic paradox in this story totally organized on the principle of romantic oxymoron: "two souls who had wept over the torments of absence at the same time; Gil and Elena, Elena and Gil, predestined to be inseparable, finally lost, in that solemn and mystic hour, their solitary, miserable individuality to embark on a future full of happiness, like two rivers that spring from the same mountain and, coursing along tortuous channels, reunite and merge in the infinite solitude of the ocean." The ocean, symbolic of their union, is a thing of "infinite solitude," as their individual lives had been. It is also a symbol of death, most famously expressed in Spanish letters in the sober beauty of Jorge Manrique's well-known lines: "[O]ur lives are the rivers that flow to the sea, which is death." Thus, their union, with all the suggestion of life and love, is symbolically called death itself.

Their wedding occurs at a dreadful time, affecting even nature herself:

> It could also be said that at that moment a period in the history of the world was coming to an end, that all of nature was bidding an eternal farewell: the bird to his nest, the zephyr to his flowers, the trees to the rivers, the sun to the mountains; and that intimate togetherness in which all had lived, lending one another color or fragrance, music or movement, and converging in the same palpitation of universal existence, had been brought to an end.
>
> It could be said, finally, that on that evening there was going to be a dissolution of the mysterious association that constitutes the unity and harmony of the worlds. . . . More than anything, and more than anybody possessed of this supreme intuition and strange delusion, Gil and Elena—still, silent, and holding hands—witnessed the august tragedy of the close of that day, the last of their misfortunes, and looked at each other with profound anxiety and blind adoration.

The passage is long, but an eloquent testimony to the possible resonance of a great text of sundered harmony, Milton's *Paradise Lost*. There too, oxymoron is fundamental, and the passionate discovery of good and evil, a closing of human beings with nature, is accompanied by a simultaneous falling away and disintegration: "She plucked, she ate: Earth herself felt the wound, and Nature from her seat Sighing through all her Works gave signs of Woe, that all was lost" (1982, 257). And the final scene, the couple's leave-taking of Paradise, sheds light on Alarcón's two brave and lost lovers: "They hand in hand with wandr'ing steps and slow, Through Eden took their solitary way" (339). "Solitary" while hand in hand, because wrenched from a wounded Mother Nature, in a sense orphaned, and cast out, are Elena and Gil. While avoiding odious comparisons, it is still possible to note in Alarcón's beautiful long story a philosophical gaze, of not inconsiderable pathos and wisdom, inherited from Milton.

The oxymoron we have just considered is part of the larger oxymoron that underlies the story's philosophical import: life-death. Life, and its principal expression, love, are countered by Death, edged by it, "defined," as it were, by it. As Death tells Gil: "Life is love, life is feeling; but the great, the noble, the revealing part of life is the tear of sadness that runs down the face of the newborn infant and the dying person, the melancholy complaint of the human heart that feels the hunger of being and pain of existing, the sweet longing for another life, or the pathetic recollection of another world. . . ."

This oxymoron is at the core of the romantic sensibility, which expresses itself in the form of contrast, but also, as we see now, in the ambiguity of the fantastic, which informs this shimmering, or shivering, story, where Death (described as neither male nor female), no longer enemy, makes life conscious of itself.

WILD FLOWERS

The story of unnatural events seems, at first sight, a strange thing in the works of the great realist writers. Benito Pérez Galdós, author of what is by consensus the greatest nineteenth-century Spanish novel, *Fortunata and Jacinta* (1886–87), wrote twelve of them, by my count, among his twenty short stories in general. Leopoldo Alas, known by his pen name "Clarín," the only possible rival to Galdós's preeminent position, with his own masterpiece, *The Regent's Wife* (1884–85), was a consummate realist, and his own fantastic stories are interspersed among his important corpus of stories (some sixty), much more significant than Galdós's, and second only to Emilia Pardo Bazán's, a very notable contemporary of theirs, in number if not in quality. Perhaps better than wild flowers, these fantastic or marvelous stories might more properly be considered wild oats, for in these the restraint, the decorous economy of mimetic verisimilitude, is unheeded. But it is a prodigality in consonance with the order of things realistic, for these stories, in their apparent disregard for realism, are truly pure manifestations of an ambiguity, a ubiquitous leavening, inherent in the best of the realists, an ambiguity that permits doubt and respect for the other, and that is expressed thematically in the narrators' own lack of authority, in highly interpretable narrated events, in dreams and visions, and formally in realism's constant debt to myth, its fundamental palimpsest.

While Galdós's two stories included in this collection, "The Mule and the Ox" and "The Princess and the Street Urchin," are both tales of children protagonists, the first might more properly be called marvelous, and the second, much more bitter, is, to a certain extent, an example of the fantastic. This disparate nature seems to me to be a characteristic of tales of unnatural events during the heyday of realism, the last quarter of the nineteenth century, in which the romantic fantastic is either eschewed or, more often than not, buffered in humor and parody, while the marvelous still made its occasional presence felt, though at times, because of ambiguous resolutions, it tiptoes on the fantastic discourse of hesitation and ambiguity, or on philosophical allegory.

"The Mule and the Ox" belongs to the editorial convention of Christmas stories, with which nineteenth-century journals often marked and celebrated the season, and because the season celebrates a baby, and is the delight of children, these tales are often childlike in their tenor, and contain child protagonists. The danger of the maudlin inherent in this convention seems to me to have been avoided by Galdós, because of the inherent honesty of his vision and wise, deft restraint; the story, for example, begins with the child protagonist's death. It is nonetheless an endearing and delicate tale, a melody if not more for the music box than the piano, certainly for this instrument's higher registers. It is a good example of Galdós's affection for children, which he shared with Dickens, and of his great skill and sympathy in depicting their fearless affirmation.

Quite another story is "The Princess and the Street Urchin," a rewriting, in small writ, of the essential romantic motif of lost love, homelessness, and the contiguity of Eros to Thanatos. Pacorrito, its boy hero, suffers more than practically any other protagonist in a Galdós short story, and seems to bear on his meager shoulders the burdens of the world, perhaps Galdós's world at the time. One of the most disturbing examples of Galdós's critical interest in the myth of Pygmalion, "The Princess and the Street Urchin" is a cautionary tale against the surrender of the will to a dreadful sculptor, in which the progression is not from statue to human, but, dreadfully, otherwise.

In contrast to Galdós's relatively small corpus of stories, as we have noted, Clarín is one of the undisputed masters of the genre, in quantity as well as quality. In both of the stories published in this collection, we see his characteristic critical vision of his contemporary society, its institutions, and its very values. "My Funeral," which appeared almost at the same time as *The Regent's Wife*, in a curious way shares some of that work's most significant characteristics: its biting social criticism and its parody of that debased vision of romanticism (though not, perhaps, of romanticism's highest achievements) which the late-nineteenth-century bourgeoisie held, confused as it became with melodramas and penny dreadfuls (the luxuriant *folletines*).

The parodic intent is obvious in the basic premise of "My Funeral": one more variation on the romantic motif of witnessing one's own burial, most famously rendered in José de Espronceda's *The Student of Salamanca* [El estudiante de Salamanca] (1836–39). While in Espronceda's vertiginous and powerful narrative poem the hero dies at the end, like Tirso's Don Juan, in Clarín we have an ambiguous ending, which the reader will enjoy discovering. Also, the serious, almost tragic import of the romantic treatment is here diluted, as it is parodied into comedy and even farce, somewhat in the Cervantine fashion.

Of course, as in Cervantes, parody is not innocent. Clarín's literary stand-in mercilessly attacks historical farce: the fake and thoroughly corrupt political process guaranteed a "peaceful" alternation of power on the part of the two bourgeois parties of Alphonsine restoration. The mendacity, cowardice, and ineptitude that the "dead" hero witnesses in his political cohorts is the same which Spain, in a way "dead," witnessed during the last quarter of the nineteenth century, and well into the twentieth.

No less biting, in fact more dreadful in its implications, because more universal, is "Socrates' Rooster." Two subtexts resonate throughout: Plato's *Phaedo* and, unmentioned, the Gospels. Crito's savagery against the rooster, his spilling of its blood, in order to fulfill his interpretation of his master's last words, reverberates with the innumerable acts of savagery perpetrated by religious institutions, as they attempted to render their founders' moving words in rigid dogmas and cemented stones. Even disguised as the thoughts of a beleaguered rooster, with all the apparent comic incongruity of that conceit, Clarín's own voice is heard: "Unworthy disciple, off with you and *you* be silent. You're unworthy of those of your ilk. All alike. Disciples of genius, deaf and blind witnesses to the sublime soliloquy of a superior conscience, through his illusions and the one you share, you believe that you can immortalize the perfume of his soul when you embalm his doctrine with drugs and prescriptions. You make a mummy of his corpse in order to have an idol. You petrify the idea and use subtle thought like a knife that makes blood flow. Yes, you are the symbol of sad sectarian humanity. From the last words of a saint and a sage you draw as the first consequence the blood of a rooster." True to his pen name, "Clarion," Leopoldo Alas's call sounds to wake up his contemporaries, as a rooster might in a village, if it is not killed.

Envoi

The dawn implied in the animal in Clarín's story, and even in its blood spilled on high, may perhaps serve to signal our parting thoughts. For the dawn Clarín wished for, though not realized in our terrible last century, was one informed by another: the twilight moment of the imagination's first light, still suffused with lingering dreams. The tales of the marvelous events, the half-light of the fantastic with its at times terrible but necessary indictments, kept, and keep, alive a world at once recognized and encountered, strangely familiar even when most shocking, and both fundamentally opposed to the convenient forgetting and self-deception of ordinary life. From Fernán's lovingly painstaking transcriptions of oral tales, to Alarcón's beautiful late romantic philosophical poem in prose, to Clarín's no less philosophical but also politically challenging stories and allegories, the story continued to recount and to account for the restlessness that must surely be a good part of our imagination's spiritual home. The marvelous and the fantastic, seemingly in opposition, may actually be both needful, wakeful dreams, invention and memory, as Plato would have it.

Boston
January 2001

Notes

1. Translations of passages from a foreign language are my own, except for passages from the stories in this edition.
2. Propp writes: "The sequence of events has its own laws. The short story

too has similar laws, as do organic formations. Theft cannot take place before the door is forced. Insofar as the tale is concerned, it has its own entirely particular and specific laws. The sequence of events . . . is strictly *uniform* [emphasis Propp's]. Freedom within this sequence is restricted by very narrow limits which can be strictly formulated: . . . The sequence of functions is always identical" (1968, 22). And again he states: "One function develops out of another with logical and artistic necessity" (64).

   3. See the introductory chapter, "Myth and Dream," in Campbell 1973.

Works Cited

Amores, Montserrat. 1997. "Tres reelaboraciones literarias decimonónicas del cuento folclórico 'La muerte padrino.'" In *Narrativa fantástica del siglo XIX (España e Hispanoamérica)*, edited by Jaime Pont, 89–105. Lleida: Mileno.

Baquero Goyanes, Mariano. 1992. *El cuento español: Del romanticismo al realismo*. Edición revisada por Ana L. Baquero Escudero. Madrid: CSIC.

Caballero, Fernán (Cecilia Böhl de Faber). 1912. *Epistolario*. Madrid: Revista de Archivos.

Campbell, Joseph. 1973. *The Hero with a Thousand Faces*. Bollingen Series 17. Princeton: Princeton University Press.

Chevalier, Maxime. 1978. *Folklore y literatura: El cuento oral en el Siglo de Oro*. Barcelona: Editorial Crítica.

Clément, Catherine, and Hélène Cixous. 1986. *The Newly Born Woman*. Translated by Betsy Wing. Foreword by Sandra M. Gilbert. Minneapolis: University of Minnesota Press.

Conroy, Patricia L. 1980. "The Art of Hans Christian Andersen's Tales and Stories." In *Tales and Stories*, by Hans Christian Andersen, xxix–xxxvi. Translated with an introduction by Patricia L. Conroy and Sven H. Rossel. Seattle: University of Washington Press.

Lang, Andrew. 1962. "*Household Tales:* Their Origin, Diffusion, and Relations to the Higher Myths." In vol. 2 of *Fairy Tales*, by Jakob Grimm and Wilhelm Grimm, 903–29. Edited by Louis and Bryna Untermeyer. Foreword by Louis Untermeyer. New York: The Heritage Press.

Milton, John. 1982. *Paradise Lost* and *Paradise Regained*. Edited by Christopher Ricks. New York: Penguin Books USA.

Nodier, Charles. 1972. Reprint. Geneva: Slatkine. Originally published as "Du fantastique en littérature," *Revue de Paris* 20 (1830): 205–26.

Propp, Vladimir. *Morphology of the Folktale*. Translated by Laurence Scott. Introduction by Svatava Pirkova-Jakobson. New introduction by Alan Dundes. Revised and edited with a preface by Louis A. Wagner. Austin: University of Texas Press, 1968.

———. 1983. *Les racines historiques du conte merveilleux*. Translated into French by Lise Gruel-Apert. Preface by Daniel Fabre and Jean-Claude Schmitt. Paris: Gallimard.

Rossel, Sven H. 1980. Introduction to *Tales and Stories*, by Hans Christian Andersen. Translated by Patricia L. Conroy and Sven H. Rossel. Seattle: University of Washington Press, 1980.

Todorov, Tzvetan. 1970. *Introduction à la littérature fantastique*. Paris: Editions du Seuil.

Trancón Lagunas, María Montserrat. 1997. "El cuento fantástico publicado en la prensa madrileña del XIX (1818–1868)." In *Narrativa fantástica del siglo XIX (España e Hispanoamérica)*, edited by Jaime Pont, 19–20. Lleida: Milenio.

Untermeyer, Louis. Foreword to vol. 1 of *Fairy Tales*, by Jakob Grimm and Wilhelm Grimm. Edited by Louis Untermeyer and Bryna Untermeyer. Essay by Andrew Lang. New York: The Heritage Press.

Stories of Enchantment from Nineteenth-Century Spain

Fernán Caballero [pseudonym of **Cecilia Böhl de Faber**]
(1796–1877)

Born in Switzerland of a Spanish mother and a German father, Fernán Caballero is frequently credited with having initiated the regional novel in Spain. The Sea Gull [La gaviota] (1849) tells of a failed marriage, and although the plot—with melodramatic highs and lows, departures and returns, a bullfighter and a singer—is inescapably romantic, there are numerous, and vivid, scenes of customs and manners that point to the realism that will be fully developed by other writers.

Having spent most of her life in Andalusia, Fernán Caballero became steeped in that province's oral traditions, and her interest in national folklore led her to give written form to tales that had been passed from generation to generation. Her source, as she wrote in the preface to Collection of Tales and Popular Andalusian *Poems [Colección de cuentos y poesías populares andaluzas] (1859), was the "inexhaustible popular muse," and from it came morality tales in keeping with the European tradition, for the reader will see immediately that "The Wishes" is a variation of Charles Perrault's "The Three Wishes."*

"The Wishes," "The Girl with Three Husbands," and "Lovely-Flower" were included under the general rubric of Stories of Enchantment *[Cuentos de encantamiento] (1877) for children.*

Fernán Caballero

"The Wishes"

ONCE upon a time there was an elderly couple who, although poor, had lived a very good life working and caring for their small piece of property. One winter evening husband and wife, content in each other's company, were sitting near the fire in their peaceful home, but instead of counting their blessings, they were enumerating the prize possessions of others and wishing that they could enjoy them too.

"If instead of my little field," the husband was saying, "which has poor soil and is only good for a donkey wallow, I had old Polainas's farm!"

"And if instead of this house," the wife was saying, "which is still standing because nobody's given it a push, I had our neighbor woman's, which is like new!"

"If instead of the burro," the husband continued, "who can no longer manage even with empty saddlebags, I had old Polainas's mule!"

"And if," the wife added, "I could slaughter a two-hundred-pound hog like the neighbor woman. To have things all those people need to do is wish for them. If only we were fortunate enough to have our wishes fulfilled!"

She had scarcely spoken these words when they saw a very beautiful woman descending the chimney, a woman so short that she was not even a foot and a half tall. Like a queen, she wore a gold crown on her head, and her long dress and veil were diaphanous and fashioned from white vapor. The sparks that shot up in a small burst and rose merrily like a joyous pyrotechnic shower settled on the husband and wife, sprinkling them with brilliant spangles. In her hand she held a small gold scepter that ended in a dazzling carbuncle.

"I'm Fortune the fairy," she said to them. "I was passing by here and heard your complaints, and since you long so to have your wishes fulfilled, I've come to grant you the fulfillment of three. One to you," she said to the wife, "another to you," she said to the husband, "and a third that has to be joint, that the two of you have to agree on.

36

I'll grant the last one in person when I return tomorrow at this same hour. Until then you'll have time to think about what it's to be."

No sooner did the lovely enchantress say this than she disappeared in a puff of smoke that rose through the flames.

I leave to my readers' imagination the good couple's joy, as well as the number of wishes that besieged them like claimants at a minister's door. So many occurred to the husband and wife that, not knowing which ones to entertain, they decided to sleep on it and leave the final choices until the morning, whereupon they began to talk about other things.

Presently their conversation turned to their fortunate neighbors.

"I was over there today. They were making blood sausages," said the husband. "What blood sausages! It was sheer pleasure to see them."

"If only I had one of them here," the wife responded, "to roast over the coals so we could have it for supper!"

She had scarcely spoken when there appeared over the coals the most beautiful blood sausage the world has ever seen or ever will see.

The woman stared at it in amazement, her mouth agape. The husband, however, sprang up in despair and paced back and forth, tearing at his hair, saying:

"Because of you, with the biggest sweet tooth and most voracious appetite on the planet, one of the wishes has been wasted. Lord, what a woman! A prize idiot! I wash my hands of you and the blood sausage and only wish that it would stick on your nose!"

No sooner had he said this than the blood sausage was hanging from the indicated spot.

Now it was the old man's turn to be amazed and the old woman's to despair.

"What a mess you've created with your big mouth!" exclaimed the latter as she made futile attempts to tear the appendage from her nose. "If I made bad use of my wish at least it was at my own expense, not someone else's. But every sin carries its own punishment, because now I wish but one thing, and one thing only, and that's the removal of the blood sausage from my nose."

"For God's sake, woman, what about the farm?"

"No."

"For God's sake woman, what about the house?"

"No."

"We'll wish for a mine and I'll make you a gold sheath for the blood sausage."

"Out of the question."

"So we're going to end up as we were?"

"That's my sole wish."

For as much as he continued pleading with her, the husband could not get his wife to budge. And as she was becoming more desperate by the minute with her double nose, only with great difficulty did she hold off the dog and cat who wanted to pounce on her.

When the fairy appeared the following night and the couple told her what their third and final wish was, she said:

"Now you see how blind and foolish people are to believe that the fulfillment of their wishes can make them happy. Happiness does not consist in fulfilling wishes, but in not having them. People who possess things are rich, but people who wish for nothing are happy."

Fernán Caballero

"The Girl with Three Husbands"

THERE was a father who had a very a beautiful, but very headstrong
and very stubborn, daughter. Three suitors, each one as dapper as
the other, came to him and asked for her in marriage, and inasmuch
as he gave his consent to all three, he said that he would ask his
daughter which of them she preferred.

And so he did, and the girl said all three.

"But, my dear, that cannot be."

"I choose all three," the girl said again.

"Be reasonable, my child," responded her father. "To which one
shall I give the nod?"

"To all three," the girl repeated, not budging.

The poor father left out of humor and told the three suitors that
his daughter wanted all of them, but that since such a thing was not
possible, he had determined that they should roam the world over in
search of something unique of its kind, and that the one who brought
back the best and rarest would marry his daughter.

They set out, each suitor by a different route, and after a very
long time they came together again beyond the seas, in a distant land,
none of them having found anything beautiful and unique of its kind.
But even in the midst of their tribulations they continued their search,
and the one who had arrived first chanced to meet a little old man
who asked him if he wished to buy a small mirror.

The suitor said no, as such a small and ugly mirror would be of
no use to him.

Then the seller told him that the mirror had one great virtue, and
it was that its owner could see in it the people that he wished to see.
And after ascertaining that such was indeed the case, he bought it
for the asking price.

The one who had arrived second was passing along a street and
chanced to meet the same little old man, who asked him if he wished
to buy a small jar of balsam.

"What good would this balsam do me?" he asked the little old man.

"God knows," the seller replied, "for this balsam has one great virtue, which is that of raising the dead."

At that very moment a funeral procession happened to pass by. The little old man went and put a drop of balsam in the mouth of the deceased, who rose in such good health that he lifted his coffin and carried it home. When the second suitor saw this, he bought the balsam from the little old man for the asking price.

While the third suitor paced back and forth along the seashore engrossed in his dilemma, he saw a huge chest riding the waves. When it approached the beach it opened, and countless passengers leaped ashore.

The last one, who was a little old man, came up to him and asked him if he wished to buy that chest.

"Why would I want it," the suitor replied, "if the only thing it's good for is to make a bonfire?"

"I beg to differ, sir," said the little old man, "for it possesses one great virtue, which is that in a few short hours it will transport its owner and those who go on board with him wherever they yearn or wish to go. This is the truth and it can be verified by these passengers, who only hours ago were on the beaches of Spain."

The gentleman suitor verified it and bought the chest from its owner for the asking price.

The following day the three met and each one pronounced himself very satisfied that he had already found what he had come to find, and was, therefore, ready to return to Spain.

The first suitor told how he had bought a mirror in which the owner saw, merely by wishing it, the absent person that he wanted to see; and to prove it, he produced his mirror, wishing to see the girl whose hand all three sought.

But imagine their astonishment when they saw her lying dead in a coffin!

"I have a balsam that would revive her," said the one who had bought the jar. "But by the time we get there she'll be buried and worm-eaten."

"Well, I have a chest that will land us in Spain in a few short hours," said in turn the one who had bought the chest.

So they hastened to embark in the chest and a few hours later leaped ashore, whereupon they headed for the town in which their intended's father lived.

They found him in the depths of despair over the death of his daughter, who was still laid out. They asked him to take them to see her, and when they were in the room with her corpse, the one with the balsam approached and sprinkled a few drops on the lips of the dead girl, who rose fit as a fiddle and with a smile on her face.

Turning to her father, she asked:

"Do you see, Father, how I needed the three of them?"

Fernán Caballero

"Lovely-Flower"

ONCE upon a time there was a father who had two sons. It fell to the older one to become a soldier, and he went off to America where he lived for many years. When he returned, he learned that his father had died and that his brother, enjoying the legacy, had become very wealthy. He went to his sibling's home and ran into him coming down the stairway.

"Don't you recognize me?" he asked him.

His younger brother answered with a rude no.

José, as the ex-soldier was called, then identified himself, and his brother told him to go to the granary, where he would find a chest that was the inheritance left to him by their father, and, saying no more, continued on his way.

So José climbed the granary and found a very old chest, and thought to himself:

What am I going to do with this broken-down chest? Well, if nothing else, I can always use it to make a fire and warm myself, since it's so cold.

José carried the chest back to his inn, where he took an ax and set about chopping it apart, when a piece of paper fell from a secret compartment. He picked it up and saw that it was the draft for a considerable sum of money owed to his father. He cashed it and became very rich.

One day as he was walking along a street he met a woman who was crying bitterly. He asked her what was wrong, and she answered that her husband was very ill, and that not only did she not have the means to treat him, but that a creditor, whom her husband was unable to pay, wanted to have him taken to jail.

"Don't worry," José said to her. "Your husband won't be taken to jail nor will your possessions be sold, because I'll stand good for everything: I'll pay his debts, his medical care, and his funeral expenses if he dies."

And he kept his word, but José realized, when paying for the funeral expenses after the indigent man's death, that he was penniless because he had spent all of his inheritance on that charitable work.

And now what do I do? he thought. *Since I have nothing to eat, I'll find a court and become a servant.*

Thus did he begin to serve in the king's palace.

José acquitted himself so well and the king took such a liking to him that he raised him from one position to another until making him his principal gentleman-in-waiting.

Meanwhile, his estranged brother had lost all his money and wrote to him asking for help, and as José was so good-hearted, he helped him, by asking the king to give his brother a position in the palace, and the king granted his request.

So he came, but instead of being grateful to his generous brother he was jealous upon seeing that José was the king's favorite, and he set out deliberately to destroy him. To this end he made inquiries to discover what he needed to know and learned that the king was in love with Princess Lovely-Flower, and that because the king was so old and ugly she had refused him and hidden in a palace concealed in underbrush. Nobody knew its location. The brother went and told the king that José knew where Lovely-Flower was and that he corresponded with her. A very angry king then summoned José and told him to leave at once to fetch Princess Lovely-Flower and said that if he returned without her he would be hanged.

Disconsolate, poor José went to the stable to saddle a horse and ride to unknown parts, without knowing where to go to find Lovely-Flower. Then he saw a very scrawny old white horse who said to him:

"Take me and don't worry."

José was amazed to hear a horse talk, but he mounted up and off they went, carrying three loaves of bread as provisions that the horse had told him to take along.

After they had gone a good stretch they came across an anthill, and the horse said to his rider:

"Toss the three loaves of bread over there for the ants to eat."

"But why, if we need them for ourselves?" José asked.

"Toss them the bread," the horse replied, "and don't ever tire of doing good works."

They went another stretch and came across an eagle that had gotten tangled in a hunter's net.

"Dismount," the horse said to him, "and cut the netting and free that poor bird."

"But aren't we going to lose time doing that?"

"Never mind. Do what I tell you and don't ever tire of doing good works."

They went another stretch and arrived at a river where they saw a small fish that had been stranded on the bank; no matter how much it moved, longing to die, it couldn't get back to the water.

"Dismount," the white horse said to José. "Pick up that poor little fish and throw it into the river."

"But we don't have any time to waste," José responded.

"There's always time to lend a helping hand," the white horse said, "and don't ever tire of doing good works."

Presently they arrived at a castle, tucked away in a dark forest, and saw Princess Lovely-Flower, who was feeding bran to her chickens.

"Pay attention," the white horse said to José. "Now I'm going to curvet and prance around, which will amuse Lovely-Flower. She'll tell you that she wants to ride me for a while and you'll let her ride me. Then I'll start to kick and neigh; she'll get frightened and you'll say it's because I'm not accustomed to women riding me, and that if you mount me I'll calm down. Then you'll get on too and I'll gallop off to the king's palace."

Everything happened just as the horse had said, and only when they left at a gallop did Lovely-Flower realize that the rider had come there with the intention of abducting her.

Then she dropped on the ground the bran that she had in her hands and told her companion that it had spread all over and asked him to gather it up for her.

"Where we're going," José replied, "there's a lot of bran."

Then, as they passed under a tree, Lovely-Flower threw her handkerchief in the air and it caught on one of the highest branches; she told José to dismount and climb the tree to retrieve it for her, but he responded:

"Where we're going there are a lot of handkerchiefs."

Then they crossed a river and she dropped a ring in it and asked José to dismount to retrieve it for her, but José told her that where they were going there were a lot of rings.

Finally, they arrived at the palace. The king was overjoyed at seeing his precious Lovely-Flower, but Lovely-Flower retired to a room and locked it, refusing to open it for anybody. The king pleaded with her to open up, but she said that she would not until the three things that she had lost along the way were returned to her.

"The only recourse, José," the king said to him, "is for you to go after them, because you know what they are. If you don't bring them back, I'll have you hanged."

Poor José went, very distressed, to tell the little white horse, who said to him:

"Don't worry. Mount up and let's go look for them."

They set off and arrived at the anthill.

"You wanted the bran, didn't you?" the horse asked.

"Of course!" José replied.

"Well, call the ants and tell them to bring it to you, because if Lovely-Flower's bran has scattered, they'll bring you what they took out of the bread, which had to be quite a bit."

And thus did it happen. The grateful ants heeded his call and brought him a mound of bran.

"Do you see," the horse asked, "how the person who does good works is sooner or later repaid in kind?"

They came to the tree where Lovely-Flower had thrown her handkerchief, which fluttered like a pennant on one of the highest branches.

"How am I supposed to reach that handkerchief?" José asked. "I would need Jacob's ladder!"

"Don't worry," the horse replied. "Call the eagle that you freed from the hunter's net and he'll get it for you."

And thus did it happen. The eagle came, plucked the handkerchief with his bill, and presented it to José.

They arrived at the river, which was very murky.

"How am I supposed to bring up that ring from the bottom of this deep river?" José asked. "I can't see and there's no way of knowing where Lovely-Flower dropped it."

"Don't worry," the horse replied. "Call the small fish that you saved and he'll bring it to you."

And thus did it happen. The small fish dove to the bottom and surfaced, very pleased, swishing his tail and holding the ring in his mouth.

José was elated and returned to the palace, but when the three items were taken to Lovely-Flower she said she would neither unlock the door nor leave her retreat so long as the villain who had abducted her from her palace was not fried in oil.

The king was so cruel that he gave her his word and told José that he would have to die fried in oil.

José, very distressed, went to the stable and related to the horse what was happening to him.

"Don't worry," said the horse, "and mount me. I'm going to run hard and perspire. Rub your body with my sweat and don't be afraid to let them throw you into the cauldron, because no harm will come to you."

And thus did it happen. When José emerged from the cauldron, he came out transformed into such a handsome, dashing youth that everybody looked at him in astonishment, and nobody more so than Lovely-Flower, who fell in love with him instantly.

Upon seeing what had happened to José and believing that he could undergo the same transformation, and that then Lovely-Flower would fall in love with him, the king, who was old and ugly, jumped into the cauldron and was burned to a crisp.

All the people then proclaimed the chamberlain their king, and he married Lovely-Flower.

When José went to thank the one who had done so much on his behalf, the little white horse said to him:

"I'm the soul of that poor devil on whose debts, medical care, and funeral expenses you spent all that you had, and upon seeing you in such a difficult and dangerous situation, I asked God's permission to be able to come to your assistance and return the favor. That's why I've told you before and will tell you again—don't ever tire of doing good works."

Antonio de Trueba (1819–89)

Fearing that their son would be conscripted to fight in a war in the Basque country, Antonio de Trueba's parents sent him, at the age of fifteen, to Madrid to work in his uncle's hardware store. In the capital he began to devote his free time to literature and by the mid-1840s had embarked on a writing career with poems, historical novels, and short stories.

Appointed archivist and historian of Biscay in 1862, Trueba spent the greater part of ten years in Bilbao, a seaport on the Bay of Biscay. Like Fernán Caballero, he became interested in the oral tradition and its morality tales, and gathered documents pertinent to the history and folklore of the entire region. In a number of the prefaces of his books Trueba wrote that he never intended to transcribe rigorously what he had gleaned from the Spanish oral tradition; he wished to preserve the tales, but by giving them, like the brothers Grimm, an acceptable literary form. So he reshaped them, so to speak, to conform to his notion of what constituted good judgment and taste.

"The Adventures of a Tailor" comes from Tales of Several Colors *[Cuentos de varios colores] (1866) and has much in common with "The Brave Little Tailor" of the brothers Grimm; and "The King's Son-in-Law" comes from* Tales of the Living and the Dead *[Cuentos de vivos y muertos] (1866).*

Antonio de Trueba

"The Adventures of a Tailor"

I

IN Whoknowswhere Valley, well-known by short story writers and even by historians, there lived a wily old witch who enjoyed such an unfavorable reputation that her life story needs to be told in some detail in order to gain a better understanding of this tale.

The witch in question made her home in a forest not far from the town, and she subsisted on the yield of a small piece of land that she farmed by herself and on that of a few chestnut trees that shaded her miserable hut. Nobody dared to approach the witch, but the ones who fled from her above all others were pregnant women. And there were powerful reasons for them to flee, because the witch was so evil that as soon as she saw a pregnant woman, instead of saying to her, "Would to God that you give birth to a saint," she would say, "Would to God that you give birth to a devil," which explained why, among the natives of Whoknowswhere, there figured a number of thieves and murderers. Such was the wickedness of the old witch!

In Whoknowswhere there were a tailor and his wife who were dearly loved by all their neighbors for their many unselfish works of charity, especially in clothing the poor. One day the tailor's wife, who was pregnant, was passing through the forest where the witch lived, beseeching God and all the saints in heaven to keep her from running into the wily old woman, when she saw a great cloud of smoke rising from where the witch's hut stood and heard the witch crying out desperately, calling for help.

The tailor's wife was so compassionate and so kindhearted that she forgot about her own well-being when presented with a chance to think about the well-being of others, and she decided immediately to help the witch, to which end she started to run toward the cloud of smoke and the sound of the cries for help. It did not take long

48

for her to discover what was happening to the witch: her hut had caught fire and she was trying in vain to put out the flames that were beginning to consume the miserable dwelling and with it the furnishings and small crop that were as miserable as the hut itself.

The tailor's wife kicked a new channel through the course of a millstream that cut across the forest at a point higher than the witch's hut, and a torrent of water then ran down toward the door with her in close pursuit, and she and the witch, with a bucket of water here and a bucket of water there, managed to put out the fire.

The witch was crying out of gratitude and could not say enough to thank the tailor's wife for the favor that she had done her.

"There's no need for thanks," the tailor's wife said to her. "I've done nothing of merit."

"You certainly have, especially considering that you're in a family way," the old woman replied.

These words reminded the tailor's wife that she was pregnant, and she trembled from head to toe. The witch, noticing her terror and guessing the reason, hastened to set her at ease, saying:

"Be happy instead of trembling, because I'm going to give you a piece of good news in return for the good deed you have done. It is this: you are going to give birth to a tiny baby, who, if he manages to kill seven with one blow, will be master of seven provinces."

"A son who's a killer!" exclaimed the tailor's wife, bursting into tears.

"Do not cry, for the deaths brought about by your son will dishonor neither humanity nor the family," said the witch, greatly consoling her.

The tailor's wife went home and related to her husband what had happened to her with the witch, without forgetting, naturally, the prediction that she would give birth to a tiny son who if he managed to kill seven with one blow would be master of seven provinces, and the tailor burst out laughing at the credulity of his wife, who believed in witches' predictions.

Not long afterward the tailor's wife gave birth to a baby boy the size of a hand, and the tailor, seeing the first part of the witch's prediction fulfilled to the letter, began to regret his incredulity.

The child grew so little that at the age of fifteen he was as small as others are at the age of six, but not on this account did he fail to become an accomplished tailor, which stood him in good stead, because at the age of fifteen he lost both mother and father and ended up on his own.

II

The little tailor knew about the forest witch's prediction, which his parents had related to him, but since his intelligence was as great as his body was small, he understood that even though one may hope to be the Great Panjandrum, it is not sufficient reason for one to live a life of leisure. He had to pin his hopes on the domain of the seven provinces, but until that domain came into his possession he toiled the whole blessed day, pushing needles and pulling thread while singing a duet with a blackbird whose cage hung from the ceiling of his workshop.

As his good or bad fortune depended on killing or not killing seven with one blow, the little tailor always had his eye out for that number. If he was walking along a road and came across a file of ants that he crushed with one stamp of his foot, he would count the dead ants to see if there were seven; if he fired his shotgun at a flock of sparrows, he would also count the dead birds to see if they numbered seven; but the number seven did not turn up, because it was always his misfortune to have killed more or fewer ants or sparrows.

One morning the little tailor was in his shop singing and sewing trousers when a woman passed by selling fresh, hot rolls, and he bought several to have them for a midmorning snack along with a glass of white wine as soon as he finished the trousers, which now only needed to have buttons put on. While he was doing so he set the rolls on the table, and a swarm of flies settled on them. Tired of trying to drive them away with his hand, the little tailor became angry and swatted the rolls with the trousers, killing a number of flies, which he counted immediately.

Oh, pleasure of pleasures, he had killed seven flies with one blow!

"Well, sir," he said, "now I have the right to take over the domain of the seven provinces, which must be a good thing. But as for the right of possession, there's many a slip twixt cup and lip, in other words, easier said than done. Nowadays to take a crown properly it's not enough to have a right to it; it's necessary to make oneself worthy of taking it by dint of one's ingenuity and effort. Where are the seven provinces whose domain belong to me? It's my obligation to find out and that is the task I am going to undertake immediately."

The little tailor sold his scant belongings, except for the blackbird, with which he refused to part, crossed his chest with a band on which he had written in big letters I KILL SEVEN WITH ONE BLOW, dressed up in a kind of overcoat that concealed the band, put the blackbird in the pocket, and set out on his journey in search of the promised land.

In the first town that he passed through he was advised to change direction, because on the mountain toward which he was heading there roamed a giant who robbed and killed all travelers. The little tailor's sole reply was to unbutton his coat and show, with a smile on his face, the words on the band.

Upon reading it, they all stepped back, frightened, but when the little tailor calmed them down by explaining that he only used his herculean strength against evildoers, they exclaimed joyfully:

"Thank heaven that rascally giant is going to meet someone who will have it out with him!"

Indeed, no sooner had the little tailor begun to cross over the mountain than he met up with the ferocious giant, who said to him imperiously:

"Stop right there, kid!"

"What do you mean . . . kid?" the tailor responded. "I'll have you know that I'm every inch a man."

The giant burst out laughing at these arrogant words and was about to give him a boot when the little tailor half-opened his coat, whereupon the giant stepped back, reading the writing on the band.

"But is it true that you kill seven with one blow?" he asked, amazed.

"Tangle with me, you and six others like you, and you'll see how quickly I'll send you on the way to eternity."

"Well, since you're so strong, show me some proof so I can believe it," said the giant.

"What kind of proof do you want?"

"Something very simple. Let's see if a stone that you throw up in the air takes as long to come down as another that I'm going to throw."

"Agreed. Throw one."

The giant picked up a stone from the ground and threw it so high that it took a full minute to come down.

"So what do you think, my friend?" asked the giant, very pleased with his feat.

"What I think," answered the little tailor, "is that without trying I can throw a stone higher than that one. Yours took one minute to come down. Take out your watch and start counting the minutes until mine comes down."

And the little tailor, who upon pretending that he was stooping to pick up a stone had actually grasped, not a stone, but the blackbird that he had in his coat pocket, flung the blackbird, which disappeared in space without the giant's being able to follow its flight, because the giant was shortsighted, and besides, night was beginning to fall.

The giant, watch in hand, was counting minutes, and the stone was not coming down.

"Hey," the little tailor said to him, "keep on counting, because I'm in a hurry and I can't wait for my stone to come down."

"God be with you," the giant replied respectfully, astonished that there was a man with such strength.

And the little tailor continued on his way.

III

The little tailor walked and walked and came to a very beautiful and vast kingdom divided by a wide, fast-flowing river.

"I wonder if this is the country where I'm to take possession of my domain," the little tailor thought to himself, but the information that he was given did not encourage him to believe that he had reached the promised land. In the first place, the kingdom did not consist of seven provinces, but fourteen; and in the second, the throne was occupied by a still very young king, and this king had an uncommonly beautiful daughter who was being courted by numerous princes, among whom undoubtedly was the one who would succeed the reigning monarch.

The little tailor arrived at the court and, while visiting the palace gardens, saw the princess leaning out a window.

"Good Lord!" he exclaimed. "What a lovely girl!" And he gazed at her as if fascinated until the princess withdrew.

As he was exhausted from so much walking, no sooner did he sit down on a bench set against a tree and lean back on the trunk than he fell asleep thinking about the princess, not without first having been mindful of unbuttoning his overcoat so that passersby could read the letters on the band and take care not to approach him.

Indeed, all those who saw him and read "I kill seven with one blow" said:

"What prodigious strength this foreigner has in spite of being so little! We need a man of his mettle to beat up on our enemies in a time of war like the one that threatens us with the neighboring kingdom."

Among those who read the words on the little tailor's band was one of the king's ministers, who told the story to His Majesty, advising him to invite such an incomparable warrior to enter into his service.

The king received this counsel as prudence prescribed on the eve of war with the neighboring kingdom.

Invited in the name of the king to join the army of the nation where his good luck had brought him, the little tailor acceded to the monarch's wishes—and I call it good luck because the little tailor himself considered it such, solely because the princess with whom he had fallen in love was from that nation.

Officers in the army were not well-disposed toward the foreigner's entrance into the service, not so much because they envied the honors and preferential treatment accorded him by the king, but because, as they said, apparently with ample justification:

"Who would want for a comrade a man as ruthless as he is? The day that we have a quarrel with him over some trifle he'll exterminate all of us with his might, because who can go up against a man that kills seven with one blow?"

A delegation of army officers appeared before the king and informed His Majesty that all of them were resolved to resign from the service, and even to swallow the bitter pill of emigration, if His Majesty did not discharge the foreigner from the army.

The king granted that his officers were in the right and judged it his duty not to part with so many and such distinguished regulars in order to retain an upstart foreigner in his service, but he said, apparently with good reason:

"And who in the devil is going to bell the cat? Who's courageous enough to tell that Sevenkiller to make himself scarce? If he starts to rain blows, killing, as he does, seven men with one blow, in one day he'll wipe out the army and me. As the saying goes, brain is better than brawn. Since the 'brawn' is dangerous, let's rid ourselves of that hellion with 'brain.'"

The king summoned Sevenkiller, the name by which the little tailor was known. When he arrived, the princess just happened to be with the king, and as His Majesty noticed that the redoubtable warrior's eyes lit up on seeing his daughter, he decided to take advantage of the fact that he was smitten by her.

"Listen," His Majesty said to the little tailor, "for some time now two ferocious outlaws have been roaming the forest beyond the river, robbing and murdering at will, and for as hard as I've tried I have been unable to exterminate them. Would you be capable of doing away with these villains who disgrace and terrorize my kingdom?"

"I'm capable of that and much more," answered the little tailor, showing His Majesty the words on the band.

"Understand that besides having the disposition of a wild beast and the slyness of a fox, they're stronger than Goliath the giant."

"I assure Your Majesty that I shall undertake responsibility for doing away with them, provided Your Majesty promises me a reward commensurate with the service."

As he spoke the little tailor did not take his eyes off the princess, a fact which was not lost on the king.

"If you keep your promise," said His Majesty, "I shall give you my daughter's hand, and with it half of my kingdom, that is, the seven provinces beyond the river."

"We are in agreement," replied the little tailor, who for his part noticed that the princess's eyes lit up when the king spoke of ending her unmarried state.

IV

The little tailor set out for the forest beyond the river, certain now that there lay the seven provinces whose domain he had been predestined from birth to oversee, and by order of the king he was being escorted by a cavalry troop.

Upon arriving at the forest he came across a very frightened woodcutter.

"What's the matter?" he asked him.

"I've spotted the two outlaws taking a nap under a big tree, over there in that opening that you can see."

"And that frightens you?"

"How could it not frighten me?" asked the woodcutter, astonished at that little man's calmness. And he went away, convinced that both the little man and the cavalry troop that accompanied him would soon pay for their boldness with their lives.

"You stay here. I can deal with these outlaws on my own," the little tailor said to the soldiers.

The latter begged him in the name of God and the Virgin Mary not to be foolish enough to enter the forest alone, but the little tailor paid no attention to them and headed for the opening that the woodcutter had pointed out.

It did not take long for him to see the two outlaws stretched out on their backs under a tree that had very dense branches, and after he filled his pockets with pebbles he climbed the tree with the agility of a squirrel.

The little tailor straddled a branch and, well-concealed by the foliage, took one of the pebbles that he carried in his pockets and dropped it on the chest of one of the outlaws.

"What in blazes!" exclaimed the outlaw, awakening and giving his partner a shove. "Why are you punching me in the chest?"

"Punching you? You're dreaming."

"No, I'm not, you are—and you punched me, no doubt, while dreaming."

"Maybe that's true."

"Well, don't let it happen again."

The two outlaws began to snore once more, and the little tailor took another pebble and dropped it on the chest of the second outlaw.

"Damn it, you've bruised me right in the chest!" the outlaw exclaimed, waking his partner.

"Me?"

"Yes, you."

"You're dreaming."

"The one who's dreaming is you."

"Maybe while dreaming I hit you the way you hit me before."

"Well, isn't that a devil of a coincidence!"

A moment later, when the little tailor heard the two men snoring again, he took a pebble in each hand and dropped them at the same time on the two outlaws' chests. Both of them awoke, furious, and, cursing and swearing, started a no-holds-barred fist fight; from punches in the face they went to dagger thrusts and soon fell to the ground, simultaneously, in the throes of death. The little tailor then came down from the tree, drew his sword, and ran them through, because the two outlaws were nearly departed and unable to defend themselves.

The little tailor, his sword still stained with blood, went to inform the soldiers that he had killed the outlaws, and, loading the bodies of the latter on two mules, returned with them to the palace.

The king, who was more desirous of ridding himself of the little tailor than of the outlaws, refused to give the princess's hand and half of his kingdom to Sevenkiller if he did not undertake another exploit, one from which the king believed the little tailor would not emerge alive.

"My daughter and the seven provinces beyond the river are worth a great deal, and what's worth a great deal costs a great deal," said His Majesty. "The secret police have informed me that the people are grumbling that the service you've rendered me is not commensurate with the reward I've promised you. What the people need, entre nous, is a carrot and a stick, which is what they get from enlightened absolute monarchs, but as modesty does not permit me to consider myself such a monarch, I have to placate the people, because it would not amuse you or me if they rose in revolt and we lost everything, you the seven provinces beyond the river and I the seven on this side."

"Your Majesty is in the right."

"Well, then. In another of the forests beyond the river there's a unicorn who has eviscerated a lot of the people and a lot of the livestock in one of my provinces, and I've tried in vain to kill it. Let's see if you'll take it on as you took on the outlaws, who were almost as fearsome as the unicorn."

"There's no more than that needed to silence the grumbling of the sovereign people?"

"No more than that."

"In that case, Your Majesty will soon see the unicorn brought here meeker than a lamb."

And so saying, the little tailor gathered a length of good hemp rope, a good olive wood cudgel, and a good ax, and set out for the unicorn's forest. No sooner did he enter it than the creature, which, to be sure, was a terrible animal, charged furiously to impale him with its horn. But the little tailor, who had studied the "science" of bullfighting, took cover behind a tree, and the beast, running at full speed, buried its horn in the trunk of the tree instead of the little tailor's insides, and could not tug it out for as much as it bucked and kicked. Whereupon the little tailor, very calmly, put the rope around the unicorn's neck, beat it with his cudgel and made it more pliable than cordovan leather, and chopped the horn with the ax, and, leading the unicorn by the rope, returned to the palace amid the applause of the people.

V

The little tailor believed that his marriage to the princess was now a *fait accompli*, but the king came out with some rot about Sevenkiller needing to undertake and execute another exploit in order for him to marry his daughter and wear the crown of the domain beyond the river. Even the princess herself, who was crazier and crazier about the little tailor, made an angry gesture when she learned of her august father's dodge.

"You've heard, have you not, that the third time is lucky?" His Majesty asked the little tailor.

"Yes, Sire, I have, but what does that have to do with us?"

"What that has to do with us is that the people are grumbling—"

"Not the people again! There's nothing that irks me more than these shamefaced kings who don't dare to be absolute or constitutional. All this concern about the people! The people approve of what's fair."

"You think it's as easy as rolling off a log. Don't talk nonsense. Who called for Christ's crucifixion?"

"That wasn't the people, that was a mob."

"Call it what you will."

"In any case, I'm not in the mood for conversation. Am I or am I not going to marry Your Majesty's daughter?"

"Yes, but the people—"

"Here we go again."

"The people are saying that it would be an unforgivable error not to take advantage of the opportunity presented to me of delivering them from a great calamity."

"And what calamity is that?"

"A bloodthirsty and monstrous wild boar that's spreading desolation and grief in one of the most beautiful provinces beyond the river."

"Well, I'll kill it as soon as I marry the princess."

"Oh, no. If you don't kill it before you'll never kill it, because my daughter will not allow her august husband to run the risk of leaving her a widow."

"All right, then, let's get down to work. Your Majesty'll see what tasty slices of boar meat we're going to have to snack on this winter."

The little tailor set out for the boar's forest, not wanting hunters or soldiers to accompany him. The only thing he did was ask for the key to a hermitage that stood halfway through the forest, the door to which he opened all the way, leaving the key in the outside lock. And he went off at once to search for the boar in the area surrounding the hermitage. The beast promptly caught a glimpse of the little tailor and chased after him furiously as soon as it did. The little tailor ran toward the hermitage and dashed into it; the boar raced in behind him, and, when it was inside, the little tailor jumped outside through the window that faced the portico and closed the door while the boar was struggling to jump through the same window. Once the boar was penned in, the little tailor called it over to the wicket of the door, and the beast came immediately, trying to put its snout through the wicket; and through the very wicket the little tailor ran his sword through its mouth.

Shortly afterward the little tailor was returning to the palace, transporting the dead boar in a cart and receiving the most enthusiastic ovation ever given to any man.

The rascal of a king still tried to avoid keeping his sacred promise, but the people rebelled in view of such villainy, and had the king not been careful his persistence would have been more trouble than it was worth.

"Sire," the little tailor said to him when he saw that the people were swearing that they would rise in revolt if the king continued to go back on his word, "I do not wish to violate Your Majesty's will. Does Your Majesty deign to grant me your august daughter's hand and the crown of the domain beyond the river?"

"A fine tailor you are!" exclaimed the king with a forced smile, and he finally decided to bring happiness to his daughter and the little tailor, who got married immediately.

When the little tailor took the crown of the domain beyond the river he would have remembered with pride, had he not been so modest, that he had been faithful to his maxim that nowadays to take a crown it is not enough to have a right to it: it is also necessary to make oneself worthy of taking it by dint of ingenuity and effort.

Antonio de Trueba

"The King's Son-in-Law"

I

THERE once lived a king who was so avaricious that, instead of spending his life engaged in making his vassals happy, he spent it crisscrossing his kingdom in search of gold and silver mines, leaving the devil at the rudder of the ship of state. A curse on such kings!

Upon passing through a village one day, he noticed that there was much joy in one wretched dwelling, inasmuch as its inhabitants were shooting skyrockets from the window and tossing coins and fruit to children. The king asked the reason behind that joy, and people told him that it was because the man and woman who lived there had had a son born feetfirst, which augured very well; and since a fortuneteller in the village prophesied that the boy would succeed in whatever he undertook, and that at the age of fifteen he would marry the daughter of a king, everybody had already begun calling the boy "the king's son-in-law."

The king, who was as superstitious as he was avaricious and evil, thought to himself:

What a turn of events it would be if the king's daughter that the boy marries is my own, so that besides the shame of being the father-in-law of a yokel, I should be deprived of the enormous riches that a son-in-law of my class would bring me!

And so he called on the parents of the newborn infant and told them to give him the child, as he was assuming the responsibility of raising him and educating him like a prince, and then of marrying him off to the daughter of one of his ministers.

At first the boy's parents refused to accede to the king's proposition, but the king offered them money, and in the end they agreed, reasoning that since the boy had been born under a lucky star and all was supposed to turn out well for him, no harm could come his way if he went to live with the king in the palace.

59

The king's idea was to drown the boy in a river that flowed close
to the village, but when he was about to throw him into the water
he noticed that the boy bore a striking resemblance to his daughter,
and he did not have the heart for such an evil deed. What he did
was place him in a big box, in which air entered only through a little
hole in the lid, and throw the box into the river, whose current swept
it away, causing the king to lose sight of it immediately.

The box floated as far as the millrace of a mill, where it was spotted
by the miller's servant, who had gone to lower the sluice gate; thinking
that there would be some kind of treasure in it, he pulled the box
ashore with a hook. Upon opening it, he found the infant, who had
slept all the way there and who, upon hearing the young man strike
repeated blows with a stone to open the box, awoke with a smile on
his rosy and beautiful little face.

The day before, the two-month-old child of the miller's wife had
died, and the servant thought that this infant would be a great consolation
to her. And he was not mistaken, for as soon as the miller's wife put
that miraculously found infant to her breast, she felt as consoled as
if she had regained her very own, and in a few short days came to
love him as if she were his mother.

II

More than fourteen years after these events, the king, as usual, was
out searching for mines that would make him even richer than he
was, because his longing for gold and silver increased with age. All
of a sudden it started raining cats and dogs, and the king ran to take
shelter from the rain at a nearby mill, where, on account of his
handsomeness, on account of how lovingly the miller and his wife
treated him, and above all on account of how much he looked like
his daughter, a boy of around fourteen or fifteen caught his eye.

"Is this boy who's so handsome your son?" he asked the miller
and his wife.

"No, Sire," they answered. "We had only one child, and he died
at the age of two months. Our servant found this boy, over fourteen
years ago, inside a big box that was floating downriver and had stopped
in the millrace."

"And you love him a great deal?"

"As if he were our very own. Of course we love him, Sire, as no
mother has given birth to a better child!"

The king had no doubt whatsoever that the boy was the selfsame one he had thrown into the river, shut up in a big box; and more fearful than ever that the fortuneteller's prophesy would be fulfilled through the boy's marriage to his daughter, he said to the miller and his wife:

"Would you mind if the boy took a letter from me to the queen?"

"Not at all, Sire," replied the miller and his wife. "Both we and the boy are entirely at Your Majesty's disposal, and it is our duty and our pleasure to serve Your Majesty."

The king wrote a letter to the queen, telling her that as soon as she received it she was to order the bearer beheaded and buried, and he gave it to the boy together with a tip of two *duros*.

The boy set out, and on the way he came across a shirtless pauper emaciated from hunger who asked him for alms, and the boy gave him one of his two *duros*, thinking: *Well, with the* duro *that's left I have enough for my journey, and with the other one this poor devil will at least be able to buy himself a sackcloth shirt and have some garlic soup for supper tonight.*

The pauper raised his eyes to heaven, weeping out of gratitude and consolation, and asking God to watch over his benefactor, and the boy continued on his way.

Shortly afterwards the boy came across a woman, also ragged and emaciated, who asked him for alms for the love of God, and he gave her his remaining *duro*, thinking: *Well, I'm young and strong and I can go without eating until I reach the court, and with the* duro *this wretch will at least be able to buy herself a sackcloth skirt and have some garlic soup for supper tonight.*

So saying and doing, the boy continued on his way, while the beggar woman implored God and all the saints in heaven to preserve him.

As night was falling and it was raining and snowing very heavily, the boy got lost in a dense and lonely wood, through which he wandered until close to midnight, unable to find his way again. It was so cold that you had to blow on your hands to warm them, and ravenous wolves howled in the depths of the forest.

"If God doesn't help me, I'm lost," said the boy. "One of those howling wolves is going to have me for supper tonight. And if not, I'll die of the cold in this dense wood. God have mercy on me!"

As he spoke, he caught a glimpse of a faint light off in the distance, through the trees, so he headed toward it somewhat encouraged, with the hope of finding a house where he could take refuge.

His hope was not groundless, as in the end he found himself at the doorstep of a small house hidden in the thickest and remotest area of the wood. He pushed the door, since he saw light inside, and came face-to-face with a little old woman who was warming herself by the fireplace.

"What brings you here?" asked the old woman, surprised at his presence.

"What brings me here?" he said in turn. "I'm very cold, very sleepy, and very tired, and I implore you to allow me to spend the night here."

"That can't be," replied the old woman, showing him the door. "Very shortly some outlaws that I serve will come, and they'll kill you if they find you here."

"If they come, intercede on my behalf."

"I will, if you insist on staying, because you seem like such a good boy that no one can look at you without loving you, but I'm advising you not to stay here."

"I have to stay even though my life may be in danger here, because if I don't stay my death is certain. The outlaws might have pity on me, because in the end they're people; but the wolves will not take pity, because in the end they're wild beasts."

"Well, stay, and I'll do what I can to save you."

The more the old woman talked with him the more fond she grew of him, so she fed the boy supper, and he fell asleep peacefully on a bench near the fireplace.

Shortly afterwards the outlaws returned, and as soon as they saw a stranger they drew their daggers to slay him, while at the same time threatening the old woman because she had allowed him to enter; but with her entreaties and her reasons she succeeded in calming them down, and in the end they consented to let the boy live, unless he awakened before dawn, when they would be leaving the house.

But if the outlaws agreed not to kill the boy, they did not give up wanting to take any money that he carried in his pockets, to which end they searched him, finding only the king's letter.

Upon seeing that the letter bore the royal seal, the two outlaws registered great surprise inasmuch as they held a grudge against the king, who had been pursuing both in order to hang them for having forged bank bills, because, it should be pointed out, one of the outlaws was an accomplished forger of all manner of official papers.

When the outlaws opened and read the letter they were filled with joy, for they had discovered the means of playing a dirty trick on the king. The outlaw most skilled at forging papers wrote a letter imitating perfectly the king's hand and seal, and telling the queen that as soon as she received it to wed the princess to the bearer, because he was positive that they would get on well and be very happy, and then the outlaw tucked the letter into the boy's pocket in place of the king's real one.

When the boy awakened at dawn, the outlaws had already departed, and after eating a delicious ham omelette prepared for him by the old woman, he continued happily on his way.

As soon as the queen read the letter, which she did not doubt was from her husband, she arranged the marriage of the bearer and her daughter, and the wedding was celebrated with great merrymaking and rejoicing, heightened by the fact that bride and groom had fallen madly in love from the moment they saw each other.

And what a catch the girl was for the miller youth! Because it should be pointed out that the princess, with her lovely eyes, pretty face, and a certain *je ne sais quoi,* could cause a saint to go astray!

What good fortune to be born feetfirst instead of headfirst!

III

At long last the king returned to the court, fit to be tied because he had not discovered a single gold or silver mine; and when he learned that the boy, far from being buried, was married to his daughter, he flew off the handle and decided to hang the queen, because she had not done what he had ordered. But the queen made excuses, showing him the letter that the boy had given her.

The king agreed that the queen was not to blame, because the letter was forged with such expertise that he himself had a difficult time becoming convinced that the handwriting was not his, and therefore he summoned his son-in-law and asked him who had forged the letter.

"Sire," answered the boy, "I do not know for certain, but it must have been some outlaws in whose lair I spent the night on my way to the court."

Upon hearing this, the king rightly suspected that the one mixed up in this affair was the outlaw whom he was pursuing for being a forger of bank bills, but now he only thought about how to rid himself of his son-in-law with a devious scheme.

"I could have you hanged," he said, "because the notion that the king reigns without governing doesn't apply to me. I'll hang anyone—I don't care how powerful he may be—if there's a need, but so as to avoid endless talk, I'm sparing your life and will only require one thing of you in order to approve of your marriage to my daughter and name you my successor. What I require of you is that you bring me three of the devil's hairs. And do not try to fob off on me some good-for-nothing's hairs, because I'll know the real ones by the smell of sulphur and the reddish *rubicundus Judas* color."

The prince, as the young miller has to be called now, was so beside himself that you could have drowned him by *one* hair as a result of the requirement that he had to bring *three* of the devil's. So he sought the counsel of his father-in-law's first minister, an old man whom everyone called Know-It-All, because he knew everything, and who had become quite attached to the prince, speculating that one day the youth would wear the crown. Know-It-All said to him:

"It's a ticklish situation, but do not fret on that account, Your Highness, as it will all come right in the end. Everywhere that you go Your Highness should say that you *know* everything, and this will suffice for Your Highness to *obtain* everything, just as I have done. I lost both parents at the age of twelve, and I decided to explore life and find my place in the world. An old woman, who had been the housekeeper of a man who rose to director of state education simply by saying that he knew everything, said to me when I set out: 'Son, you do not know anything, but I'm going to reveal a secret to you, and with it you will obtain everything, and it is that you should always say you know everything.' In the first town that I reached there was a gentleman who needed a valet, and I went to him, asking to be taken into his employ. 'What is it that you know?' the gentleman asked me, and I replied that I knew everything. With the confidence that my master had because I had said I knew everything and with what I learned out of necessity, I managed to please my master, who ended up recommending me for a position as scribe in government offices, where, by saying that I knew everything, I rose to department director. Hearing one day that I knew everything, the king summoned me before him and asked if what people said concerning me was true. 'Yes, Sire,' I answered, 'I know everything.' And he immediately offered me a ministerial post, which is a cushy job. So do not forget the lesson, Your Highness, and you shall see how you obtain whatever you wish with it."

The prince set off for hell, resolved to make the journey in the shortest time possible, because the Constitution forbade the king to remain outside of the kingdom for more than one year, and princes for more than two, under penalty of the king losing the crown and the princes all their rights to inherit it. Of course, as the prince was taking leave of his wife the infanta, she admonished him about not "getting entangled along the way with some rascal of a woman," and about other things that are inevitable in such cases.

IV

Walking nonstop, the prince came across a band of outlaws who would murder anyone, and who, as soon as they saw him, made ready to do away with him.

"Where are you going?" asked the outlaws' leader while he was cocking his blunderbuss to blow the prince's brains out.

"To hell," replied the prince, who was incapable of lying to anyone.

Upon hearing this answer, the leader uncocked his blunderbuss and embraced him, saying:

"That arrogant answer saves you, because we appreciate brave men, who, like you, talk big even though they may be looking death in the eye."

The prince continued on his way, and, walking nonstop, arrived at a city where only laments and pleas were heard. He did not ask anyone what was going on, since by asking he would have confessed that he did not know everything, but he learned everything from the people's conversations. There was such a marvelous fountain in the city that nearly all illnesses were cured by drinking its waters, and as a result the city always found itself full of strangers who came to drink them, and in exchange for the health that they regained, they left a fortune there. But the fountain had not flowed for eight days, and although a donkey loaded with gold had been offered to whoever succeeded in making it flow again, no one had been successful and there was no longer hope that anyone would be. Naturally, every stranger who arrived in the city was asked what it was that he knew, to see if someone among them knew about plumbing. The prince was also asked this question, and he answered that he knew everything, but when the people then inquired why the fountain had stopped flowing, he said that he was in a great hurry and that upon his return he would give the longed-for answer and win the donkey loaded with gold.

The inhabitants of the city were much consoled with the hope given them by the prince, who continued on his way.

Walking nonstop, he arrived at another city, where everything was also laments and pleas, because in that city there grew an enormous apple tree, whose apples were so marvelously luscious in smell, color, and taste that representatives from all the foreign kingdoms came to buy them for the tables of kings, and the city sold them for their weight in gold. But the apple tree, whose fruit brought in a veritable fortune, was drying up and no remedy was in the offing, despite the fact that the city had offered a donkey loaded with gold to whoever managed to remedy that public calamity.

There, as in the first city, all strangers were asked what it was that they knew, to see if someone among them knew about arboriculture, and the prince was also asked. He answered that he knew everything, but that, as he was in a great hurry, he would defer treating the apple tree and winning the donkey loaded with gold until his return.

The prince continued on his way, leaving the inhabitants of the second city also filled with hope and consolation, and, walking nonstop, arrived at an inn near a river and spent the night there. When he had already gone to bed, two peasants leading a donkey loaded with gold nuggets arrived at the inn, and also spent the night there. Those two peasants were elated because they had discovered a gold mine so rich that, working it with what little they knew about mining operations, they had extracted enough gold to load the donkey.

Of course, they refrained from telling a soul that they had discovered it, but hearing the innkeeper say that there was a traveler at the inn who was a well of knowledge, and seeing that their pleasure was lessened by the difficulty in finding someone who could direct the excavation of the mine, it occurred to them that perhaps they would find in that sage the one they needed, and they decided to pump him in the morning to see if he understood about mines.

Sure enough, in the morning they called the prince aside and asked him what he knew.

"I know everything," answered the prince.

The peasants believed that by this he meant that he knew about the discovery they had made, and they looked at each other as though saying: *My friend, he's seen through us and it's futile now to use pretexts with him. Let's speak frankly to see if he wishes to take charge of working the mine, and if he doesn't, then let's buy his silence, even if it's with all the gold we've brought on the donkey, because we'll not want for gold as long as we keep the mine a secret.*

"Well, since you know everything," they said to the prince, "let's speak frankly. Do you want to take charge of working the mine we've discovered?"

"That can't be," answered the prince, "because I'm in a big hurry."

"Well, where are you going?"

"To hell."

Upon hearing this, the peasants believed that the sage was very short-tempered, and they only thought about buying his silence so that he would not divulge their secret. They offered him the donkey loaded with gold if he swore not to say anything to anyone about the mine; the prince swore it, and shortly afterward continued on his way, leaving the gold-laden donkey at the inn until his return, and thinking to himself: *Where in the devil can the mine discovered by those peasants be? I'm sorry I don't know, because it would be great news for my father-in-law.*

Walking nonstop, he arrived at the bank of the river, which one crossed by boat. The boatman there found himself in a very particular set of circumstances. Although he was already sixty years old, he had been working since the age of twelve because he could not find anyone to replace him in that occupation, which he utterly hated. When he was still a boy, his mother, who was a saint, saw with profound sorrow that he was fond of spending time in taverns, and she feared that he would become corrupted in them and be damned. So that he would never go to taverns, and, consequently, not be damned, she asked God for a favor, which he granted in view of her saintliness, and it was that her son not be able to leave the boat as long as no one got in who had steered one more clumsily than he. As soon as any man got in the boat, the boatman would put the oar in his hands and then try to get out. But he had been putting all of them to this test for more than forty years, and he had been doing so in vain. How very clumsy the boatman must have been!

Curiosity spurred him to learn if he was destined to end his days there or if he would at long last find someone to replace him, and he asked the prince, as he asked everyone, if he knew how to dispel his doubts.

"I know everything," answered the prince, "but we'll talk upon my return, because I'm in a great hurry now."

"Well, where are you going in such a great hurry?"

"To hell."

The boatmen did not dare to ask more questions of someone who answered so disagreeably, and the prince continued on his way.

V

The prince had heard that hell is hot country, and with this sign he hoped to find the place he was looking for. Walking nonstop, he began to feel so oppressively warm that he had no alternative but to take off little by little almost all his clothes. When he had only his shirt on, and was about to take it off too, he discovered a cave and had no doubt, judging by all the people who were entering it, that it was the approach to hell.

He also entered, and, walking nonstop, reached the apartment of the devil, who by chance was not at home at the time, as he was very involved in the formation of political parties of some sort.

The devil had many servants, and one of them sent word to his lady, who had the prince come to her drawing room at once. He found her sitting on a sofa, crammed into a hoopskirt that took up half of the seating area.

"Is that gentleman not in?" asked the prince, somewhat embarrassed by his dishabille.

"No, sir," answered the lady with a winsome smile, gathering the hoop skirt a little so that he could sit beside her. "And give thanks to God that he isn't, because he has such a diabolic temper that if he were in you wouldn't leave here alive."

"Why?"

"Because he's jealous as the devil."

"He likes women, does he?"

"How could he not like us!"

"It's true that you're of great use to him."

"We're his hands and feet for everything."

"Well, before he comes, I'm going to tell you what brings me here, for it's truly a thorny predicament."

Encouraged by the tender glances and tempting smiles given him by the devil's lady, the prince asked her assistance in obtaining, in the first place, three hairs from the horned one's head, and in the second, the solution to the three problems he had left unresolved on the way, namely, that of the fountain, that of the apple tree, and that of the boatman.

The lady, who was more and more cordial and helpful to the prince, and who had studied with the devil to solve the most formidable questions, was racking her brains in order to find the means to oblige her visitor, when, lo and behold, the devil knocked on the door, and in order to save the prince from his clutches she had no alternative but to hide him under her hoopskirt.

"It smells of a Christian here!" exclaimed the devil as he entered and contracted his nostrils like someone taking snuff. "It smells of a Christian, and may Satan and his followers take me if there isn't one around here!"

"Go to the devil with your apprehensions!" the lady said to him, as if it were the most natural thing in the world. "When are you going to stop making this place hell with your damned jealousy?"

"I'm telling you it smells of a Christian . . ."

"It probably smells of horns, God forgive me!"

The horned one finally settled down, because women are capable of deceiving the devil himself, and since he was exhausted from all the work given to him by politicians, he sat on a low little chair and rested his head on the lady's knees so that she could smooth out his hair, which had stood on end from fright when he imagined that the apartment smelled of a Christian.

No sooner did he rest his head than he fell asleep and began to snore, to the great satisfaction of the prince, whose blood ran cold up to that point. The lady then took a hair between her index finger and thumb, and . . . in a trice pulled it out and gave it to the prince, slipping her hand through the slit in her dress and whatever else was there that I don't know about.

The devil awoke in pain when his hair was pulled, exclaiming:

"The devil! You hurt me!"

"Be quiet," said the lady. "The fact is that I pulled your hair while I was dreaming, because I had fallen asleep, and I was dreaming the strangest thing . . ."

"And what was it that you were dreaming?" asked the devil, who was curious as the devil.

"That in a city it's all laments and pleas because a fountain has stopped flowing."

"And it won't flow again as long as they don't kill a toad that has gotten stuck in the piping."

And he fell asleep again.

As soon as the devil started snoring again, the lady took hold of another hair, and . . . in a trice pulled it out and also gave it to the prince through the slit in her dress and whatever else was there.

"The devil! You made me see stars!" shouted the devil, waking up again.

"Be quiet," said the lady. "I was dreaming this time too, since I had fallen asleep again and was having the strangest dream . . ."

"And what was your dream?"

"I was dreaming that in another city it's all laments and pleas because an apple tree is drying up."

"And it will dry up for sure if they don't kill a mouse that is gnawing its roots."

When the lady heard him snoring, she took another hair, and . . .
in a trice pulled it out and gave it to the prince through the slit.

"What in the name of Satan are you doing!" exclaimed the furious
devil, waking up again in pain.

"Be quiet," said the lady. "I pulled your hair while I was dreaming,
since I had fallen asleep again and I was having the strangest dream
. . ."

"And what were you dreaming?"

"That a very clumsy boatman is itching to know whether or not
he'll find someone to replace him."

"And nothing less than a king will replace him."

And again the devil fell asleep.

The prince, very quietly, then came out from under the lady's
hoopskirt, where he had not suffocated from the heat thanks to his
flimsy dress, and if he did not make off with the lady's soul at his
departure, it was because the lady's soul belonged to the devil.

VI

The prince embarked on his homeward journey, donning more clothes
again as he put distance between himself and hell, which is hot country.
When he came to the aforementioned boat, he filled the boatman's
heart with joy by announcing that he was going to be replaced, and
by none other than a king. The grateful boatman told him that the
day before he passed by there, two peasants had crossed with a gold-
laden donkey, which proved that somewhere on the other side there
had to be a very rich mine.

A good piece of news for my father-in-law, the prince thought to
himself.

At the inn the prince collected the donkey loaded with gold, and,
walking nonstop with the donkey ahead of him, arrived at the city
of the apple tree. He searched for the mouse that was gnawing the
roots of that valuable tree, and killed it, and the following day the
apple tree began to flourish, in view of which the city, overjoyed and
grateful, gave him the promised donkey loaded with gold.

Walking nonstop, with his two gold-laden donkeys ahead of him,
the prince arrived at the city of the fountain. He searched for the toad
caught in the piping, and killed it, and the fountain started flowing
again, for which reason the city, filled with joy and gratitude, gave
him another donkey loaded with gold.

Walking nonstop with his three gold-laden donkeys, the prince arrived at court, embraced his wife the infanta, without telling her of course that he had gotten entangled in the hoopskirt of a rascal of a woman, and presented the king his father-in-law with the devil's three hairs, which the king recognized as authentic.

When the king saw the three donkeys loaded with gold, he opened his eyes wide and asked his son-in-law where the mine was that produced all that gold, and since his son-in-law told him that it had to be on the other side of the aforementioned river, the king immediately set out to cross it and search for the mine.

In the meantime the prince thought to himself:

Why the devil do I need three donkeys loaded with gold, if for my modest ambition my wife's love and the principality's revenue are enough for me? I'll go with them by the mill where I grew up, in order to bestow riches on those who raised me so lovingly, and if on the way I run across the two beggars to whom I distributed the two duros that my father-in-law gave me as a tip, they won't go away with their hands empty, because I believe that I owe all my good fortune to the blessings they asked on my behalf.

Walking nonstop with his three gold-laden donkeys, the prince passed through a village, and at the doorway of a squalid house he saw an old man and an old woman sunning themselves. Upon taking a good look at their faces, he recognized in them the two beggars whom he had aided when he was delivering the king's letter, and he gave them one of the donkeys loaded with gold. As he continued on his way, the old people blessed him and cried with joy, saying:

"Now we have the means to journey to court and learn the whereabouts of the beloved son that the king took from us!"

What can those good old people be saying? the prince thought to himself upon hearing them. *It must be about some rascally trick played by my father-in-law, who's a real gem!*

And walking nonstop downriver with his two gold-laden donkeys, he arrived at the mill where he had been raised, and after spending several days in the loving company of the man and woman who had acted as his parents, he left them the two donkeys loaded with gold, and returned to court, where his wife the infanta, more and more in love with him, awaited her husband the prince.

Nearly a year had gone by since the king's departure and he had not returned, which was a serious matter, because in accordance with the Constitution he lost the crown if he did not return by the expiration of one year after his exit from the kingdom. The one year expired without the king returning, and the crown passed to the head of his son-in-law, who devoted himself heart and soul to the happiness of his vassals, who stood in great need of him, as the previous monarch had turned everything upside down on account of his intemperate zeal in searching for gold and silver mines.

But what happened to the king? The king had replaced the boatman, because he had steered the ship of state more clumsily than the boatman his craft, and for the rest of his days was unable to leave the boat, because no one more clumsy than he got into it. A curse on such kings!

Juan Eugenio Hartzenbusch (1806–80)

The son of a German father and a Spanish mother, Hartzenbusch was born in Madrid, where he worked during his youth as a cabinetmaker, his father's trade, before turning to journalism. Schooled in Spain's capital by Jesuits, he studied rhetoric, philosophy, and languages, which was how he came to translate French and Italian dramatists. A gifted scholar, writer, and prosodist, Hartzenbusch prepared editions of works by Spain's Golden Age authors, became a member of the Royal Spanish Academy, and for over a dozen years served as director of the Biblioteca Nacional in Madrid.

Hartzenbusch owes the lion's share of his literary fame to The Lovers of Teruel *[Los amantes de Teruel] (1837), far and away the best of his plays, and one of the best of Spanish romantic plays of the nineteenth century. He also wrote poetry, essays,* Fables in Castilian Verse *[Fábulas en verso castellano] (1848), and* Stories and Fables *[Cuentos y fábulas] (1861).*

The first story of the latter book is "Beauty as Punishment" [La hermosura por castigo], a tale rich in human vanity and extrahuman occurrences. Another well-known story of his is "The Golden Bride" [La novia de oro], which is written in old Spanish, and for which Hartzenbusch took the trouble to include a glossary or vocabulary of old Spanish that runs to six compact pages in the 1863 Leipzig edition of his Selected Works *[Obras escogidas].*

Juan Eugenio Hartzenbusch

"Beauty as Punishment"
A Moral Tale

THE "Marvel of the East," people called Emperor Teodosio's daughter, the incomparably beautiful Pulqueria, who enjoyed such flattering renown from nearly the tender age of thirteen. The gentle disposition of the princess, born, like her father, in Itálica,* the soft comeliness of her virginal countenance, the Spanish gracefulness of her figure, her clear mind, and above all her decorous life attracted numerous devoted admirers of high station from near and far, but nary a one noticed a very grave flaw that must have greatly overshadowed the outstanding charms of the august maiden. The daughter of Valentinian's successor, the sister of Arcadio and Honorio, the idol of the imperial family, had never seen her parents, nor her brothers, nor any*one*, nor any*thing*. Pulqueria, whose bewitching, almond-shaped eyes were the envy of the most genteel ladies of Constantinople, could not see them; Pulqueria had been born blind and lived sightless throughout her youth. As a blind child she heard the loving words spoken by her mother Flaccila when she nursed; as a blind child she received the blessing of that most saintly of women when the Lord called her to accept, in the company of angels, the due reward for her sublime virtues; and as a blind child she listened to the devoted and amorous entreaties of Prince Favencio, who sought and obtained the promise of the father and the daughter of being able to call her his wife when she was a maiden of fifteen summers.

Pulqueria was happy because she was the daughter of such a father, happier because of the feminine pulchritude and the spirit with which Providence had endowed her, and still more happy because of her family's love for her, but so many and such superlative gifts meant nothing to her from the time that, in the fullness of youth and giving ear to the universal voice that proclaimed her the loveliest of all beauties, there took root in her heart the vain and vehement desire to see in

74

order to see herself. Persuaded, and rightly so, that her mother dwelled in glory in the abode of the blessed, every night she fervently implored her to intercede with the Almighty for the gift of sight.

And one night Flaccila appeared to Pulqueria in her sleep, or rather, one night Pulqueria felt that Flaccila was miraculously embracing her. The happy matron, whose immortal brow was wreathed with the divine laurel of virtuous wives, held a palm leaf in her right hand and a crown formed by stars in her left. "My dear daughter," Flaccila said to her in a mellifluous voice, "God, who knows better than man what's in man's interest, continually refuses to satisfy your imprudent wishes, because if he satisfied them they would irremediably bring you harm. When the Lord who gave you life keeps you blind, it's a sign that he wants you to remain blind. And as the Divine Majesty can only want what's best and just, you can be certain that deprivation of sight was as great a blessing for you as having it is for us. Nevertheless, the Lord, moved by my entreaties, as I was by yours, has decided at last to grant it to you, by virtue of his infinite wisdom and power. But so that this gift, instead of causing you harm, will serve to gain you the rich crown and imperishable palm of martyrs, victorious insignias that I hold out to your hands for you to touch, it's necessary, my daughter, for you to resign yourself to not seeing, until the very moment of your death, what you most earnestly wish to behold. Say if at that price you wish to receive eyesight, and tomorrow at noon it will be granted to you supernaturally."

With that swiftness with which the soul of man, in witness of his celestial origin, sometimes ponders over everything to be pondered in a difficult matter and resolves it with a single thought, in the imperceptible space of time that she used to speak nine words followed by a "Yes," this lengthy reasoning went through Pulqueria's mind: *If the Lord gives me a precious gift that I've longed for so much, and this gift, limited in part, is to bring me, besides happiness on Earth, the happiness of the just, I would in truth be insane if I didn't accept it. What do I love most in the world? First, my father; next, my future husband; and then, my brothers. It would be hard for me not to see my Favencio, the emperor, and Arcadio and Honorio until the hour of my death. But I'll see the sun from which the day is born and the stars that illuminate the night; I'll see the sea, whose roars I hear from my bed; I'll see the Earth that I walk and the creatures that inhabit it, the grandeur and splendor of this magnificent palace. It is a small sacrifice to always remain blind to a single thing if I am able to fill my sight with the vastness of creation in its entirety.* "I accept the condition, Mother. I want to see. Yes." No sooner did she utter this monosyllable, with the dull articulation of someone who talks in her sleep, than the celestial vision vanished or withdrew.

The joys that come from Heaven differ from purely human pleasures in one notable respect: the latter, when they are especially intense, fatigue us and sometimes wear us out, like the most acute pain; the delights that the Almighty sends to his favorites, as intense as they may be, are enjoyed calmly, without detriment to our weak physical makeup. Thus did Pulqueria, after the disappearance of her mother, continue to sleep peacefully; and peacefully and joyfully she awoke at the usual hour; peacefully and joyfully she let her maids dress her; and then she went to the emperor's room, but in order for the surprise to be greater, she wished to keep from her father, as well as from her brothers, the marvelous visit that she had received the night before.

The inner jubilation that Pulqueria savored produced a single visible effect—that of animating her face with such a new enchantment, her voice with such a sweet ring, her gestures and movements with such an admirable combination of dignity and charm that never, not even on the day she learned that Favencio returned her love, had those around her seen her so happy and so beautiful. Sitting across from the emperor in a magnificent salon, with her brothers on one side and her lover on the other, all of them, even Teodosio himself, affectionately praised her wondrous beauty, never more dazzling than at that moment, when the sun reached the midway point of its journey.

Instantaneously and marvelously, as though she were opening her eyes after a brief, peaceful sleep, and without the light offending them, the beautiful daughter of Flaccila and Teodosio, the loveliest of the daughters of Itálica, found herself with the divine gift offered by her mother, and she discovered what it was to see, what it really was to live, what it was to get drunk with joy and grow weak out of sheer contentment.

Her surprise and delight were voiced with a prolonged *Ooooh!*, as were the admiration and joy triggered by the discovery and possession of a happiness that was greater than hope could imagine it, greater than desire wished it would be. Three times she closed and immediately opened her eyes; three times she thought she had died and revived. She got to know Favencio, she got to know Teodosio, she got to know her brothers, the sun, the sky, the clouds, the fields, the sea, statues, paintings, the brilliance of jewels, the iridescence of silk . . . and she wished, finally, to know herself. Teodosio brought her a mirror made of burnished gold . . . she looked at herself in it . . . and saw in the polished convex surface a robe and cloak over it, and above them she also saw a necklace, and, higher up, an earring on either side, and higher still, a diadem or headband adorned with precious stones, and all these images of the robe, cloak, necklace, earrings, and headband moved simultaneously in the mirror as Pulqueria moved her body and her head, but of a human figure . . . not a trace was to be seen in the mirror.

The princess raised her right hand to her forehead, and then part of the diadem disappeared as if it had been covered with something; appearing in the mirror were the bracelet and ring that adorned the hand placed on the forehead, but neither the forehead nor the hand could be seen. After several very quick trials, she became convinced that the mirror reflected all the objects that were placed in front of it, save the image of the princess from head to foot.

She then tried other mirrors of different substances, and the same thing occurred with all of them. Pulqueria wanted to explain to those present the terrible wonder and relate the conversation that she had had with Flaccila, but against her will her tongue refused to reveal the secret, which by divine order was to be kept hidden for many years.

She asked her father and everybody else if they saw her in the mirror, and they said yes, because for them it reproduced Pulqueria's image the same as that of any other person. She realized, then, that the object that was not to be visible to her in her life was her body, her charms, and therefore that what she loved most, and most earnestly longed to see in the world, was not her father, nor her brothers, nor the man to whom she had devoted her first and only love: it was she herself.

And if Pulqueria entertained any manner of doubt, the unspeakable torment that she began to feel from the instant she saw no reflection of herself in the burnished gold disk would have made her understand that a celebrated beauty, to which all paid homage, naturally—perhaps without realizing it, and even without consciously wishing it—would ultimately come to worship itself. Eyes, mouth, skin, hair, neck, bosom, waist, hands, elegance, voice, smile, her walk, her sitting posture, her carriage posture, her church posture—Pulqueria had heard all of them praised to the skies thousands of times; she wished, therefore, to take pleasure in her smile, to admire the flutter of her eyelids, to observe the onset and purple hues with which a blush tinged her cheeks, to ponder the most appropriate coiffure to flatter the rich mass of her hair, and the most suitable dress to set off the delicacy of her neck and arms and her graceful waistline; she wished, in short, to know herself and enjoy herself. She believed that the time had come, and she found that she had sight for everything except for seeing herself. The delusion could not have been greater, the agony more cruel!

The momentary pleasure that she derived from the inestimable acquisition of sight immediately turned into tears of bitterness and sobs of grief, but—oh wonder!—with the anguish and weeping, which all those who saw it attributed to jubilation, she looked more lovely than before, when she only exuded joy. Favencio told her that she was more beautiful when weeping, and this praise wounded her like a spear thrust.

So as to escape from a long series of sufferings that she guessed lay in store for her, she might have wished then that a dreadful ugliness would disfigure her face . . . provided that, being visible to her, it would not be to anyone else.

From that day on, which was to have been so happy for the beautiful Pulqueria, her smile fled from her face and her contentment from her heart, but her seriousness, although sad, was lovely—everybody told her so, and she begged them in vain to silence their praise. How much she suffered as poets lauded her on the occasion of her marriage to the loving prince, now in the language of Pindar, now in the metrics of Horace! How much she envied the lot of beggars and cripples to whom she charitably distributed alms! They saw her, but for Pulqueria not even the generous hand that she extended to them was visible. She gave birth to a son, to a daughter, to two . . . "Perhaps I'll see my likeness in this baby," she would exclaim on feeling life in her womb. Vain hope! They all resembled Favencio.

Desperate and frantic, many times she tore off her rich finery, tousled her hair, and dressed in a penitent's coarse tunic . . . and never was she more seductive than in that disheveled state. Going into seclusion in the palace to avoid the applause of the people, she even ordered her servants and family, and Favencio himself, not to look at her so as not to praise her. She was obeyed, but how could she control the eyes and tongues of her little ones? And those innocent offspring, admiring in Pulqueria's face the features that set her apart from all the other women they saw, could not help exclaiming in the passionate, ingenuous language of children: "Mother, dearest Mother, you're the most beautiful of them all!" "Yes," she would say to herself, sighing, "I'm the most beautiful one in the world, but such is my misfortune that I cannot see what I am."

So as to unburden herself in some way, she once wrote a letter to her husband recounting Flaccila's appearance and the harsh rule to which her eyes were subject, but the moment she finished the missive it disappeared from her hands.

As the rebellious victim of an unsatisfied vanity, Pulqueria was miserable for many years, until at length she remembered the crown and the palm that her mother had offered her when she announced that her daughter would see. Pulqueria considered that if she did not bear patiently the deprivation of seeing herself in her lifetime, not only would she not gain the palm of martyrdom, she would not even have the consolation of knowing herself when she did die, and so, in order to satisfy her curiosity, at least at the hour of her death, she determined to suffer the martyrdom of her wish with resignation, for as long as the Lord kept her in the world.

Her excessive love of self had turned her away from virtue, and, consequently, from happiness, and that love, now on the straight and narrow, was finally guiding her to virtue and contentment, proof of the fact that human passions are only bad or good, only harm us or benefit us, in accordance with the use that we make of them.

Thus, as her curiosity abated somewhat with time, Pulqueria gradually became accustomed to hearing her praises sung, first without anger, next with tolerance, then with forbearance, and lastly with reverent humility. She always experienced a painful sensation upon hearing a laudatory remark or an admiring glance, but she recovered quickly and would say: "When I die, I'll see myself. In the meantime, let us submit to the will of the Lord." She no longer hid from people in order to avoid hearing congratulations and compliments; she no longer dressed poorly in order to tarnish her beauty; but now she did go out frequently in public, arrayed as befitted the daughter and sister of a Caesar, seeking occasions to triumph over herself.

It occurred to her a number of times that in the natural scheme of things her beauty ought to decline as she aged and that therefore the mortification it caused her would cease, but she was also mistaken in this surmise: Pulqueria was condemned to be beautiful at every stage of her life. At fifteen, she flowered with the delicate beauty of a maiden; at thirty, she stood out with the perfect, mature beauty of a wife; at forty, she exhibited the august gracefulness of the mothers who are the queens of the human race. She was about to turn fifty, surrounded by children and grandchildren, and her indestructible beauty, although it was different, had not diminished. Teodosio had already died, and in that half century everything around Pulqueria had grown old, save Pulqueria—Pulqueria had her beauty as punishment.

To celebrate the fiftieth anniversary of the felicitous birth of his wife, Favencio arranged to have all their children, daughters-in-law, sons-in-law, and respective families come to the palace in the morning. Seated in her dressing room, whose walls were covered, in between strips of marble, by enormous sections of polished obsidian that served as mirrors, Pulqueria was being attended to by her ladies-in-waiting not far from one of the shining pieces that reflected, for her, her attire but not her body, when the illustrious swarm invaded the apartment. After Pulqueria gave her blessing to all of them, they expressed their mutual affection with hugs and kisses, and then daughters, daughters-in-law, and granddaughters contended for the honor of dressing the august Spanish princess. One put on her sandals; another tied her sash; a third fastened her necklace; a fourth arranged a cloak on her shoulders; a fifth fixed her diadem in place.

It was one of those moments of supreme happiness that can occur only once in a man's or woman's life; nevertheless, Pulqueria had enjoyed another exactly like it when her eyes were given sight. "Look at yourself in the wall, Señora," the oldest and most beautiful of her granddaughters said to her with tender effusiveness. "Look at yourself and you'll see how you still surpass all of us in beauty." Pulqueria looked to please the granddaughter, who was her favorite, even though she had no expectation of seeing herself, but for the first time in her life she beheld in the black obsidian an image that had to be hers. First she saw a recently born baby girl, who, nonetheless, was already beautiful; and then the baby's features gradually changed and took on the loveliness of a lovely one-year-old child, a two-year-old, and . . . in succession there appeared on the smooth specular stone fifty different looks and likenesses of the same face, all equally beautiful, so that in a few very brief moments Pulqueria came to know all that she had been, all the degrees of beauty through which she had passed from the time of her birth to that very day. "So this is what I've been?" she said in an indefinable tone of voice that puzzled her family, who only saw in the mirror the image of the grandmother just as it would naturally be reflected at that moment. "So this is me?" she said again, even more moved and now stammering.

And a voice from Heaven answered her words, the voice that had spoken to her in her sleep thirty-five years ago, Flaccila's voice, and it said to her clearly and tenderly: "That's what you were, my daughter, but look what you're going to be now." All of a sudden the princess's worldly finery disappeared in the mural mirror; in it a marvelous tunic made of white light covered her body. Her tresses came loose from the knots and adornments that held them in place, and they fell free down her back; her face radiated an ineffable beauty, distinct from what is called beauty on Earth, because it was the one that distinguishes the inhabitants of Empyrean; in her right hand the palm of triumph appeared, and on her head the crown of stars, the brilliant symbol of perpetual happiness. Two dazzlingly white wings, golden in parts, sprouted from her shoulders, and thus, represented in the figure of an angel departing our wretched globe to return to his brotherhood, his eyes fixed on the heights of the celestial Jerusalem, Pulqueria, after having seen her physical charms in the black mirror, saw the image of her soul.

A sweet smile showed on her lips; then she closed her eyes, squeezing Favencio's hand, and let her head gently come to rest on her beloved granddaughter's bosom, as her spirit, in the arms of Flaccila, rose to the regions of never-ending happiness.

The mural obsidian, which was not to be desecrated with another image, lost its brilliance and became transformed into another stone, white and unpolished, as writing appeared on its surface—the words of the letter that Pulqueria wrote to reveal the secret of her afflictions, the letter that disappeared from her hands as soon as she finished it. The sorrow experienced by Favencio and his children on losing Pulqueria was alleviated when they understood from those words that the ever beautiful princess occupied a seat in the glorious choir of martyrs.

An eighteenth-century Madrilenian lady, who had the peculiar custom of reading this story to her daughters as they dressed and made ready for a dance, always added these brief words of her own at the end: "Indeed, my dears, the greatest anguish for a woman is the one that torments her vanity, just as the greatest punishment for a man is the one that brings down his pride."

Luis Coloma, SJ (1851–1914)

When he was twenty or twenty-one, a shot in the chest changed Coloma's life. It is not known for certain whether he fired the pistol accidentally and wounded himself or whether he was wounded by another party. But after his recovery, he became a Jesuit and devoted himself to writing.

His most well-known work is Trifles [Pequeñeces] *(1891), a roman à clef that attacks nineteenth-century Madrilenian aristocracy and its dissolute life. The novel stirred considerable controversy, and several prominent writers took him to task for his one-sided portrayal of high society, most notably Juan Valera, in a critique entitled* Currita Albornoz to Father Luis Coloma.

If Coloma's novels and historical writings are the obverse of his literary coin, then his children's literature is the reverse. A friend of Fernán Caballero in her old age, he shared her interest in fairy tales and stories of wonder with a didactic twist. "Green Bird," dedicated to the infante Don Antonio de Orleáns y Borbón, and "Pérez the Mouse," written for Alfonso XIII, king of Spain (1886–1941), were published in Stories for Children [Cuentos para niños], *volume 6 of his* Complete Works.

Luis Coloma, SJ

"Green Bird"

WELL, sir, there once was a very prosperous gardener who lived with his only child, a daughter named Manolita, whom everybody called *Lela* or *Lelita*.

Across from the house of Señó Miguel, as the gardener was called, stood another where Lelita went to school. The teacher's name was Señá Andrea, and she had two daughters as ugly as sin who were considerably older than Lelita. One day, the latter, who could be a little devil, was going over her lesson with Señá Andrea and began to review the alphabet:

"A—e—i—o—u . . . ," and she added, pointing at the teacher with her finger: ". . . a little donkey like you."

Señá Andrea put her in a pillory and did not allow her to go home to eat. Seeing that she was late, Señó Miguel went in search of her and the teacher released the girl immediately. The following day, Lelita, who was a revolutionary worthy of modern times, recited *a—e—i—o—u* without stumbling, but upon concluding *b—c—d*, she said resolutely:

> B, c, d,
> My primer I no longer see,
> But don't punish me, teacher,
> Because tomorrow I'll bring it
> Tied to my knee.

"Oh, what an adorable little girl!" exclaimed Señá Andrea, laughing heartily and smothering Lelita with kisses. Leading her to the kitchen, she took a half bread roll, removed the white inside, and sprinkled olive oil and sugar in the crust; she then inserted the white mass and handed the appetizing treat to Lelita, who devoured it instantly. While the girl was eating, Señá Andrea said to her:

"Let's see if you can deliver an important message from me."

"I'm at your service, teacher," she said with her mouth full.

"It's to ask your father if he wants to marry me."

As soon as she arrived at home, Lelita, who still had the pleasant taste of the bread with oil and sugar in her mouth, relayed the message to Señó Miguel, who replied:

"And give you a stepmother? Think twice, sweetie. I've considered remarrying on more than one occasion, and haven't only to spare you that kind of grief."

"Really, Father. Seña Andrea says she'll take very good care of me and I'll always be playing with her daughters."

"If you're of the same opinion when you're fifteen, then I'll do it. Don't worry."

The following day, Seña Andrea stood behind the door, on the lookout. No sooner did Lelita arrive than she asked her:

"What did he say?"

"He said that if I'm of the same opinion when I'm fifteen, then he'll marry you."

Seña Andrea pulled a face, because a long wait like that would be hard on her. But, embracing Lelita, she said:

"Oh, my dear child, it's going to seem longer than Lent to wait so much time before having you at my side and looking upon you as a daughter!"

But time, which never stands still, flew by and Lelita turned fifteen, with the looks of a Saint Teresa and the virtues of a Saint Rita. Seña Andrea and her daughters, who all this time had pampered Lelita like a queen, or as a poor nephew would a rich uncle, reminded Lelita of her father's promise. The girl, who was innocent, good, and affectionate, had grown fond of the teacher, because since there was no ill will at all in her, she believed Seña Andrea's deceitful flattery. As a result, she again urged her father to enter into the marriage so desired by all. Señó Miguel raised other considerations to Lelita, but she rejected them as though it was she and not her father who would marry.

"Well, inasmuch as you're so insistent, I'll do it," he finally said. "But don't complain if bad things happen as a result, and remember that our actions come home to roost."

"Come, now, Father. You do carry on. Why, Seña Andrea is dying to call me her daughter, and she treats me like a queen."

Señó Miguel and Seña Andrea got married, and the latter, along with her two daughters, whose ugliness had increased in direct proportion to their growth, moved to Señó Miguel's garden to live. During the first month everything went as smooth as silk because Lelita continued to be indulged by all of them; the innocent thing believed that the affection they were showing her was real. But no sooner did Señá Andrea and her daughters settle in than they began to curb their gentle treatment of Lelita and dump all the work on her, and to such a degree that the wretched girl even found herself unable to complain to her father, since they always waited for him to be absent to abuse her.

One day Señá Andrea ordered Lelita to scrub a gallery that over-looked the garden. The poor thing had no alternative but to pick up a bucket that she could barely manage and begin the arduous task. The floor was full of cracks and stains, and Señá Andrea, seated next to Lelita, ran out of patience, saying from time to time:

"Press down on that stain. Rub hard, girl, you're so clumsy . . . You're not rubbing, you good-for-nothing! Press down until your wrists drop!"

Lelita lost her temper and, clutching the scrub cloth, said to her stepmother:

"If I was rubbing your face, you'd see whether or not I'm pressing down. Go somewhere else and tell people what to do, because you aren't going to boss me around."

"So the brat's being disrespectful to me?" exclaimed the harpy, furious. And pouncing on Lelita, she slapped her in the face.

Lelita burst into tears and waited for her father to come so that she could relate to him her well-founded complaints. When he arrived, she told him what had happened; the harpy and her daughters contradicted her. But the five livid finger marks that stood out on the girl's face vouched for the truth of her account.

"If you had listened to me, this wouldn't be happening now," Señó Miguel said to her, "but I'll put a stop to this once and for all."

And taking Lelita by the hand, he led her to a cottage that stood at the far end of the garden. The girl settled in there, and Señá Andrea and her daughters were strictly forbidden to set foot near the place; only Lelita's father visited her, three or four times a day, and he always took her numerous gifts when he did.

One day, as he was passing by a secondhand shop, Señó Miguel saw a number of old books for sale in the doorway. He decided to buy a few for Lelita's amusement in her leisure hours, but since he didn't know how to read, he chose four of the thickest and most well bound. Among them was one with a parchment cover that had some very strange symbols on it—symbols drawn in vivid colors.

Lelita was greatly pleased with the books, and as soon as she finished her chores that afternoon she sat by a small window that overlooked the garden and began to leaf through one of them. It was the story of the chaste Joseph.

The following afternoon she picked up the one with the magnificent parchment binding, and as soon as she opened the first clasp, she saw a beautiful green bird fly into the room and alight on her table.

"Oh, how pretty!" exclaimed Lelita, eager to have it. And she approached the bird slowly, her body bent, and her hands extended with her apron in order not to frighten it, inching her way to reach out and grab it.

The green bird tilted its little head, staring at her with eyes that shone like diamonds. When it all of a sudden shook its green feathers, an astounded Lelita saw that a shower of stunning pearls slipped through them and, rolling on the table, fell to the floor where, bouncing here and there, they scattered all over. Lelita stooped down to gather them, but when she raised her head the green bird had disappeared, and in its place she saw the handsomest of youths dressed in the old Spanish manner—a white satin frock coat embroidered in gold, a satin vest, and breeches secured with pearl-studded buckles.

"Oh!" exclaimed Lelita, frozen in a crouch and turning as red as a beet.

"Am I so ugly that I frighten you, Lelita?" asked the youth in a voice as dulcet as the notes of a harp.

"No."

"Then I strike you as beautiful?"

Lelita said nothing, but she looked at him out of the corner of her eye, and if the bird struck her as beautiful, the youth struck her as more beautiful.

"Do not be frightened, Lelita," said the latter. "I'm Prince Pretty-Look, whom a fairy enchanted and changed into a green bird and whom she foretold was to marry the first woman who opened that book."

"So I—" blurted out Lelita without finishing her reply, but blushing more scarlet than ever.

"Yes, Lelita, you will marry me, because thus is it ordained."

Prince Pretty-Look and Lelita were silent at first, and then they talked about the cold, the temperature, and the changeable weather, and gradually and imperceptibly they stood up straight. Whereupon Prince Pretty-Look asked Lelita:

"Have you ever loved, Lelita?"

"But I didn't know you!" she exclaimed with the innocence of her fifteen years, fixing her sky-blue eyes on the prince's beautiful brown eyes.

The two lovers—since now they indeed were—looked out the window and, leaning on the sill, talked a good while, then fell silent, then gazed at each other, and the sweet song of a nightingale warbling in the garden engulfed them in a somewhat dangerous rapture—dangerous if Lelita had not been a good, innocent girl and if Prince Pretty-Look had not been a very different youth from those who take pride in deceiving maidens. The stroke of twelve midnight on the church clock made both lovers snap out of their ecstasy.

"Good-bye, Lelita," said the prince, squeezing her hand, "until tomorrow. Be careful to guard my secret, because it will be your undoing and mine."

And, all of a sudden changing into a green bird, he disappeared through the window, his sweet whistle, like a tender and eloquent farewell, gladdening the ears of the enamored Lelita.

The following afternoon Lelita opened the clasp of the book, and the green bird appeared forthwith, greeting her with his merry chirping. He alighted on the table, shook his feathers, causing a thousand pearls to scatter, and Prince Pretty-Look appeared, even more richly attired than the day before—in pink satin highlighted by silver embroidery, with pearls and diamonds sewn all over.

Lelita and the prince, engrossed in their delightful conversation, did not notice the time going by, and when it struck twelve, the prince asked if the bells were ringing for vespers.

Thus did they spend several days, happy in their secret love. One morning, having gathered all the pearls scattered by the green bird upon being transformed into a prince, Lelita was making a magnificent string, when, all of a sudden, her father entered the cottage, and she did not have time to hide the precious stones.

"Where did you get these magnificent pearls, my child?" asked Señó Miguel, astonished.

Lelita blushed deeply, and not knowing how to lie, she confessed the truth of the matter to her father. Señó Miguel scratched his head with an expressive gesture of distrust and said to her:

"This enchantment business makes me suspicious, but you have a good head on your shoulders, and as long as passion doesn't cause you to lose it, you'll know what's best."

Lelita was as relieved as someone who's had a weight taken off her mind, for such was the necessity of hiding their secret from Señó Miguel. That very afternoon she told Prince Pretty-Look what had happened, and he said, nodding his head:

"You would have been wrong to lie to your father, for lying is a vice. But you *were* also wrong to reveal our secret, because a secret among three people is no longer a secret. Take care, nonetheless, that your stepmother and her daughters do not discover it, because then I would lose you and you would lose me. Remember what Saint Teresa said: 'Secrecy is the key to good sense. How do you expect your friend to keep a secret if you yourself don't do so?'"

It shouldn't surprise Your Highness to hear a quote from the illustrious Doctor of the Church on the lips of Prince Pretty-Look, because the youth was God-fearing, deeply religious, and averse to all those readings forbidden to us by superior intelligence and paternal prudence. Lelita gave him her solemn promise, and the prince withdrew at the stroke of twelve midnight.

Meanwhile, Señá Andrea and her daughters were dying to go and see Lelita, not because they would take pleasure in it, but because they were more curious than justice, politics, and the police, which, according to an anonymous writer, are the three most curious parties that exist. But Señó Miguel refused to take them to the cottage and would only give his daughter their regards, for which Lelita—whose heart, like the petals of a rose open to the breeze, was susceptible—expressed profound gratitude. One day she made three magnificent necklaces with the green bird's pearls and sent them as a gift to Señá Andrea and her daughters.

They were amazed by that generosity and agreed to thank her, but since ingratitude has no memory, they began to ponder where she might have acquired the pearls.

"We must find out," said Señá Andrea. "We have to know."

"Maybe the little hypocrite's found a suitor," said the older of the sisters, who, like a good fool, was very malicious. "But I'll get to the bottom of it."

"And I'm going to hide under the table," added the younger one, "when she goes out in the afternoon to water her flowerpots. I'll have to be pretty careless for her to detect me."

Mother and daughters continued to knock the innocent Lelita, because Your Highness should know that backbiting is typical only of mean-spirited souls, and it always recognizes jealousy and envy as its source.

The following afternoon, when Lelita was watering her flowerpots, the younger of Señá Andrea's daughters furtively passed through the garden gate, entered the cottage, and hid under a table covered by a rich green cloth. Shortly afterwards Lelita came in, and, after sitting by the window, opened the mysterious book, whereupon the green bird appeared. The curious onlooker, squatting under the table, had to remain in her uncomfortable position until the stroke of twelve midnight, when Prince Pretty-Look withdrew. But she considered all the hours of hardship under the table as well spent, inasmuch as she now possessed Lelita's secret. Upon leaving the cottage, she went in search of her mother and related to her everything that she had seen.

The three envious vixens decided to destroy Lelita's happiness, because envy corrupts hearts as rust corrodes steel. The younger daughter proposed a plan adopted by all. She offered to slip inside Lelita's cottage again and fill the windowsill with pieces of glass, in such a way that the green bird would be injured all over upon flying in. That same afternoon the young shrew, with a handkerchief full of pieces of glass from a bottle that they had broken, slipped inside Lelita's cottage and spread them along the ledge and frame of the window, and then ran to her hiding place.

Shortly afterwards Lelita arrived and opened the book, and the green bird, who came immediately and flew into the pieces of glass, was injured on the windowsill, where he uttered a pitiful moan instead of the merry chirping with which he customarily greeted Lelita. The beautiful bird tried shaking his feathers, but in place of pearls, blood issued from them, and, taking wing again toward the garden, he disappeared. Filled with agony, the astounded Lelita extended her arms to him, only to hear these words:

"If you wish to see me, you must wear out three pairs of iron shoes!"

Lelita put her hands to her head and wailed over and over in desperation. Suddenly her vision dimmed, her legs buckled, and she slipped and grabbed the table cover in order not to fall down, but it came off and exposed Señá Andrea's daughter, who, squatting under the table, looked like the live image of confusion and remorse.

Lelita then understood everything that had happened, and in a voice that reflected her sweet, long-suffering disposition, she spoke only these words to her tormentor, words laced with tears:

"What did I ever do to you for you to treat me so cruelly?"

Señá Andrea's daughter fled, livid with shame and fury, because nothing can counter envy and meanness like scorn, or victims who return good for evil.

After the first few moments of bitter hurt had passed, Lelita was roused to action by remembering the green bird's words—*If you wish to see me, you must wear out three pairs of iron shoes*—and hope rose anew in her heart. She had three pairs of iron shoes made; she donned the pilgrim's dress of coarse tunic, cloak with scallop shells, and cloth hat; she took up a staff with a water gourd tied to the top; and, making the sign of the cross in the name of the Father, the Son, and the Holy Spirit, she set out to roam the world.

At the end of a year she had worn out the first pair of shoes and not heard a word about Prince Pretty-Look. Ever constant, nonetheless, she continued passing through cities, climbing mountains, and wading across rivers, and at the end of another year she had worn out the second pair of iron shoes, and still had no news of the beautiful prince. So she put on the third pair, but without losing heart; quite the contrary, with her hopes even stronger and more alive, she set out again.

One night, out in the country, Lelita was caught unawares by a frightful storm and had no choice but to take refuge under the branches of a tree. A flock of cranes had also sought shelter in the very same spot, and, while the storm lasted, engaged in animated conversation:

"Oh, what a night!" exclaimed one of the birds. "Why, it's raining harder than when Mustache was buried!"

"And when was that, neighbor?"

"To tell the truth, I don't know, but it had to be one time when it rained so much that the water rose above men's mustaches."

"So what's the latest, neighbor?"

"A very big piece of news. I'll have you know that Prince Pretty-Look—"

Lelita's heart skipped a beat and she listened for all she was worth.

"—that Prince Pretty-Look is dying."

"What're you saying?"

"What you hear, my friend."

"Oh, what a shame! What's wrong with him?"

Then Lelita, half-dead with anxiety and grief, listened to every word as the first crane related all that had happened between her and the prince, as well as the infamy of Señá Andrea and her daughters.

"And so," continued the talkative crane, "when the green bird flew out of Lelita's cottage injured all over—so much so that it broke your heart to see him—he turned back into a prince, but the pieces of glass have stayed inside him and the poor thing is suffering miserably."

"Oh, what a shame! Such a glorious youth he was. And tell me: there's no cure?"

"Yes, there is! And I wish I myself could bring it about. Because I'll have you know that His Royal Majesty, who has only that one son, is beside himself with sorrow, and has promised whoever cures him his weight in gold. And he's very right to do so, for I would give my bill and my feathers and even my crest to keep any of my chicks from having even a little bellyache."

And since the mother crane was moved by the mere thought of such an occurrence, with her foot she brushed away a tear that had welled up in her eye. Even mother cranes are tender when it comes to their children!

"Oh, good heavens, neighbor! God forbid! But, tell me, why don't *you* go and cure the prince? In addition to the work of charity, you'll bring back money."

"Never, my friend. Where can a poor devil of a crane go without being looked down upon? It would be for naught. You know our motto: Each one with his own kind."

"Don't say such a thing, because I've been told that under the Constitution we're all equal."

"Oh, what a joke, my friend!" and the talkative crane laughed so spontaneously and so sincerely that it didn't take long for her companion and Lelita and even us to laugh with her. Moreover, if Your Highness had heard how the chatterbox of a crane laughed, it's more than likely that you too would have joined in the merriment.

"Empty talk, I'm afraid," she added, laughing again. "That's what those who are down say to be equal to those who are up, but those who are up do whatever's necessary to keep them down. I'm telling you, my friend, that what occurs to man occurs to no one else."

And given over to another fit of merriment, the crane again burst into laughter in such an open and spontaneous manner that, unable to help it, we joined her once more.

"Well, neighbor, I say it's a lack of charity to let such a good and beautiful prince die."

"He's done for if Lelita doesn't go to his aid, for she's the only one who has the power to cure him."

"What she wouldn't give to know what has to be done."

"I'll say! She has only to enter the prince's bedroom, take a vial from the closet, dip a feather in the balm contained therein, and anoint the prince's body, and the pieces of glass will come out on their own."

"Oh, heavens! If only I could tell Leli—"

A terrifying thunderclap cut her off, causing her to exclaim devoutly as she beat her chest with her left foot:

> Lord God, omnipotent God, immortal God,
> Deliver us, Lord, from all evil.

"Neighbor, let us stop gossiping and pray the Trisagion."

"You're right, because we have more than enough to do with taking care of ourselves."

The two birds began to pray the Trisagion, but soon thereafter the storm ended and the moon shone in the sky. Whereupon both cranes shook their feathers and flew off in search of their nests.

Meanwhile, not a single word spoken by them had escaped Lelita. So after their departure, she praised God, who had furnished her with that chance encounter, brushed off her drenched clothes, and set out for the palace of Prince Pretty-Look.

Lelita arrived at the prince's court and immediately headed for the royal residence. Eight gentlemen, all of them fat, potbellied, and bald, were coming out of the palace carrying gold-handled walking sticks and talking animatedly. They were the royal doctors who had given up hope for His Highness, and they were withdrawing to let him die a peaceful death.

Believing that she had arrived too late, a weak Lelita leaned against a column. When she staggered forward, she felt a stab of pain in both feet and realized instantly that the last pair of iron shoes were worn out.

"I've saved him!" she exclaimed, discarding the heavy iron pieces and resolutely entering the palace barefoot.

A guard blocked her way, but after explaining that she was a pilgrim from Jerusalem and that she bore a sure cure for His Highness's affliction, she was taken to the queen. The disconsolate mother believed Lelita readily, because whoever has lost everything is willing to believe whatever offers a shred of hope. She herself accompanied Lelita as far as the door of the prince's bedroom and withdrew, because the beautiful pilgrim told her that she needed to be alone.

Lelita stood in front of the door for a moment, pressing both hands over her heart, which seemed as though it was going to jump out of her chest. She finally drew the rich damask curtain that covered the door and entered the bedroom.

Prince Pretty-Look lay, in a half-light, on a magnificent ebony bed inlaid with precious metals. His head reclined on soft pillows, whose ever so fine down was not as fine as the prince's golden curls; his closed eyes had bluish rings around them; and his hands, which rested on the crimson velvet bedspread, appeared to be of marble. Lelita had stopped in the middle of the room, and her oppressed heart seemed to have risen to her throat as if it were going to suffocate her. She tried to take a step and fell to the floor on her knees, covering her head with her hands and exclaiming from the depths of her soul:

"Thank heavens! Thank heavens!"

After this initial moment of ecstatic joy—so natural in their love, in their misfortune, and in their particular circumstances—Lelita turned decisive and began to search for the vial of balm. Behind a damask curtain she found the closet mentioned by the crane, and inside it the silver vial, which she took in her hands drunk with joy. She rang a bell and a page came; Lelita ordered him to bring a feather and a silver salver.

"Hold the salver here," she said to the page as soon as her orders were carried out.

And, dipping the feather in the vial, Lelita anointed certain parts of the prince's body. As the feather touched them, they opened, and by virtue of the balm there issued from each and every one a piece of glass, which Lelita, crying tears of compassion, placed on the salver held by the page. When this operation was completed, she said to him:

"His Highness is out of the woods and only needs rest. Take these pieces of glass to the queen and tell her they were the source of her son's illness."

The page left, and Lelita, after covering the prince and making him comfortable, because he still had not come to, slipped out through a concealed stairway and began her homeward journey.

"If he loves me," she said to herself on the way, "he'll come for me, and if he doesn't love me. . . . Why am I going to compel him to be happy with me when he could be happy with someone else? Let him be happy, because. . . ."

And, turning around, Lelita said good-bye to the palace's cupola, which was hidden behind a hill, with one sigh of hope and two tears of apprehension.

The first afternoon that Lelita spent at home after her return, she opened the mysterious parchment book, but the green bird did not appear.

"God's will be done," she said sadly.

And Lelita continued opening the book every afternoon, but the green bird never came. She suffered without forgetting. And she took pleasure in recalling her love, which was the life of her spirit. Finally, the anniversary of the day that she cured the prince arrived, and she opened her parchment book late in the afternoon. At that very instant a confused noise of carriages and horses reached Lelita's ears. The girl stiffened, her face pale, and turned toward the door, which opened all of a sudden, and Prince Pretty-Look dashed into the room and swept her into his arms. Weak with joy, Lelita fainted, and the prince carried her to his carriage and took her to his palace, where he married her posthaste.

Thus did Lelita become a queen, as a result of the constancy of her love. Because although a French author has said that constancy in love is the interval between two passing fancies, a Spanish writer says that waiting is the advice given by constancy in order to gain one's ends.

Luis Coloma, SJ

"Pérez the Mouse"

BETWEEN the death of the king who suffered terribly and the accession to the throne of Queen Maricastaña,* there exists a long and obscure hiatus in the chronicles, and no record of it has come down to us. It is clear, however, that a king thrived in that age, King Buby I, a great friend of poor children and a resolute protector of mice.

For the former he had a doll and cardboard horse factory built, and it is known for certain that from this factory came the three ponies with four white feet that King Bermudo the Deacon gave to the children of Hissén I, after the Battle of Bureva.

It is also known that King Buby strictly forbade the use of mousetraps and passed very sensible laws to contain within the limits of self-defense the hunting instincts of cats, which can be seen in the grave disturbances that took place between Queen Goto, or Gotuna—the widow of Don Sancho Ordóñez, king of Galicia—and the jurisdiction of Ribas de Sil, because of the fact that in the latter an attempt had been made to apply King Buby's laws to the cat of Pombeyro convent, where said queen lived in seclusion.

The case was grave and long remembered, and while some authors say that the cat in question was named Rusaff Mateo, others simply call him Minini. In any event, the deed is a proven fact, even though good old Don Lucas de Túy acts as if he's forgotten the matter, perhaps, perhaps, for the sake of convenience.

It is also known that King Buby began to reign at the age of six, under the tutelage of his mother, a very Christian and prudent lady who guided his steps and watched at his side, as guardian angels do with all good children.

King Buby was a real delight at that time, and when on ceremonial occasions he donned his gold crown and his royal embroidered robe, the gold of his crown was not any brighter than that of his hair, nor were the ermine furs of his robe any softer than his cheeks and his

96

hands. He looked like a Sèvres-ware doll who, instead of having been placed on the fireplace mantel, had been placed in a sitting position on the throne.

Now then, it turned out that one day, while the king was eating some soup, a tooth of his loosened. The whole court became alarmed, and the royal doctors appeared, one after another. The matter was grave, as all indications were that the time had arrived for His Majesty's new teeth to come in.

The entire school of physicians gathered in consultation; a telegram was sent to Charcot* in the event of a nervous complication; and finally it was decreed that His Majesty's tooth would be pulled. The doctors wanted to administer chloroform to him, and the president of the Council of State stubbornly supported this opinion, as he himself was so impressionable that he never did without it whenever he had his hair cut.

But King Buby was brave and stouthearted and insisted on facing the danger resolutely. Nevertheless, he wished to go to confession first, because it was better to be safe than sorry—after all, the soul can escape through the gap of a tooth just as it can through a wound from a lance.

So they tied a red silk thread to it, and the most senior doctor began to pull so steadily and so adroitly that halfway through the operation the king screwed up his face and out popped the tooth, as white, as clean, and as pretty as a small pearl without a setting.

It was retrieved on a gold tray by the first gentleman-in-waiting, who went to present it to Her Majesty the queen. The latter at once convened the Council of Ministers, and there resulted a divergence in opinion.

Some wanted to mount the tiny tooth in gold and keep it in the Crown's treasure; others proposed setting it in the center of a precious piece of jewelry and giving it to the statue of the Blessed Virgin, patron saint of the kingdom. In both views those ministers revealed more of a desire to please the mother than to serve the queen.

But this lady, who as a bright woman did not trust flatterers and was very prudent and mindful of tradition, decided that King Buby would write a polite letter to Pérez the Mouse, and that he would put the tooth under his pillow that very night, as has been and is the common, continual practice of all children from time immemorial, because no one knows of an instance when Pérez the Mouse did not come to fetch a tooth and leave a splendid gift in its place.

Innocent Abel did as much in his time, and even villainous Cain hid his first tooth, which was yellow and fetid like a clove of garlic, beneath the black dog hide that served as his pillow. Nothing is known about Adam and Eve, which nobody finds strange, because since they were born full-grown obviously no new teeth came in.

King Buby was hard put to write the letter, but he finally managed it, and not without a good deal of luck, as he smudged with ink only the five fingers of both hands, the tip of his nose, his left ear, a little of his right shoe, and all of his lace bib—from top to bottom.

That night he went to bed earlier than usual, and gave orders for all the candelabra and chandeliers in the bedroom to be left burning. He very carefully put the letter with the tooth inside under his pillow, and then he sat on it, prepared to wait for Pérez the Mouse, even though it might be necessary to stay awake until dawn.

But Pérez the Mouse was a long time in coming, so the little king amused himself thinking about what he would say to him. Shortly afterwards Buby opened his eyes wide, fighting sleep, which was shutting them, but in the end they shut completely, and his little body slumped, seeking the warmth of the blankets, while his head came to rest on the pillow, hidden under an arm as birds hide theirs under a wing.

All of a sudden he felt something soft brushing his forehead. He sat up on the spot, startled, and saw in front of him, standing on the pillow, a very small mouse with a straw hat, gold spectacles, coarse cloth shoes, and a red satchel slung over his shoulder.

King Buby, very frightened, stared at him, and Pérez the Mouse, upon seeing the little king awake, doffed his hat, sweeping it down to his feet, after which he bowed his head, in keeping with court etiquette, and in that respectful posture waited for His Majesty to speak.

But His Majesty said nothing, because suddenly he forgot his prepared speech, and, after giving his predicament considerable thought, all he managed to say, somewhat flustered, was:

"Good evening."

To which Pérez the Mouse, deeply moved, responded:

"May God grant Your Majesty the very same."

And with these polite exchanges Buby and Pérez became the best of friends. You could tell a mile away that the rodent was a very worldly mouse, accustomed to walking on carpets and to social dealings with people of distinction.

His conversation was varied and instructive, and his learning astonishing. He had traveled through all the pipes and cellars of the court, and had made his home in all the archives and libraries; at the Royal Spanish Academy alone he ate up, in less than a week, three unpublished manuscripts that had been stored there by a certain illustrious author.

He also talked about his family, which was not very large: two marriageable daughters, Adelaida and Elvira, and one teenage son, Adolfo, who pursued a diplomatic career in the very drawer in which the Secretary of State kept secret notes. He had little to say about his wife, and as though in passing, for which reason the king suspected that there might a *messa alleanza*, or perhaps marital discord.

King Buby listened in fascination, automatically extending his hand from time to time to catch him by the tail. But Pérez the Mouse, with a rapid, ceremonious swing, moved his tail to the other side, thwarting the child's attempt without showing disrespect to the monarch.

It was late already, and as King Buby gave no sign of dismissing him, Pérez the Mouse, without violating protocol, cleverly insinuated that he had no choice but to pay a visit to 64 Calle de Jacometrezo that very same night, to collect the tooth of another child, a very poor little boy named Gilito. The way there was arduous and to a certain extent dangerous, because in that neighborhood there lived an ill-intentioned cat named Don Gaiferos.

King Buby took it into his head to accompany him on that journey, and he voiced his request to Pérez the Mouse most earnestly. The latter turned pensive, smoothing his mustache; it was a very big responsibility, and he needed, in addition, to make a stop at his house to pick up the gift that he planned to leave Gilito in exchange for his tooth.

To which King Buby responded that he would be highly honored to rest for a moment at such a respectable house.

Vanity got the better of Pérez the Mouse, and he hastened to offer King Buby a cup of tea to reciprocate for winning the right to put chains on the door of his house, as was done in those days to proclaim that its owner had the honor of entertaining a monarch.

Pérez the Mouse lived at 8 Calle del Arenal, in the cellars of Carlos Prast,* directly opposite a huge stack of wheels of Gruyère cheese, which offered a nearby and well-stocked larder to the Pérez family.

Beside himself with joy, King Buby hopped out of bed and started putting on a blouse. But all of a sudden Pérez the Mouse jumped up on his shoulder and inserted the tip of his tail into Buby's nose; the little king sneezed loudly, and by means of a marvelous transformation, which to this day no one has been able to explain, he was changed, by the very force of the sneeze, into the most handsome and darling little mouse ever dreamed up by a fairy's imagination.

All of him was as bright as gold and as soft as silk, and his little eyes were as green and lustrous as two cabochon emeralds.

With less ceremony than before, Pérez the Mouse took him by the hand, and, quick as a wink, they shot through a hole that was under the bed, concealed by the carpet.

Their run was wild and their way dark, dank, and sticky, and at every turn they came across bands of tiny vermin that haphazardly pricked and bit them.

At times Pérez the Mouse stopped at an intersection and explored the terrain before going forward, all of which made King Buby a little nervous and put him in a bad humor because he began to feel, from his snout to the tip of his tail, certain faint shivers that struck him as signs of fear. He remembered, nevertheless, that

> Fear is natural in one who is prudent,
> and knowing how to overcome it is being valiant,

and he overcame his and was valiant by virtue of reason, which is what characterizes true valor.

Only once, upon hearing a frightful racket overhead that sounded as though dozens of train cars were passing by, did he very softly ask Pérez the Mouse if that was where Don Gaiferos lived. Pérez the Mouse answered with a negative shake of his tail, and they continued on.

Shortly afterwards they came upon a smooth esplanade that led into a wide and very well tiled cellar, where one breathed a tepid atmosphere, scented with cheese. They turned at an enormous pile of wheels of Gruyère and found themselves in front of a big Huntley's cookie box.

That was where Pérez the Mouse's family lived, under the banner of Carlos Prast, as comfortably and as well-off as could have lived the legendary rat of the fable in Dutch cheese.

Pérez the Mouse introduced King Buby to his family as a foreign *touriste* who was visiting the court, and the lady mice received him with that elegant *aisance* of women accustomed to habitual social contact.

The señoritas were doing needlework with their governess, Miss Old-Cheese, a very learned English mouse, and Señora Pérez was embroidering a pretty cap for her husband by the warmth of a fireplace where raisin stems burned merrily.

King Buby was very pleased by that placid interior of a bourgeois family, which in all of its particulars revealed that *aurea mediocritas* of which the poet speaks as the most suitable state to find peace and happiness in this life.

Adelaida and Elvira served tea in exquisite bean pod cups, and afterwards there was a bit of music. To harp accompaniment Adelaida sang Desdemona's aria *Assisa al piè d'un salice** with a relish and intonation that delighted King Buby.

Adelaida was not pretty, but she had very refined manners, and she made her tail swing with a certain wistful coquetry that no doubt denoted a secret sorrow of some sort.

Elvira, on the contrary, was vivacious and a little unpolished, but she overflowed with an energetic spirit, and King Buby thought he saw before him a Spartan woman repeating the hymn of Thermopylae when, to piano accompaniment, she sang with tragic modulation and vigorous, mouselike indignation:

> In the King's Hospital
> there's a mouse with tertian fever
> and a Moorish kitten
> is commending its soul.

At this point Adolfo returned from the Jockey Club where, to the profound regret of his parents, he lost time and money playing poker with the mice attached to the German embassy.

The continual contact with these diplomats had made him vain and caused him to adopt foreign customs, and his only topics of conversation were polo and lawn tennis.

King Buby would have gladly prolonged the soiree, but Pérez the Mouse, who had absented himself for a moment, returned with the satchel slung over his shoulder—a satchel, to all appearances, absolutely crammed—and respectfully indicated to him that it was time to go.

Whereupon King Buby bade gracious and polite farewells. Señora Pérez, in a somewhat bourgeois burst of cordiality, planted a loud kiss on each of his cheeks; Adelaida extended one of her paws with a certain sentimental air that seemed to say "Until we meet again"; Elvira shook his hand, English style; and Miss Old-Cheese curtsied ceremoniously to him, as they did in bygone days, after which she watched him depart through her tortoiseshell lorgnon.

Adolfo was also warmly expressive. He accompanied them as far as the entrance to the pipes, where he reiterated his offer to introduce Buby at the Polo Club and recommended to him for the third time the J. Tate racquets, size 12, or at most the 12½. The 13 was a little too heavy for a mouse's hands.

The little king thanked him profusely and said good-bye thinking that Adolfo could really be quite elegant, but that he undoubtedly had mush for brains.

Buby and Pérez the Mouse began their wild run anew, and with so many precautions that the king became alarmed.

The advance guard was a sizable detachment of husky mice, warriors all, whose sharp-pointed steel bayonets occasionally flashed in the darkness. Another detachment formed a no less numerous rearguard, also armed to the teeth.

Pérez the Mouse then confessed that he would not have agreed to set out on that expedition without being able to safeguard, with that veteran escort of light infantry, the person of the young monarch who so nobly had entrusted himself to his care.

All of a sudden King Buby saw that the entire vanguard was disappearing through a narrow hole from which escaped threads of tenuous light.

The moment of danger had arrived, and Pérez the Mouse, shaking the tip of his tail, very slowly and very gradually raised his snout to that fearful opening; he glanced around for a second, took two steps backwards, advanced again cautiously, and, abruptly grasping King Buby by the hand, darted through the hole swift as an arrow, raced like a blue streak across a spacious kitchen, and vanished through another hole located directly behind the stove.

Just as train travelers nowadays look out their windows and see telegraph poles file by, King Buby saw a frightening scene pass before his eyes. The feared Don Gaiferos was asleep by the warmth of the embers in the fireplace. He was an enormous Andalusian tomcat whose bristly whiskers rose and fell in time to his slow, even breathing.

The mouse brigade, motionless, silent, and on the alert, practically biting the tomcat's tail, shielded King Buby's passage, forming a formidable wedge from the dozing Don Gaiferos to the entry and exit holes, like the triangle of Roman legions at the Battle of Cape Economus.*

It was an impressive, hair-raising sight . . .

An old woman ugly as sin was asleep in a chair, her half-finished knitting having fallen onto her lap.

Once Pérez the Mouse and King Buby cleared the exit hole, the danger passed, and they only needed to climb up to the topmost attic of that very same house, which was where Gilito lived. The whole of his miserable room, open to the elements, constituted an entrance, as mice invaded it through cracks, fissures, and holes as one invades a leveled city.

King Buby perched on the wing of a seatless chair, the only one there, and from that vantage point surveyed the entirety of all that horrible destitution, which he never would have been able to even imagine.

It was a foul hovel in which ceiling and floor joined on one side, and did not separate sufficiently on another to enable a grown person to stand up. The freezing wind blew in through innumerable cracks, and as the day grew lighter you could see big lumps of ice on the underside of the ceiling tiles of the roof.

The only pieces of furniture were the chair that served as King Buby's observatory, an empty bread basket hanging from the ceiling within arm's reach, and, in the corner least exposed to wind and weather, a bed of straw and rags on which Gilito and his mother slept in an embrace.

Hand in hand with Buby, Pérez the Mouse approached them, and when the king saw poor Gilito up close, his stiff little hands showing outside the wretched rags that covered them, his beautiful little face pressed against his mother's bosom to seek warmth, it broke his heart with sorrow and surprise, and he started crying bitterly.

Never had he seen such a sight! How was it possible that he had not known that there were poor children who were hungry and cold and dying from want and grief in a horrible garret? He no longer wanted to have blankets on his own bed so long as there was even one little boy or girl in his kingdom who did not have at least one complete outfit of clothes!

Pérez the Mouse, also deeply touched, furtively wiped away a tear with his paw, and attempted to relieve King Buby's pain by showing him the bright gold coin he was going to put under Gilito's pillow in exchange for his first tooth.

At this point Gilito's mother awoke and sat up in bed, gazing at her sleeping child. Dawn was already breaking, and she had to get up in order to earn a mere pittance of a day's wage doing wash in the river. She lifted Gilito and set him on his knees, half asleep, in front of a print of the Infant Jesus of Prague that she had affixed to the wall by the bed.

King Buby and Pérez the Mouse also went down on their knees, with the greatest respect, and even the light infantry mice knelt inside the empty basket where they were quietly searching for booty.

The little boy began to pray.

Our father, who art in heaven . . . !

King Buby looked greatly surprised upon hearing him and gaped at Pérez the Mouse.

The latter understood his astonishment and riveted his piercing eyes on the little king, but he did not say a single word, hoping, no doubt, that someone else would say them.

Silent and preoccupied, they started their return journey, and a half hour later King Buby entered his bedroom accompanied by Pérez the Mouse.

The latter again inserted the tip of his tail into the king's nose, and once more Buby sneezed loudly and found himself in his bed, in the arms of the queen who was awakening him, as she did every day, with a mother's loving kiss.

At first he believed that it had all been a dream, but he quickly raised the pillow, searching for the letter to Pérez the Mouse that he had put underneath it the night before, and the letter had disappeared.

In its place there was an exquisite jewelry box with the emblem of the Golden Fleece, overlaid with diamonds—a magnificent gift generously given to him by Pérez the Mouse in exchange for his first tooth.

Nonetheless, the little king dropped it on the rich bedspread, almost without looking at it, and was pensive for a long time, his elbow on the pillow. Then he abruptly said, in the serious and thoughtful tone that children sometimes assume when they are reflecting and anguishing:

"Mama, why do poor children pray the same as I do, *Our father, who art in heaven . . . ?*"

The queen replied:

"Because God is their father the same as he's yours."

"Then," said Buby still more pensively, "we're brothers . . ."

"Yes, son, they're your brothers."

Buby's eyes then overflowed with profound wonder, and, his voice choked with tears and his chest heaving with a sob, he asked:

"And why am I king and have everything and they're poor and have nothing?"

The queen held him to her heart with immense love and, kissing him on the forehead, said:

"Because you're the *older brother*, that's what being a king is. Do you understand, Buby? And God has given you everything so that, as far as possible, you can see that your *younger brothers and sisters* do not want for anything."

"I didn't know that," said Buby, shaking his head sorrowfully.

And no longer remembering the Golden Fleece, he started saying his morning prayers, as he did every day. And as he prayed it seemed to him that all the poor, destitute children of the kingdom gathered around him, also raising their little hands to God, and that he, as the older brother, was leading them:

Our father, who art in heaven . . . !

And when King Buby was a man and a great warrior, and had to petition God for help in times of hardship and give him thanks in times of joy, he always said, leading his subjects—rich and poor, good and bad—in prayer:

Our father, who art in heaven . . . !

And when, an aged man already, King Buby died and his virtuous soul arrived at the gates to heaven, he knelt and said, as always:

Our father, who art in heaven . . . !

And when he spoke these words, the gates were opened to him by thousands and thousands of poor Gilitos, whose king—that is, *older brother*—he had been here on Earth.

Gustavo Adolfo Bécquer (1836–70)

One of the major literary figures of the century, Bécquer's fame rests on his Poems [Rimas] (published posthumously, 1871), literary letters, and Legends [Leyendas] (which originally appeared in newspapers between 1858 and 1864). Orphaned at an early age and plagued by poverty most of his life, Bécquer struggled to make ends meet as a social columnist. In 1861 he married Casta Esteban Navarro, with whom he had three children, but separated from her in 1868. He died at age thirty-four, a victim of pneumonia.

Bécquer studied both painting and music in Seville, the city of his birth, and the "colors" of the former and the "sounds" of the latter form part of the tapestry of his linguistic imagery, in poetry and prose alike. The Poems are seventy-six brief compositions, some as delicate as a whisper, some as exquisite as filigree, all of them a variation on one theme, love—all of them composed in a romanticism shorn of strident exultation, in a purified romanticism rich in pictorial and musical metaphor. Only the Nicaraguan writer Rubén Darío did more to advance the age of modern poetry in Spain.

The Legends, fewer than twenty, are a singular type of short story: journeys to a bygone time, mostly the Middle Ages, with its attendant superstitions and supernatural occurrences. They are a world of heroic architecture, exotic personages, haunted ruins, majestic cathedrals, and divine intervention; a world in which the protagonist pursues the impossible, the ephemeral, the beautiful, the ethereal, and the mysterious; a world in which the protagonist—in search of love, which is to say in search of woman—frequently risks madness or death.

Gustavo Adolfo Bécquer

"Believe in God"

†

I WAS THE TRUE TEOBALDO DE MONTAGUT, BARON OF FORTCASTELL. LORD OR SERF, NOBLE OR COMMONER, YOU, WHOEVER YOU MAY BE, WHO STOP FOR A MOMENT AT MY GRAVE, BELIEVE IN GOD AS I BELIEVED AND PRAY FOR ME.

I

YOU noble adventurers who, lances in holders, visors lowered, and riding powerful steeds, travel the world seeking honor and glory in the profession of arms with your illustrious reputations and broadswords as your only patrimony: if on crossing the craggy valley of Montagut* you have been surprised by a storm and nightfall, and have taken refuge in the ruins of the monastery that can still be seen at one end, hear me.

II

You shepherds who slowly follow your white sheep as they graze and scatter about hills and plains: if on leading them to the edge of the clear brook that runs, leaps, and fights its way through the rocks of the valley of Montagut you have found, in the hottest time of summer and on a blistering afternoon, shade and repose at the base of the demolished monastery arches whose moss-covered pillars are caressed by waves, hear me.

III

You girls from nearby villages, wild lilies who grow up under the protection of your humility: if on the morning of the patron saint of this region, going down to the valley of Montagut to gather clover and

108

daisies with which to adorn his shrine, overcoming the fear instilled in you by the gloomy monastery that rises among its rocks, you have entered its silent, deserted cloister to wander among its abandoned tombs, at whose edges grow deep blue hyacinths and double daisies, hear me.

IV

You, noble knight, perhaps by the brilliance of a flash of lightning; you, wandering shepherd, tanned by the sun's rays; and lastly you, pretty little girl, still covered with dewdrops like tears: all of you must have seen in that holy place a tomb, a modest tomb. Previously it consisted of a rough stone and a wooden cross; the cross has disappeared and only the stone remains. In that tomb, whose inscription is the refrain of my song, rests in peace the last baron of Fortcastell, Teobaldo de Montagut, whose strange story I am now going to tell you.

の の の

I

WHEN the noble Countess of Montagut was pregnant with her firstborn son, Teobaldo, she had a mysterious and terrible dream. Perhaps a warning from God; perhaps a vain fantasy that time made come true. She dreamt that she had given birth to a serpent, a monstrous serpent that emitted shrill hisses and slithered through the low grass and coiled on itself to spring; it fled from her sight, hiding, finally, in a bramble patch.

"There it is, there it is!" the countess screamed in her horrible nightmare, pointing out to her servants the bramble where the repulsive reptile had hidden.

When her servants arrived on the run at the spot where the noble lady, motionless and panic-stricken, was still pointing with her finger, a white dove flew out of the patch and soared away to the clouds.

The serpent had disappeared.

II

Teobaldo came into the world. His mother died giving birth to him; his father met his end several years later in an ambush, fighting valiantly against the enemies of God.

From this point on, the youth of the scion of Fortcastell can only be likened to a hurricane. Wherever he went his path was strewn with a trail of blood and tears. He hanged his villeins, fought with his fellow nobles, chased after maidens, beat monks, and, in his blasphemies and oaths, left no saint unsullied and no sacred object unprofaned.

III

One day when he went out hunting and, as was his wont, sought shelter from the rain in a village church of his domain along with his diabolical retinue of licentious pages, barbarous archers, and debased serfs, as well as dogs, horses, and gyrfalcons, a venerable priest, braving his fury and not cowering before the violent outbursts of his impetuous character, implored him, in the name of heaven, while carrying the consecrated host in his hands, to leave that holy place and go on foot with a pilgrim's staff to ask the pope for forgiveness for his sins.

"Leave me alone, you crazy old man!" exclaimed Teobaldo upon hearing him. "Leave me alone or, since I haven't come across a single piece of game all day, I'll let my dogs loose and hunt you like a wild boar to amuse myself."

IV

Teobaldo was a man of his word. The priest, nonetheless, spoke his piece.

"Do as you like, but remember that there is a God who punishes and forgives, and that if I die by your hands He will erase my sins from the book of His righteous anger to write your name and make you atone for your crime."

"A God who punishes and forgives!" the sacrilegious baron scoffed, bursting into laughter. "I don't believe in God, and to prove it, I'm going to carry out what I promised to do, because although prayer isn't high on my list, I always keep my word.

"Raimundo! Gerardo! Pedro! Set the pack on him, give me my javelin, sound the chase on your horns, and let's hunt this imbecile down, even if he climbs on top of the retables of his altars."

V

After hesitating for an instant and hearing a second command from their lord, the pages began to unleash the greyhounds, whose barking created a cacophony in the church. The baron had already cocked his crossbow, laughing satanically, and the venerable priest, mumbling a prayer, had raised his eyes to heaven and was calmly awaiting death when they heard outside the sacred walls an awful din, blasts on horns to beat the bushes, and shouts of "After the boar! Get the boar! By the bramble! Toward the mountain!" Teobaldo, at the report of the coveted game, ran to the doors of the sanctuary, beside himself with joy; with him went his servants, and with his servants, the horses and dogs.

VI

"Where's the boar headed?" asked the baron as he leaped onto his steed without using the stirrups or uncocking his crossbow.

"Toward the glen that stretches to the foot of those hills," they answered him.

Without hearing the last word, the impetuous hunter dug his gold spur into the flank of his horse, which galloped off. His retinue followed at his heels.

The village inhabitants, who were the first ones to sound the alarm, and who had taken refuge in their huts when the terrible animal appeared, timidly put their heads out windows, and when they saw the infernal hunting party disappear in the foliage of the dense wood, made the sign of the cross.

VII

Teobaldo raced ahead of all the others. His steed, fleeter or ridden harder than those of his servants, followed the quarry so closely that two or three times, dropping the bridle on top of the fiery beast's neck, Teobaldo stood up in the stirrups and raised the crossbow to his shoulder to take aim. But the boar, which he glimpsed only now and then in the close thickets, would disappear from view only to reappear beyond the range of his arrow.

Thus did he ride for many hours, passing through gorges in the valley and crossing the stony riverbed; then he penetrated an immense forest and lost his way in the dark turns, his eyes always on the coveted quarry, always believing he would catch up with it, and always finding himself outsmarted by its marvelous agility.

VIII

Finally seeing an opportunity, Teobaldo took aim and shot the arrow, which sank into the terrible animal's back and vibrated; the boar jumped and let out a hair-raising squeal.

"It's done for!" the hunter exclaimed with a joyful shout while digging his spur for the hundredth time into the bloody flank of his horse. "It's done for and fleeing in vain! And the blood that it's losing is marking a trail." Teobaldo then began to blow on his trumpet to signal his success to his servants.

At that very moment the steed pulled up, its legs gave way, a slight shudder shook its wasted muscles, and it collapsed, spouting a jet of blood through its swollen, foam-covered nostrils.

The horse had died of exhaustion, had died just when the wounded boar was beginning to slow down, just when a single effort would have been enough to bring it to heel.

IX

To describe the furious Teobaldo's rage would be impossible. To repeat his curses and blasphemies, just to repeat them, would be scandalous and sacrilegious. He called out to his servants at the top of his voice, and his only answer in that vast stretch of solitude was an echo, and he tore at his hair and pulled at his beard, prey to the most dreadful despair.

"I'll run after it myself even if I meet my end," he exclaimed at last, cocking his crossbow once again and preparing to follow his quarry. But at that moment he heard a noise at his back and tangled branches opened, and there appeared before him a page leading, by the halter, a steed as black as night.

"A gift from heaven!" said the hunter as he leaped, nimble as a gazelle, onto its back.

The page, who was thin, very thin, and pallid like death, smiled strangely upon handing him the reins.

X

The horse neighed with a force that made the forest shake; then he made an incredible jump, a jump that lifted him more than thirty feet off the ground, and as a stone hurled by a slingshot hums, so did the air begin to hum in the rider's ears. Teobaldo had set off at a gallop, but at such a swift one that, fearful of losing the stirrups and falling to the ground from dizziness, he had to close his eyes and hold on to the streaming mane with both hands.

And the steed raced on and on, without his rider pulling on the reins, digging his spurs, or urging him on with shouts. How long did Teobaldo race along with him ignorant of where, feeling branches hitting him in the face as he dashed by, brambles tearing at his clothes, and the wind whistling about him? Nobody knew.

XI

When, having regained his fortitude, he opened his eyes for a moment to glance around anxiously, Teobaldo found himself far, far away from Montagut, in places completely unknown to him. The steed continued to race along, and trees, rocks, castles, and villages passed by him like lightning. A host of new horizons unfolded before his eyes—horizons that receded to make way for others more and more unfamiliar. Narrow valleys, studded with colossal fragments of granite that storms had ripped from mountain peaks; pleasant stretches of countryside covered with a carpet of greenery and dotted with white hamlets; limitless deserts where sand baked, calcined by the rays of a burning sun; vast wildernesses, immense plains, eternally snowbound regions where gigantic ice floes, standing out against a dark gray sky, looked like white ghosts extending their arms to grab him by the hair as he sped by: all this, and thousands of other things that I am incapable of describing, he saw in his fantastic chase, until, enveloped in a dark fog, he did not hear the noise made by the horse's hooves as they pounded the ground.

∽ ∽ ∽

I

YOU noble knights, simple shepherds, and pretty girls who listen to my story: if you are astonished by what I'm telling you, do not think it is a tale spun at my whim to take your credulity by surprise. This tradition has come down to me by word of mouth, and the inscription on the tomb which still lies in the monastery of Montagut is unimpeachable testimony of the truthfulness of my words.

Believe, then, what I have told, and believe what I have yet to tell, for it is as true as the preceding events, albeit more marvelous. Perhaps I'll embellish the bare skeleton of this simple and terrible story with some poetic finery, but I'll never knowingly depart one whit from the truth.

II

When Teobaldo stopped hearing the hoofbeats of his steed and felt himself thrown into the void, he could not repress an involuntary shudder of terror. Until then he had truly believed that the objects passing before his eyes were figments of his imagination, an imagination unbalanced by vertigo, and that his steed raced out of control, but without leaving the confines of his seigneury. Now he had no doubt that he was the plaything of a supernatural power that was sweeping him, he knew not where, through those dark patches of fog and clouds of fantastic, whimsical forms, at whose center—which would light up now and then with the brilliance of lightning—he thought he made out fiery thunderbolts about to streak across the sky.

The steed raced, or rather swam, in that ocean of misty, crimson vapors, and the wonders of the firmament began to unfold, one after another, before its rider's frightened eyes.

III

Teobaldo saw angels, ministers of the Lord's wrath, cross the wings of a tempest like a mighty army; they were dressed in long tunics with fringes of fire, their glowing hair streaming in the hurricane, and they rode over the clouds and brandished their swords, which flashed and threw off sparks of purple light.

And he rose higher and thought he perceived in the distance stormy clouds similar to a sea of lava, and he heard thunder roar beneath him as the ocean roars when beating against the rock from which the amazed pilgrim looks on.

IV

And Teobaldo saw the archangel who, as white as snow, sits on an immense crystal globe that he steers on clear nights like a silver ship over the surface of a blue lake.

And he saw the blazing sun revolve on its gold axles in a kaleidoscopic atmosphere of fire, and at its center the igneous spirits who dwell unscathed among the flames and who, from their burning core, chant hymns of joy to the Creator.

And he saw the imperceptible threads of light that bind people to the stars and he saw the rainbow, spread out like a colossal bridge over the abyss that separates the first heaven from the second.

V

He saw souls descend to Earth by a mysterious ladder; he saw many go down and few come up. Every one of those innocent souls was accompanied by a resplendent archangel who covered them with the shadow of his wings. The angels who returned alone returned in silence with tears in their eyes; the rest came up singing like larks on an April morning.

Afterwards, the pink and blue mists, which were floating in space like curtains of transparent gauze, vanished like the veils that are removed from the altars of our churches on the day of glory, and the paradise of the righteous, dazzling and magnificent, opened up before his eyes.

VI

Teobaldo beheld there the holy prophets whom you have seen crudely sculpted on the stone façades of our cathedrals; luminous virgins whom the painter attempts in vain to copy from his dreams onto the stained glass of ogival windows; cherubim with their long, flowing robes and gold halos, like those depicted on altars; and, lastly, crowned with stars, dressed in light, surrounded by all the celestial hierarchies, and beautiful beyond all conception, Our Lady of Montserrat, the Mother of God, the Queen of Archangels, the refuge of sinners and the consolation of the afflicted.

VII

Beyond the paradise of the righteous, beyond the throne where the Virgin Mary sits, Teobaldo's spirit was overcome with fear, and a profound dread possessed his soul. Eternal solitude and eternal silence dwell in those regions that lead to the mysterious sanctuary of the Lord. From time to time his brow was whipped by a blast of wind, cold like the blade of a dagger, that made his hair stand on end and penetrated to the marrow of his bones, a wind like those that announced to the prophets the coming of the divine spirit. Finally, he reached a point where he thought he heard a dull noise similar to the distant hum of a swarm of bees when, on fall afternoons, they flit about the season's last flowers.

VIII

Teobaldo was crossing that fantastic region where all the speech from Earth goes, and all the sounds that vanish after we make them, all the words that we think are lost in the atmosphere, all the laments that we believe no one hears.

There, in a harmonious circle, float the prayers of children and virgins, the psalms of pious hermits, the petitions of the humble, the chaste words of the pure of heart, the resigned wails and cries of those who suffer, and the hymns of those who hope. Teobaldo heard among those voices, which still quivered in the luminous ether, that of his saintly mother, who was praying to God for him, but he did not hear his own voice.

IX

Further on, his ears were offended by the discordant din of thousands and thousands of rough, harsh accents, and by blasphemies, vengeful shouts, bacchanalian lyrics, curses of despair, threats of powerlessness, and sacrilegious oaths of impurity.

Teobaldo crossed the second circle, with the swiftness of the meteor that streaks across the sky on a summer afternoon, to avoid hearing his own voice, which vibrated there, resounding, deafening, drowning the other voices in the middle of that infernal concert.

"I don't believe in God! I don't believe in God!" his voice was still saying and reverberating in that babel of blasphemies.

But Teobaldo was beginning to believe.

X

He left those regions behind and crossed other vast stretches full of terrible visions, which he failed to comprehend and which I am unable to conceive, and arrived, finally, at the last circle of the spiral of the heavens, where seraphim adore the Lord, prostrate at His feet, their faces covered with their triple wings.

He tried to look at Him.

A breath of fire burned Teobaldo's face, a sea of light blinded his eyes, a tremendous thunderclap boomed in his ears and, pulled off the steed and hurled into the void like a white-hot stone belched by a volcano, he felt himself descending and descending without ever falling—burned, blinded, and deafened, as the rebellious angel must have plunged when God knocked over the pedestal of his pride with one puff from His lips.

∽ ∽ ∽

I

NIGHT had fallen and the wind was moaning as it stirred the leaves of the trees, through whose foliage a soft moonbeam shone, when Teobaldo, sitting up on his elbows and rubbing his eyes as if he had awakened from a deep sleep, glanced around and saw that he was in the same forest where he had wounded the boar, where his steed had breathed his last, and where he had been given the fantastic mount that carried him to mysterious, unknown regions.

A deathly silence reigned all around, a silence that was only broken by the distant snorting of deer, the faint rustle of leaves, and the echo of a faraway bell that came now and then on gusts of wind.

"I must have dreamed," said the baron, and he set off through the forest and came out, at last, on the plain.

II

In the distance, and above the rocks of Montagut, he saw the black silhouette of his castle standing out against the transparent blue background of the night sky.

"My castle is far away and I'm tired," he mumbled. "I'll wait for day in a nearby village," and he went to a village and knocked at a door.

"Who are you?" he was asked.

"The baron of Fortcastell," he replied, and they laughed in his face. He knocked at another door.

"Who are you and what do you want?" he was asked again.

"Your lord and master," the nobleman insisted, surprised that people did not recognize him. "Teobaldo de Montagut."

"Teobaldo de Montagut!" the speaker, an old woman, scoffed. "Teobaldo de Montagut, the one in the story. Bah! Off with you and don't come around waking decent people, telling them tasteless jokes."

III

Teobaldo, dumbfounded, left the village and headed for the castle, whose gates he reached when it was scarcely growing light. The moat was stopped up with the ashlars of the ruined battlements; the drawbridge, useless now, was rotting and still hung by its strong braces, which the years had covered with rust; in the keep a bell was tolling slowly; in front of the fortress's main arch, and on a granite base, rose a cross; at the parapets not a single soldier was to be seen; and, muffled and indistinct, a religious hymn that sounded like a distant hum, seemed to rise from the castle's depths—a grave, solemn, sublime hymn.

"This is beyond question my castle!" exclaimed Teobaldo, looking anxiously from one end to another, unable to fathom what was happening to him. "That is my coat of arms still engraved above the keystone of the arch! That's the valley of Montagut! These are lands ruled by the baron of Fortcastell!"

At that moment the heavy leaves of the door swung on their hinges and a monk appeared at the threshold.

IV

"Who are you and what are you doing here?" Teobaldo asked the monk.

"I am," the latter replied, "a humble servant of God, a monk of the monastery of Montagut."

"But . . . ," the baron interrupted, "is not Montagut a seigneury?"

"It used to be," the monk answered, "a long time ago. Its last lord, so the story goes, was carried off by the devil, and as he had no one to succeed him in the fief, the sovereign counts granted these lands to the monks of our rule, who have been here for around one hundred to one hundred and twenty years. And you, who are you?"

"I . . . ," stammered the lord of Fortcastell after a long, silent pause, "I am . . . a miserable sinner who, sorry for his sins, comes to confess them to your abbot, and to ask him to be admitted into the bosom of your religion."

Gustavo Adolfo Bécquer

"The Devil's Cross"

I

TWILIGHT was beginning to extend its light, vaporous wings over the picturesque banks of the Segre River* when, after a tiring day's ride, we arrived at Bellver, the last leg of our journey.

Bellver is a small town located at the foot of a hill, behind which soar, like the steps of a colossal granite amphitheater, the steep, misty crests of the Pyrenees.

The white houses that surround the hill, and which here and there dot an undulating sheet of greenery, look from afar like a flock of doves who have interrupted their flight to quench their thirst with the water of the riverbank.

A smooth rock, around whose base the Segre River winds its course and on whose pinnacle the vestiges of construction can still be seen, marks the old dividing line between the countship of Urgel and the most important of its fiefs.

To the right of the torturous path that leads to this point, paralleling the flow of the river and following its bends and luxuriant banks, stands a cross.

The upright and the transverse are made of iron; the round base to which it is anchored is marble; and the flight of steps that lead to it are dingy, ill-fitting pieces of masonry.

The destructive effect of time, which has covered the metal with rust, has split and eaten away at the stone of this monument, and in its cracks grow climbing plants that twist all the way to the top, while a massive old holm oak acts as a canopy.

I had gotten ahead of my traveling companions and, stopping my scrawny mount, gazed in silence at the cross, a mute, simple expression of the beliefs and devotion of other times.

A thousand and one ideas flashed into my mind at that moment.

119

Indeterminate, elusive ideas that fused together, like an invisible thread of light, the profound solitude of those villages, the intense silence of the approaching night, and the vague melancholy of my spirit.

Driven by an indefinable and spontaneous religious impulse, I dismounted without thinking, took off my hat, and began to search in the recesses of my memory for one of those prayers that I was taught as a child, one of those prayers that, when they involuntarily tumble off our lips as adults, seem to alleviate a heavy heart and, like tears, relieve pain, which also assumes bodily form only to vanish.

I had already begun to mumble it when all of a sudden I felt someone shaking my shoulders furiously. I turned around: there was a man at my side.

It was one of our guides, a native of the area, who, with an indescribable expression of terror stamped on his face, was struggling to pull me away with him and cover my head with the felt hat that I still held in my hands.

My initial glance, half surprise and half anger, was tantamount to a forceful, albeit silent, question.

The poor man, without letting up in his efforts to pull me away from that spot, answered it with these words, which I failed to comprehend at the time, but which had a ring of truth that startled me:

"By all that's sacred! By all that you hold most dear in the world, master, cover your head and get away from this cross as fast as you can! You're so desperate that, not content with God's help, you petition the devil too?"

I stood there for a time looking at him in silence. Frankly, I thought he was mad, but he continued in the same impassioned tone:

"You're looking for the border. Well, if you ask heaven for help in front of this cross, the tops of the nearby mountains will rise to the invisible stars overnight just to prevent us from finding the boundary for the rest of our days."

I couldn't help smiling.

"This amuses you? Do you perchance believe that this is a holy cross like the one in the atrium of our church?"

"Can there be any doubt?"

"Well, you're dead wrong, because this cross, although a symbol of Christianity, is damned. This cross belongs to an evil spirit, and that's why it is called *The Devil's Cross*."

"The devil's cross!" I repeated, giving in to his insistence without becoming aware of the involuntary dread that began to take possession of me, and which was pushing me away from that site like an unknown force. "The devil's cross! Never has a more absurd combination of two such opposite notions jarred my mind! A cross and . . . the devil's! Well, well! When we reach town you must explain this monstrous inconsistency to me."

During this brief exchange our companions, who had spurred their horses, joined us at the foot of the cross. I explained to them in a few words what had just happened to me and remounted my nag. The bells of the parish church were slowly calling to prayer when we alighted at the most secluded and gloomy of Bellver's inns.

II

Blue and red tongues of flame emitted sparks and wound along the big oak log that was burning in the wide hearth. Our shadows, which quivered on the blackened wall, became smaller or took on gigantic shapes depending on the intensity of the fire's blaze. The elderwood cup, drained and then replenished and not with water like a noria's buckets, had been passed three times around the group that sat together in a circle next to the fire. All of us were waiting impatiently to hear the story of *The Devil's Cross*, promised to us as dessert to the frugal supper that we had just eaten, when our guide coughed twice, took a last swig of wine, wiped his mouth with the back of his hand, and began like this:

"What I'm going to tell you occurred a long, long time ago. I don't know how long, but the Moors still occupied the greater part of Spain, our kings were called counts, and towns and villages belonged in fief to certain nobles who, in turn, paid tribute to others more powerful than they."

After making this brief historical introduction, the man of the hour kept silent for a few seconds, as if ordering his thoughts, then continued:

"Well, to begin with, back in those times this town and several others constituted a part of the heritage of a noble baron whose seignorial castle stood for many centuries on the crest of a large rock washed by the Segre River, from which it takes its name.

"Atop the rock there still exist, to testify to the truth of my story, shapeless ruins covered with hedge mustard and moss that can be seen from the road that leads to this town.

"For his cruelty this noble was detested by his vassals, and for his depravity, refused admittance to court by the king and shunned by his neighbors. As luck would have it—fortunately or unfortunately, I don't know—he got bored living alone with his bad temper and crossbowmen in the stone aerie built by his forebears.

"Night and day he racked his brain in search of some distraction in keeping with his character, which proved quite difficult, weary as he had become of making war on his neighbors, beating his servants, and hanging his subjects.

"At last, the chronicles record, he came up with a felicitous, although not unprecedented, idea.

"Knowing that Christians from other powerful nations were preparing to set sail together on a formidable fleet and go to a faraway land to recover the Holy Sepulcher, which was in the hands of Moors, he decided to join up with them.

"If he acted on this idea with the aim of atoning for his sins, which were considerable, and shedding his blood in such a just cause, or with the aim of removing to a place where his evil ways were not known, nobody can say. But the truth of the matter is that, much to the delight of young and old, of vassals and peers, he amassed as much money as he could, released towns from his seigniory for a king's ransom, and, retaining only the Segre rock and the castle that stood on it, a legacy from his parents, disappeared overnight.

"The entire region breathed freely for a time, as if it had awakened from a nightmare.

"No longer did clusters of men, instead of fruit, hang from the trees in his groves; no longer were girls from the town afraid to go out with their jugs on their heads to fetch water from the roadside fountain; no longer did shepherds lead their flocks to the Segre River along nearly impassable and hidden paths fearful of encountering at every bend the crossbowmen of their beloved lord.

"Thus did three years pass. The story of the *Evil Noble*, the only name used to refer to him, was beginning to be the exclusive property of old women who, on endless winter evenings, would tell astonished children his fiendish deeds in a hollow, fearful voice, and of mothers who would scare their whiney or unruly little ones by saying to them 'Here comes the baron of Segre!,' when out of the blue—I don't know if one day or one night, if fallen from heaven or expelled from the depths of hell—the much feared baron did indeed appear and, as the saying goes, in the flesh, in the midst of his former vassals.

"I shall refrain from describing the effect of this pleasant surprise. You'll be able to imagine it better than I can relate it simply by my saying that he returned and reclaimed the rights he had sold. So if he went away bad, he came back even worse, and if he was poor and had no credit before going off to war, the only resources that he could count on now were his indifference, his lance, and a handful of adventurers as heartless and dissolute as their leader.

"The towns, naturally enough, balked at paying tributes that they had redeemed at such great cost, but the baron set fire to their property, farmhouses, and cornfields.

"Then they sought royal justice, but the baron made a mockery of the sovereign count's edicts, nailing them to the postern of his castle and hanging the heralds from an oak tree.

"Infuriated, and finding no other way to save themselves, they finally banded together, put their trust in Divine Providence, and took up arms, but the baron rallied his followers, enlisted the aid of the devil, withdrew to the top of his rock, and prepared to do battle.

"It had a terrible, bloody beginning. They fought with all kinds of arms, in all kinds of places, and at all hours—with swords and fire, in the mountains and on the plain, by day and by night. They weren't fighting to stay alive; they were staying alive to fight.

"In the end, the cause of justice triumphed. Listen how:

"One dark, pitch-black night, when not a single sound could be heard on Earth and not a single star shone in the sky, the lords of the stronghold, puffed up by a recent victory, were dividing booty. They were in the middle of a wild, deafening orgy, drunk from the fumes of their spirits and singing sacrilegious songs in praise of their diabolic leader.

"Nothing, as I've said, could be heard around the castle except for the echo of blasphemies that vibrated and disappeared in the inky bosom of night, like the souls of the damned that cry out wrapped in the folds of hell's hurricane.

"The careless sentries had already looked a number of times in the direction of the town, which was resting in silence, and, not fearing a surprise, had fallen asleep leaning against the stout shafts of their lances, when lo and behold several peasants, prepared to die and protected by the darkness, began to scale the towering Segre rock, whose peak they reached at exactly midnight.

"Once on the peak, what they needed to accomplish took very little time. The sentries went from sleep to death in two shakes of a lamb's tail. Fire, set with resin torches to the drawbridge and portcullis, spread with lightning speed to the walls, and the climbers, aided by the confusion, made their way through the flames and did away with the inhabitants of that lair in a wink. They all perished.

"When the approaching day began to cast a soft light on the junipers' crowns, the charred rubble was still smoking. Through wide holes in the gutted towers it was easy to make out, sparkling as the sun hit it and hanging from one of the black pillars in the banquet hall, the armor of the dreaded leader whose body, covered with blood and dust, lay together with his unrecognizable companions among the tattered tapestries and hot ashes.

"Time passed. Brambles began to crawl along the bailey and deserted courtyards, ivy tangled around dark pilasters, and blue harebells swung from dilapidated battlements. Erratic breezes, the cawing of nocturnal birds, and the rustling of snakes that slithered through the tall grass disturbed only occasionally the deathly silence of that cursed spot where the unburied bones of the castle's former dwellers were turning white in the moonlight. And you could still see the baron of Segre's suit of armor hanging from the black pillar in the banquet hall.

"Nobody dared touch it, but countless legends centered around that abandoned object which was an endless source of rumors and scares for those who saw it flash in the sun during the day, or thought they heard in the small hours the metallic sound of its pieces as they clinked together when the wind moved them with a prolonged, mournful howl.

"Despite all the stories that were fabricated about the suit of armor, and which the inhabitants of the surrounding area repeated to one another in a low voice, they were only stories; the only clear evil that resulted from them amounted to no more than fear, which everyone tried to hide as much as possible, while keeping, as the saying goes, a stiff upper lip.

"If the situation had gone no further, nothing would have come of it. But the devil, who apparently was not satisfied with his handiwork, intervened in the matter—and undoubtedly with God's leave—to make the region atone for a number of its sins.

"From that moment on, the stories, which until then were little more than idle talk and contained not a shred of truth, began to seem credible and appeared more and more probable.

"And, in fact, for several nights the whole town had observed a strange phenomenon.

"Off in the distant shadows, either moving up the twisting slopes of the Segre rock or wandering amid the ruins of the castle or seeming to hover overhead, fantastic and mysterious lights—whose source nobody could explain—were seen shooting, crisscrossing, disappearing, and then appearing again to move off in different directions.

"This was repeated for three or four nights during the space of a month, and the bewildered townspeople anxiously awaited the outcome of those diabolic assemblies; it was not long in coming. Three or four farmhouses set on fire, several missing head of cattle, and the bodies of a few wayfarers—thrown over cliffs—terrified everybody for ten leagues around.

"Now there was no doubt whatever. A band of villains was living in the underground passages of the castle.

"These cutthroats, who in the beginning let themselves be seen only very rarely and only at certain places in the forest that even to this day stretches along the riverbank, ended up controlling almost all the mountain passes; they lay in ambush on the roads, looted the valley, and descended like a torrent of lava on the plain, where they butchered people left and right, sparing no one.

"The murders multiplied, girls disappeared, and children—in spite of their mothers' screams—were snatched from their cradles for use in the villains' diabolic feasts, during which, most everybody believed, the sacred vessels stolen from desecrated churches served as wineglasses.

"People became terrified to such an extent that at the Angelus bell they didn't dare to leave their homes, although not even there were they always safe from the brigands of the rock.

"But who were they? Where had they come from? What was the name of their leader? That was the enigma that everybody tried to explain, the puzzle that nobody could solve. People realized, however, that at one point the feudal lord's suit of armor had disappeared from where it had been hanging, and afterwards several peasants stated that the captain who rode at the head of that heartless band wore one that, if not the same suit, looked exactly like it.

"If stripped of the fantastic elements with which fear magnifies and elaborates its favorite creatures, there is nothing inherently supernatural or strange in what I've just related.

"What could have been more normal for a group of brigands than the acts of savagery that they committed, or more natural than their leader's taking possession of the baron of Segre's abandoned suit of armor?

"Nevertheless, the confession of one of his followers, taken prisoner in the last skirmish, was the last straw, causing even the biggest skeptics to become concerned. Here, more or less, are his dying words:

"'I come,' he said, 'from a noble family. My misconduct as a youth, my profligate ways, and, lastly, my transgressions, earned me the fury of my relatives and the curse of my father, who disinherited me on his deathbed. Finding myself alone and penniless, the devil doubtless suggested to me the idea of bringing together a few youths who were in similar straits, and they, seduced by the promise of a future of dissipation, freedom, and plenty, didn't hesitate to endorse my plan. And my plan consisted of forming a band of high-spirited young men, carefree and heedless of danger, who would thereafter live happily off the outcome of their bravery and at the expense of the land until such time that it pleased God to pass judgment on each one according to His will, which time for me is today. Having agreed on our purpose, we selected this region as the scene of our future expeditions and chose as the most suitable site for our meetings the abandoned Segre castle, a safe place not so much for its advantageous and well-fortified location as for the protection afforded by the superstitions and fear of the peasants.

"'One night when we gathered under the dilapidated arches, around a bonfire that illuminated the deserted galleries with its reddish glow, a heated argument broke out over which of us was to be elected leader. Each one stated his merits, and I set forth my claims. Some were beginning to grumble amongst themselves and dart threatening looks, and others, their angry voices brought on by drunkenness, had put their hands on the hilts of their daggers to settle the matter, when all of a sudden we heard a strange rattling of armor accompanied by hollow, resounding footsteps that became more and more distinct. We all looked around warily, got up, and bared our swords, determined to sell our lives dearly, but we couldn't help stopping dead in our tracks on seeing a man approach us with steady, measured strides—a tall man, completely armed from head to foot, his face covered by the visor of his helmet. He proceeded to unsheathe his broadsword, which two men would have difficulty wielding, and, setting it on one of the disintegrated fragments of the broken arcades, exclaimed in a deep, hollow voice, like the sound of an underground waterfall: "If one of you dares to be the leader while I inhabit Segre castle, pick up that sword, the symbol of power." We all kept silent until the first moment of astonishment had passed, and then we loudly proclaimed him our captain and offered him a glass of wine; he refused our offer by means of signs, perhaps to avoid showing his face, which we tried in vain to make out through the iron ventail that hid it from our eyes.

"'All the same, that night we took the most horrendous of oaths, and on the following one began our nocturnal forays. When we raid, our mysterious leader always rides at the head of the band. Fire doesn't stop him, danger doesn't intimidate him, and tears don't move him.

He never utters a word, but when blood is streaming on our hands, when churches collapse consumed by flames, when frightened women flee through ruins, and children scream in pain and old men die from our blows, he responds with a guffaw of savage joy to their moans, curses, and laments. He never ungirds his sword, and neither raises the visor of his helmet after victory nor takes part in the celebration nor surrenders to sleep. Blades that strike him penetrate the layers of his armor, but they neither kill him nor come out covered with blood; fire turns his cuirass and coat of mail red-hot, and he still carries on in the flames, undaunted, searching for new victims. He spurns gold, detests beauty, and is unaffected by ambition. Some in the band think he's a maniac and some think he's a down-and-out nobleman who keeps his face covered out of a lingering sense of shame, and there are some who are convinced that he's the devil incarnate.'

"The outlaw who made these disclosures died with a sneering smile on his lips, unrepentant. Several of his cohorts suffered, at different times, the same punishment as he, but the dreaded leader, who continually attracted new followers, did not desist in his pillage.

"The miserable inhabitants of the region, increasingly more weary and desperate, were unable to find the resolve needed to put an end once and for all to that state of affairs, more unbearable and disastrous with each passing day.

"Right next to the town, and concealed in the depths of a dense woodland, there lived at this time, in a small hermitage dedicated to St. Bartholomew, a holy man who led a devout, exemplary life; the townspeople always looked upon him as a saint thanks to his beneficial counsel and unfailing predictions.

"This venerable hermit, to whose prudence and proverbial wisdom the people of Bellver entrusted the solution of this pressing problem, implored divine mercy through his patron saint, who, as you all know, is quite familiar with the devil and on more than one occasion has put him in his place. The holy man then counseled them to lie in ambush one night at the foot of the stony trail that snaked its way up to the rock on top of which stood the castle; at the same time he instructed them, once there, not to make use of any weapon to catch him other than a wondrous prayer that he made them memorize, and with which the chronicles affirm that St. Bartholomew had made the devil his prisoner.

"When the plan was put into effect it exceeded everybody's fondest hopes, inasmuch as the early morning sun had yet to light up the tall tower of Bellver when its inhabitants, grouped in the main square, were already telling one another with an air of mystery how that night the famous captain of the brigands of Segre, bound hand and foot, had ridden into town on a stout mule.

"Nobody, not even the participants themselves, could say what arts were employed to bring this undertaking to a successful conclusion, but the fact was that, thanks to the saint's prayer or to the courage of his devotees, the baron was overcome in the manner described.

"No sooner did the news begin to spread from person to person and from house to house than all the people noisily rushed outside and congregated at the doors of the prison. The church bell summoned the town council, and its members convened as everybody anxiously awaited the hour when the criminal would appear before his improvised judges.

"These men, who were empowered by the counts of Urgel to administer, on their own, swift and strict justice to those cutthroats, deliberated briefly and then ordered the villain brought in so they could deliver their sentence.

"As I've already said, in the main square as well as in the streets that the prisoner needed to cross to go where the judges were, the impatient crowd teemed like a tightly packed swarm of bees. Especially at the entrance to the prison, disturbance among the people reached ever greater proportions. The lively conversations, the veiled grumbles, and the menacing shouts were beginning to worry his guards when, fortunately, the order came to bring out the offender.

"When he appeared under the massive arch of the prison doorway, in a full suit of armor and his face covered by the visor, a low, prolonged murmur of admiration and surprise rose from the dense throng, which only with difficulty opened up to let him through.

"Everybody had recognized the suit of armor as that of the baron of Segre, the suit of armor that had been the object of hair-raising stories while it hung from the ruined walls of the ill-fated stronghold.

"There was no doubt whatever that it was the same armor. All of them had seen the black plume streaming from the crest in battles that they had once fought against their lord; all had seen it fluttering in the breeze at daybreak, like the ivy on the charred pillar where the suit was hung after its owner's death. But who could this unknown individual be who was now wearing it? They were soon going to find out—at least they thought they were. Events will demonstrate how this prospect, like many others, was frustrated, and why fresh and more incomprehensible confusion arose from this solemn act of justice, which should have answered all the questions surrounding the armor.

"The mysterious brigand finally entered the Council Chamber, and a profound silence followed the buzz made by the onlookers when they heard the metallic sound of his gold spurs echo under the hall's high domes. One of the members of the tribunal, in a slow, shaky voice, asked him his name, and everyone listened anxiously so as not to lose a single word of his answer, but all the warrior did was shrug his shoulders slightly, with an air of contempt and disdain that couldn't help irritating his judges, who looked at each other in surprise.

"He repeated the question three times and three times received the same or similar response.

"'Make him raise his visor! Make him show his face! Make him show his face!' the townspeople who were witnessing the proceedings began to shout. 'Make him show his face! Then we'll see if he dares to insult us with his disdain as he is now, hiding behind his armor!'

"'Show your face,' he was commanded by the same judge who had questioned him earlier.

"The warrior remained impassive.

"'I order you in the name of this tribunal.'

"The same response—not a word.

"'In the name of our sovereign lord.'

"When that had no effect either, indignation reached its peak—to the point where one of the guards, flinging himself at the brigand whose persistence in remaining silent was enough to try the patience of a saint, opened the visor with a violent jerk. A cry of general surprise escaped from the assembled crowd, momentarily struck by an inconceivable feeling of awe.

"And with reason. The helmet, with the upper half of the iron visor raised and the lower resting on the shining steel gorget, was empty, completely empty.

"After the initial moment of terror had passed, they tried to touch it; the armor quaked slightly and, separating into its component parts, fell to the floor with a strange muffled sound.

"At the sight of that new marvel, most of the onlookers stampeded from the room and ran to the square, frightened to death.

"The news spread like wildfire among the crowd that was impatiently awaiting the result of the trial, and such was the alarm, the commotion, and the uproar that no one doubted any longer what was being said openly—that the devil, at the death of the baron of Segre, had inherited the fiefs of Bellver.

"Finally, the tumult subsided and the tribunal decided to return the marvelous arms to a dungeon.

"The judges then immediately dispatched four emissaries, who, as representatives of the beleaguered town, were charged with explaining the occurrence to the count of Urgel and to the archbishop. The four returned in a matter of days with the decision of those august personages. It was brief and to the point.

"'Hang the armor,' they were told, 'in the main square of the town, because if the devil does occupy that suit, he'll either have to abandon it or be hanged himself with it.'

"Delighted with such an ingenious solution, the tribunal convened once again and ordered a gallows raised in the square; when the crowd lined the streets that led to it, the judges went to the jail, ex officio and with all the formality that the occasion demanded.

"When the estimable body arrived at the massive arch that led into the building, a pale, agitated man threw himself to the ground in the presence of the stunned bystanders, exclaiming with tears in his eyes:

"'Mercy, my lords, mercy!'

"'Mercy? For whom?' several of them inquired. 'For the devil who dwells inside the baron of Segre's suit of armor?'

"'For me,' continued in a shaky voice the hapless man whom everybody recognized as the warden, 'for me . . . because the armor has . . . disappeared.'

"On hearing these words all the people in the portico stared at him in consternation. They would have remained speechless and motionless God knows how long if the terrified warden hadn't told the following story, which caused them to gather round and listen eagerly.

"'Forgive me, my lords, forgive me,' the poor man repeated, 'forgive me and I shan't keep anything from you, even if it speaks ill of me.'

"They all kept silent and he continued thus:

"'I doubt if I'll ever be able to explain why, but I never gave credence to the story of the empty suit of armor. It always seemed to me like a myth invented on behalf of some noble whom, perhaps for serious reasons of state, you could not reveal or punish. This belief, which I held from the beginning, was confirmed for me when the armor did not move even once after it was brought here for the second time at the tribunal's order. Night after night I tried in vain to discover the armor's secret, if it had one, so little by little I would advance and press my ear to the cracks in the dungeon's iron door, but not a sound could be heard. I tried in vain to observe it through a small hole made in the wall. Dumped on top of some straw, and in one of the darkest corners, it sat there day after day, in pieces and unmoving. Finally, spurred by curiosity and wanting to become convinced that there was nothing mysterious about that object of terror, one night I lit a torch, descended to the underground cells, raised the double crossbars, and, not even taking the trouble to close the doors behind me (so persuaded was I that the whole thing was just a figment of the imagination), I entered the dungeon. I wish I hadn't! After I took but a few steps my torch light went out, for no apparent reason, and my teeth began to chatter and my hair stood on end. Then I heard something break the profound silence that surrounded me, something like the shifting and clinking of iron parts that were coming together in the dark. The first thing I did was throw myself at the door to block the exit, but as I grasped the leaves I felt a powerful hand on my shoulders, a hand inside a gauntlet, that shook me violently and threw me to the threshold. I lay there until the following morning, when my staff found me unconscious. All I could remember was that after my fall I thought I heard, in a haze, something like clanking footsteps with the jingling sound of spurs, which grew fainter and fainter until finally dying out.'

"When the warden finished, a profound silence reigned, a silence that was followed by an infernal clamor of moans, shouts, and threats.

"The more peaceable ones in the crowd found it difficult to restrain the people who were enraged by the new development and who called for the death of the curious author of their new setback.

"In the end the disturbance was brought under control and everybody began to plan for another chase, which, like the previous one, had a satisfactory result.

"Several days later the suit of armor was once again in the hands of its pursuers. Now that they knew the formula and had St. Bartholomew's help, retrieval was no longer a problem.

"But another one had yet to be resolved, because in vain did they attempt to secure the armor by hanging it from a gallows; in vain did they keep very careful watch to eliminate chances for escape to wherever it chose. As soon as the separated pieces saw the slightest opportunity, they would join together and slowly go off to make forays anew in highland and lowland, which, of course, was a real godsend. There was no end to it.

"Given the urgency of the situation, the townspeople divided the pieces of armor amongst themselves, in their hands now for perhaps the hundredth time, and implored the devout hermit who had assisted them earlier with his counsel to decide what they should do with the suit of armor.

"The holy man ordered them to do a general penance. He then shut himself up for three days in the depths of the cave that served as his shelter, at the end of which time he instructed them to melt the diabolical armor and erect a cross with it and ashlars taken from Segre castle.

"The plan was brought into effect, although not without new and terrifying marvels that frightened the dismayed inhabitants of Bellver out of their wits.

"When the pieces thrown into the flames began to get red-hot, prolonged and deep moans seemed to arise from the huge blaze, while the armor shot up from between the burning logs as if it were alive and experiencing excruciating pain. A swirl of red, green, and blue sparks danced at the apex of the bright tongues of flame, and twisted and writhed as if a legion of devils were riding them and fighting to free their lord from that torment.

"It was a strange, horrible operation during the time that the red-hot suit of armor lost its shape to assume that of a cross. Hammers pounded and rang out with a frightful racket on the anvil, where twenty muscular workers held the bars of molten metal that throbbed and moaned under the blows.

"The arms of the symbol of our redemption were already formed and the upright was beginning to take shape when the diabolical, glowing mass twisted itself again as in a dreadful convulsion and, encircling the hapless workers who fought to escape its deadly embrace, coiled like a snake or contracted like bead lightning.

"Continuous work, faith, prayer, and holy water succeeded, at last, in subduing the demonic spirit, and the suit of armor became a cross.

"It's the one that all of you saw today, the cross to which the devil, who lends it his name, is bound. Girls don't place bouquets of lilies before it in the month of May, nor do shepherds uncover on passing by, nor do the aged genuflect—even priests' warnings are barely sufficient to keep boys from pelting it with stones.

"God has turned a deaf ear to all the prayers that are offered to Him in its presence. In winter, wolves gather in packs alongside the juniper that rises above it to attack livestock; outlaws wait in its shade for travelers whom they bury at its foot after murdering them; and when a storm breaks, flashes of lightning stray from their path to whiz and wrap around the cross's upright and part the ashlars of its base."

Pedro Antonio de Alarcón (1833–91)

If he had written nothing else, Pedro Antonio de Alarcón would be justly celebrated for The Three-Cornered Hat *[El sombrero de tres picos] (1874), a short novel as familiar to the Spanish public as Juan Ramón Jiménez's* Platero and I *[Platero y yo]. Born in Guadix (province of Granada), Alarcón eventually made his way to Madrid, fought as a volunteer in the army (and was wounded in Africa), traveled to Italy, and returned to Madrid.*

A liberal and revolutionary who edited an anticlerical newspaper, Alarcón's life was spared in a duel, and afterwards he became a staunch conservative and vigorous champion of Catholicism. This about-face materialized in several long novels that turned into works of thesis. The Scandal *[El escándalo] (1875), for example, is a novel of romantic excesses that defends the Catholic religion as the basis of morality and argues that it is the path to salvation.*

But Alarcón, a born storyteller with a gift for plot, movement, and rapid characterization, gained renown in short fiction. Well-respected critics like his contemporary Emilia Pardo Bazán, José Montesinos, Mariano Baquero Goyanes, and Juan Luis Alborg have nothing but praise for "The Nun," "The Nail," "The Tall Woman," "Moors and Christians," and "Death's Friend." And Montesinos considers the latter "one of . . . Alarcón's masterpieces" [una de . . . las obras maestras de Alarcón].

Pedro Antonio de Alarcón

"Death's Friend"

A FANTASTIC TALE

I
VIRTUES AND SERVICES

THE friend was a tall, skinny, unfortunate youth with a sallow complexion, big black eyes, an open face, and the most beautiful hands in the world; he was shabbily dressed, had a haughty bearing, and an intolerable disposition. He was nineteen and his name was Gil Gil.*

Gil Gil was the son, grandson, great-grandson, great-great-grandson, and God knows what else, of the best cobblers in Madrid, and on coming into the world caused the death of his mother Crispina López, whose father, grandfather, great-grandfather, and great-great-grandfather also honored the same profession.

Juan Gil, the lawful father of our melancholy hero, did not begin to love him from the moment he learned that the boy had been conceived, only from the moment he was informed that the boy had left the womb and deprived him of his wife, which leads me to conclude that the hapless master shoemaker and Crispina López typified brief but bad marriages.

Theirs was so brief, in fact, that it could not have been briefer, if we keep in mind that it bore fruit . . . to a certain extent. What I mean to say is that Gil Gil at seven months was premature, or rather, that he was born seven months after his parent's marriage, which does not always prove the same thing. Nevertheless, and judging only by appearances, Crispina López deserved to be mourned more than she was by her husband, because when she moved to his shoe shop from her father's she brought to him in dowry, besides an almost superabundant beauty and considerable bed linen and clothing, a very well-to-do customer, a count no less, the count of Rionuevo, who for a number of months (we believe seven) inexplicably took to wearing on

134

his small, delicate feet good Juan's crude work, work that made Juan the most unworthy of representatives of the martyrs Crispín and Crispiniano, patron saints of shoemakers.

But none of this has anything to do with my story titled "Death's Friend."

What *is* important for us to know is that Gil Gil lost his father, that is to say, the honest shoemaker, at the age of fourteen, when he himself was becoming a good cobbler, and that the noble count of Rionuevo, either feeling sorry for the young orphan or captivated by his great intelligence—nobody ever learned the real reason—had him brought to his palace in the capacity of a page, notwithstanding the strong aversion of the countess, who already knew about the child delivered by Crispina López.

Our hero had received some education—reading, writing, arithmetic, and catechism—so that he was, of course, able to tackle Latin under the direction of a Hieronymite monk who frequented the count's home, and the truth be said, these were the happiest years of Gil Gil's life, happy not because the poor devil suffered no misfortunes (the countess supplied him with major ones, continually reminding him of the shoemaker's stirrup and awl), but because in the evenings he would accompany his protector to the home of the duke of Monteclaro, and the duke of Monteclaro had a daughter, sole presumptive heiress of all his goods and property and current and future income, and uncommonly beautiful besides, even though the father was rather ugly and ungainly.

Elena was nearly twelve when she and Gil Gil met, and as the young page passed in the Rionuevo household for the son of a very noble although down-and-out family—a white lie on the count's part—the aristocratic girl deigned to play children's games with him, to the point, and as a joke of course, of calling him her "boyfriend," and even granting him an occasional show of affection when her twelve years of age turned into fourteen and his fourteen into sixteen.

Thus did three years go by.

The shoemaker's son lived all this time in an atmosphere of luxury and pleasure: he became a member of the court, associated with the nobility, acquired the latter's tastes, spoke broken French (a highly fashionable language then), and learned, in short, riding, dancing, fencing, a little chess, and a little necromancy.

But Death came upon the scene a third time, and more heartless than the first two, to lay waste our hero's future. The count of Rionuevo died intestate and the widowed countess, who cordially hated the deceased's protégé, instructed him, with tears in her eyes and venom in her smile, to leave their home without delay, because his presence reminded her of her husband, which could not help but sadden her.

Gil Gil believed that he was awakening from a beautiful dream, or that he was the victim of a cruel nightmare. The fact is that he tucked under his arm what little clothing he was allowed, and, crying his eyes out, quit what had ceased to be a hospitable roof.

With little money, no family, and no home to go to, the poor devil remembered that on a certain side street in the Vistillas district he owned a humble stand and some shoemaker's tools locked in a chest, all of which had been left in the custody of the oldest old woman in the neighborhood, in whose home the miserable thing had found affection and even sweetmeats during the lifetime of the virtuous Juan Gil. So he went there: the old woman was still alive; the tools were in good condition; and the rental of the stand had, during those years, earned some seven doubloons, which the good woman gave to him, not without first wetting them with tears of joy.

Gil decided to live with the old woman, to devote himself to the shoemaker's craft, and to forget all about riding, fencing, dancing, and chess. But by no means Elena de Monteclaro! That he would have found impossible.

He realized, nonetheless, that he had died for her, or that she had died for him, but before placing the gravestone of despair over that inextinguishable love he wished to say a final good-bye to the one who for so long had been the soul of his soul.

Therefore one night he put on his best gentleman's clothes and set out for the duke's house.

At the door there was a diligence with four mules already harnessed. Elena was getting into it, followed by her father.

"Gil!" she exclaimed fondly upon seeing her former companion.

"Let's move out!" the duke shouted to the coachman, neither hearing his daughter nor seeing the erstwhile page of the count of Rionuevo.

The mules pulled out.

The dejected youth extended his arms toward his idol without even having time to say good-bye.

"All right," the doorman grumbled. "I have to lock up."

Gil recovered from his bewilderment.

"They're going away." he said.

"Yes, sir. To France," the doorman responded curtly, closing the door in his face.

The ex-page went back home more desperate than ever, undressed, and stored away his finery; he then put on his shabbiest clothes, cut his hair, shaved the beginnings of a mustache, and the following day took possession of the rickety chair that Juan Gil had sat in for forty years in the midst of lasts, cutters, awls, and wax.

Thus do we find him at the beginning of this story, which, as has been said, is titled "Death's Friend."

II
MORE SERVICES AND VIRTUES

The month of June 1724 was drawing to a close.

Gil Gil had been a shoemaker for two years, but do not for this reason think that he had become resigned to his fate.

He had, of necessity, to work night and day in order to earn a living, and never stopped deploring the consequent damage done to his beautiful hands. He would read when no customers came, and not even accidentally did he tread on the doorstep of his out-of-the-way lodgings during the week. He lived alone, taciturn, hypochondriac, with no other distraction than occasionally hearing the old woman extol the beauty of Crispina López or the generosity of the count of Rionuevo.

On Sundays, however, a total transformation took place. Gil Gil would put on the clothes—never touched during the rest of the week—that he used to wear as a page and go to the steps of San Millán Church, the one nearest the Monteclaro mansion, where his unforgettable Elena used to attend Mass in happier times.

This went on for one year, then two, and he never saw her. On the other hand, he usually ran into students and pages whom he had met as a child, and they kept him informed of all that occurred in the high circles that he no longer frequented; it was they in fact who told him that his idol continued in France. Of course, nobody in that quarter suspected that our young hero was a poor cobbler in another; on the contrary, they believed him the beneficiary of a bequest from the count of Rionuevo, who in his lifetime had shown too much of a preference for the young page for people to believe that he had not thought about safeguarding his future.

Such was the state of affairs at the time mentioned at the outset of this chapter when one feast day Gil Gil stood waiting by the entrance of the aforesaid church. He saw two elegantly dressed ladies arrive with a large entourage, and they passed sufficiently close to him that he recognized in one of them the countess of Rionuevo, his implacable enemy.

Our young hero was going to hide in the crowd when the other lady raised her veil, and . . . oh, good fortune! Gil Gil saw that it was his adored Elena, the sweet cause of his bitter sorrows. He let out a cry of frantic joy and advanced toward his lovely companion of old.

Elena recognized him immediately and exclaimed with the same tenderness of two years ago:

"Gil!"

The countess of Rionuevo clasped the arm of the Monteclaro heiress, and turning to Gil Gil, said:

"I've told you: I'm happy with my shoemaker and I don't wear cobblers' secondhand articles. Leave me alone!"

Gil Gil turned as white as a sheet and collapsed on the stone floor of the atrium.

Elena and the countess proceeded into the church.

Two or three students who had witnessed the encounter laughed boisterously, even though they did not really understand.

Gil Gil was carried home.

There another blow awaited him.

The old woman who constituted his entire family had died of old age.

He took to bed with acute brain fever and was, as the saying goes, at death's door.

When he recovered he discovered that a neighbor on his street, even poorer than he, had cared for him during his long illness, but in order to pay the doctor and the pharmacy the man had had to sell the furniture, tools, stand, books, and even the fine clothes of our young hero.

At the end of two months, Gil Gil was dressed in rags, hungry, debilitated by the illness, and penniless; he had no family, no friends, no old woman whom he had come to love as a mother, and, worst of all, no hope of ever again approaching the friend of his early youth, the dreamed-of and blessed Elena, and so he abandoned the stand (refuge of his ancestors and already the property of another shoemaker) and headed along the first street he came across, without knowing where he was going, what to do, to whom to turn, how to work, or for what reason to live.

It was one of those rainy, dismal afternoons when it seems that even clocks are tolling, when the sky is covered with clouds and the earth with mud, when the air, damp and biting, stifles sighs in the human heart, when all the poor are hungry, all orphans cold, and all the unfortunate envious of those who have already died.

Night fell, and Gil Gil, who was running a temperature, curled up in a doorway, burst into tears, and cried disconsolately.

The idea of death then presented itself to his imagination, not as the darkness of fear and convulsion of agony, but pleasant, beautiful, and bright, as Espronceda* describes it.

The poor devil crossed his arms over his heart as if to retain this sweet image which brought him so much rest, so much peace, and so much bliss, but on making this movement his hands felt something hard in his pocket.

The reaction was swift. The idea of life, or its preservation, which coursed distressfully through Gil Gil's mind, fleeing from the other idea that we have mentioned, latched with all its strength onto that fortuitous circumstance which materialized at the very edge of the grave.

Hope murmured a thousand seductive promises in his ear, which led him to speculate whether that hard something which he had touched might be money or an enormous precious stone or a talisman, something, in short, that might contain life, fortune, happiness, and glory (which for him came down to Elena de Monteclaro's love), and, saying to death, "Wait," he put his hand in his pocket.

But, oh, the hard something was the phial of sulphuric acid, or to put it more clearly, oil of vitriol, that he used to make blacking, the last of his shoemaker's materials, and which by some inexplicable coincidence turned up in his pocket.

Consequently, there where the poor devil thought he had seen a sheet anchor, his hands came across a poison, and one of the most lethal.

"So let's die!" Gil Gil then said to himself.

And he raised the phial to his lips.

. . . .

And a stone-cold hand settled on his shoulder, and a sweet, tender, divine voice murmured these words above his head:

"HELLO, FRIEND!"

III
How Gil Gil Learned Medicine in One Hour

No words could have astounded Gil Gil as much as the ones he had just heard:

"Hello, friend!"

He had no friends.

But he was surprised much more by the horrible sensation of cold that the hand of that shadow produced in him, and even the tone of its voice, which penetrated, like an arctic wind, to the marrow of his bones.

We have said that it was a very dark night.

The poor orphan could not, as a result, distinguish the features of the newcomer, but he could make out its black, full-length attire, which did not clearly belong to either sex.

Filled with doubts, mysterious fears, and even an intense curiosity, Gil rose from the doorway where he was still curled up and murmured in a faint voice broken by the chattering of his teeth:

"What do you want of me?"

"That's my question for you!" replied the stranger, locking arms with Gil Gil with affectionate familiarity.

"Who are you?" inquired the poor shoemaker, who felt his life ebbing from the cold contact of the stranger's arm.

"I'm the person you're looking for."

"Who . . . ? That I'm . . . ? I'm not looking for anyone!" Gil responded, trying to break loose.

"Well, why have you summoned me?" asked that *person*, clutching Gil's arm more tightly.

"Oh! Let me go."

"Calm down, Gil, I don't intend to harm you in the least," the mysterious stranger added. "Come! You're shivering with cold and hunger. I see an inn over there, where, it turns out, I have things to do tonight. So let's go in and you can have something to drink."

"Fine . . . but, who are you?" asked once again Gil Gil, whose curiosity was beginning to get the better of him.

"I've already told you: *we're friends*. And be advised that you are the only person on earth to whom I give this name. I am bound to you by remorse. I've been the cause of all your misfortunes."

"I don't know you," the shoemaker said.

"Nevertheless, I've been to your home many times. Because of me you became a motherless child at birth; I was the cause of the stroke that killed Juan Gil; I had you thrown out of the Rionuevo mansion; I did away one Sunday with the old woman who took you in; I, in short, put that phial of sulphuric acid in your pocket."

Gil Gil shook like a leaf; he felt his hair stand on end; and he thought that his taut muscles were snapping.

"You're the devil!" he exclaimed with unspeakable fear.

"Boy!" rejoined the stranger dressed in mourning in a tone of friendly reproach. "What gives you that idea? I am something more and better than the forlorn creature whom you name."

"Who are you, then?"

"Let's go inside the inn and you'll find out."

Gil entered hurriedly, positioned the stranger in front of the modest lamp that lighted the room, scrutinized him from head to toe . . . and saw a person about thirty-three years old, tall, handsome, pale, dressed in a full tunic and black cape, whose long hair was held in by a Phrygian cap, also black.

And although he had not a trace of a beard there was nothing womanish about him. Nor did he resemble a man, despite the virile and energetic facial features.

What he really appeared to be was a human being without sex, a body without a soul, or rather a soul without a definite mortal body. You might say that he was a negation of personality.

No brightness at all shone in his eyes. They brought to mind the blackness of midnight. Indeed, they were shadowy eyes, grief-stricken eyes, dead eyes. But so gentle, so inoffensive, so profound in their muteness that you could not look away from them. They attracted like the sea; they fascinated like a bottomless abyss; they consoled like oblivion.

So it was that Gil Gil, shortly after fixing his own eyes on those inanimate ones, felt a black veil enveloping him, the world returning to chaos, and the Earth's noise like a storm carried by the air.

Then that mysterious creature spoke these awesome words:

"I am *Death*, my friend. I am Death, and it is God who sends me; God, who has a glorious place reserved for you in heaven. Five times have I caused you misfortune, and I, the implacable deity, have taken pity on you. Tonight when God ordered me to bring your impious soul before His tribunal, I pleaded with Him to commit your existence to my care and allow me to be at your side for a time, undertaking to deliver you to Him in the end with your spirit cleansed of sin and worthy of His glory. Heaven did not turn a deaf ear to my request. You are, as a result, the first mortal I've approached whose body did not change into cold ashes. You are my only friend. Listen now and learn the way to your happiness and eternal salvation."

At this point Gil Gil uttered a barely intelligible word to Death.

"I understand," the latter responded. "You speak to me of Elena de Monteclaro."

"Yes!" exclaimed the youth.

"I swear to you that no other arms will embrace her but yours or mine. And besides, I say again: I shall make you happy in this world and in the next. And to do so what follows will be enough. But, my friend, I am not Omnipotence; my power is very limited, very slight. I do not have the ability to create. My knowledge amounts to destruction. Nevertheless, it is in my hands to give you a strength, a power, a wealth greater than that of princes and emperors. I am going to make you a doctor, but a doctor who is a friend of mine, a doctor who will know me, see me, and talk to me. You guess the rest."

Gil Gil was astounded.

"Can it be true?" he exclaimed, as if struggling with a nightmare.

"All of it is true, and something more that I shall explain as time goes on. For now I will only say that you are not the son of Juan Gil. I hear the confessions of all dying people, and I know that you are the natural son of the count of Rionuevo—your deceased protector— and Crispina López, who conceived you two months before marrying the unfortunate Juan Gil."

"Oh, say no more!" the poor boy exclaimed, covering his face with his hands.

Then, suddenly struck by an idea, he asked with indescribable horror:

"So one day you'll kill Elena?"

"Calm down," the deity replied. "Elena will never die for you. Answer me therefore: do you or do you not wish to be my friend?"

Gil answered with a question of his own:

"Will you, in exchange, give me Elena?"

"I've told you I will."

"Then here is my hand!" Gil Gil added, extending it to Death.

But another idea more horrible than the previous one occurred to him at that moment.

"With these hands that grasp mine," he said, "you killed my poor mother!"

"Yes. Your mother died," Death said. "Understand, however, that I did not cause her any pain at all. I do not make anybody suffer! The one who torments you until you breathe your last is my rival, Life, that life which you all love so much."

By way of an answer Gil threw himself into Death's arms.

"Let's go, then," said the creature in mourning.

"Where to?"

"The palace at La Granja,* to take up your duties as a doctor."

"But whom are we going to see?"

"The former King Philip V."*

"Why? Is Philip V going to die?"

"Not yet. He will reign again, and you are going to provide him with his crown."

Gil's head drooped, overwhelmed by the weight of so many new ideas. Death took him by the arm and led him out of the inn.

They had yet to reach the door when at their backs they heard screams and laments.

The innkeeper had just died.

IV
A Digression That Is Beside the Point

From the moment that Gil Gil left the inn he began to observe such a transformation in himself and in his whole nature that, were he not gripped by an arm as strong as Death's, he undoubtedly would have fallen to the ground, overcome.

And it was because our hero was feeling what no other man has felt: the double movement of the Earth around the sun and round its own axis.

On the other hand, he did not detect that of his own heart.

Furthermore, anyone studying the former shoemaker's face by the magnificent light of the moon would have noticed that the melancholy beauty that always made it admirable had grown in an extraordinary manner. His eyes, a velvety black, already reflected the mysterious peace that reigned in those of the personification of Death. His long, silky locks, as dark as a raven's wings, framed a face as pale as the alabaster of tombs, radiant and opaque at the same time, as if a funeral light burned inside that alabaster and glowed faintly through its pores. His expression, his attitude, his look, his entire being had changed and taken on a certain stately and timeless air totally alien to any notion of human nature, and which undoubtedly would make Gil, wherever he went, superior to the most insensitive women, the most arrogant rulers, and the most valiant warriors.

The two friends continued to walk toward the sierra, sometimes following the road and sometimes veering off it.

Whenever they passed through a town or village, the slow, plaintive tolling of a bell would remind our young hero that Death was not wasting his time, that his long arm reached everywhere, and that not because Gil felt it heavy on his heart like a mountain of ice did it cease to cover the vast face of the Earth with mourning and devastation.

All the while Death was telling his protégé great and strange things.

An enemy of history, he took pleasure in speaking disparagingly of its supposed usefulness, and to support his view he presented the facts as they occurred and not as documents and accounts record them.

The enigmas of the past were unraveled before Gil Gil's engrossed imagination, and the disclosures brought him highly important revelations about the fate of empires and all of humanity. He came to fathom the great mystery of life and the no less great and frightening end toward which all we misnamed mortals march, and he understood, in the light of such lofty philosophy, the laws that govern the development of cosmic matter and its manifold manifestation in those passing and short-lived forms which we call minerals, plants, animals, stars, constellations, nebulae, and worlds.

Physiology, geology, chemistry, and botany were all explained to the former shoemaker, and he learned the mysterious bases of life, movement, reproduction, passion, feeling, thought, conscience, reflection, memory, will, and desire.

God, only God, remained hidden in the depths of those seas of enlightenment.

God, only God, was alien to life and death, removed from universal human concerns, one and higher in essence, unique as substance, independent and free and almighty as a force. Death was unable to envelop the Creator in its infinite shadow. God was God. His eternity, His immutability, and His impenetrability dazzled Gil Gil, who bowed his head and adored and believed, plunged into even greater ignorance than before descending to the abysses of death.

V

CERTAINTY IN EXCHANGE FOR UNCERTAINTY

It was ten o'clock in the morning, 30 August 1724, when Gil Gil, painstakingly instructed by that negative power, entered the palace of San Ildefonso and requested an audience with Philip V.

It would be well to remind the reader of this monarch's status at the time and day just mentioned.

The first Bourbon of Spain, grandson of Louis XIV of France, he had accepted the Spanish crown when he could no longer dream of succeeding to the French crown. But other princes were dying, uncles and cousins of his who kept him from the throne of his native land, so in order to occupy it, were his nephew Louis XV also to die (and said nephew was not at all well and only fourteen years old), Philip V abdicated the throne of Castile in favor of his son Louis I* and retired to San Ildefonso.

At this juncture, not only did the health of Louis XV improve somewhat, but Louis I fell gravely ill from such a severe attack of smallpox that they feared for his life. Ten couriers, stationed at intervals between La Granja and Madrid, carried hourly dispatches to Philip with news of his son's condition, and the ambitious father, further incited by his celebrated second wife, Isabel Farnesio (much more ambitious than he), did not know what to decide in such an unforeseen and grave conflict.

Was the throne of Spain going to fall vacant before that of France? Should he declare his intention to reign again in Madrid and prepare himself to take up the legacy of his son?

But what if the latter did not die? Would it not be a celebrated blunder to have divulged to all of Europe the dark depths of his soul? Would it not discredit the sacrifice of having lived seven months in solitude? And would it not be to renounce forever the sweet hope of occupying the coveted French throne of Saint Louis? What, then, was to be done? To wait was tantamount to wasting precious time. The Government Council despised him and challenged all his influence in affairs of state. Making just one move could compromise his lifetime ambition as well as his name in posterity.

False Charles V: the temptations of the world were harrying him in the desert, and in those hours of doubt the hypocrisy of his abdication cost him dear!*

Such were the circumstances in which our friend Gil Gil announced himself to the pensive Philip, saying that he was the bearer of extremely important information.

"What do you want of me?" the king, without rising or looking at him, asked when he sensed Gil's presence in the royal chamber.

"Sire, Your Majesty, look at me," replied a self-assured Gil Gil. "Do not be afraid of my reading your thoughts, for they are no mystery to me."

Philip V abruptly turned toward that man whose voice, dry and cold like the truth it revealed, had frozen the blood in his heart.

But his anger came up against the funereal smile of Death's Friend.

As a result, a superstitious terror gripped him when he fixed his eyes on those of Gil Gil, and, raising a trembling hand to the small bell on the escritoire, he repeated his first question:

"What do you want of me?"

"Sire, I am a doctor," the young man calmly answered, "and I have such faith in my science that I dare tell Your Majesty the day, the hour, and the very moment when Louis I is to die."

Philip V looked more closely at the tattered visitor whose face was as beautiful as it was supernatural.

"Speak," was all that the king said.

"Not just like that, Your Majesty!" exclaimed Gil Gil with a certain amount of sarcasm. "First we must agree on the price."

The Frenchman shook his head on hearing these words, as if he were awakening from a dream; he saw their exchange in another light and was almost ashamed of having tolerated it.

"Captain!" he called out, ringing the bell. "Arrest this man!"

A captain appeared and put his hand on Gil Gil's shoulder.

The latter remained impassive.

The king, his superstition again taking hold of him, looked at the strange doctor out of the corner of his eye. He then rose with great effort, for the languor from which he had been suffering for a number of years had recently become aggravated, and said to the captain of the guard:

"Leave us alone."

Finally, standing in front of Gil Gil, as if attempting to lose his fear of him, the king asked with feigned calm:

"Who the devil are you, owl face?"

"I am Death's Friend," our young hero replied without batting an eye.

"Why, of course you are," said the king, poking fun in order to mask his childish fear. "And what were you saying about our son?"

"I was saying, Sire," continued Gil Gil, taking a step toward the king, who moved back involuntarily, "that I have come to bring you a crown. I will not say if it is that of Spain or of France, because for this secret you must pay me. And I say that we are losing precious time, and that consequently I need to speak to you soon and clearly. So listen to me with care: Louis I is dying, but his illness is one that can be cured. Your Majesty is the dog in the fable."*

Philip V interrupted Gil Gil.

"Say it. Say whatever you like. I want to hear it all. In any event, I am going to have you hanged."

Death's Friend shrugged his shoulders and continued:

"I was saying that Your Majesty is the dog in the fable. You wore the crown of Spain on your head; you bent over to pick up that of

France; yours fell upon the cradle of your son; Louis XV took his; and you ended up with neither the one nor the other."*

"That is true!" exclaimed Philip V, with his expression if not with his voice.

"Today," continued Gil Gil, noticing the king's expression, "today when you are closer to the crown of France than to that of Spain, you are going to expose yourself to the same fate. Louis XV and Louis I, the two boy kings, are ill. You can succeed both, but you need to know several hours in advance which of the two is going to die first. Louis I is in greater danger, but the crown of France is more attractive. Hence your dilemma. It's quite obvious that you are wary. You do not dare reach for the scepter of Saint Ferdinand, Spain's crown, for fear that your son will recuperate, that history will ridicule you, and that your French partisans will abandon you. More clearly: you dare not let go of the prey in your clutches for fear that the other one you see will be a simple illusion or wishful thinking."

"Speak . . . speak!" Philip said anxiously, believing that Gil had finished. "Speak, because in any case from here you are going to a dungeon where only the walls will hear you. Speak. I want to know what the world is saying about my thoughts."

The former shoemaker smiled disdainfully.

"Prison! Gallows!" he exclaimed. "That is all you kings know. But I am not frightened. Listen to me a little longer, for I am going to finish. I, Sire, need to be named a court doctor, granted the title of duke, and given, today, the sum of thirty thousand *pesos.* Your Majesty laughs? Well, I need what I ask for just as much as Your Majesty needs to know if Louis I will die from smallpox."

"And do you know?" the king asked in a low voice, unable to overcome the terror that that youth caused him.

"I will know tonight."

"How?"

"I have already told you that I am Death's Friend."

"And what is that? Explain it to me."

"It's . . . something that I myself don't understand. Take me to the palace in Madrid. Arrange for me to see the reigning king, and I shall tell you the sentence that the Eternal has written on his forehead."

"And what if you are wrong?" asked the descendant of Anjou, drawing close to Gil Gil.

"You can hang me . . . to which end you will keep me under arrest for however long you wish."

"So you are a sorcerer!" exclaimed Philip to justify in some way the credence that he gave to Gil Gil's words.

"Sire, there is no sorcery these days," he responded. "The last sorcerer was named Louis XIV, and the last bewitched was Charles II. The crown of Spain, which we sent to you in Paris twenty-five years ago wrapped in the will of an idiot, ransomed us from the captivity of the devil, in which we had been living since the abdication of Charles V. Nobody knows that better than you."

"A court doctor . . . a duke . . . and thirty thousand *pesos* . . ." murmured the king.

"For a crown that is worth more than you imagine," Gil Gil retorted.

"You have my royal word," Philip added solemnly, overpowered by that voice, by that face, by that mystery-filled demeanor.

"Does Your Majesty swear it?"

"I promise," replied the Frenchman. "I promise if first you prove to me that you are something more than a man."

"Elena, you'll be mine," Gil mumbled.

The king summoned the captain and gave him several orders.

"Now," Philip V said, "while your journey to Madrid is being arranged, tell me your story and explain your knowledge."

"I shall indulge you, Sire, but I fear that you will understand neither the one nor the other."

. . . .

An hour later the captain was riding post to Madrid alongside our hero, who, for the time being, had discarded his rags and was dressed in a magnificent black velvet outfit accented by colorful lace; he also wore a dress saber and a hat trimmed with braid.

Philip V had given him the clothes and a good deal of money after learning of his extraordinary friendship with Death.

Let us follow the good Gil Gil no matter how fast he rides, for he just might happen upon his beloved Elena de Monteclaro or the odious countess of Rionuevo in the queen's apartment, and we surely do not want to be ignorant of the details of such interesting encounters.

VI
PRELIMINARY CONFERENCE

It was about six o'clock in the afternoon when Gil Gil and the captain dismounted at the doors of the palace.

An immense crowd had gathered in the area, aware that the young king's life was in danger.

When our friend stepped inside the royal palace, he unexpectedly ran into Death, who was leaving in a hurry.

"Already?" Gil asked, panic-stricken.

"Not yet," the sinister deity replied.

The doctor breathed a sigh of relief.

"Well, when?" he asked after a short pause.

"I can't tell you."

"Oh, do! If you knew what I've been promised by Philip V!"

"I can imagine."

"Well, then. I need to know when Louis I is going to die."

"You'll know in due course. Come in. The captain has already entered Louis's chamber. He brings instructions from the king father. At this moment you are being announced as the foremost doctor in the world. People are crowding the stairway to watch your arrival. You are going to meet Elena and the countess of Rionuevo."

"Oh, what happiness!" exclaimed Gil Gil.

"Six-fifteen . . . " Death went on, taking his pulse, which was his sole and infallible timepiece. "They're waiting for you. So long."

"But tell me—"

"That's right. I forgot. Listen: if I'm in the king's chamber when you see Louis, he has an incurable disease."

"And will you be there? Or are you going elsewhere?"

"I don't know yet if I'll be in attendance. I'm ubiquitous, and if I receive *higher* orders, you'll see me there, as you would wherever I might be."

"What were you doing here now?"

"I just killed a horse."

Gil Gil shrank back, taken by surprise.

"What?" he asked. "You also have to concern yourself with irrational beings?"

"Irrational? What do you mean? Do you humans by chance possess true reason? There is but one *reason*, and it cannot be seen from Earth."

"Then tell me," Gil continued, "animals, brutes, creatures that we call irrational here—do they have a soul?"

"Yes and no. They have a spirit with neither freedom nor responsibility. But go to the devil! You're full of questions today. Good-bye for now. I'm off to a certain noble house . . . where I'm going to do you another favor."

"Do *me* a favor? Please explain yourself. What's this about?"

"Thwarting a certain wedding."

"Oh!" exclaimed Gil Gil, a horrible suspicion coming over him. "Can it possibly be—?"

"I can't tell you any more," Death replied. "Go inside. It's getting late."

"You're driving me mad!"

"Put yourself in my hands and you'll be better off. You have my word that you'll enjoy total happiness."

"Ah! So we *are* friends? You don't intend to kill me or Elena?"

"Don't worry," replied Death with such sadness and solemnity, with such tenderness and joy, with so many and varied inflections in his voice, that Gil immediately gave up any hope of understanding his answer.

"Wait!" Gil finally said, seeing that the creature in mourning was going off. "Tell me the times again because I don't want to make a mistake. If you're in the room of a sick person but don't look at him, it means that the patient will die of that sickness."

"Exactly. But if I'm facing him he'll die that very day. If I am lying in the same bed, he has three hours left. If you find him in my arms, he has but one hour. And if you see me kiss his forehead, say a prayer for his soul."

"And you won't say a single word to me?"

"Not a one. I am not permitted to reveal to you in such a manner the intentions of the Eternal. Your advantage over the rest of men consists only of the fact that I am visible to you. So good-bye, and don't forget me."

With these words he vanished into space.

VII

THE ROYAL CHAMBER

Gil Gil reached the royal domicile neither regretful nor pleased at having entered into relations with the personification of Death.

But no sooner did he begin to climb the palace stairs and remember that he was going to see his beloved Elena than all of his lugubrious thoughts disappeared like nocturnal birds at daybreak.

Accompanied by a brilliant retinue of courtiers and other noble personages, Gil Gil passed through galleries and salons to reach the royal chamber, and all who saw him admired, to be sure, the strange beauty and tender youth of the famous doctor whom Philip V had sent from La Granja as the final recourse of human ability to save the life of Louis I.

The two courts, that of Louis and that of Philip, were in attendance.

They were, in a manner of speaking, rival powers who had been living in constant warfare for a week; they were the old servants of the first Bourbon branch and the new ones whom the regent of France, Philip the "Generous" of Orleans, had gathered around the throne of Spain to keep the ambitious former duke of Anjou from using it as a stepping-stone to the throne of his grandfather; they were, in short, the courtiers of the docile boy who hovered near death, and those of his lovely wife, the indomitable daughter of the regent, the renowned duchess of Montpensier.

The followers of Isabel de Farnesio, stepmother of Louis I, wanted the latter to die in order for the sons of Philip V's second marriage to be closer in line to the throne of Saint Ferdinand.

The partisans of the young queen from Orleans, the daughter, wanted Louis I to recover, not out of love for the mismatched couple, but out of hatred for Philip V, whom they did not want to see reign again.

The friends of the unfortunate Louis trembled at the thought that he might die, because, having induced him to reject the guardianship in which the recluse from La Granja held him, they knew full well that if Philip reclaimed the throne his first act would be to exile them or arrest them.

The palace was, therefore, a maze of conflicting desires, opposing ambitions, intrigues and suspicions, and fears and hopes.

Gil Gil entered the chamber with his eyes seeking only one person: his unforgettable Elena.

Near the king's bed he saw her father, the good friend of the deceased count of Rionuevo, the duke of Monteclaro, talking to the archbishops of Santiago and Toledo, the marquis of Mirabel, and Don Miguel de Guerra, the four bitterest enemies of Philip V.

The duke of Monteclaro did not recognize the former page, childhood companion of his charming daughter.

In another part of the room, not without a certain feeling of fear, Death's Friend saw, among the ladies who surrounded the young and beautiful Luisa Isabel de Orleans, his implacable and eternal enemy: the countess of Rionuevo.

Gil Gil passed by and almost brushed against her dress as he went to kiss the queen's hand.

The countess did not recognize her husband's natural son either.

At this point a tapestry rose behind the group made up of the above-mentioned ladies, and there appeared, with two or three others whom Gil Gil did not know, a tall, pale, exceptionally beautiful woman.

It was Elena de Monteclaro.

Gil Gil stared at her, and the young woman shuddered on seeing that funereal and noble countenance, as if she were contemplating the ghost of a beloved dead person, as if she had before her eyes, not Gil, but his shadow wrapped in a shroud, as if, in short, she were seeing a being from the other world.

Gil at court! Gil consoling the queen—that haughty, mocking princess who disdained everything! Gil in those splendid clothes, respected and esteemed by all the nobility!

Oh! No doubt it's a dream! thought the charming Elena.

"Come, Doctor," said the marquis of Mirabal at this point. "His Majesty has awakened."

Making a painful effort to shake the ecstasy that paralyzed his entire being upon finding himself in the presence of his beloved, Gil approached the bed of the ravaged king.

The second Bourbon of Spain was a youth of seventeen, tall and weak and rachitic, like a plant that grows in the shade.

His face (which had not lacked a certain fineness of expression in spite of the irregularity of his features) was now frightfully swollen and covered with ashen pustules. He looked like a crude sculpture model fashioned from clay.

The boy king directed an anguished look at that other adolescent who was approaching his bed, and when he saw Gil's silent, somber eyes, unfathomable like the mystery of eternity, he wailed softly and hid his face under the sheets.

Gil Gil, meanwhile, was looking all around the room to see if Death was there.

But Death was not there.

"Will he live?" Gil was asked in a low voice by several courtiers who thought they had glimpsed a sign of hope on his face.

He was going to say "Yes," forgetting that he was to express his opinion only to Philip V, when he felt someone tugging at his sleeve.

He turned around and saw next to him a person dressed entirely in black, his back to the king's bed.

It was Death.

He'll die from this disease, but not today, thought Gil Gil.

"What is your impression?" asked the archbishop of Toledo, feeling, like everybody, that insuperable respect generated by our young hero's supernatural countenance.

"Excuse me," the former shoemaker answered. "My opinion is reserved for the person who sent me."

"But you are so young," added the marquis of Mirabal, "that you cannot have learned so much medical science. Undoubtedly God or the devil has ingrained it in you. Maybe you are a saint who works miracles or a wizard friend of witches."

"As you wish," said Gil Gil, "but one way or another, I read into the future of the prince who lies in this bed, and it is a secret you would dearly love to learn, as it resolves whether tomorrow you will be the favorite of Louis I or the prisoner of Philip V."

"What?" sputtered the marquis, pale with anger, but smiling thinly.

At this point Gil Gil noticed that Death, not content to lie in wait for the monarch, took advantage of his presence in the royal chamber to sit next to a lady, almost in the same chair, and stare at her.

The sentenced one was the countess of Rionuevo.

Three hours! thought Gil Gil.

"I need to speak with you," continued meanwhile the marquis of Mirabal, who had taken it into his head to buy, no less, the strange doctor's secret.

But one glance and one smile from Gil, who had read the marquis's thoughts, disconcerted him to such an extent that he moved back a step.

That glance and that smile were the same ones that had held Philip V in his sway in the morning.

Gil took advantage of Mirabal's momentary bewilderment to make a big advance in his career and establish his reputation at court.

"Your Excellency," he said to the archbishop of Toledo, "the countess of Rionuevo, whom you see peaceful and alone in that corner (we already know that Death was visible only to Gil Gil), will die within three hours. Advise her to prepare to meet her Maker."

The archbishop shrank back in alarm.

"What is it?" asked Don Miguel de Guerra.

The prelate related Gil Gil's prophecy to several people, and all eyes fixed on the countess, who, in fact, was beginning to turn horribly pale.

Gil Gil, meanwhile, was approaching Elena.

Elena was standing on the marble floor in the middle of the room, still and silent like a noble piece of sculpture.

From there the beautiful young woman—frenzied, fascinated, possessed of a terror and happiness impossible to define—followed every movement made by her childhood friend.

"Elena," the youth murmured as he passed by her.

"Gil," she responded automatically. "Is it you?"

"Yes, it's me!" he said adoringly. "Have no fear."

And he left the room.

The captain was waiting for him in the antechamber.

Gil Gil wrote several words on a piece of paper and said to Philip V's faithful servant:

"Here. Do not lose a moment. Take this to La Granja."

"But . . . and you?" asked the captain. "I can't leave you. You're in my custody."

"And I will continue to be, on my word," Gil said with dignity, "because I cannot accompany you."

"But . . . the king—"

"The king will approve of your conduct."

"Impossible."

"Listen, and you'll see that I'm doing the right thing."

At that moment a noisy disturbance was heard in the royal chamber.

"The doctor! The doctor!" several people came out shouting.

"What's going on?" asked Gil Gil.

"The countess of Rionuevo is dying," said Don Miguel de Guerra. "Come! This way. They have taken her to the queen's apartment."

"Go, Captain," Gil Gil said softly. "I'm telling you to go."

And he accompanied his words with such an expression and such a gesture that the soldier left without further protest.

Gil followed Guerra and entered the apartment of Louis I's wife.

VIII

REVELATIONS

"Listen!" a voice said to Gil Gil as he was walking toward the bed on which the countess of Rionuevo lay.

"Oh! It's you!" our young hero exclaimed, recognizing Death. "Has she passed away already?"

"Who?"

"The countess."

"No."

"Then, why are you leaving her?"

"I haven't left her, my friend. As I've already told you, I am to be found in all places at all times in different forms."

"Fine. So what do you want from me?" asked Gil with a certain displeasure on hearing this statement.

"I've come to do you another favor."

"You don't say! What is it?"

"Do you know that you're growing disrespectful toward me?" Death asked with considerable sarcasm.

"It's natural," replied Gil. "The familiarity, the complicity—"

"Complicity? What are you suggesting?"

"Nothing. I'm alluding to a painting I saw when I was a child. It depicted Medicine. In a bed lay two people, or rather, one man and his illness. The doctor had entered the room blindfolded and armed with a club, and when he reached the bed he began to swing out wildly and strike the patient and his illness. I don't remember exactly which one received the first blows. I believe it was the patient."

"An amusing allegory. But let's get down to business."

"Yes, let's, because everybody is surprised to see me like this, all alone, standing in the middle of the room."

"Leave them be. They'll think you're meditating or awaiting inspiration. Listen to me for a moment. You know that the past belongs to me by right, and that I can reveal it to you. The same is not true of the future."

"Get on with it!"

"Be a little patient. You're going to speak to the countess of Rionuevo for the last time, and it's my duty to tell you a certain story.

"It's pointless. I forgive the woman."

"It concerns Elena, you idiot!" exclaimed Death.

"What?"

"I say it concerns your being noble and being able to marry her."

"I'm already a nobleman. King Philip V has made me a duke."

"Monteclaro will not be content with an upstart. You need ancestors."

"So?"

"I've already told you that you are the last Rionuevo offspring."

"Yes. But adulterous."

"You're wrong. Natural, and very natural!"

"All right, but who can prove it?"

"That's exactly what I'm going to tell you."

"Please do."

"Listen, and don't interrupt me. The countess is the awful sphinx in your life."

"I know."

"She holds all your happiness in her hands."

"I know that, too."

"Well, the time has come to snatch it away from her."

"How?"

"You'll see. Since your father loved you so much—"

"Ah! He loved me very much?" asked Gil Gil.

"I told you not to interrupt me. Since your father loved you so much, he did not depart this world without thinking very seriously about your future."

"Are you certain? Didn't the count die intestate?"

"What gave you that idea?"

"Everybody thinks so."

"Out-and-out fabrication on the countess's part in order to seize all the count's money and name a certain nephew as her heir."

"Oh!"

"Take it easy. Everything can be worked out. Your father possessed a declaration by Crispina López and another by Juan Gil, besides a medical verification in due form that confirmed conclusively that you are the natural son of the count of Rionuevo and Crispina, and were conceived when both were single. This is what your father confessed on his deathbed to a priest and notary whom I saw there and know very well. Moreover, the priest . . . But that I can't tell you. In short, the fact is that the count named you his sole and universal heir, which he was able to do very easily as he had no relatives, close or distant. Nor did this bequest end the solicitude with which that loving father laid the groundwork of your happy future from the very edge of the grave."

"Oh, my father!" Gil Gil uttered softly.

"Listen. You know of the great friendship which for so many years joined the honorable count and the duke of Monteclaro, his comrade in arms during the War of Succession."

"Yes, I know."

"Well, then," Death continued, "your father, seeing the love that you professed for the lovely Elena, wrote a long and heartfelt letter to the duke shortly before he died, and in it he related everything, and asked the hand of his daughter for you, his son, reminding him of numerous and signal tokens of friendship that they had always shown each other."

"And that letter?" asked Gil with unwonted vehemence.

"That letter alone would have convinced the duke, and you would have been his son-in-law . . . many years ago."

"What's become of that letter?" the youth asked again, shaking with love and bursting with rage.

"That letter would have kept you from making a pact with me," Death continued.

"Oh! Don't be cruel! Tell me that the letter exists!"

"That's the truth."

"So it does exist?"

"Yes."

"Who has it?"

"The same person who intercepted it."

"The countess?"

"The countess."

"Oh!" exclaimed the youth, taking a step toward the deathbed.

"Wait," said Death. "I haven't finished yet. The countess also has in her possession the count's will, which she almost snatched from my hands."

"From you?"

"I say from me because the count was already half dead. As for the priest and the notary, I'll tell you where they live, and I believe they will attest to the truth."

Gil Gil reflected a moment.

Then, staring at the funereal creature, he said:

"In other words, if I manage to get hold of those documents—"

"Tomorrow you can marry Elena."

"Oh, God!" the youth uttered, taking another step toward the bed.

There he turned around again to face Death.

The courtiers were oblivious of Gil Gil's agitation. They thought he was alone, or struggling with the miraculous vision to which he owed his bizarre knowledge, but such was the terror that he awakened in them that nobody dared to interrupt him.

"Tell me," the former shoemaker asked his dreadful company, "why hasn't the countess burned those papers?"

"Because the countess, like all criminals, is superstitious; because she feared that one day she might repent; because she suspected that those papers might, in such a situation, be her passport to eternity; because, in short, it has been shown time and again that no sinner erases the tracks of his crimes for fear of forgetting them at the moment of his death and being unable to retrace his steps until finding the path of virtue. I repeat: those papers exist."

"So if I get hold of them, Elena will be mine," Gil insisted, always doubting that Death could bring him happiness.

"There would still be one more obstacle to overcome," Death said.

"What obstacle?"

"Elena has been promised by her father to a nephew of the countess, the viscount of Daimiel."

"What? And she loves him?"

"No, but it's all the same, as they were betrothed two months ago."

"Oh! So everything is futile!" exclaimed Gil in despair.

"It would have been without me," Death said. "But I already told you at the entrance to this palace that I was trying to thwart a wedding."

"How? Have you killed the viscount?"

"I? Kill?" asked Death with a certain sarcastic terror. "Heaven forbid! I haven't killed. He's died."

"Oh!"

"Sh! Nobody knows it yet. His family believes right now that the poor youth is taking a nap. So . . . watch your behavior! Elena, the countess, and the duke are just steps away from you. Now or never!"

And so saying, Death approached the sick woman's bed.

Gil Gil followed him.

Many of the people present in the room, among them the duke of Monteclaro, already knew Gil's prediction that the countess of Rionuevo would die within three hours; therefore, on seeing it almost come true, because the lady who a short time before had been healthy and jovial had suddenly turned into an inert mass jolted at intervals by violent convulsions, all of them began to look upon our friend with superstitious terror and fanatical veneration.

For her part, no sooner did the countess make out Gil than she extended to him a trembling, imploring hand, while with the other she signaled that they be left alone.

Everybody moved away from the bed, and Gil sat down next to the dying woman.

IX
THE SOUL

Even though the countess of Rionuevo, Gil Gil's terrible enemy, plays such an odious role in our story, she was not, as many may have imagined, an ugly or old woman, or ugly and old simultaneously. Physical nature is also misleading on occasion.

At the time, the illustrious woman on her deathbed was about thirty-five years old and at the height of a magnificent beauty. She was tall and robust and had a good figure. Her eyes, blue like the sea and treacherous like the sea, concealed vast chasms under her soft, languid appearance. The freshness of her mouth and the delicacy of her features revealed that neither grief nor passion had ever disturbed that enduring beauty. So to see her now weak and stricken, overwhelmed by terror and overcome with suffering, the least compassionate person would have experienced a singular kind of sympathy, much like fright or dread.

Gil Gil, who hated that woman intensely, could not help feeling this complex sensation of pity and astonishment, and, spontaneously taking the beautiful hand extended by the sick countess, asked with more sadness than bitterness:

"Do you know me?"

The dying woman ignored Gil Gil's question and exclaimed:

"Save me!"

At this point another personage slipped from behind the curtains and positioned himself between the two speakers, leaning his elbow on the pillow and his head on his hand.

It was Death.

"Save me!" repeated the countess, to whom intuition born of fear had revealed that our hero detested her. "You are a sorcerer. They say you talk to Death. Save me!"

"You are very afraid of dying, madam," responded the youth indifferently, letting go of the sick woman's hand.

That stupid cowardice, that animal terror which shut out all other ideas, all other feelings, upset Gil Gil profoundly and showed the extent of the selfish spirit of the originator of all his misfortunes.

"Countess!" he then exclaimed. "Think about your past and about your future! Think about God and about your fellow man. Save your soul, now that your body is no longer yours."

"Oh, I'm going to die!" exclaimed the countess.

"No, Countess, you are not going to die."

"I'm not going to die!" the poor woman screamed with savage joy.

The youth continued in the same serious vein:

"You are not going to die, because you have never lived. On the contrary, you are going to be born into the life of the soul, which for you will be eternal torment, as for the just it is eternal bliss."

"Oh, so I'm not going to die!" said the sick woman once again, shedding tears for the first time in her life.

"No, Countess, you are not going to die," said the doctor a second time with indescribable majesty.

"Oh, have pity on me!" the poor woman exclaimed, regaining hope.

"You are not going to die," the youth continued, "inasmuch as you are showing remorse. The soul never dies, and repentance can open for you the doors to eternal life."

"Oh, my God!" exclaimed the countess, overcome by that cruel uncertainty.

"You do well to call upon God. Save your soul. I repeat, save your soul. Your beautiful body, your worldly idol, and your sacrilegious existence have ended forever. This temporal life, these earthly joys, this health, this beauty, this luxury and fortune that you tried so hard to preserve; the possessions that you usurped; the air, the sun; the world that you have known until now—you are going to lose them all. They have disappeared already, and tomorrow everything for you will be dust and darkness, unreality and decay, solitude and oblivion. You have only your soul, Countess. Think of your soul."

"Who are you?" the dying woman asked in an imperceptible voice while staring at him in amazement. "We've met before. You detest me. You are the one who's killing me. Ah!"

At that moment Death placed his pale hand on the sick woman's head and said:

"Finish up, Gil, finish up; her last hour is approaching."

"I don't want her to die!" exclaimed Gil. "She can still mend her ways, she can still atone for all the evil she has done! Save her body and I will answer for her soul!"

"Finish up, Gil, finish up," Death repeated, "her last hour is going to strike."

"You poor woman!" the youth commiserated softly with the countess.

"You pity me," said the dying countess with inexpressible tenderness. "I've never been grateful, I've never loved, I've never felt what I feel for you. Pity me. Tell me you do. My heart is moved at the sound of your sorrowful voice."

And it was true.

The countess, carried away by terror in her final moments, afflicted by remorse, fearful of punishment, and stripped of everything that had constituted her pride and joy on earth, was beginning to feel the first stirrings of a soul, which until then had remained hidden and silent, deep in the recesses of her consciousness. It was a soul continuously scorned, but rich in patience and heroism, a soul, in short, comparable to the miserable daughter of criminal or dissolute parents who watches, says nothing, keeps out of their sight, and sheds tears in private until one day, when she notices the first sign of repentance in them, she recovers her courage, runs into their arms, and lets them hear her pure, divine voice, which is the song of a lark, music from heaven, and which appears to greet the dawn of virtue after the darkness of sin.

"You ask me who I am," said Gil, understanding all of this. "I myself don't know now. I was your mortal enemy, but I no longer hate you. You've heard the voice of truth, the voice of death, and your heart has responded. God be praised! I came to this bed of misery to ask you for the happiness of my life, and now I would leave without it, and willingly, because I believe I have brought about your happiness, because I have saved your soul. Oh, Divine Lord, I have forgiven offenses and pardoned my enemy! I'm satisfied. I'm happy. I ask no more."

"Who are you, mysterious and sublime boy? Who are you, so good and so beautiful, that you come like an angel to the head of my deathbed and make my final moments so sweet?" asked the countess, anxiously taking Gil Gil's hands.

"I am Death's Friend," answered the youth. "Do not be surprised, therefore, that I calm your spirit. I speak to you in the name of Death, and for that reason you have believed me. I have come to you as the delegate of that merciful divinity who is the peace of Earth, who is the truth of worlds, who is the redeemer of the spirit, who is the messenger of God, who is everything, except forgetfulness. Forgetfulness is in life, Countess, not in death. Think and you will remember who I am."

"Gil Gil!" exclaimed the countess, fainting.

"Has she died?" the doctor asked Death.

"No. She has a half hour yet."

"But, will she be able to speak?"

"Gil!" the dying woman sighed.

"Finish up," Death added.

The youth bent over the countess, whose face shone with another beauty, an immortal, divine beauty; and from those eyes, where the fire of life was flickering and growing weak; from that half-opened, feverish mouth that gasped for breath; from those soft, burning hands; from that white neck that stretched toward him with infinite anguish— from all this Gil Gil received such an eloquent expression of repentance and tenderness, such an intimate caress and frantic entreaty, such an infinite and solemn promise that, without a moment's hesitation, he withdrew from the bed, summoned the duke of Monteclaro, the archbishop, and three of the many other nobles who were in the bedroom, and said to them:

"Listen to the public confession of a soul that is returning to God."

The interested parties approached the dying woman, drawn more by Gil Gil's inspired face than his words.

"Duke," murmured the countess on seeing Monteclaro, "my confessor has a key. Your Excellency," she continued, turning to the archbishop, "ask him for it. This boy, this doctor, this angel, is the *natural, recognized* son of the count of Rionuevo, my deceased husband, who, shortly before his death, wrote you a letter, Duke, asking Elena's hand for him. With that key. . . in my bedroom . . . all the papers . . . I beg of you! I command you!"

Thus she spoke, and her head fell on the pillow, no light in her eyes, no breath on her lips, no color in her face.

"She's dying," said Gil Gil. "Stay with her, Your Excellency," he added, speaking to the archbishop. "And you, my lord duke, listen to me."

"Wait," Death whispered in our young hero's ear.

"What else?" asked Gil.

"You haven't forgiven her."

"Gil Gil! Your forgiveness!" stammered the dying woman.

"Gil Gil!" exclaimed the duke of Monteclaro. "Is it you?"

"Countess, may God forgive you as I have. Die in peace," said the son of Crispina López with religious ardor.

At this point Death bent over the countess and touched his lips to her forehead.

The kiss echoed in the chest of a corpse.

One cold, cloudy tear ran down the dead woman's face.

Gil wiped his away and answered Monteclaro:

"Yes, my lord duke, it is I."

The archbishop was saying the prayers for the dead.

Meanwhile, Death had disappeared.

It was midnight.

X
UNTIL TOMORROW

"Look for those papers, my lord duke," said Gil Gil, "and do me the favor of speaking to Elena."

"Come, Doctor, come! The king is dying!" exclaimed Don Miguel de Guerra, interrupting Death's Friend.

"Follow me, my lord duke," said the youth most respectfully. "It

has struck twelve, and I can inform you of some very important news—
I don't know if good or bad. It's this: I can tell you if Louis I will or
will not die on this day that is just beginning."

Which was the case, for the 31st of August, the day that Louis
I was to surrender his spirit to his Maker, had already dawned.

Gil Gil became certain of it when he saw that Death was standing
in the middle of the room, watching the royal patient.

"The king will die today," Gil Gil whispered in Monteclaro's ear.
"This news is my wedding present to Elena. If you know the value
of such a present, keep it a secret and proceed accordingly in your
dealings with Philip V."

"Elena is promised to someone else," the duke said.

"The countess of Rionuevo's nephew died this afternoon," Gil Gil
interrupted him.

"What is happening to us?" asked the disturbed duke. "Who are
you? We met when you were a child and now you frighten me with
your power and knowledge."

"The queen is calling you," a lady said at that moment to the duke
of Monteclaro, who remained lost in thought.

That lady was Elena.

The duke approached the queen, leaving the two lovers alone in
the middle of the room.

Not alone, because Death was three steps away from them.

Elena and Gil Gil stood there looking at each other, as if fearful
that their joint presence might be a dream from which they would
awaken on extending a hand or sighing ever so slightly.

Upon meeting in that very same place one other time, the previous
afternoon, both had experienced, in the middle of their indescribable
joy, a certain secret anguish similar to what would be felt by two friends
who, after being apart for a long, long time, recognized each other in
a prison, at dawn on the day of execution, unknowing accomplices
in a fatal crime, or both of them victims of the same persecution.

It might also be said that the painful joy with which Gil and Elena
recognized each other was similar to the bitter pleasure with which
the corpse of a jealous husband (if corpses feel) would smile inside
the tomb on hearing the door of the cemetery open one night and
realizing that it was the corpse of his wife that was brought for burial.

You're finally here! the poor man would say. *You're finally here!
For four years I've been counting the nights and days alone, wondering
what you were doing in the world, you, so beautiful and so ungrateful
that you stopped dressing in mourning one year after my death. You've*

taken a long time! But you're finally here. If love is no longer possible
between us, on the other hand neither is infidelity, and much less,
forgetfulness. We belong to each other in a negative way. Although
nothing unites us, we are united, because nothing separates us. An
eternity of love or recollection has replaced jealousy, uncertainty, and
the anxieties of life. I forgive you for all of it.

These ideas, although softened somewhat by the gentleness of Gil's
and Elena's characters, by her innocence, by his acute intellect and
the elevated virtue of both, shone in the souls of the two lovers like
funeral torches by whose light they saw a limitless future of peaceful
love that nobody could disturb or destroy, unless everything that was
happening to them was a fleeting dream.

So for a long time they regarded each other with blind adoration.

Elena's blue eyes became absorbed in Gil Gil's dark eyes, as the
firmament projects its brightness on the darkness of our nights, while
Gil Gil's black eyes disappeared in the unfathomable transparency of
the pure, untainted azure of Elena's eyes, as sight and thoughts, and
even feelings, grow weary in vain when they measure the infinite vastness
of space.

They would have stayed that way for nobody knows how long—
for all eternity?—if Death had not attracted Gil Gil's attention.

"What do you want of me?" murmured the youth.

"What am I going to want?" replied Death. "For you to stop looking
at her."

"Oh! You love her!" exclaimed Gil with unspeakable anguish.

"Yes," Death said softly.

"You plan to snatch her away from me."

"No. I plan to bring you together."

"You once told me that no arms other than yours or mine would
embrace her," said Gil Gil despairingly. "Whose will she be first? Mine
or yours? Tell me."

"You're jealous of me?"

"Horribly."

"It's unwise of you," said Death.

"Whose will she be first?" repeated the youth, clutching the frozen
hands of his friend.

"I cannot answer. You, God, and I are contending for her, but we
are not incompatible."

"Tell me that you don't intend to kill her. Tell me that you'll bring
us together in this world."

"In this world," Death repeated ironically. "It'll be *in this world.*
I promise you that."

"And afterwards?"

"Afterwards . . . she'll belong to God."

"And yours? When?"

"Mine . . . she's already been mine."

"You're driving me mad. Is Elena alive?"

"The same as you," answered Death.

"But . . . am I alive?"

"More than ever."

"Tell me, for pity's sake!"

"I have nothing to say to you. You still wouldn't be able to understand
me. What is death? Do you by any chance know? What is life? Have
you ever been able to understand it? If you don't know the meaning
of these words, why are you asking me if she's dead or alive?"

"But, will I ever understand them?" asked a desperate Gil Gil.

"Yes, tomorrow," replied Death.

"Tomorrow? I don't understand."

"Tomorrow you will become Elena's husband."

"Ah!"

"And I will be your best man," continued Death.

"You? Do you plan to kill us?"

"Nothing of the kind. Tomorrow you'll be rich, noble, powerful,
happy. Tomorrow you'll also know everything."

"So you do love me?" Gil Gil asked.

"You ask if I love you?" replied Death. "You ingrate! How can you
doubt it?"

"Until tomorrow, then," said Gil Gil, giving his hand to the terrible
divinity.

Elena continued to stand in front of Gil Gil.

"Until tomorrow," she responded, as if she had heard his words
of farewell, as if she were answering another secret voice, as if she
were divining the youth's thoughts.

And she turned around slowly and left the royal chamber.

Gil approached the king's bed.

The duke of Monteclaro went over and stood alongside our friend
and said to him in a low voice:

"Until tomorrow. If the king dies, tomorrow your marriage to my
daughter will take place. The queen has just notified me of the death
of the viscount of Rionuevo. And I have informed her of your and Elena's

wedding, and she approves wholeheartedly. Tomorrow you will be the foremost personage of the court if Louis I does indeed breathe his last today."

"Have no doubts, my lord duke," said Gil in a mournful tone.

"Until tomorrow, then," Monteclaro repeated solemnly.

XI
Gil Is Happy Again and the First Part
of This Story Comes to an End

The following day, 1 September 1724, at nine o'clock in the morning, Gil Gil was striding back and forth in a room of the Rionuevo palace.

The palace belonged to him now that he was the count and legitimized by virtue of the will and other papers of his father's, which the duke of Monteclaro and the archbishop of Toledo found in the place indicated by the countess.

Moreover, the night before, a messenger had brought him, from Philip V, who had in the end decided to return to the throne of Saint Ferdinand, an appointment as court physician, the title of duke of Veracity, and thirty thousand *pesos* in gold.

And the following day his marriage to Elena de Monteclaro was to take place.

As for Death, Gil Gil had lost sight of him totally since the previous morning when he left the palace, taking with him the soul of Louis I.

Nevertheless, our young hero remembered that the relentless deity had offered to act as his best man in his marriage to Elena, and therein lay the reason for his pensive mood.

Here I am, he thought, *noble, rich, and powerful. Here I am, about to possess the woman I adore. And, nevertheless, I'm not happy. Last night, as I looked at Elena, and later during my final talk with Death, I thought I caught a glimpse of inexplicable and terrifying mysteries. I have to break off relations with the sinister numen who has protected me. It may be ingratitude, but so be it. In time he'll have an opportunity to avenge himself. No. I don't want to see Death again. I'm too happy.*

The new duke began to reflect on ways to keep his distance from Death until the last moment of his life.

It's a fact, he reasoned, *that I won't die until God so ordains. Death, by and of himself, can do me no harm, given that he does not have the power to hasten my demise or Elena's. The aim, therefore, is to not see him and hear him at all hours. His voice frightens me, his revelations distress me, and his speeches inspire me with contempt for life and material objects. What can I do to keep him from being my nightmare? Oh, what an idea! Death never appears except where he has something to kill. Living in the country, not seeing people, alone with Elena, my enemy would leave me alone until, by decree of the Most High, he went straightaway in search of one of us. And meanwhile, in order not to see him in Madrid either, I'll live with my eyes blindfolded.*

Excited by this last thought, our young hero radiated with joy, as if he had just come out of a long illness and believed himself safe on Earth until the end of time.

. . . .

The following day at six o'clock, Gil Gil and Elena de Monteclaro were married in a beautiful villa located at the foot of the Guadarrama mountain range, a villa owned by the new count and duke.

At six-thirty the wedding party returned to Madrid, and our newly married couple were left alone in a lush garden.

The former Gil Gil did not see Death again.

And although our story could end here, it is at this point that it will truly begin to be interesting and clear.

XII
SUNSET

> She loved, and was beloved—she adored,
>   And she was worshiped after Nature's fashion—
> Their intense souls, into each other poured,
>   If souls could die, had perished in that passion.
>
> —Lord Byron, *Don Juan*, Canto the Second, CXCI

Gil and Elena loved each other and belonged to each other; they were free and they were alone.

The memories of their childhood, the pulsations of their hearts, the wishes of their parents, their fortune and birth, God's blessing—everything united them, everything knitted them together.

Two souls who had looked upon each other with delight since childhood; two souls who had been captivated by each other's beauty since adolescence; two souls who had wept over the torments of absence at the same times; Gil and Elena, Elena and Gil, predestined to be inseparable, finally lost, in that solemn and mystic hour, their solitary, miserable individuality to embark on a future full of happiness, like two rivers that spring from the same mountain and, coursing along tortuous channels, reunite and merge in the infinite solitude of the ocean.

It was evening, but it did not seem like the evening of a single day; it seemed like the evening of the world's existence, like the evening of all the time that had elapsed since Creation.

The sun was gradually sinking below the horizon. The magnificent lights in the western sky gilded the front of the villa, streaking through the luxuriant green vines of a broad grape arbor, a kind of canopy that sheltered the newly married couple. The mild, still air, the last flowers of the year, the motionless birds on the branches of trees— all of nature, in short, witnessed, in silence and amazement, the close of that day, and of that sunset, as if it might have been the last one taken in by human eyes, as if the sun-king might not return the following day so generous and so joyous, so overflowing with life and youth, as it had morning after morning during so many thousands of centuries.

It could be said that at that point time had come to a standstill, that the hours, exhausted from their continuous revolutions, had sat down on the grass to rest and were telling each other moving tales of love and death, like young boarding school girls who, tired of playing, form a circle in the garden of a convent and recount their childhood adventures and adolescent fantasies.

It could also be said that at that moment a period in the history of the world was coming to an end, that all of nature was bidding an eternal farewell: the bird to his nest, the zephyr to the flowers, the trees to the rivers, the sun to the mountains; and that the intimate togetherness in which all had lived, lending one another color or fragrance, music or movement, and converging in the same palpitation of universal existence, had been brought to an end and that in future each one of those elements would be subject to new laws and influences.

It could be said, finally, that on that evening there was going to be a dissolution of the mysterious association that constitutes the unity and harmony of the worlds, an association that precludes the demise of the most inconsequential of created things, which transforms and continually revitalizes matter, which disregards nothing, which identifies and renews and beautifies everything.

More than any*thing* and more than any*body* possessed of this supreme intuition and strange delusion, Gil and Elena—still, silent, and holding hands—witnessed the august tragedy of the close of that day, the last of their misfortunes, and looked at each other with profound anxiety and blind adoration. Neither knew what the other was thinking, but both were oblivious to the entire universe, and both were ecstatic and spellbound, like two portraits, like two statues, like two corpses.

Perhaps they believed they were alone on Earth; perhaps they believed they had departed it.

Ever since their wedding guests had left, ever since the sound of their footsteps had died away in the distance, and ever since the world had completely abandoned them, they had said nothing—nothing! All they did was delight in looking at each other.

There they were, sitting on a grass bench, surrounded by flowers and greenery, with an infinite sky before their eyes, free and solitary like two seagulls perched on algae that are rocked by waves in the middle of the ocean's void.

There they were, engrossed in mutual contemplation, greedy for happiness. The cup of bliss was in their hands, but they did not dare raise it to their lips for fear that it might all be a dream or that they might lose the good fortune they already had by coveting even more.

There they were, in short, ignorant, chaste, beautiful, immortal, like Adam and Eve in paradise before sin.

Elena, the nineteen-year-old maiden, was at the height of her extraordinary beauty, or rather, at that fleeting moment in a woman's youth when, in full possession of all her charms, judge of her own nature, and overflowing with blessings from heaven and promises of happiness, she can feel everything even though she has felt nothing, and is at once woman and child. A rose half-opened by the generous warmth of the sun, which has already spread all its petals, displayed all its delights, and received the caresses of the zephyr, but which still preserves the shape, the color, and the perfume that are only retained by modest buds.

Elena was tall, graceful, statuesque, and her whole being lovely, artistic, and seductive. Her round head, crowned with blond hair that turned golden toward the temples and hazel where her waves thickened, protruded nobly over a white neck shaped like that of Juno. Her blue eyes seemed to reflect the infinite nature of eternal thought. It could be said that as much as one gazed at those eyes, one never fathomed them. They had something of heaven besides their color and purity.

Indeed, in Elena's glance there was a light of eternity, of pure spirit, of immortal passion, that was not of this world. Her complexion, white and pale like water at nightfall, had the transparency of mother-of-pearl, but it did not reflect the flush of blood, and only an occasional sky-blue vein broke the serene, placid whiteness. It could have been said that Elena was made of marble.

Her angelic face did have, however, a woman's mouth, and that mouth, the vermilion of a pomegranate's blossom, moist and sparkling like a bed of pearls, was, in a manner of speaking, bathed in a tepid, voluptuous vapor like the sigh that kept it half open. Elena might also have been compared to the statue carved by Pygmalion when, for the first time and in order to kiss the sculptor, Galatea moved her be-witching lips.*

Lastly, Elena wore white, which intensified the dazzling magnifi-cence of her loveliness, but she was one of those women whom finery never succeeds in masking. The same thing happened to her as to noble pagan Minervas: her attire hinted at enough for the mind's eye to behold the pure form of Olympian beauty. And thus the consummate and supreme comeliness of the new wife also showed itself in all its splendor, even under silk and lace. It seemed as if her body radiated among the folds of her white dress, after the manner in which Naiads and Nereids illuminate the depths of the waters with their burnished limbs.

Thus was Elena the evening of her marriage to Gil Gil.

And thus did she appear to Gil Gil, thus was she his!

XIII
LUNAR ECLIPSE

> Never would the shepherds have ended
> Their sad lament nor brought to a close
> Songs heard only by the mountain
> If, looking at the reddish clouds edged with gold
> As they passed by the sun,
> They had not seen that the day was done.
> Darkness could be observed
> Approaching swiftly along the
> Dense slopes of the
> Soaring mountain . . .

—Garcilaso de la Vega, verses from the
First Eclogue, last stanza.*

Oh, yes! The youth was gazing at her as the blind contemplate the sun—not seeing the daystar but feeling its warmth on their dead pupils.

After so many years of loneliness and grief, after so many hours of nightmarish fantasies, he, DEATH'S FRIEND, found himself plunged in a sea of life, in a world of light, hope, and happiness.

What was he to say, what was he to think, if he still could not bring himself to believe that he existed, that the woman was Elena, that he was her husband, that both had escaped the clutches of Death?

"Speak to me, my Elena! Tell me everything!" Gil Gil exclaimed in the end, when the sun had set and the birds had broken the silence. "Speak to me, my love!"

Elena then told him all that she had thought and felt during those last three years: her sorrow when she stopped seeing Gil Gil; her despair on leaving for France; how she caught a glimpse of him, on departing, at the door of their palace; how the duke of Monteclaro had opposed their love, of which he had been informed by the countess of Rionuevo; how much she delighted in running across him in the vestibule of San Millán three days ago; how much she suffered on seeing him cut to the quick by the countess's cruelty. Everything, she told him everything, because everything had increased her love, not made it ebb.

Night was falling, and, as the darkness grew, the secret anguish that clouded Gil Gil's happiness was being dispelled.

Oh! thought the youth, gathering Elena in an embrace. *Death has lost my trail, he doesn't know where I am. He won't come here! Our everlasting love would drive him away. What could Death do in our midst? Come, come, dark night, and envelop us in your black veil. Come, even if you are to last forever. Come, even if tomorrow never dawns.*

"You're trembling, Gil!" Elena exclaimed. "You're crying!"

"My wife!" the youth murmured. "My darling! My joy! I'm crying from happiness."

And with these words he took his bride's bewitching head in his hands and stared intensely, deliriously, and wildly into her eyes.

A deep, burning sigh, a cry of heady passion intermingled on Gil's and Elena's lips.

"My love!" they both exclaimed in the delirium of that first kiss, at whose rapturous sound the invisible spirits of solitude shuddered.

At this point the moon suddenly came into view, full, magnificent, and brilliant.

Its fantastic, unexpected light startled both husband and wife, who turned simultaneously toward the east, drawing away from each other by some unknown and mysterious instinct, but not letting go of their trembling, twitching hands, as cold at that moment as the alabaster of a tomb.

"It's the moon!" the two of them muttered in hoarse voices.

They looked at one another in ecstasy, and Gil extended his arms toward Elena with the utmost solicitude, with as much love as despair.

But Elena was as white as a sheet.

Gil shuddered.

"Elena, what's the matter?" he asked.

"Oh, Gil!" she responded. "You're so pale!"

At that moment there occurred a lunar eclipse, as if a cloud had come between the luminary and the newlyweds.

But, oh! It was not a cloud!

It was a long black shadow, which, seen by Gil from the grass where he was reclining, extended from Earth to the heavens, casting into mourning nearly the entire length of the horizon.

It was a colossal figure, which was perhaps magnified by his imagination.

It was a terrible being, wrapped in a long, dark cloak, and it stood at his side, motionless, silent, enveloping both of them in his shadow.

Gil Gil guessed who it was.

Elena did not see the mournful personage. Elena continued seeing the moon.

XIV
At Last, a Doctor!

Gil Gil found himself between his beloved and Death, or rather between death and life.

Yes, because that gloomy shadow which had come between him and the moon, clouding the resplendence of passion on Elena's face, was the Deity of Darkness, our hero's faithful companion since that sorry night when the then miserable shoemaker contemplated suicide.

"Hello, friend," he said, as he did on that occasion.

"Sh!" uttered Gil Gil, covering his face with his hands.

"What's wrong, my love?" asked Elena, noticing her husband's distress.

"Elena! Elena! Don't leave my side!" exclaimed the youth in despair, throwing his left arm around his bride's neck.

"I have to talk to you," Death continued, taking Gil Gil's right hand and gently drawing him away.

"Come, let's go inside," Elena said as she pulled him toward the villa.

"No, you come with me," Death murmured to Gil as he pointed to the garden gate.

Elena neither saw Death nor heard him.

Only the duke of Veracity enjoyed this sad privilege.

"Gil, I'm waiting for you!" added the sinister personage.

The hapless Gil shook from head to toe. From his eyes fell copious tears, which Elena wiped away with her hand. He then freed himself from her arms and ran wildly through the garden, crying out between heartbreaking sobs:

"To die, to die now!"

Elena wanted to follow him, but no doubt because of the terror into which her husband's state had plunged her, she fell to the ground, unconscious, when she took her first step.

"To die, to die!" Gil kept exclaiming in despair.

"Have no fear," Death said, approaching him amicably. "Besides, it's useless for you to run away from me. Chance has brought us together and I don't intend to let go of you just like that."

"But, why have you come here?" the youth asked heatedly, wiping away his tears like someone who is renouncing supplication, and perhaps prudence, and confronting Death somewhat defiantly. "Why have you come here? Answer me!"

And he glanced around angrily as if looking for a weapon.

There was a hoe near him that belonged to the gardener. He grabbed it convulsively, held it high as if it were a light stick (his strength doubled by despair), and repeated for the third time and more irately than before:

"Why have you come here?"

Death let loose a peal of laughter that we should characterize as philosophical. Its echo lasted a long time, reverberating around the four walls of the garden and imitating, with its strident sound, the rattle of skeletons bumping together.

"You want to kill me!" the figure in black finally exclaimed. "So Life dares to take on Death? This is curious. All right, let's fight."

With these words he threw his long black cape over his shoulder, uncovered the hand with which he held another kind of hoe (which looked more like a sickle or scythe), and assumed his guard opposite Gil.

The moon took on the yellowish hue of the wax candles that illuminate churches on Good Friday; a cold wind arose, making fruit-laden trees creak with sorrow; the distant barking of many dogs was heard, or maybe they were long howls of funereal portent; and it even seemed possible to hear on high, in the upper reaches of the clouds, the discordant sound of countless bells that were tolling death.

Gil Gil noticed all these things and dropped to his knees in front of his adversary.

"Pity me! Forgive me!" he said with indescribable anguish.

"You're forgiven," Death replied, hiding his scythe.

And as if all that funereal display of nature had stemmed from the fury of the black deity, no sooner did a smile play on his lips than the cold of the atmosphere abated, the bells fell silent, the dogs stopped howling, and the moon again shone as softly as it had earlier that night.

"You tried to fight with me!" exclaimed Death good-naturedly. "*At last, a doctor!* Get up, you poor devil; get up, and give me your hand. I've already told you not to fear anything *tonight.*"

"But, why have you come here?" the youth repeated with growing alarm. "Why have you come here? Why are you in my house? You enter only where you have to kill someone. Whom are you looking for?"

"I'll tell you everything. Let's sit down a while," Death replied, stroking Gil Gil's frozen hands.

"But, Elena," murmured the youth.

"Let her be. Right now she's *asleep*—I'm watching out for her. So let's get down to business. Gil Gil, you're an ingrate. You're like all the others. Once at the top you kick away the ladder used to make the climb. Oh! Your behavior toward me will be frowned on by God. How much you've made me suffer these last few days! How much! How much!"

"Oh! I adore her!" Gil Gil exclaimed.

"You adore her. That's it. You had lost her forever; you were a miserable shoemaker and she was going to marry a baron; I intervene on your behalf and make you rich, noble, and famous; I deliver you from your rival; I reconcile you with your enemy the countess and carry her off; I give you, finally, Elena's hand. And what do you do? You turn your back on me, you forget me, you put on a blindfold to avoid seeing me. You're foolish. As foolish as other men who should always be seeing me in their thoughts. But no, these others are blinded by the world's vanities and live without paying me the slightest attention until I call on them. My fate is a most unhappy one. I don't remember having approached a mortal without causing fright and surprise, as if the person had never expected me. Even old people over a hundred think they can escape me. For your part, you have the privilege of being able to see me and you can't forget me just like that, but the other day you put a physical obstruction over your eyes—a blindfold—and today you shut yourself in a lonely garden and believe yourself free of me forevermore. You idiot! You ingrate! You false friend! You *man* . . . which says it all."

"But," stammered Gil, whose suspicious curiosity had not been quelled by confusion and shame, "why do you come to my house?"

"I come to carry out the mission that the Eternal has entrusted to me concerning you."

"But, you're not coming to kill us?"

"Not at all."

"Well, then—"

"However, now that I've managed to see you, or rather, managed to have you see me, I need to take certain precautions so you won't forget me again."

"What precautions?" asked Gil, trembling more than ever.

"I also need to make certain extremely important revelations to you."

"Oh! Come back tomorrow!"

"No, no. Impossible. This meeting of ours is providential."

"My friend!" exclaimed the poor youth.

"I am indeed your friend," Death responded in kind. "And because I am, you need to follow me."

"Where?"

"To my house."

"To your house? So you do come to kill me! Ah, how cruel! And such is your friendship! Dreadful sarcasm! You have me know happiness and then snatch it away from me at once. Why didn't you let me die that night?"

"Be quiet, you poor devil," Death replied with some sadness. "You say you know happiness. How mistaken you are. My aim is that you *will* know it."

"My happiness is Elena. I renounce everything else."

"You will see things more clearly tomorrow."

"Kill me, then!" Gil shouted in despair.

"It would be futile."

"Then kill her! Kill us both!"

"You are raving."

"*Go to your house.* My God! Let me at least say farewell to my beloved wife. Let me say good-bye."

"Very well. Wake up, Elena! Come! I command you. Look at her there. She's coming."

"Good. What do I tell her? At what time will I be able to return tonight?"

"Tell her . . . that you'll see each other at dawn."

"Oh, no! I don't want to be with you so long! Today I'm more afraid of you than ever."

"Careful."

"Don't be angry!" exclaimed the disconsolate husband. "Don't be angry and tell the truth. Will Elena and I really see each other at dawn?"

Death solemnly raised his right hand and looked at heaven as he answered in his sad voice:

"I swear it."

"Oh, Gil! What's this?" Elena exclaimed, coming through the trees, pale, graceful, and radiant like a mythological personification of the moon.

Gil, also pale like an exhumed corpse, with his hair disheveled, his expression grim, and his heart heavy, kissed Elena on the forehead and said in a gloomy voice:

"Until tomorrow. Wait for me, my life!"

"His life!" Death muttered with profound compassion.

Elena, her eyes brimming with tender tears, looked toward heaven, clasped her hands in a fit of mysterious anguish, and repeated in a voice that was not of this world:

"Until tomorrow."

And Gil and Death left while she stayed there, standing among the trees with her hands clasped and her arms hanging down— motionless, magnificent, and resplendent by the light of the moon.

She looked like a noble statue without a pedestal, forgotten in the middle of the garden.

XV
Time in Reverse

"We have a long way to go," Death said to our friend Gil as soon as they left the villa. "I'm going to order my chariot."

And he stamped the ground.

A dull noise, like the one that precedes an earthquake, rumbled below the surface of the earth. There then arose around the two friends an ash gray mist, and through its haze appeared a kind of ivory chariot, in the style of those we see in the bas-reliefs of pagan antiquity.

Anyone who regarded it (we shall not keep this from the reader) would have noticed in short order that that chariot was not of ivory, but purely and simply of human bones that had been polished and joined together with exquisite skill so as to retain their natural shape.

Death gave his hand to Gil and they got in the chariot, which rose through the air like today's balloons, the only difference being that it was steered by the will of those who rode in it.

"Although we have a long way to go," Death continued, "we have time to spare, because this chariot will fly as fast as I want it to. As swiftly as the imagination. By that I mean we'll alternate between fast and slow, trying to circumnavigate the earth in the three hours we have at our disposal. Right now it's nine o'clock in the evening in Madrid. We'll travel northeastward and that way avoid running into sunshine immediately."

Gil remained silent.

"Marvelous. You persist in keeping quiet," Death continued. "Then I'll do the talking. But you'll see how soon you're going to be intrigued, and your silence broken, by the sights you're about to take in. Here goes."

The chariot, which had been hovering in the air, directionless, since our travelers got in it, took wing and nearly grazed the earth, but with incredible speed.

At his feet Gil saw mountains, trees, rivers, cliffs, plains—all in jumbled confusion.

From time to time a fire identified the mountain hut of simple shepherds, but more often than not the chariot passed somewhat slowly over great rocky masses piled in rectangular shapes through which crossed an occasional shadow preceded by a light, while at the same time one heard the peals of bells that were tolling the dead or striking the hour, which is almost the same thing, and the call of the night watchman who repeated it. Death would laugh then and once again the chariot would speed away like a blue streak.

As they headed toward the east the darkness was denser, the tranquility of the cities more profound, and the silence of nature greater.

The moon was fleeing westward like a frightened dove, while the stars changed places in the sky like an army in disarray.

"Where are we?" asked Gil Gil.

"In France," Death replied. "We've already crossed over a considerable portion of the two bellicose nations who fought so fiercely at the beginning of this century. We've seen the entire theater of the War of Succession. Conquerors and conquered alike have gone to bed. My apprentice, Sleep, reigns over the heroes who didn't die in battle, nor afterwards of illness or old age. I don't understand why all you men down below aren't friends. The similarity of your misfortunes and weaknesses, the fact that you all need one another, the brevity of human life, the spectacle of the infinite greatness of the heavenly bodies and the comparison of the same to your insignificance—all these things should bring mankind together in a fraternal bond as the passengers of a vessel threatened with shipwreck join together. Among them there is no love, no hatred, no ambition; no one is a creditor or a debtor; no one is great or small, ugly or beautiful, happy or unhappy. The same danger surrounds them . . . and *my* presence makes everyone equal. So then: what is Earth, seen from this height, but a ship that is sinking, a city stricken by the plague or fire?"

"What are those ignes fatui that I've seen twinkling at various points on Earth ever since the moon disappeared?" asked the youth.

"They're cemeteries. We're over Paris. Alongside every living city, town, or village, there's always a dead city, town or village, as our shadow is always alongside our body. Geography, consequently, is two-sided, even if all of you speak only of the half that strikes you as more pleasant. Making a map of every cemetery on Earth would suffice to explain the political geography of the world. Nevertheless, you would be mistaken in the amount or number of the population: the dead cities are much more inhabited than the living, for in the latter there are barely three generations, while in the former hundreds are some-times stacked together. As for those lights you see shining, they're the phosphorescent glow of corpses, or rather, the last flashes of a thousand vanished existences; they are twilights of love, ambition, anger, genius, charity; they are, in a word, the last streaks of light that is extinguished, of individuality that disappears, of the being that returns its matter to mother earth. They are, and now I'm happening upon the right words, the foam that the river produces as it empties into the ocean."

Death paused.

At the same time Gil Gil heard a frightful racket beneath his feet, like the passage of a thousand chariots over a long wooden bridge. He looked toward Earth and did not sight it, but in its place saw a kind of movable sky into which they were sinking.

"What is that?" he asked in amazement.

"It's the sea," Death said. "We've just crossed over Germany and now we're above the North Sea."

"Oh, no!" murmured Gil, overcome with an instinctive terror. "Take me in another direction. I'd like to see the sun."

"I'll take you to see the sun even if we go backwards to do so. This way you'll observe the highly unusual spectacle of time in reverse."

He turned the chariot in space and they sped southwestward.

A moment later Gil Gil again heard the sound of waves.

"We're above the Mediterranean," Death said. "Now we're crossing the Strait of Gibraltar. And here's the Atlantic Ocean."

"The Atlantic!" Gil uttered in awe.

And now he saw only sky and water, or rather, sky and only sky.

The chariot seemed to roam through the void, beyond the terrestrial atmosphere.

Stars shone everywhere: beneath his feet, above his head, all around him, wherever he looked.

Thus did another minute elapse.

At the end of it he glimpsed in the distance a purple line that separated those two skies, one of them stationary and the other floating.

This purple line turned red, then orange, and afterwards it became as bright as gold, illuminating the vast seas.

The stars gradually disappeared.

It looked like dawn was going to break.

But then the moon reappeared.

However, it had shone only a moment when the light of the horizon eclipsed its brightness.

"Dawn is breaking," said Gil Gil.

"On the contrary," Death corrected him, "it's getting dark. It's just that since we're moving behind the sun, and much more rapidly, the west is going to act as our east and the east as our west. Here are the lovely Azores."

Indeed, a delightful cluster of islands appeared in the middle of the ocean.

The dreamy evening light, breaking through clouds and filtering through fluvial mist, lent the archipelago an enchanting appearance.

Gil and Death passed over those oases in the marine deserts without stopping even for a moment.

Ten minutes later the sun emerged from the bosom of the waves and rose a little above the horizon.

But Death stopped the chariot and the sun set again.

They started anew, and the sun came out once more.

Two dawns merged into one.

All this caused our hero considerable amazement.

They journeyed further and further, becoming engulfed in the day and in the ocean.

Gil's watch, however, said nine-fifteen—at night, if we can speak in such terms.

Several minutes later North America loomed on the seas.

As they passed overhead Gil saw the activity of men who were already tilling the fields, sailing along coasts in ships, and swarming through the streets of cities.

In some place or other he made out a great cloud of dust. It was a battle.

In a different spot Death called his attention to a great religious solemnity devoted to a tree, the idol of that particular town.

Further on he pointed out two young savages, alone in a forest, regarding each other lovingly. Then the Earth vanished again and they came upon the Pacific Ocean.

On Bird Island it was noon.

Thousands of other islands appeared before their eyes everywhere.

On every one of them there were different customs, religions, and pursuits, and different clothes and different ceremonies.

Thus did they arrive at China, where dawn was breaking. But for our travelers this dawn was a nightfall.

Other stars different from those they had seen earlier dotted the firmament.

The moon shone again in the east and hid itself at once.

They continued to fly faster than the Earth turns on its axis.

At last they traversed Asia, where it was nighttime. They passed over the Himalayas, which rose on their left and whose eternal snows glisten in starlight; they crossed the shores of the Caspian Sea; and then they turned slightly leftward, stopping on a hill next to a certain city, where at that moment it was midnight.

"What city is this?" asked Gil Gil.

"We're in Jerusalem," said Death.

"Already?"

"Yes. We've nearly gone around the world. I'm making a stop here because I hear it striking twelve midnight and I always go down on my knees at this hour."

"Why?"

"To worship the Creator of the universe."

And so saying, he got down from the chariot.

"I too wish to contemplate the city of God and meditate on its ruins," said Gil, kneeling alongside Death and folding his hands devoutly.

When both had finished praying, Death recovered his talkativeness and cheerfulness, and, preceded by Gil Gil, got back in the chariot and said:

"The village you see over there on that mountain is Gethsemane.

It's where the Mount of Olives was. On this other side you can make out a rise crowned by a temple that stands out against a field of stars. That's Golgotha, where I spent the greatest day of my life. I thought I had vanquished God Himself, and vanquished I did have Him for many hours. But, ah, it was also on this mountain where, at dawn on a Sunday three days later, I found myself disarmed and incapacitated. Christ had risen! These sites also witnessed, on the same occasion, my great personal battle with Nature. Our duel took place here—at three in the afternoon, I remember everything perfectly—that terrible duel when, as soon as She saw me brandish Longinus's spear against the Redeemer's chest, She began to fling stones at me, disturb cemeteries, resurrect the dead. How should I know! I thought poor Nature had gone mad!"

Death paused a moment, and then, raising his head, added with a more serious expression on his face:

"Time's up! Midnight has passed. Let's go to my house and deal with what we have to discuss."

"Where do you live?" Gil Gil asked timidly.

"At the North Pole," Death replied. "There where no human has ever set foot nor ever will. In the middle of snow and ice as old as the world itself."

With that Death changed his course northward, and the chariot flew more swiftly than ever.

Asia Minor, the Black Sea, Russia, and Spitsbergen disappeared beneath its wheels like fantastic visions.

The horizon was presently illuminated by brilliant flames, reflected by a landscape of rock crystal.

Silence and whiteness blanketed the Earth.

The rest of the sky was purple, sprinkled with almost imperceptible stars.

The aurora borealis and ice. Such was the extent of life in that dreadful region.

"We're at the Pole," said Death. "We have arrived."

XVI
Death Turns Serious Again

If Gil Gil had not already seen so many extraordinary things during his aerial journey; if the memory of Elena had not completely filled his mind; if the desire to know where Death was taking him had not troubled his saddened spirit, it would have been a propitious occasion to study and solve the greatest of geographic problems: the shape and arrangement of Earth's poles.

The mysterious limits of the continents and of the polar sea, blurred by eternal ice; the prominence or abyss that, according to diverse opinions, is supposed to mark the course of the rational axis about which our globe turns; the appearance of the star-spangled firmament, where he would have made out every heavenly body that adorns the skies of North America, Europe in its entirety, Asia—from Troy to Japan—and the northern reaches of the two oceans; the glowing center of the aurora borealis, and, in short, many other phenomena that science has vainly pursued over many centuries at the expense of a thousand illustrious navigators who have perished in those terrifying regions—all these would have been things as clear and manifest to our hero as the light of day, and we would now be able to pass them on to our readers.

But as Gil was not in the mood for such observations, we cannot take up a matter that has nothing to do with our story, so let the human race remain in ignorance as regards the Pole and let us continue this account.

Furthermore, by reminding our readers that at that time it was the beginning of the month of September, they will understand that the sun was still shining in a sky where there had been no night, not even for an instant, for more than five months.

By its pale and oblique light our two travelers got down from the chariot. Then, taking Gil Gil by the hand, Death said most affably:

"Welcome to my house. Let's go in."

A mammoth ice floe rose before their eyes.

In the middle of that floe, which resembled a glass wall affixed to a mass of snow as old as the world, there was a kind of long, narrow opening barely able to accommodate one man.

"I'll show you the way," said Death, going through the opening.

The duke of Veracity stopped, not daring to follow his companion.

But what was he to do? Escape to where in that endless wasteland? Take what direction in those white and interminable icy plains?

"Gil. Aren't you coming in?" Death asked.

Gil shot one final, momentous glance at the pale sun and entered the opening in the ice.

A spiral staircase, sculpted of the same frozen matter, led him to an immense square room, also of ice, with neither furniture nor decoration, which brought to mind the great salt mines of Poland and the marble chambers of the baths of Isfahan and Medina.

Death had squatted in a corner, sitting on his legs Oriental style.

"Come here, sit beside me, and we'll talk," he said to Gil.

The youth obeyed automatically.

There reigned such a profound silence that one would have heard the breathing of a microscopic insect if any living thing could have existed in that region without relying on Death's protection.

As for the cold, no words of ours would do it justice.

Imagine a total absence of heat, a complete negation of life, the absolute stoppage of all movement, death as a way of being, and still you will not have formed an exact idea of that cadaverous world, or more than cadaverous, since it neither decayed nor became transformed, and consequently provided neither nourishment for worms, nor manure for plants, nor elements for minerals, nor gases for the atmosphere.

It was chaos without the embryo of the universe; it was nothingness under the appearance of centuries-old ice.

Nevertheless, Gil Gil withstood that cold thanks to Death's protection.

"Gil Gil," exclaimed the latter in a quiet, majestic voice, "the time has come for the unadulterated truth to shine before your eyes in all its magnificence. I'm going to summarize briefly the history of our relationship and reveal to you the mystery of your destiny."

"Speak," Gil Gil said bravely.

"There is no doubt, my friend," Death continued, "that you wish to live, that all my efforts, all my thoughts, and all the revelations that I make to you all the time are unavailing to extinguish the love of life in your heart."

"You mean love for Elena," the youth interrupted.

"Love of love," Death said. "Love is life, life is love, make no mistake. And if not, think about something that you probably understood in your glorious career as a doctor and during the journey we have just completed. What is man? What does his life mean? You've seen him sleeping from sunset to sunrise and dreaming while asleep. Between these periods of sleep he had at his disposal twelve or fourteen hours daily of wakefulness, which he did not know how to use. On the one hand, you found him, arms in his hands, killing his fellow man; on the other, you saw him sailing the seas to trade food. There were some who strove to dress in this or that color, some who dug holes in the earth and took out metals with which to adorn themselves. In one place a man was being executed, in another a man was being blindly obeyed. In some parts, virtue and justice consisted of one thing, while in others they consisted of just the opposite. What one group held to be the truth, another judged to be an error. Beauty itself quite likely struck you as conventional and imaginary depending on whether you passed over the Caucasus, China, the Congo, or Eskimo country. It must also be evident to you that science is a highly unwieldy experiment to determine the most immediate effects or foolish conjecture about the most obscure causes, and that glory is an empty word appended by chance, by sheer chance, to the name of this or that corpse. You must have realized, in short, that everything man does is child's play to pass the time; that his misfortune and greatness are relative; that his civilization, his social organization, and his most serious interests lack common sense; that fashions, customs, and hierarchies are airs, pretensions, vanity of vanities. But what am I saying? Vanity? Even less. They're the playthings with which all of you occupy your spare time. They're the ravings of one laid up with fever, the hallucinations of a madman. Children, old people, nobles, commoners, the learned, the uneducated, the beautiful, the deformed, slaves, rich and poor, kings and queens—they're all the same to me, they're all handfuls of dust that are undone by my breath. And you still clamor for life. And you still tell me that you wish to remain in the world. And you still love that transitory appearance."

"I love Elena!" Gil Gil exclaimed.

"Ah, yes!" Death continued. "Life is love, life is desire. But the ideal of that love and that desire should not be some kind of beauty fashioned from clay. Dreamers! You always take the near for the far. Life is love, life is feeling; but the great, the noble, the revealing part of life is the tear of sadness that runs down the face of the newborn infant and the dying person, the melancholy complaint of the human heart that feels the hunger of being and pain of existing, the sweet longing for another life, or the pathetic recollection of another world. The displeasure and unease, the doubt and worry of the great souls who are not satisfied with the vanities of Earth, are but a premonition of another order, of a higher mission than science and power, of something, in a word, more infinite than the temporal greatness of men and the fleeting charms of women. Let's concentrate now on you and your history, which you do not know; let's penetrate the mystery of your anomalous existence; let's explain the reasons behind our friendship. Gil Gil, you've made yourself clear: of all the supposed forms of happiness offered by life, you desire but one, and that is the possession of a woman. I have, as a result, made great conquests in your spirit! But nothing—not power, not wealth, not honor, not glory—appeals to your imagination. You are, therefore, a consummate philosopher, a perfect Christian, and it's to this point that I've wanted to bring you. Now then, tell me: if this woman were dead, would you regret dying?"

Gil Gil jumped to his feet, panic-stricken.

"What?" he cried out. "Elena is—?"

"Calm down," Death continued. "Elena is as you left her. We're speaking hypothetically, so answer me."

"Before taking Elena's life, take mine. That's my answer."

"Magnificent!" exclaimed Death. "And tell me: if you knew that Elena was in heaven waiting for you, wouldn't you die peacefully, happily, praising God and commending your soul to Him?"

"Oh, yes! Then death would be resurrection!" exclaimed Gil Gil.

"So long as Elena is at your side," continued the terrible personage, "nothing else matters to you."

"Nothing!"

"Well, then, know it all. Today is not the 2nd of September, 1724, in the Catholic world, as perhaps you imagine. You and I have been *friends* for many, many more years."

"Good heavens! What are you telling me? What year am I in?"

"The eighteenth century has passed, and the nineteenth, and the twentieth, and a few more. Today the church is celebrating the feast of Saint Anthony, and the year is 2316."

"So then I'm dead!"

"For almost six hundred years."

"And Elena?"

"She died when you did. And you died the night we met."

"What? I drank the sulphuric acid?"

"To the last drop. As for Elena, she died of grief when she learned of your unfortunate end. The two of you have, therefore, been in my clutches for six centuries."

"Impossible! You're driving me mad!" exclaimed Gil Gil.

"I don't drive anyone mad," said Death. "Listen to me and you'll hear all I've done on your behalf. Elena and you died the day I've said: Elena, destined to ascend to the abode of the angels on the day of the Last Judgment, and you, deserving of all the agony of hell; she, for her innocence and purity, you, for having forgotten God and harbored base ambitions. Now then: the Last Judgment will take place tomorrow, as soon as it strikes three in the afternoon in Rome."

"Oh, my God! So the world's coming to an end!" exclaimed Gil Gil.

"It was time!" said the formidable being. "I'm finally going to rest."

"The world's coming to an end!" Gil repeated with indescribable fear.

"It's nothing to do with you. You have nothing to lose now. Listen. Seeing that the Last Judgment was approaching, Elena, who loved you in heaven as much as she had loved you on Earth, and I, who have always felt a fondness for you, as I said the first time we spoke, implored the Eternal to save your soul. 'I shouldn't do anything for one who committed suicide,' the Creator said. 'I commit his spirit to you for one hour; cleanse it if you can.' For her part, Elena said to me: 'Save him!' I promised her I would and went down to your tomb where you'd been sleeping for six centuries. I sat there, at the head of your coffin, and made you dream about life. Our meeting, your visit to Philip V, your appearances at the court of Louis I, your marriage to Elena—you've dreamed it all in your tomb. You believed that three days of life elapsed in a single hour as six centuries of death had elapsed in a single instant."

"Oh, no! It wasn't a dream!" exclaimed Gil Gil.

"I understand your astonishment," said Death. "It seemed real to you. That'll tell you what life is. Dreams seem like realities and realities seem like dreams. Elena and I have triumphed. Knowledge, experience, and philosophy have purified your heart, ennobled your spirit, and made you see the splendors of Earth in all their disgusting futility, and it turns out that by fleeing death, as you did yesterday, you were fleeing the world, and by crying out for an eternal love, as you are today, you're crying out for immortality. You're redeemed."

"But, Elena—" Gil Gil murmured.

"This has to do with God. Do not think about Elena. Elena does not exist nor has she ever really existed. Elena was beauty, the reflection of immortality. As the Star of Truth and Justice is retrieving His brilliance today, Elena is uniting with Him forever. It is to Him, therefore, that you should direct your entreaties."

"It was a dream!" exclaimed the youth with indescribable anguish.

"And that is what the world will be within a few hours—a dream of the Creator."

With these words Death stood up, uncovered his head, and raised his eyes to heaven.

"Dawn is breaking over Rome," he said. "The *last day* is beginning. Good-bye, Gil. Farewell, forever."

"Oh, don't abandon me!" exclaimed the wretched creature.

"*Don't abandon me*, you say to Death. And yesterday you fled from me."

"Oh! Don't leave me alone here in this region of grief. This is a tomb!"

"What?" the black divinity asked ironically. "You've gotten along that badly in it for six hundred years?"

"How's that? I've lived here?"

"*Lived.* Call it whatever you wish. You've slept here all that time."

"Then this is my tomb?"

"Yes, my friend, and as soon as I disappear, you'll become convinced of it. Only then will you feel all the cold in this dwelling."

"Ah! I'll die instantly!" exclaimed Gil Gil. "I'm at the North Pole."

"You can't die because you're already dead, but you *will* sleep until three in the afternoon, when you'll awake with all generations."

"My friend!" Gil Gil cried out with indescribable bitterness. "Don't leave me alone or let me continue to dream. I don't want to sleep. It frightens me. This tomb is suffocating me. Take me back to the villa in the Guadarrama where I imagined I saw Elena, and let the destruction of the world surprise me there. I believe in God, I defer to His justice, and I appeal to His mercy, but take me back to Elena!"

"What tremendous love!' said the divinity. "It has triumphed over life and is going to triumph over death. It scorned Earth and will scorn heaven. It will be as you wish, Gil Gil, but don't forget your soul."

"Oh, thank you, thank you, my friend. I see that you are going to take me to Elena."

"No, I'm not going to take you to her. Elena is asleep in her tomb. I'll have her come here so she can sleep alongside you during the final hours of her death."

"One day we shall be buried together. It's too much for my glory and my happiness. Let me see Elena, let me hear her say that she loves me, let me know that she'll be forever at my side, on Earth or in heaven, and the long night of the tomb will not matter to me."

"Come then, Elena. I command it!' said Death in a deep voice, communicating with Earth by stamping.

Elena, dressed in her white robes, seemingly the same as she was in the garden of the Guadarrama, but as pale as alabaster, appeared in the middle of the room of ice where this marvelous scene was occurring.

Gil Gil received her on his knees, his face covered with tears and his hands folded as he gazed with profound gratitude upon Death's gentle face.

"Good-bye, my friends," said the latter.

"Your hand, Elena," asked a moved Gil Gil.

"My Gil," she said softly, kneeling at her husband's side.

And with their hands joined and their eyes raised to heaven, they answered Death's "Good-bye" with another melancholy "Good-bye."

The black divinity, meanwhile, was slowly withdrawing.

"Farewell forever!" murmured the Friend of man as he took his leave.

"Mine forever!" exclaimed Elena, gazing at Gil Gil. "God has forgiven you, and we shall live together in heaven."

"Forever!" the youth repeated with ineffable joy.

At this point Death disappeared.

A horrible cold invaded the room and Gil Gil and Elena were frozen instantaneously—petrified and immovable in that religious attitude, on their knees, holding hands, their eyes raised to heaven like two magnificent sepulchral statues.

CONCLUSION

A few hours later the Earth exploded like a grenade.

The stars closest to it attracted and assimilated fragments of the shattered mass, not without the fusion causing them tremendous cataclysms like deluges and deviations from their polar axes.

The moon, nearly intact, became a satellite of either Venus or Mercury.

Meanwhile, the Last Judgment of the family of Adam and Eve had taken place, not in the Valley of Jehoshaphat, but on the comet named Charles V, and the souls of the damned were banished to other planets, where they had to begin a new life. What greater punishment?

Those who are cleansed in this second existence will achieve the glory of returning to God's bosom the day those planets disappear.

Those who are not cleansed will continue to migrate to a hundred other worlds, where they shall wander the same as we did through ours.

As for Gil and Elena, that afternoon they entered the Promised Land, hand in hand, forever free of sorrow and penance, saved and redeemed, reconciled with God, partakers of His blessedness and heirs to His glory, neither more nor less than the rest of the righteous and cleansed.

Whereupon I can end my story the same way that old women end all theirs, by saying, "And that's all there is to tell."

Juan Valera (1824–1905)

One of nineteenth-century Spain's most respected authors, Juan Valera spent much of his life in the diplomatic service, with postings to Naples, Lisbon, Rio de Janeiro, Dresden, St. Petersburg, Washington, Brussels, and Vienna. Cosmopolitan, cultured, and urbane, Valera read six languages, including Greek, from which he translated Longus's Daphnis and Chloe *into Spanish.*

A serious student of his own and foreign literatures, Valera wrote novels, short stories, poetry, essays, and literary criticism, in addition to carrying on a voluminous correspondence with several of his fellow Spanish writers. The unifying thread of his work is "art for art's sake," that is, beauty as the end and purpose of inspiration and creativity. Two examples of this aesthetic credo in his long works are the eponymous novels Pepita Jiménez *(1874) and* Doña Luz *(1879).*

Valera cultivated the short story early and late in his life: "The Green Bird" came out in 1860 and "The Wizard" in 1894. In an article titled "Doctor Fastenrath [a German Hispanist]" (1870) he wrote: "Spain has contributed very little till now to this literary treasure [compilations of folktales]. Although our Count Lucanor *is one of the oldest collections of stories, the genre has been neglected." And in a letter to a friend he wrote: "We're trying to publish a collection of stories, legends, and popular tales from Spain along the lines of the fairy tales published in Germany by the brothers Grimm." Valera and the other person who made up the "we" never brought the project to fruition, but "The Green Bird" and "The Wizard" came from the oral tradition that they sought to preserve.*

Juan Valera

"The Green Bird"

I

ONCE upon a time there was, in an age very remote from the one in which we live, a powerful king, loved in the extreme by his subjects and possessor of a vast, productive, and populous kingdom in one of the far-off regions of the Orient. This king, who owned immense treasures and gave splendid fetes, had in attendance at his court the most genteel ladies and the most discreet and valiant knights to be found anywhere in the world at that time. His army was numerous and battle-hardened; his ships roamed the seas as if in triumph; and the parks and gardens in which he was disposed to hunt and take his ease were marvels on account of their magnitude and luxuriance, and on account of the abundance of animals and birds that fed and lived in them.

But what shall we say about his palaces and their contents, the magnificence of which exceeds the most fertile imagination? They contained sumptuous pieces of furniture, silver and gold thrones, and porcelain services, which were much less common then than now; there were dwarfs, giants, jesters, and other freaks for the entertainment and amusement of His Majesty; there were eminent and expert cooks and confectioners who looked after his bodily nourishment; and there were no less eminent and expert philosophers, poets, and legal experts who looked after him with spiritual nourishment, who attended his private council, who decided the most thorny questions of law, who sharpened and exercised their genius with charades and logogriphs, and who sang the glories of the dynasty in stupendous epics.

This king's subjects rightly called him "Fortunate," for everything kept getting better and better during his reign. His life had been a tissue of happy occurrences whose brightness dimmed only with the black shadow of sorrow occasioned by the early death of the queen,

190

a very upright and beautiful person whom His Majesty loved with all his heart. Imagine, reader, how he must have wept, and all the more so having been, because of his pure devotion to her, the innocent cause of her death.

Histories of the country relate that the king had been married seven years without producing offspring, although he vehemently desired children, when war broke out in the neighboring country. The king departed with his troops, but not before saying good-bye most affectionately to the queen. Embracing him, his wife spoke in his ear:

"Don't tell anyone, so that people won't laugh if my hopes aren't fulfilled, but I think I'm pregnant."

With this piece of news the king's joy knew no bounds, and since all turns out well for a joyful person, he triumphed over his enemies in the war, killed with his own hands three or four kings who had played we don't know what dirty tricks on him, laid waste cities, took captives, and returned to the beautiful capital of his monarchy laden with booty and glory.

Several months had been spent on these activities, so that while the king was passing through the city with great pomp, amidst the acclamations and applause of the multitude and the lively pealing of bells, the queen was giving birth, and delivered felicitously and easily, despite the noise and excitement and even though this was her first child.

What unalloyed happiness His Majesty must have experienced when, as he entered the royal chamber, the chief male midwife of the realm presented him with a beautiful princess who had just been born! The king gave his daughter a kiss and, filled with jubilation, love, and satisfaction, headed for the room of the queen, who was in bed as ruddy, as fresh, and as pretty as a May rose.

"Dearest wife!" exclaimed the king, and he squeezed her in his arms. But the king was so strong and the outpouring of his affection so intense that, without further ado, he unintentionally suffocated the queen. There then ensued shouts, desperation, and his calling himself a beast, along with other eloquent demonstrations of pained feeling. But not on this account did the queen revive, and although dead, she looked divine. You might say that a smile of ineffable delight still played about her lips. Undoubtedly her soul had flown through them, wrapped in a sigh of love and proud to have known how to inspire enough affection to produce that embrace. What woman truly in love would not envy the lot of this queen!

The king showed how greatly devoted he was to his wife, not only during her life but also after her death. He took a vow of perpetual widowerhood and chastity, and kept it. He commanded poets to compose a funeral panegyric, which people still say is considered the most precious jewel in the national literature of that kingdom. The court was in mourning for three years. And so spectacular was the mausoleum erected to the queen that the one built subsequently in Caria was but a poor imitation of it.

But since, as the saying goes, time heals all wounds, at the end of a number of years the king shook off the melancholy and considered himself as fortunate or more fortunate than before. The queen would appear to him in his dreams and tell him that he enjoyed God's favor, and the princess was growing and developing so much that it was a delight to see her.

When his daughter turned fifteen, she was, owing to her beauty, intellect, and way with people, the admiration of all who saw her and the wonder of all who heard her. The king had her sworn as heiress to the throne, and then tried to marry her off.

More than five hundred diplomatic couriers, each one mounted on a post zebra, set out simultaneously from the capital with dispatches for as many other courts, inviting all princes to come and seek the hand of the princess, who was to select from among them the one she liked most.

The fame of her prodigious beauty had by now spread throughout the entire world, so that no sooner did the couriers begin arriving at the various courts than there was not a single prince, as contemptible and useless as he may have been, who did not decide to journey to the capital of the Fortunate King to compete in jousts, tournaments, and exercises of ingenuity in order to gain the princess's hand. Each one asked his father—a king—for his blessing, arms, horses, and money, and then set out at the head of a brilliant retinue.

The arrival of all these gentlemen of high station at the princess's court was a sight worthy to behold, as were the soirées held at the royal palaces. And worthy of admiration were the riddles that the princes posed in order for each one to demonstrate his keen mind; the verses they wrote; the serenades they gave; the archery, boxing and wrestling contests, and the chariot and horse races in which each one tried to best the others and win the love of the sought-after fiancée.

But the princess, who despite her modesty and discretion was endowed with an indifferent, hard-to-please, sullen disposition, and unable to help it, overwhelmed the princes with her disdain, and she cared not a whit for any of them. Their discretion struck her as coldness, their riddles as simpleness, their submissiveness as arrogance, and the love that they showed her as vanity or greed for her riches. She barely condescended to observe their knightly exercises, or listen to their serenades, or smile in appreciation at their love verses. The magnificent gifts that each one brought her from his native land lay forgotten in a garret of the king's palace.

The princess's indifference was glacial for all her suitors. Only one, the son of the Khan of Tartar, had managed to escape her indifference, and then only to incur her hatred. This prince suffered from a sublime ugliness. His eyes were slanted, his cheeks and chin prominent; his hair was kinky and tangled, his body small and squat, although of titanic strength; and he had a haughty, mocking, anxious temperament. Not even the most inoffensive people were free from his gibes, and the chief butt of them was the Fortunate King's foreign affairs minister, whose gravity, conceit, and limited intelligence, as well as how terribly he spoke Sanskrit, the language of diplomacy at that time, lent themselves somewhat to ridicule and jokes.

Such was the state of affairs, with the festivities at court becoming more and more brilliant by the day. The princes, however, were despairing of being loved, and the Fortunate King was beside himself seeing that his daughter was nowhere near making up her mind, while for her part the princess stubbornly continued to ignore them all, except the Tartar prince, whom she taunted and openly loathed, thereby avenging a thousandfold her father's famous minister.

II

It happened, then, that on a beautiful spring morning the princess was in her boudoir, her favorite maid combing her long, silky, golden tresses. The doors of the balcony, which faced the garden, were open to let in a fresh breeze and with it the fragrance of the flowers.

The princess seemed melancholy and pensive and did not speak a single word to her servant.

The girl already held in her hands the cord with which she was getting ready to tie together her mistress's blond locks, when unexpectedly the loveliest of birds entered through the balcony, a bird whose feathers looked like the color of emeralds and whose grace in flight enthralled the lady and her maid. Swiftly passing by the latter, the bird snatched the cord from her hands and flew back out of the room.

Everything was so instantaneous that the princess scarcely had time to see the bird, but his boldness and beauty created the strangest impression on her.

Several days afterward the princess, in an attempt to dispel her melancholy moods, was weaving through a dance with her maids, in the presence of the enraptured princes who were all in the garden watching her. All of a sudden the princess felt a garter coming untied and, stopping the dance, quietly slipped away to a nearby wood to retie it. Her Highness had already bared her shapely leg, already stretched her white silk stocking, and was preparing to secure it with the garter that she had in her hand, when she heard the sound of wings and saw, flying toward her, the green bird, who snatched the garter from her with his eburnean bill and disappeared at once. The princess screamed and fell into a faint.

Her father and the suitors rushed to her side. She regained consciousness and the first thing she said was:

"Find me the green bird. Bring him to me alive. Don't kill him. I want to possess the green bird alive!"

But in vain did the princes search for him. In vain, despite the princess's command that they not think about killing the green bird, did the princes give it chase with falcons, gyrfalcons, sakers, and even golden eagles, domesticated and trained in hawking. The green bird did not show up, dead or alive.

The unfulfilled wish to possess it tormented the princess and aggravated her bad humor. That night she was unable to sleep. The best thing she thought about the princes was that they were worthless.

Day had scarcely broken when she rose from her bed and, scantily clad, wearing neither a corset nor a criniline, pale and with rings under her eyes, but more beautiful and interesting in that dishabille, she went with her favorite maid to the shadiest section of the forest at the back of the palace, where her mother's tomb stood. She started to cry there and to lament her fate.

"What good are all my riches if I despise them?" she said. "What good are all the princes in the world if I don't love them? What good my kingdom if I don't have you, dearest Mother, and what good all my finery and jewelry if I don't possess the beautiful green bird?"

Whereupon, and as if to console herself somewhat, she unlaced the top of her gown and removed from her breast an exquisite locket in which she kept one of her mother's curls, which she began to kiss. But no sooner did she begin to kiss it than the green bird, flying more swiftly than ever, brushed the princess's lips with his eburnean bill and snatched the locket, which for so many years had rested against her heart, and where, in such a hidden and desired place, it had remained. The robber disappeared immediately, soaring skyward and getting lost in the clouds.

This time the princess did not faint; on the contrary, she stopped, her cheeks flushed, and said to the maid:

"Look at me, look at me. That insolent bird has injured my lips, because they're on fire."

The maid looked at them and saw no bite, but the bird had undoubtedly deposited something poisonous, because the traitor did not turn up again afterwards, and the princess's health went downhill by degrees, until she fell gravely ill.

A peculiar fever was consuming her and she almost never spoke except to say:

"Don't kill him. Bring him to me alive. I want to possess him."

The doctors agreed that the only medicine to cure the princess was to bring her the green bird alive. But where were they going to find him? It turned out to be fruitless to have the most skillful hunters go after him; and it turned out to be fruitless to offer an enormous sum to whoever brought him in.

The Fortunate King then assembled a great congress of sages for the purpose of ascertaining, under pain of incurring his just indignation, who the green bird was and where the green bird lived, because the recollection of it was tormenting his daughter.

The sages were gathered together for forty days and forty nights, meditating and discoursing continuously, stopping only to sleep a little and take nourishment. They delivered very learned and eloquent speeches, but they determined nothing.

"Sire," they said humbly at his feet as their respectable foreheads struck the ground, "we are a group of half-wits. Have us hanged. Our knowledge is a sham. We do not know who the green bird is, and we only dare to wonder if perhaps it may be the phoenix of Arabia."

"Rise," said the king with noteworthy magnanimity. "I pardon you and thank you for the information about the phoenix. Without delay, seven of you will depart with valuable presents for the queen of Sheba, and with all the means at my disposal to hunt live birds. The phoenix must have its nest in Sabean land, and you are to bring him to me from there, lest my regal anger punish you, even if you should try to avoid it by hiding in the bowels of the earth."

Thus there left for Arabia seven sages who were the most well versed in languages, and among them was the minister of foreign affairs, which gave the Tartar prince cause for much laughter.

This prince also sent letters to his father, who was the most famous magician of the age, consulting him about the case of the green bird.

The princess, meanwhile, continued in very poor health and wept such copious tears that every day she needed more than fifty handkerchiefs to soak them up. As a result the palace laundresses were kept very busy, and since back then not even the most powerful person had as much linen as is used nowadays, all they did was go to the river to do washes.

III

One of these laundresses, who was, to use a fashionable expression, a "very likeable lass," was returning one day at nightfall from washing the princess's tear-stained handkerchiefs in the river.

Halfway back, but still quite distant from the city gates, she felt a little tired and sat down at the foot of a tree. She took an orange from her pocket and was going to peel it in order to eat it, when the fruit slipped from her hands and began to roll downhill with exceptional speed. The girl ran after her orange, but the more she ran the more the orange got ahead, without ever stopping and without her catching up, even if she did not lose sight of it. Tired of running, and suspecting, although little experienced in the things of the world, that that orange on the run was not altogether natural, the poor thing stopped now and then and considered giving up her chase, but the orange also stopped, and instantly, as if it had already halted its movement and was inviting its owner to pick it up again. She would manage to touch it with her hand, but the orange would slip away from her anew and continue on its way.

The little laundress was engrossed in this extraordinary chase when she finally noticed that she was in a dense forest, and that night was falling, as black as pitch. Fear gripped her then and she burst into tears of distress. The darkness grew rapidly, not allowing her to see the orange or get her bearings or find the path to retrace her steps.

So on she went, wandering aimlessly, disconsolate, dying of hunger, and dog-tired, when she glimpsed a few brilliant points of light not very far away. She imagined that they were from the city, and, giving thanks to God, made her way toward them. But how great must have been her surprise upon finding herself, after a short stretch and without exiting the dense forest, at the doors of the most sumptuous of palaces, which shone so brightly that it looked like a glittering diamond, and in comparison with which the splendid castle of the Fortunate King would pass for a squalid hut.

There was neither a sentry nor a doorman, not even servants to prevent entry, and the girl, who was not fainthearted, and who felt moreover the stimulus of curiosity and the desire to find shelter and eat something, crossed the threshold, climbed a wide and luxurious polished jasper staircase, and began to roam about the most magnificent and most elegant salons imaginable, although always without seeing a soul. The salons were, however, profusely illuminated by a thousand gold lamps, whose scented oil emitted a delicate fragrance. The exquisite furnishings and *objets d'art* found in the salons were sufficient to take away the breath not only of the little laundress, but of Queen Victoria herself, who would have confessed the relative inferiority of English industry, and would have given patents and medals to the inventors and makers of all those articles.

The laundress admired them at her leisure, and while admiring them she progressed little by little toward a spot from which came the rich, luscious, and delicious aroma of food. Thus did she arrive at the kitchen, but there were neither chefs, nor undercooks, nor scullions, nor dishwashers in it—everything was deserted, like the rest of the palace. Nonetheless, the hearth, the oven, and the firepans were all burning, and cooking in them were an infinite number of pots, casseroles, and other vessels. Our adventurous lass lifted the cover of one casserole and saw in it several eels; she lifted another one and saw a deboned boar's head stuffed with pheasant breasts and truffles; in short, she saw the most exquisite dishes that grace the tables of kings, queens, emperors, and popes. And she even saw some dishes alongside which regal and papal blancmange would be rustic, as would be alongside the latter stewed kidney beans or gazpacho.

Cheered by what she saw and smelled, the girl armed herself with a knife and fork and flew at the boar's head. But no sooner had she reached it than she received a blow on her hands, a blow seemingly administered by another hand, powerful and invisible, whereupon she heard a voice saying to her, so close that she felt the movement of air and the warm, live breath of the words:

"Stop, because it is for my lord the prince!"

She then headed for some salmon trout, considering them a less princely dish and one that she would be allowed to eat, but the invisible hand again punished her boldness, and the mysterious voice repeated to her:

"Stop, because it is for my lord the prince!"

Finally, she tried her luck with a third, fourth, and fifth dish, but the same thing always happened; wherefore she had to resign herself, with considerable regret, to fasting, and left the kitchen in despair.

Then she passed again through the salons, where the same mysterious solitude always reigned and where the most profound silence seemed to have its dwelling, and she arrived at the prettiest of bedrooms, in which only two or three candles, contained and dimmed in alabaster vases, shed a vague, voluptuous light that invited repose and sleep. In this bedroom there was such a soft, comfortable bed that our laundress, who was exhausted, could not resist the temptation of stretching out on it and resting. She was going to put her intention into effect and had already sat down and was getting ready to stretch out, when on the same part of her body with which she had just touched the bed, she felt a painful sting, as if she were being pricked with a good-sized pin, and again heard a voice saying:

"Stop, because it is for my lord the prince!"

Needless to say, the little laundress became alarmed and grieved over this, resigning herself to not sleeping, as she had resigned herself to not eating, and in order to take her mind off her hunger and sleepiness she began to inspect every object in the bedroom, and her curiosity even led her to raise the draperies and tapestries.

Behind the latter our heroine discovered an exquisite little secret door made of sandalwood, with mother-of-pearl inlay. She pushed it gently, and when it gave way she found herself on a spiral staircase of white marble. She descended it without stopping at what looked like a greenhouse, where the most exotic plants and aromatic flowers grew, and at whose center stood an immense basin, fashioned, by the look if it, from a single, clear, diaphanous topaz. From the middle of the basin rose a jet of water as gigantic as the one in place today at Madrid's Puerta del Sol, but with the difference that the water of the Puerta del Sol is natural and ordinary, whereas that of the basin was scented, and had in it furthermore all the colors of the rainbow and its own light, which, as the reader can imagine, gave it a most alluring appearance.

Even the murmur made by the water as it fell sounded more musical and melodious than the ones produced by other waters, and it seemed as though the jet sang some of Mozart's or Bellini's most love-inspired songs.

The laundress was absorbed in gazing at all that beauty and enjoying all that harmony when she heard a great racket and saw a glass window open. She hurriedly hid behind a mass of greenery so as not to be seen and to be able to see the people or creatures who were undoubtedly approaching.

And they were three extremely rare and pretty birds, one of them all green, and bright like an emerald. In him the laundress thought she saw, with noteworthy contentment, the one who was the cause, according to what everybody maintained, of the persistent ailment of the Fortunate Princess. The other two birds were not, by any means, as lovely, but they did not want for a singular kind of attraction. All three flew in very swiftly, and all three swooped down on the topaz basin and dived into it.

Shortly afterward the laundress saw, rising from the diaphanous bosom of the water, three youths who were so handsome, well-built, and fair that they looked like exotic statues carved by an expert hand from rose-tinted marble. For the sake of truth it ought to be said that the girl had never seen naked men, and that from seeing her father, her brothers, and their friends, both fully dressed and partially dressed, she could not deduce to what degree masculine human beauty was capable of being elevated; she imagined, therefore, that she was gazing at three immortal genies or three angels from heaven. So without blushing she continued to gaze at them with considerable pleasure, like saintly and in no wise sinful objects. But the three youths came out of the water at once and dressed in elegant clothes.

One of them, the handsomest of the three, was wearing an emerald diadem on his head, and was revered by the others as sovereign. If when naked he looked, by virtue of his handsomeness, like an angel or a genie to the little laundress, when dressed he dazzled her with his majesty, and he looked, in her eyes, like the emperor of the world and the most adorable prince on Earth.

Those gentlemen went straight off to the dining room and sat down at a splendid table, where three place settings had been laid. Invisible, subdued music greeted them upon arrival and gladdened their ears as they ate. Servants, also invisible, came and went with the dishes, serving the table admirably. All this was witnessed and observed by the little laundress who, without being seen or heard, had followed those gentlemen and was hiding in the dining room behind the curtains.

From there she managed to overhear some of the conversation, and learned that the handsomest of the youths was the crown prince of the great empire of China, and that one of the other two was his secretary and one his most beloved page, all three of whom were enchanted and transformed into birds during the day, and only at night regained their natural state, following the bath in the fountain.

The curious laundress likewise observed that the Prince of Emeralds barely ate, even though his intimates begged him to do so, and that he appeared melancholy and entranced, at times exhaling a passionate sigh from the depths of his beautiful chest.

IV

The chronicles that we are extracting relate that at the end of that sumptuous but not very gay feast, the Prince of Emeralds, coming around as if from some dream, raised his voice and said:

"Secretary, bring me the little box of my amusements."

The secretary rose from the table and shortly thereafter returned with the most stunning little box that mortal eyes have ever seen. The one in which Alexander enclosed the *Iliad* was, by comparison with it, cruder and tackier than a nougat box from Jijona.

The prince took the little box in his hands, opened it, and spent a long time contemplating its contents. Then he put his hand in the little box and withdrew a cord. He kissed it passionately, shed tears of tenderness over it, and exclaimed these words:

> Ay, little cord of my lady fair!
> If only I could see her there!

He replaced the cord in the little box and removed from it an immaculate, embroidered garter. He kissed it, caressed it, and also exclaimed while putting it to his lips:

> Ay, lovely garter of my lady fair!
> If only I could see her there!

Finally, he took out a precious locket, and if he kissed the cord and garter a lot, he kissed the locket more and caressed it still more than he kissed it, saying in a tone so doleful that it broke hearts and even stones:

> Ay, locket of my lady fair!
> If only I could see her there!

Shortly afterwards the prince and his two intimates retired to their bedrooms, and the little laundress did not dare to follow them. Seeing herself alone in the dining room, she approached the table where there still remained, almost untouched, the rich dishes, sweets, fruits, and full-bodied, sparkling wines; but the recollection of the mysterious voice and invisible hand stopped her and obliged her to content herself with looking and smelling.

In order to enjoy this incomplete delight, she got so close to the dishes that she ended up standing between the table and the prince's chair. Then she felt, not just one, but two invisible hands resting on her shoulders and clutching her. The mysterious voice said:

"Sit down and eat."

Whereupon she found herself seated in the same chair as the prince, and, authorized by the voice, started eating with a ravenous appetite, which the novelty and exquisiteness of the food made even greater, and after eating she fell into a deep sleep.

When the laundress awoke, it was well past dawn. She opened her eyes and found herself in the middle of the country, stretched out at the foot of the tree where she had wanted to eat her orange. The clothes that she had brought from the river were there, and even the fleet-footed orange was there.

Could it all have been a dream? wondered the little laundress. "I would like to return to the palace of the crown prince of China to make sure that those magnificent things are real and not dreamed up."

So saying, she began throwing the orange to the ground to see if it would again show her the way, but the orange would roll a little and stop in a hole or at some obstacle, or when it lost momentum. In short, the orange did what all oranges, in identical circumstances, ordinarily do. There was nothing strange or marvelous about its conduct.

Turning indignant, the girl split the orange and saw that on the inside it was like all others. So she ate it and it tasted the same to her as every orange she had eaten previously.

Now she scarcely doubted that she had been dreaming.

"I haven't a single thing," she said, "with which to convince myself of the reality of what I've seen. But I'll go to the princess and tell her the whole story because it might be important to her."

V

While the not very ordinary events that have been related were occurring, in dreams or in reality, the Fortunate Princess, exhausted from so much crying, slept peacefully; and although it was already eight o'clock in the morning, an hour when everybody was usually up and had even breakfasted in that age, the princess did not stir and remained in bed.

So undoubtedly her favorite maid considered the news very interesting indeed when she dared to awaken her. The girl entered her bedroom, opened the window, and exclaimed joyfully:

"My lady, my lady, wake up and rejoice, for there is someone here who brings you news of the green bird."

The princess awoke, rubbed her eyes, sat up, and said:

"Have the seven sages who went to Sabean country returned?"

"Nothing of the sort," the maid replied. "The person bringing you the news is one of the laundresses who wash Your Highness's tear-stained handkerchiefs."

"Send her in at once."

As she was already behind a door awaiting this permission, the laundress entered and began to relate in great detail and ease of manner all that had happened to her.

Upon hearing of the appearance of the green bird, the princess was overcome with joy, and upon learning of his emergence from the water transformed into a handsome prince, she turned as red as a lobster, a heavenly and loving smile played about her lips, and her eyes closed gently, as if to become absorbed in herself and see the prince with the eyes of her soul. Lastly, upon finding out about the high esteem, veneration, and fondness that the prince had for her, and the love and care with which he guarded the three stolen articles in his precious little box of amusements, the young princess, despite her modesty, could not contain herself; she hugged and kissed the laundress and the maid and indulged in other no less excusable, innocent, and sensitive extremes.

"Now," she said, "I really can call myself the 'Fortunate Princess.' This whim to possess the green bird wasn't a whim, it was love. It was and is a love that by a mysterious and not customary route has penetrated my heart. I've not seen the prince, and I believe he's handsome. I've not spoken to him, and I presume he's discreet. I don't know about the events of his life, except that he's enchanted and that he has me enchanted, and I take it for granted that he's brave, generous, and loyal."

"My lady," said the laundress, "I can assure Your Highness that the prince, if my vision is not a vain dream, cuts a splendid figure, and he has such a sweet, kind face that it's a joy to behold. The secretary isn't bad-looking either, but the one—and I don't know why—that I've taken a liking to is the page."

"You shall marry the page," replied the princess. "My maid, if she pleases, shall marry the secretary, and both of you shall be mandarins and ladies-in-waiting in my court. Your dream was not a dream, but reality. My heart tells me so. What matters now is disenchanting the three bird youths."

"And how will we be able to disenchant them?" asked the favorite maid.

"I myself," the princess answered, "shall go to the palace in which they live and there we shall see. You will guide me, my laundress."

The latter, who had not finished her story, told the rest of it and explained why she could not serve as a guide.

The princess listened to her very attentively, meditated a while, and then said to the maid:

"Go to my library and bring me the book entitled *Contemporary Kings* and the *Astronomical Almanac.*"

When these volumes were brought to her, the princess leafed through that of the *Kings* and read aloud the following lines:

The same day that the Emperor of China died, his only son, who was to succeed him, disappeared from the court and all of the empire. His subjects, believing him dead, have had to submit to the Khan of Tartar.

"What do you make of this, my lady?" asked the maid.

"What am I to make of it," replied the Fortunate Princess, "except that the Khan of Tartar is the one who enchanted my prince to usurp the crown from him? This explains why I loathe the Tartar prince so much. Now I understand everything."

"But it's not enough to understand it; we must also set it right," said the laundress.

"That is my intention," the princess continued, "and to do so, we must send two hundred armed men at once, men who inspire the greatest trust, to all the roads and crossroads along which can travel the mail that the Tartar prince sent to his father the king to consult him about the case of the green bird. Their letters shall be seized and turned over to me. If the messengers resist, they shall be killed; if they yield, they shall be imprisoned and held incommunicado, so that nobody will learn what is happening. Not even the king my father is to know. We shall arrange everything amongst the three of us with the greatest secrecy. Here's enough money to buy the silence, loyalty, and energy of the men who are to execute my plan."

And indeed, the princess, who had already risen and was in a dressing gown and slippers, took from a cabinet two big bags filled with gold and gave them to her confidantes.

The maid and laundress left at once to get things under way, and the Fortunate Princess stayed behind deep in study of the *Astronomical Almanac*.

VI

Five days had passed since the action of the previous scene. The princess had not cried in all that time, provoking not a little amazement and pleasure in her father the king. She had even been jovial and jestful, thereby giving a glimmer of hope to the suitor princes that she would finally decide on one of them, because suitors always have high expectations.

No one had suspected the cause of such a sudden turnaround and such unforeseen relief in the princess.

Only the Tartar prince, who was diabolically astute, feared, albeit in a very vague way, that the princess had received some news of the green bird. This same prince had, moreover, the mysterious premonition of a great misfortune, and had divined by magic, which his father had taught him, that in the green bird he should see an enemy. Figuring, furthermore, like a Tartar who knew the road and the amount of time needed to cover it, that the messengers he sent to his father should be returning that very day, and anxious to learn what the latter had to say about his consultation, he mounted his horse at dawn and, with forty of his men, all of them well-armed, left to meet up with the above-mentioned messengers.

But although the Tartar prince left in great secrecy, the Fortunate Princess, who had spies and, to quote a popular saying, "had her ear to the ground," learned at once of his departure, and summoned the laundress and maid to a council.

When they were present, she said to them in an anguished voice:

"My situation is dreadful. Three times I have gone to throw an orange under the tree where the laundress threw hers, but to no avail, because the orange has refused to guide me to my lover's castle. I have neither seen him nor been able to learn how to disenchant him. I have only learned, through the *Astronomical Almanac*, that the night the laundress saw him was the spring equinox. Mayhap it won't be possible to see him again until the next equinox of the same season, and by then the Tartar prince will have killed him. The prince will kill him as soon as he receives the letter from his father, and he has gone after it with forty of his men."

"Grieve not, beautiful princess," said the favorite maid. "Three parties of one hundred men are waiting for the messengers at various points to seize the letter from them and bring it to you. The three hundred are valiant, carry well-tempered arms, and will not let themselves be defeated by the Tartar prince despite all his magic."

"Nevertheless, I am of the opinion," added the laundress, "that more men ought to be sent against the Tartar. Even though, in truth, the prince has only forty of his with him, all of them, it is said, have cuirasses and enchanted arrows that make each one the equivalent of ten."

The laundress's prudent counsel was adopted immediately. The princess had her father's most gallant and skilled general come secretly to her room. She related to him everything that was happening, opened her troubled heart to him, and asked his support. He offered it to her and, hastily gathering a large troop of soldiers, left the capital determined to die in the attempt or to bring to the princess the Khan of Tartar's letter as well as the Khan's son, dead or alive.

After the general's departure, the princess deemed it advisable to inform the Fortunate King of all that had occurred. The monarch flew into a rage. He said that the entire story of the green bird was a ridiculous dream that she and the laundress had had, and he bemoaned the fact that his daughter, acting on the basis of said dream, had sent so many assassins against an illustrious prince, thereby trampling the laws of hospitality, peoples' rights, and all moral precepts.

"Ay, my daughter!" he exclaimed. "You have attached a bloody stigma to my honorable name if this is not remedied."

The princess also became distressed and regretted what she had done. Despite her passionate love for the crown prince of China, she now preferred to leave him eternally enchanted to having a single drop of blood spilled over that love.

Thus it was that dispatches were sent to the general instructing him not to join battle, but it was all in vain. The general had ridden so fast that there was no way to overtake him. They did not have telegraphs back then and the dispatches could not be delivered. When the messengers arrived where the general was, they saw all the king's soldiers fleeing and so they followed suit. The forty in the Tartar escort, who were so many more genies, were giving them chase, transformed into horrible, fantastic monsters spouting fire from their mouths.

Only the general, whose gallantry, calmness, and skill at arms bordered on the superhuman, remained undaunted in the face of that most excusable terror. The general went for the prince, the only nonfantastic enemy with whom he could have it out, and began to wage the fiercest and most singular battle with him. But the Tartar prince's arms were enchanted, and the general could not wound him. Recognizing then that it was impossible to finish the prince off without resorting to a stratagem, he retreated a considerable stretch from his adversary and quickly untied a long and strong silk sash that girded his waist; unnoticed, he made a running knot with it, rode back toward the prince with incredible speed, looped the knot around his neck, and continued pressing his horse at a gallop, pulling the prince off his mount and dragging him along the ground.

And in this way the general strangled the Tartar. No sooner did he die than the genies disappeared, and the soldiers of the Fortunate King regrouped and rejoined their commander. The latter waited with them for the envoys who were bringing the Khan of Tartar's letter, and who did not make them wait long.

At nightfall of that very same day the general entered the palace of the Fortunate King with the Khan of Tartar's letter in his hand. Making a graceful and respectful bow, he gave it to the princess.

The anxious maiden broke the seal and began to read, but to no avail, for she did not understand a word. The same thing happened to the Fortunate King. They then summoned all the employees who worked as interpreters, and they could not decipher that script either. Afterwards members of the twelve royal academies came, and they found themselves similarly stymied.

The seven sages, so expert in linguistics, who had just arrived without the phoenix, and who were therefore condemned to death, also tried their luck; but although they were promised a pardon if they read that letter, they failed to do so, and could not even say in what language it was written.

The Fortunate King then believed himself the most unfortunate of all kings; he regretted having been an accomplice in a useless crime, and feared the revenge of the powerful Khan of Tartar. That night he did not fall asleep until very late.

Even so, his sorrow became much more acute when, upon awakening very early the following morning, he learned that the princess had disappeared, leaving him this note:

Father, do not search for me and do not attempt to find out where I am going if you do not want to see me dead. Let it be enough for you to know that I am alive and that I am in good health, although you will not see me again until I have deciphered the Khan's mysterious letter and disenchanted my beloved prince. Farewell.

VII

The Fortunate Princess had gone with her two friends, on foot and on pilgrimage, to visit a saintly hermit who lived in the wilderness and ruggedness of some towering mountains that rose a short distance from the capital.

Even if the princess and her friends had wished to ride to the hermitage, it would not have been possible. The way was more suited to goats than camels, elephants, horses, mules, and asses, if the reader will pardon the last word, which were the quadrupeds usually ridden in that kingdom. For this reason, and out of devoutness, the princess went on foot with no other retinue than her two confidantes.

The hermit they were going to visit was a very penitent old man in the odor of sanctity. The common people also claimed that the hermit was immortal, and they did not lack reasonable grounds for such a claim. There was no recollection anywhere in those parts of when the hermit went to settle in the depths of that sierra, where only rarely did humans lay eyes on him.

The princess and her friends, attracted by the fame of his virtue and his knowledge, searched for him for seven days in that rough, craggy terrain. During the day they walked through scrub and undergrowth; at night they took refuge in the hollows of the rocks. There was nobody to guide them, as much because of the dense patches of brushwood, where not even goatherds trod, as because of the fear inspired by the curse of the hermit, who was quick to cast it on whoever invaded his temporal domain, or on whoever disturbed him in his prayers. It should be noted that the hermit was pagan, and that despite the natural goodness of his soul, his terrible, somber religion obliged him to call down curses and utter imprecations. But the three friends, imagining, as though by inspiration, that only the hermit could decipher the letter for them, decided to brave his curses and searched for him, as has been said, for seven days.

On the night of the seventh, the three pilgrims were going to take refuge in a cave in order to sleep, when they came upon the hermit himself, praying at the back. A lamp illuminated that mysterious retreat with a melancholy, unsteady flame.

The three trembled at the prospect of being cursed, and almost regretted having gone there. But the hermit, whose beard was whiter than snow, whose skin was more wrinkled than a raisin, and whose body resembled a wasted skeleton, fixed a penetrating gaze on them with eyes that, although deep-set, shone like two live coals, and said in a soft, glad, clear voice:

"Thank heaven you're finally here. I've been waiting for you for one hundred years. I've wished for death, but could not die until fulfilling with you an obligation imposed on me by the king of genies. I am the only sage who still speaks and understands the exceptionally rich language that was spoken in Babel before the confusion. Each word of this language is an effective conjuration that compels or causes the infernal powers to serve whoever speaks it. The words of this language have the virtue of tying and untying all the knots and laws that unite and govern natural things. The cabala is but a highly crude imitation of this fertile, incommunicable tongue. Its extremely imperfect and impoverished dialects are today's most beautiful and complete languages. Contemporary science is a lie and charlatanism compared with the science that was intrinsic to that language. Every utterance in this tongue contains in its letters the essence of the thing named along with its hidden properties. All things, hearing themselves called by their real names, obey whoever calls them. Such was the power of humankind when it possessed this language that it attempted to scale heaven, and would undoubtedly have succeeded if heaven had not ordained that the primitive language be forgotten.

"Only three well-meaning sages, of whom two have already died, preserved that tongue in their memories. By special privilege of the devils, Nemrod and his descendants likewise preserved it. But the last of the latter died a week ago, which was your doing, oh Fortunate Princess, and now there remains only one person in the world who can decipher the Khan of Tartar's letter. That person is I, and in order to do you this service, the king of genies has preserved my life for centuries."

"Here is the letter, oh venerable and profound sage!" said the princess, placing the mysterious piece of writing in the hermit's hands.

"I am going to decipher it for you at once," responded the hermit, who put on his spectacles and drew close to the lamp in order to read. And for more than two hours he read aloud in the language in which the letter was written. With each word that he spoke, the universe shook, the stars clouded over with mortal pallor, the moon trembled in the sky, as its image trembles on the waves of the ocean, and the princess and her friends had to close their eyes and cover their ears to keep from seeing the specters that appeared and hearing the sorrowful, terrible, or portentous voices that rose from the very bowels of a disturbed nature.

When he finished reading, the hermit removed his spectacles and said in a quiet voice:

"It is not right or fitting or possible, oh Fortunate Princess, for you to know everything contained in this abominable letter. It is neither right nor fitting, because in it there are frightful and fiendish mysteries; it is not possible, because in all the human languages that are spoken nowadays these mysteries are ineffable, inexpressible, and even inexplicable. Humankind, through its incomplete and feeble sense of reason, will come to know, when millions of years pass, some of the rudiments of things, but it will always be ignorant of the substance that I know, that the Khan of Tartar knows, and that the early sages knew, the sages who availed themselves, for their 'lucubrations,' of this perfect language which is now intransmissible on account of our sins."

"Well, we're in a pretty pickle," said the laundress, "if after what we've gone through to find you, what with you being the only person who can translate that muddled letter, you now tell us that you don't want to translate it."

"I neither want to nor ought to," retorted the venerable and centuries-old hermit, "but I will say what the letter contains of interest to all of you, and I will say it in few words, without going into chapter and verse, because the minutes of my life are numbered and my death approaches.

"The prince of China, because of his virtues, talent, and handsomeness, is the favorite of the king of genies, who has rescued him a thousand times from the attempts made on his life by the Khan of Tartar. Seeing that it was impossible for him to kill the prince, the Khan decided to avail himself of a spell to keep him far away from his subjects and reign in his place in the celestial empire. The Khan would certainly have wanted this spell to be indestructible and everlasting, but he could not manage it in spite of his marvelous knowledge of magic. The king of genies opposed his evil designs, and although he could not completely negate his enchantments and conjurations, he knew how to divest them of a great part of their wickedness.

"The prince, although transformed into a bird, was given the faculty for regaining his real form at night. The prince also had a palace where he could live and be accorded all the honors, luxury, and attention due to his august station. Lastly, his disenchantment was agreed to if the following conditions were met, conditions which the Khan considered impossible to meet because of the bad opinion that he holds of women, and because of how perverted and depraved the human race is in general.

"The first condition, already met, was that a twenty-year-old woman, discreet, spirited, and passionate, and of the lowest social class, see the three enchanted youths, who are the handsomest ones in the world, emerge from the basin naked, and that the purity and chastity of her soul be such that they would not be disturbed or tarnished by the slightest stimulus of lewdness. This test was to be undertaken on the spring equinox, when all of nature excites love. The woman was to have felt it for their handsomeness, and to have admired the handsomeness intensely, but in a saintly, spiritual way.

"The second condition, also met already, was that the prince, able to show himself for only three brief moments, and then in the shape of a green bird, inspire in a princess of his class a love that was as fervent and chaste as it was enduring.

"The third condition, which is being met now, was that the princess get hold of this letter, and that I interpret it.

"The fourth and last condition, which to be met calls for the intervention of all three of the maidens who are listening to me, is as follows. I have only two minutes of life left, but before dying I will place you in the prince's palace, beside the topaz basin. The birds will go there and dive into it and be transformed into extremely handsome youths. The three of you will see them, but you are to preserve, when seeing them, all the chastity of your thoughts and all the virginity of your souls, loving, nonetheless, each of you one of them, with an innocent, saintly love. The princess already loves the prince of China, and the laundress the page, and both have shown the innocence of their love; now the princess's favorite maid needs to fall in love with the secretary in the same manner. When the three enchanted youths go to the dining room, you will follow them, without being seen, and you will stay there until the prince asks for the box of his amusements and says, kissing the little cord:

> Ay, little cord of my lady fair!
> If only I could see her there!

The princess, then, and the two of you with her, will show yourselves at once, and each of you will plant a tender kiss on the left cheek of the object of your love. The spell will be broken instantaneously, the Khan of Tartar will die all of a sudden, and the prince of China will not only possess the celestial empire, but will likewise inherit all the khanates, kingdoms, and provinces possessed in his own right by that diabolical enchanter."

No sooner did the hermit finish saying these words than he made a very odd face, started to open his mouth, stretched his legs, and breathed his last.

Suddenly the princess and her friends found themselves behind a mass of greenery, beside the topaz basin.

Everything came true as the hermit had said.

The three maidens were in love, and were as chaste and innocent as could be. Not even at the awkward moment of giving the soft, tight-lipped kiss did they feel more than a deep stirring that was all mystical and pure.

Thus it was that the three youths became immediately disenchanted. China and Tartar were happy under the prince's scepter; and the princess and her friends were even more happy married to such good-looking men. The Fortunate King abdicated and went to live at his son-in-law's court, which was in Peking. The general who killed the Tartar prince received all the decorations of China, the title of first mandarin, and a pension of thousands and thousands for him and his heirs.

Lastly, it is said that the Fortunate Princess and the emperor of China lived happily for many, many years, and had half a dozen children, each one as beautiful as the other. The laundress and the maid, with their respective husbands, always continued to enjoy their Majesties' favor and to be the foremost personages in all of that land.

Madrid, 1860

Juan Valera

"The Wizard"

THE castle stood on top of the hill, and although on the outside it appeared to be half in ruins, it was said that on the inside there were still very elegant and comfortable, if not spacious, accommodations.

Nobody dared to live there, no doubt on account of the terror produced by anything that had to do with the castle. For centuries a cruel tyrant, the powerful Wizard, had lived in it. With his dark arts he had managed to prolong his life way beyond the limits that nature normally grants to human beings.

People claimed something still more extraordinary. People claimed that the Wizard had not died, but had only changed the conditions of his life—from open, clear ones to hidden, sinister, and barely or rarely perceptible ones. And woe betide the person who chanced to see him wandering through the woods, or suddenly glimpsed his face, illuminated by a moonbeam, or, without seeing him, heard him singing in the distance, in the silence of the night! Whoever experienced such an occurrence either lost his mind or underwent a thousand other tragic misfortunes. Thus it was that for upwards of seventy-five miles around it became a commonplace to declare that every girl who was downcast, absentminded, and haggard, everyone who was melancholy and emaciated, everyone who died young, and everyone who sought death or committed suicide, had seen or heard the Wizard.

With such an evil reputation, which persisted and spread in an age when people were more credulous than today, nobody dared to occupy the castle, and solitude and wilderness reigned on all sides. At its back were the highlands, with deep valleys, twisty gullies, and narrow gorges, as well as several tall mountains covered with dense thickets, in front of which the hill on which the castle rose looked like an advance guard.

No human dwelling could be sighted anywhere in a radius of five or six miles, save a modest farmhouse, almost at the end of a pine grove, that had a view of the main façade of the castle. The farmhouse's owners, who had been living in it for twelve years, were a still relatively young married couple who came from the nearest village.

The husband had spent years traveling, trading, or soldiering, according to what people claimed, far off in the Indies. And the fact is that he had returned with some of fortune's riches.

Over and above the prestige that wealth usually brings (and his comfort and leisure were considered wealth in the humble village where he had been born), several good qualities stood out in this man, whom the locals, because they assumed he had been in the Indies, called the *Indiano*. And this *Indiano*, who was still young, strong, and adept at all physical exercises, had a very proud bearing and seemed to be brave and discreet.

Almost all the single girls in the village wanted him for a husband. So he was able to select, and did select, the one who passed for and undoubtedly was the prettiest, taking her for his wife, with not a little envy and even bitter sorrow on the part of some other aspirants.

No sooner did he marry than the *Indiano* went with his wife to live in the farmhouse that he had bought shortly before the wedding. There he owned, grew, or obtained with little effort all that one requires for country comfort and healthy pleasure. A clear brook, whose water was fresher and more plentiful in the summer on account of the melting snow, emptied into several channels and irrigated the vegetable and flower garden. On the hillside he had almond, cherry, and other fruit trees, and on the banks of the brook and the irrigation channels, apple mists, violets, and a thousand fragrant herbs flourished. There were beehives, in which the industrious bees made wax and honey scented by the rosemary and thyme that sprouted on the surrounding slopes. The poultry pen, at a remove from the house, was full of hens and turkeys; the cattle shed sheltered three magnificent cows that gave delicious milk, and the stable housed two splendid horses; and in a separate pen wallowed a small drove of pigs that fed now on beans, now on the tasty acorns of an adjacent oak grove. There were, in addition, a few small fields sown with wheat, chickpeas, and kidney beans, and lastly, down in the hollow a luxuriant little copse full of black poplars and willows toward whose center ran the brook, first forming foamy waterfalls and then still ponds. And since the *Indiano* was a skilled hunter, rabbits, partridges, wild ducks, and even big game appeared on his table.

Thus had husband and wife been living, as I've said, for twelve years, their solitude gladdened by their only child, a pretty girl going on eleven. The histories that we have consulted do not give the daughter's name, but so as to facilitate our narrative we shall call her Silveria.

It can be stated outright, without any exaggeration, that Silveria was a gem, a truly delightful girl. She had grown up in the outdoors, but neither the sun's burning rays nor other kinds of inclement weather had ever adversely affected the delicacy of her fresh and still childish beauty. As if by magic, the rosy whiteness of her complexion stayed clear and resplendent. Her eyes were blue like the sky, and her hair golden like ears of corn in August.

Mayhap, when we were children, we were pampered and spoiled a great deal by our parents. In any event, who has not known pampered, spoiled children? And nonetheless, it would not be easy for anyone to imagine and emphasize sufficiently just how pampered and spoiled Silveria was. The mother, by reason of sweet apathy and weakness of character, let her do whatever she felt like; and the father, who was imperious, who worshiped his daughter and took pride in the fact that she resembled him in her resolve and determination, and in the brave decisiveness with which she always tried to do exactly as she pleased, far from restraining her, would as a matter of course encourage her and give her free rein. Thus it was that when the father went away, and he went away often to go hunting and on other outings, it looked as though he tacitly transmitted all of his authority to the girl. As a result Silveria seemed like an absolute little queen, but so generous and noble was the natural state of her spirit that her absolutism did not lessen the love and respect that she had for her mother, nor did she ever take advantage of the wide freedom that she enjoyed to do anything bad.

The only servants at the farmhouse were the mistress's old wet nurse, who doubled as cook and housekeeper; her grown-up daughter, who, although very simple, worked hard and washed and ironed well; and the wet nurse's elderly husband, who acted as farmhand, swineherd, and cowman.

Silveria, inasmuch as she had been raised in that rustic isolation, speaking to practically no one except the servants and her parents, was a singular example of naive innocence. She had formed a very carefree and poetic concept of nature, and instead of suspecting or distrusting something, she was game for everything and mistrusted nothing. She imagined that whatever was natural existed for her pleasure, and that it did its utmost to gratify her. How, then, was the supernatural to be less obliging and benign? Hence, without an exact realization of such reasoning, but rather from instinct, Silveria did not get frightened at nocturnal darkness or at the vague and mysterious noises made by water as it runs and wind as it stirs leaves. She had heard a thousand horrors about the Wizard himself, and instead of causing her dread, he instilled in her a desire to come upon him and get to know him and have contact with him. She imagined that he was being maligned, and that he couldn't be as wicked as people claimed.

Her mother said that the Wizard no longer tormented her, but that during the early years of her marriage and her residence at the farmhouse, he had done so considerably. Mayhap, at night, she had heard his voice singing melancholy songs; mayhap the sad, magical sound of his melodious violin had reached as far as her ears; mayhap she had caught a glimpse of him, in the glimmer of starlight, as he crossed the forest and arrived at a clearing, where there were no oak, pine, or fir trees. Then the mother said that her blood would run cold, and that she felt anxiety, the kind of anxiety that must be caused by remorse over the offense of seeing and hearing, and that she would close doors and windows so that the Wizard would not come in search of her.

Silveria did not understand what her mother said, or she understood it the wrong way; neither in the singing nor in the playing of the violin could she discern anything frightful or sinful, and the only thing that grieved her was that said music—the source, in her view, of groundless fears—never sounded any more, or at least never reached her ears.

Without the slightest apprehension, then, Silveria would leave the house, where her mother was distracted and caught up in chores, and explore all those hills and dells, jumping and frolicking like a nimble doe. One of the things she liked most was going to the foot of the castle, which wasn't far, and whose battlements and towers, and even the main façade, with its big ogival windows, looming above the mass of greenery, could be made out clearly from the very room in which she slept.

In front of the castle there was a broad pool with clear, pure water, because the abundant brook that irrigated the garden, flowing in and out, replenished the water continually. In that pool, like in a mirror, one could look with pleasure at the castle's reflection. And, fantastically lighting up its bottom and lending it the appearance of infinite depth, the divine breadth of the heavens shimmered on its surface. All around there were, besides the ilexes and oaks of the woods, willow, fig, pomegranate, and locust trees, along with the lush growth of other plants and herbs.

One cool April morning, Silveria was wandering about that secluded, solitary spot, picking lilies, violets, and roses that flourished in abundance and filled the atmosphere with their scents.

Unexpectedly she heard a sudden noise and went to hide in some bushes. Then she saw a man arrive on horseback, dismount, and tie the horse's reins to a branch. He was in the prime of life, and dressed in black, his very handsome face visible under his wide-brimmed, plumed hat. He had a genteel bearing and his gold spurs jingled with each graceful step that he took.

The stranger's look was not calculated to frighten anyone, so Silveria, who didn't have a timid bone in her body, came out of her hiding place and, approaching the newcomer, said to him:

"A good morning to the gentleman."

Surprised by that sudden appearance, the stranger asked:

"And who might you be, little girl?"

"I'm Silveria," she replied. "I'm the *Indiano*'s daughter and I live only a stone's throw from here. If the grove wasn't in the way, my house could be seen. And is the gentleman, by some chance, the magician that people talk about so much?"

"No, I'm not the magician, but I am looking for him. And tell me, what are you doing here?"

"Me? What would I be doing except . . . gathering flowers. There are scads of them here. And such pretty ones! Look, look at how many I've gathered!" And extending her arms and spreading her apron, she showed him the flowers that she had. "Take the ones you want."

"Thank you," said the gentleman. And taking from the apron two of the lilies with the longest stems, he removed his hat, inserted the flowers alongside the feathers, and put his hat back on.

Mayhap the girl noticed, when the gentleman's head was bare, that his hair was black and curled into ringlets, his brow white and serene, and his eyes gentle and sad. In any case, feeling more confident, Silveria said to him:

"Even though he may accuse me of being excessively curious, will the gentleman please tell me what the devil he's doing in this out-of-the-way place?"

Silveria's imperious assurance and innocent self-confidence amused the gentleman, and, with a smile on his face, he answered:

"I've bought this castle, my dear, and I'm coming to live here. My servants will arrive with the baggage. Since I was impatient to see it, I got ahead of them at a gallop."

"Ay! And I've never seen the castle because it's locked up. Let me see it."

"How so? You're not afraid?"

"Of what?"

"Then come with me. Here are the keys. We'll unlock the door, go in, and see all of it."

Said and done. The young gentleman unlocked it, and, accompanied by Silveria, surveyed the inside of the castle. As soon as they climbed the elegant staircase, they saw finely furnished rooms on the second floor, although everything was covered with cobwebs and dust. From the central window, located above the entry door and in the best room, both became enraptured upon contemplating the magnificent view. They looked out over rivers and brooks, pleasant expanses, farms and distant villages, and, on the horizon, blue mountains whose peaks were outlined or faded away in the spotless azure of the diaphanous sky, clear of clouds and gilded by the sun at that hour. All around there rose, like a sea of greenery, the packed crowns of the trees that surrounded the castle, and, not very far away, at the end of the woods, Silveria's small farmhouse.

"That's where I live," she said to the stranger, pointing to the dwelling with her slender little index finger.

The stranger looked at the farmhouse, but before he could say a word, Silveria exclaimed:

"I must have my head in the clouds! For sure it's almost nine o'clock . . . breakfast time. My father's going to cry bloody murder and be upset if I'm not home. Good-bye, good-bye!"

And she bolted from the room and bounded down the steps.

The gentleman didn't want to stop her or pursue her, but he did shout from the top of the staircase: "Be careful, girl. Don't fall. And come back whenever you wish."

"I will, if I'm not in the way," she responded.

And then, looking out the window again, he watched the girl run from the castle, cross by the bank of the pond, and disappear from view under the branches that covered the shortest path leading to her house.

Silveria spent more than a week without returning to the castle, although she longed to go back, keen on a desire to know what was happening there. She had hoped that the stranger would have come to visit her parents, as his only neighbors, or that she would have come across him, on horseback or on foot, on her walks through the countryside. But these hopes of hers had been frustrated. The young gentleman had no doubt sought out the most complete solitude, a solitude in which he took so much pleasure that he spent his time shut up in his new mansion, invisible to everybody.

In the end, Silveria could not resist her desire to see him again. She remembered that he liked flowers, and, gathering many of the prettiest and most fragrant ones to be found then in her garden, she made a bouquet and off she went with it to the castle.

There was an old servant at the door.

"I'm bringing these flowers for the master," Silveria said to him.

The old servant reached for the flowers in order to take them to him.

"Oh no you don't!" said the girl, laughing. "I'll take the flowers myself. Tell your master that Silveria's here."

Laughing in turn at the girl's despotic brazenness, the old man left to carry out her command. Silveria followed him to the foot of the staircase, and inasmuch as he heard footsteps overhead, the servant shouted:

"Master, Silveria's here."

"Have her come up, have her come up," the master responded at once.

Nothing more was needed. Silveria gave a slight push to the old man, who was in front of her and cutting her off, climbed the steps two at a time, curtsied gracefully to the stranger, who was waiting for her upstairs, and presented him with the bouquet. He took it, thanking her profusely, and kissed Silveria on the forehead. Then he turned to the servant, who had joined them, and said:

"Juan, take these flowers, and be careful not to lose the petals. Put them in a glass of water. And bring biscuits, candy, and muscatel to treat my guest."

Afterwards they entered the salon, where Silveria found everything prettier. There were no longer cobwebs or dust; the furniture looked better; the fabrics had more vivid coloring; and the woodwork, cleaned and polished, shone. Next to the main window there was a desk, with a writing case, and numerous books and pieces of paper. Silveria, lolling in an armchair, was eating one of the biscuits that Juan had offered her on a silver tray.

"It's very good," she said, and ate two more.

When the servant left and Silveria found herself alone with the master, she answered with unaffected naturalness several questions that he asked her. Considering herself authorized thereby to ask questions of her own, she subjected the stranger to an amusing exchange:

"What's the gentleman's name?"

"My name is Ricardo, to serve you."

"To serve God," she said. "And tell me, how does the gentleman spend his time, shut up here the livelong day without seeing a soul?"

"Writing."

"Writing what?"

"Plays, novels . . . I'm a poet."

"Oh . . . I get it. Funny plots and intrigues to entertain idle people."

"Exactly, my child."

"Well . . . how does the gentleman manage to invent so many tangled arguments? By dreaming them up? It must be a difficult profession. Who taught it to you?"

"The Wizard, about whom you've heard so many things."

"And where and how did the gentleman see him?"

"I saw him years ago. Then I lost track of him, and now I'm afraid I'll never find him again."

Silveria understood none of this, and admitted as much to the stranger with innocent candor.

"You'll understand it with time," he said to her. "You're still very young."

And as he gave her no further explanations, she felt hurt and offended in the depths of her soul that not only did he think her ignorant, but for the present, and God only knew until when, incapable of learning, unworthy of having any mystery revealed to her.

And in her opinion there was a mystery in his words. In truth, the immediate and distinct notion that she formed of Ricardo's profession was that he spun inoffensive, ingenious tales that could act as mild entertainment. But Silveria reflected a great deal, and her thoughts raced and flew as she reflected, imagining beautifully confused things, inasmuch as she did not succeed in expressing them with words, or even ordering them in her mind so as to perceive them better. Only vaguely, as she roamed through a certain intellectual penumbra, did she note that the poet's fictional writings were not a mere imitation of what we all see and hear, but that they penetrated the deep significance of it, revealing not a little of the invisible and unheard-of, and showing clearly a thousand treasures that nature hides in her bosom. But who loaned the poet the key to open the chest in which those treasures are kept? Who gave him the code to interpret the hidden meaning of what people say? What does the wind talk about when it whispers among leaves? What does the brook murmur? What do little birds sing about? What do the stars tell, what do they say when they illuminate us with their light? Surely there must be an angel, an elf, a genie, a familiar spirit who would come to us in all this. Ricardo had to be in contact with it, had to know incantations that obeyed him, conjurations that abided by his orders.

Such fantasies, and a thousand others like them, altogether indescribable, arose in Silveria's imagination and piqued her curiosity. Ricardo, however, had said that she was too young to deal with other matters of seemingly less importance. How, then, was she to deem herself fit to be initiated into and schooled in something even more recondite and obscure?

Silveria was modest and prudent, despite her self-assurance and boldness, and did not insist on asking. For her consolation and peace of mind, she injected a strange delight in what was unexplained, and, in what was unknown, searched for and found an inexhaustible lode of fantastic suppositions that entertained and enthralled her.

Henceforth her visits to Ricardo were not as frequent. Silveria was proud and did not want to be in the way, or to be importunate or tiresome, but Ricardo treated her very hospitably, like an amusing, indulged, bright little girl, and so she continued to visit him every now and then, bringing him flowers and eating his biscuits. And since he encouraged her, saying that she should look upon him as her older brother, Silveria ended up using the familiar form of address with the castle's owner.

When she was by herself and thinking about Ricardo, sometimes she envied him greatly, imagining as she did that he had to be on intimate terms with genies of the air or with other beings and superhuman intellects; and sometimes she pitied him greatly upon regarding the isolation and retirement in which he lived, with neither a father nor a mother to care for and indulge him as hers cared for and indulged her. Thus did the days roll by until winter arrived with its frosts and freezing temperatures.

The Indiano wished to present his daughter with something special on Christmas Eve, so he bought her a beautiful Nativity scene. Jerusalem, with Solomon's temple and Herod's palace, all made of painted cardboard, was in the highest part, above numerous rocks, also made of cardboard; bits of glass represented rivers and brooks; the star that guided the Magi was tied to a wire; and the crèche appeared in the foreground.

More than forty clay figurines gave life to the scene: Herod was talking to the queen, both of them on a balcony; Melchior, Balthazar, and Caspar rode along a path on horseback, guided by the wondrous star; the infant Jesus was in the crèche with the Virgin Mary, Saint Joseph, the ox, and the mule; shepherds and shepherdesses were bowed low in adoration of the newborn child; others tended the sheep or a flock of turkeys; and six or seven angels, showy in the extreme and with their wings spread, wings seemingly of gold, were all announcing the Good News to the world by blowing their trumpets. And because the entire scene was illuminated by at least two dozen wax tapers, it took on a dazzling appearance, glittering like a diamond.

Silveria experienced immense joy upon seeing her Nativity lighted. There ensued a family celebration in the farmhouse. The wet nurse played a hand drum, and the master and mistress and their daughter and the servants sang Christmas carols, and in patriarchal and primitive fashion they supped together, on almond soup, bream, and lentil stew, and for dessert they had roasted chestnuts, sweet-smelling pears, and other well preserved fruit from the fall.

When the celebration ended, everybody withdrew to go to bed long before midnight, but Silveria was not at all sleepy and a thousand reveries and fantasies kept her wide awake, agitating her spirit. Alone in her room, she opened the wood window louvers and gazed at the heavens and the silent, solitary countryside. Not even the slightest breeze moved limbs. The cloudless sky allowed the moon to bathe the mountains and treetops with its pale glow, while a mysterious darkness prevailed where the crowns cast their shadows. Patches of snow, on branches and scattered on the ground, glistened like pieces of polished silver, and as moonbeams fell on it, now they gave off adamantine flashes, now they formed fleeting rainbows. Silveria contemplated it all, but she also looked at the castle, which stood out amid the trees, and saw light through the panes of the main window. The lamp was still burning on the desk, and her friend was no doubt writing or reading.

She was then moved to great compassion for Ricardo in his loneliness and, upon considering that she had had such a good time while he had been so alone, tears welled up in her eyes. Deep down Silveria pondered and moreover heightened the magnificence and exquisiteness of her Nativity scene, and sincerely regretted that he had not seen it. She felt overcome by an irresistible desire to show off to her friend the artistic marvel of which she was the owner, thanks to her father's generosity, and without giving it a second thought she made the most daring decision.

Silveria bundled up as best she could, descended the stairs on tiptoe, took the key, opened and then closed the door, and found herself outside, feeling the cold and carrying in her arms the extinguished Nativity, which, fortunately, weighed very little even though it was somewhat bulky.

Since she was strong and nimble, she reached the castle door in fewer than ten minutes, toting the three Magi, angels, the infant Jesus, sheep, turkeys, Jerusalem, and shepherds. Setting her load on the ground, she gave two loud knocks on the door and soon heard old Juan's voice saying:

"Who's there?"

"A friend. Open up!"

Juan recognized the voice and opened the door in a dither, repeatedly making the sign of the cross.

"Good Lord! What's happened? Have you taken leave of your senses?"

"Don't be silly," Silveria replied. "I'm in my right mind. I've come to show your master this beautiful piece of work. Let's light it quickly."

And, using Juan's candle, she quickly lighted all the wax tapers.

"Hold your tongue and don't say that I'm here. I'm going to surprise your master." And lifting the Nativity again, all aglow now, Silveria climbed the stairs.

The poet, his elbows on the desk and lost in thought, had not heard anything. Silveria entered, approached noiselessly, and, when she was nearly on top of him, remembered the writing on a piece of pasteboard that hung from the head angel's trumpet, and in a silvery, melodious voice, said by way of a greeting:

"Glory to God in the highest and peace on Earth to men of good will!"

Amazed at the sight, the poet jumped to his feet, and the girl, moving swiftly, set the luminous but simple representation of the sacred mystery on the desk.

"Come on!" she exclaimed. "Admit that it's really pretty."

Ricardo glanced at the Nativity without saying a word. Then he turned to Silveria and said:

"I should say so. It's a marvel!"

And grasping the girl by the waist with both hands, he lifted her firmly in the air, chided her, bounced her up and down, and planted a half dozen loud kisses on her ruddy cheeks. At once he gently and paternally admonished her for the bold folly of having slipped out of her house and come alone through the pinewood in the dead of night. She listened to him, shamefaced, but not contrite.

Not for that reason did Ricardo refrain from looking again at the Nativity, praising it profusely. Afterwards he blew out all the tapers, put on his cape and hat, instructed Juan to follow him carrying the Nativity, and, taking Silveria by the hand, accompanied the girl to her parents' house, which he made her enter, where Juan left the Nativity, and from which he did not withdraw until Silveria was inside and had locked the door.

Time passed, and Silveria's visits and conversations with the poet did not become more frequent. Saddened, although not moved to anger, she could not help noticing that he always spoke to her about trivialities, that he did not deign to read to her any of his work, and that he never got around to explaining to her the arcane processes of his art.

But Silveria, who was very proud, attributed it all to her youth and did not regret it overmuch, because she was trusting, jovial, and cheerful, and did not mope except for a good reason. She never talked to the poet about his writings, contenting herself with learning from Juan that they were becoming more and more celebrated in the kingdom's capital, thereby according their author enviable fame.

Ricardo absented himself frequently; he would journey to the capital, spend several months there, and return to his retreat. No sooner would he come back than Silveria would go to see him, and he would find her as young, as amusing, and as innocent as he had left her.

But it happened that Ricardo went on one of those trips and took a long time to return. Silveria repeatedly asked Juan, who had stayed behind watching the castle, when his master would come back, and, judging from his answers, she came to believe that the poet would be gone for a long time, that mayhap he would never return.

Thus did more than five years elapse, not two or three months, like on other occasions, but Silveria was very far from forgetting the poet. She always had him on her mind, and she even dreamed about him. And although she despaired of seeing him again in the flesh, which caused her bitter sadness, the healthy energy and noble serenity of her spirit overcame all her sorrow. Furthermore, she knew from Juan, and this consoled her, that Ricardo was in good health and that he was achieving brilliant triumphs in remote countries.

She was also triumphing, in her own way, in that isolated retreat in which she lived, because a springlike development brought about a glorious transformation in her. She turned into another person, although more lovely. She grew until she was almost as tall as her father; her head seemed, in proportion to the rest of her body, smaller and better positioned on her graceful neck, whose elegant outline could be seen through her blond hair, which no longer fell in plaits on her back, but was gathered in a bun; little ringlets, which hung loose on her nape, made her neck even prettier, as if they were shedding threads of golden chain and powdered cinnamon over fresh, rose-tinted milk; the striking majesty of her bearing and carriage indicated the good health and vitality of all her limbs; and the divine harmony of her figure showed through close-fitting clothes, with her firm breasts rising in a soft curve. In a word, Silveria was now a very beautiful woman, but as innocent and virtuous as when she was a girl.

Upon seeing Silveria in such a blooming, ripe age, her mother implored the *Indiano* to pull up stakes and forsake that solitude and go to live in a village or the largest, richest town, so as to find a good suitor whom the girl could marry, but the *Indiano* always opposed such a move and condemned it as an abominable desecration. Although he used plainer terminology, he reasoned as follows: something still lay dormant in Silveria, and it was cruel to brusquely shatter her angelic dream; it was unkind, without waiting for the angel herself to come down from heaven to fulfill her mission, to send her forth all of a sudden on Earth, however great the happiness that Earth might bring her.

On the contrary, it was advisable for that early rose to open its petals with due deliberation and not give out precipitately the perfume and honey of its calyx. The *Indiano* argued, lastly, that there was no fear of their daughter losing chances. On account of her unparalleled beauty she could aspire to marry a prince, and since, moreover, the *Indiano* had managed his assets wisely, he had saved a fair amount and could provide Silveria with a munificent dowry; whenever he decided, suitors would come in droves, like sheep to a meadow.

It is not known whether or not the *Indiano*'s reasoning convinced his wife, but she had to yield, as was her custom. So their daughter continued to be rustic and almost withdrawn from all human contact and exchange, like a ringdove, like a hidden desert flower.

One pleasant afternoon in the month of May, Silveria went up to the castle to see the elderly Juan, who lived there alone. Great was her joy, and her surprise, when she learned that the night before Ricardo, without prior notice, had returned after a five-year absence.

As when she was eleven years old, with the same straightforwardness, although with greater impetuosity, Silveria shunted the servant aside, bounded up the stairs, and, excited, breathless, and with flushed cheeks, rushed into the salon, where, happily, she found the poet.

Remembering then, all of a sudden, the angelic greeting of the Christmas Eve of years ago, she repeated it:

"Glory to God in the highest and peace on Earth to men of good will!"

Ricardo was astonished, speechless, ecstatic, as though a marvelous deity had come to visit him.

"What? You mean you don't recognize me?" she added, flying with heartfelt joy into his arms.

Gently he moved her away from him, with honest fear, with a wonder and an amazement that Silveria did not understand.

"Are you no longer my brother?" she asked him wistfully.

Then she gazed at him briefly and thought she noticed a veil of sadness clouding his face, but she found it even more beautiful than in former times.

Ricardo affectionately took her hands in his and talked to her about things that she listened to with a half-open mouth and eyes that, because of the interest and astonishment with which she gazed at him and took in his words, looked sweeter and brighter and bigger.

Silveria did not fully grasp the meaning of everything that he was saying, but she did understand that he was lamenting how very unlucky he was, that he could no longer make any woman happy, that his heart was shriveled, and that, although the Wizard could still restore to him all his youthful vigor, he had searched for him in vain in his long travels and had been unable to find him.

Such painful confessions distressed Silveria in the extreme. Two fat tears welled up in her eyes and slipped down her fresh cheeks. Eager then to console the poet, and with the same innocence, with the same pure abandon with which she showed affection to her mother, she approached Ricardo and began to caress him.

At that point, and with annoyance identical to that felt by the person who suspects that someone is trying to incite him to commit a crime, the poet violently repulsed Silveria, exclaiming:

"Don't touch me! Don't kiss me! Leave here at once!"

The lovely maiden, without fathoming the reason for that evident and highborn disdain, considered herself deeply aggrieved. She did not complain; she did not plead; she did not cry. Her pride stopped up the source of her tears and drowned protests and entreaties, but she fled, flying like an injured dove, running away like a hind hurt by a poisoned arrow sunk in her insides.

The poet had fallen into a profound stupor upon noticing the disastrous effect of the coldness he had just shown because of a thoughtless initial outburst. But it must be said that no sooner did he shake it off than he cast aside all scruples and regretted and even became ashamed of his conduct. He laughed at himself nervously and called himself an imbecile. And so as to remedy what he now regarded as a mistake, he ran after Silveria but it was too late.

How would he discover her tracks? How would he recognize the path along which she had fled? The woods were extremely dense and vast. Ricardo wandered through that labyrinth and kept calling out to Silveria, but only an echo answered him.

Night soon fell, moonless, and with clouds that blocked out the starlight. Complete darkness reigned in the woods. Mayhap its solemn silence was broken now and then by the hooting of owls or the tenuous moan of the mild breeze that continually stirred the leaves. Going around in circles like a madman, the poet finally ended up near the farmhouse. Cheerful premonitions and gratifying schemes all of a sudden restored his serenity.

Silveria, he thought, *won't have gone anywhere else. She must be home. I'll go inside. I'll tell her parents everything, and I'll ask Silveria her forgiveness in front of them, assuring her that, far from disdaining her, I'm hers forevermore.*

At the farmhouse nobody yet knew of the poet's return. With singular amazement the *Indiano* and his wife greeted a man whom they knew only by hearsay and about whom they had scarcely heard a word in over five years. But everything there was consternation and commotion. The *Indiano* had just come back from a long trip and his wife had informed him, weeping and sobbing, that Silveria had not returned, that Silveria was nowhere to be seen.

Not waiting for further explanations on account of their worry and anxiety, they all hurried out into the countryside to look for Silveria. They searched high and low for her until dawn, but in vain, and when daybreak came upon them they were exhausted and desperate. The mother imagined that the Wizard had stolen her daughter from her; the *Indiano*, that wolves had devoured her; and the servants, that the Earth had swallowed her. Suspecting that mayhap she had fallen in a pond, they stirred every one and probed the bottom of every one, not finding her dead or alive.

Scarcely resting that entire day, master, mistress, and servants made inquiries and a beating of sorts through several sections of the forest, which stretched for miles and miles. They sent out notices of the flight, along with a description of the fugitive, to the nearest towns and villages, but to no avail. And although there were no telegraph and no telephone back then, and no police, or police who were less efficient than they are nowadays, so diligent were they in searching for Silveria that her continuing disappearance was taking on the semblance and guise of something miraculous, or outside of the natural, normal order of things.

But let us go back in time, inasmuch as we have gotten ahead of ourselves, and return to when Silveria fled, believing herself aggrieved.

Delirious with rage and rancor, at first she ran without stopping and without realizing that she had penetrated a wild and dense labyrinth of wood through which she had never before passed, and where there were no paths or traces of human feet, only an abundance of heather, bracken, rockrose, and other plants that grew among the trees, forming tangled thickets. Then she stopped for a moment, took stock of her situation, and realized that she had lost her way. A terrible worry gripped her as she imagined the grief she was going to cause her parents if she did not return home soon. She struggled to retrace her steps, looking for the trail, first in one direction, then in another, but with each step she became more disoriented and found herself on more unfamiliar ground. The inhospitable forest soon turned more ominous and solemn, and the blackness of night enveloped her there.

Fortunately, Silveria did not know what fear was. Despite her sorrow and anger, she experienced a certain sublime delight upon feeling herself surrounded by darkness and mystery in the middle of woods she had never explored. Mayhap the Wizard was going to appear to her there all of a sudden.

Very different ideas and feelings arose in her spirit. Her anger at the poet changed into pity. She considered him heartsick, forgave him, and excused his coldness. The Wizard had caused that evil, and it was necessary that the Wizard bring him a cure.

Silveria then improvised a daring evocation, an imperious conjuration, and said aloud and bravely:

"Come, Wizard, come to console and heal my poet and make him happy!"

Her voice faded into the darkness, with neither an answer nor an echo, restoring the silence. All of creation slept or was deaf and dumb. Our heroine continued walking aimlessly, although slowly. Her pupils

had dilated and she was almost able to see in the inky night as she
went on negotiating obstacles and snags and going up and down hills,
because the terrain was becoming more and more rough and uneven.
At last dawn began to break.

Silveria's fatigue was immense. She could not stand. But she
managed, nonetheless, to get to the top of a crag, where she hoped
to escape the dampness, and, trusting in heaven's protection, sought
repose and soon fell asleep.

Her dreams were not gloomy. Mayhap they augured well and lent
themselves to favorable interpretations. She dreamed that, while her
mother was teaching her to read in prayer books, the genies of the
air came and flew off with her to teach her more agreeable reading
in the coded and sealed book of nature, whose seals they broke, so
that she could decipher and read it.

When Silveria awoke the sun was shining, culminating in the ether.
Its bright rays bathed, gladdened, and gilded everything. She rubbed
her eyes and glanced around. She found herself in a deep ravine with
rocks and bramble patches everywhere. The peaks of the hills limited
the horizon. That site had to have been the heart of the mountain
range. Silveria thought that it was almost impossible that she had
reached it without having tumbled down a precipice, without having
torn her body to pieces among the hawthorns and cistuses, or without
the assistance of those genies of the air about whom she had dreamed.

Why remain in that desolate spot? With renewed determination,
although without knowing where she was headed, Silveria continued
her trek.

After walking for more than two hours, she came across a somewhat
worn path. The luxuriance of gigantic trees formed a canopy all along
it, and only an occasional ray of sun filtered through their branches.
Silveria took the path and was climbing a low hill when she heard close
by the pitiful howls of a dog. She quickened her step, reached the
vantage point, where there was a rise, and saw below a cluster of huts.

Near the huts five dirty, disheveled women, or rather, five furies,
each one armed with a cudgel, surrounded a dog and were beating
it to death. Fourteen or fifteen children dressed in rags and covered
with grime were celebrating that merciless execution with wild shouts
of cruel joy. From a distance a pathetic-looking old man with a long
white beard was running toward the women with an unsheathed dagger
in his hand in order to defend or avenge the dog. A violin hung from
his back and he was blind. He was an itinerant musician.

The women withdrew toward their huts, watching him come. The children, lined up in a row, started throwing stones at him while one boy rolled on the ground and shrieked like someone possessed of the devil. The dog, hounded by all of them, had given him a little nip, which brought on the women's wrath and the canine tragedy.

The blind man arrived late, for the dog had died. Flinging himself on the animal, the oldster wailed such laments and wept so inconsolably that he mitigated somewhat the ferocity of those people. The children stopped throwing stones at him, but they and their mothers continued to hurl insults at him. They called him a sorcerer, a shameless beggar, and a cursed wizard. And at this point Silveria appeared, an unexpected and strange personage in the middle of such a scene.

It could be considered a stroke of good fortune that that ragged, unruly band's husbands and fathers, who, in the guise of charcoal burners and woodcutters were perhaps smugglers or outlaws, had gone off that day to ply their trades or engage in marauding raids. If they had been there, the blind man and Silveria, who very bravely began to defend him, would have been in grave danger, because those men were bound to be perverse and cruel.

Whatever the reason, Silveria, turning into an intrepid amazon, seized the dagger that the old man could not wield on account of his feebleness and blindness and let it be known that she would keep all the rabble at bay.

The prudent course, however, was to begin a speedy retreat, which the blind man requested, saying to Silveria in a shaky voice:

"Let us get out of here, my child. I'm dying and I can hardly walk. You're an angel. Act as my guide and my support. I'll describe the trail we need to follow and you'll see it, you'll see it with your eyes, which I'm sure are very beautiful, and you'll take me along it until we reach the place where, with resignation, I'll await my rapidly approaching death."

And the old man did in effect have the countenance of a person *in extremis*. Violent passions and continual ailments, both physical and moral, had worn away his life.

"Without the dog," he said, "I couldn't have gone anywhere if you, my child, hadn't come to my aid. Help me to get home, where I have shelter and a refuge. It's not far from here, and at that I don't know if I'll make it alive. My strength's failing me."

Overcome with compassion, Silveria supported the old man, and he, leaning on his staff and Silveria's arm, set out with the gallant young woman, indicating to her the way.

As they tramped along, the old man told her astonishing secrets.

"No sooner did you speak than I recognized you by your voice. I thought I was listening to your mother when, twenty years ago, she deluded herself as she persuaded me with honeyed words that she really loved me, and flattered me with the hope of being my wife. But, unluckily for me, the *Indiano* came to the village and your mother fell madly in love with him. I forgive her. I understand that she was not to blame for my misfortune, and that it was the insuperable influence of fate. Back then my soul was more fervent, more forceful. My soul was unjust, and I didn't forgive her. On more than one occasion I planned to kidnap her or kill her, and then my integrity . . . or my cowardice dissuaded me and scared me. Like a lunatic, I prowled around your farmhouse, I hid in the castle. I tormented your mother like a living regret. I frightened her by making her believe that I was the Wizard. God, undoubtedly, wished to punish me and left me blind. From then on I no longer frequented your farmhouse. My life became more and more disastrous. I wandered through mountains and valleys, playing my violin and begging."

The old man's revelations, his squalid poverty, and his illnesses, which were clearly draining him, filled Silveria with a powerful aversion, but in her noble spirit even more powerful were compassion and the stimulus not to abandon the helpless blind man until putting him out of harm's way.

Furthermore, Silveria could not resist the beggar's insistent questions, and told him the story of her life, her flight, and her determination to find the Wizard in order to heal and console the poet.

Meanwhile, the trek continued with laborious slowness through even more rugged terrain. They had penetrated a narrow and deep gorge. On both sides rose inaccessible mountains and sheer crags where not even wild goats would be able to climb. Spontaneous fertile vegetation carpeted all of it with uncultivated beauty, which provoked fear and delightful amazement at the same time.

The old man, utterly exhausted, paused often, lay down on the ground, and rested. During one of these stops he took from his pouch a few chunks of dark bread and several pieces of cheese, and by the side of a spring shared his not very appetizing and rustic meal with his guide. Other times Silveria took a brief nap and recovered from her tiredness.

"We still have a ways to go," said the old man.

Taking a little lantern from the same pouch, and flint, tinder, and a spill from his pockets, he lit the candle end that was inside the lantern. Then he handed the lantern to Silveria, along with other candle ends that he carried with him, for when the lighted one burned down. And in this manner they continued on their way.

It must have been around midnight when Silveria heard the sound of water running rapidly and rushing over rocks.

"We're getting close to my house now," said the blind man. "I live with my sister, who's older than I am. Her character is violent and embittered. She hated your mother. I don't want her to see you. She could recognize you and harm you. Besides, her two sons are outlaws, and I should fear the worst from them. As soon as we reach the bank of the river you'll have to leave me. By following the sound of the current I'll get home without any trouble. It's not far from there. You be brave and go upstream, trying to avoid any contact with human beings. The lantern will light your way. In the end you'll come to the source of the river, which rises among the crags. A short distance from that spring you'll see, if you look carefully, the entrance to a cave. Enter it without fear and go all the way to the back, and I assure you that you'll find the Wizard, as is your wish."

And sure enough, they soon arrived at the edge of that fast-flowing river. There the old man slipped away and disappeared in the darkness like an airy, fanciful illusion. Silveria found herself utterly alone. For a period of several hours her trek was more arduous and more risky than before. The nearly obliterated path that Silveria was following rose, in more than a few places, above the level of the water, from which it was separated by a black chasm. The pass through the mountains, in which the river had channeled its course, became more and more narrow, and the peak of the sierras seemed to soar, reducing the view of sky and stars.

Day finally broke and the uncertain light of dawn penetrated the ravine. Everything cheered up and brightened as the darkness gradually faded. Birds awoke and greeted the dawning day with their warbles.

Silveria then arrived at the source. Sheets of limpid water were gushing forth over a mass of enormous, smooth rocks, and on all sides there rose steep hills that looked like colossal walls. The wayfarer thought she had plunged into a big hole, because the turns in the path concealed the point of entry that she sought. She searched anxiously for the grotto, separating the branches and brambles that covered it, and finally came across the opening.

Without hesitating a single moment, and with heroic bravery, she penetrated the cavern, scaring away the owls and bats that nested there. After walking for more than twenty minutes in darkness, lessened somewhat by the little lantern, and following a crooked path, Silveria saw that she was not coming to the end and got impatient. Remembering her evocation, she shouted courageously:

"Come, Wizard, come to heal and console my poet!"

Nobody responded to the evocation, which echoed and reverberated in all those hollows and bends. The last candle end that was burning spluttered and died out, and the bold pilgrim found herself enveloped in jet-black darkness.

She groped her way along, going uphill, and the more the slope rose the steeper it became even as the ceiling of the cavern became lower. Silveria had to walk in a deep crouch while touching the ceiling with her hands to keep from bumping her head. All of a sudden, instead of stone, she discovered wood on the ceiling. She felt carefully and noticed that there were boards joined by two iron bars. Then she felt with even greater care and realized that the boards were secured to the ceiling with four strong hinges.

So she mounted the three steps at the terminus of the climb, put her back to the joined boards, and pushed hard. They had neither a padlock nor a bolt, which meant that there was no key that could be inserted, but they resisted Silveria's push, and she nearly despaired of raising them. Nevertheless, she made a supreme effort, and the boards rose, swinging up on their hinges and precipitating, through the wide opening, the fall of dirt, nettle, wall rocket, and other plants with which they were covered. At the same time the beautiful light of the clear day streamed into that end of the cavern.

"God be praised!" exclaimed Silveria.

And, jumping with joy, she found herself in an untended, deserted little garden that was surrounded by very high walls that did not have a single window.

She only made out, next to one of the corners of that square enclosure, a small ogival arch, and beneath the arch, the first few steps of an extremely narrow spiral staircase. As swift as an arrow she passed beneath the arch and bounded up the steps to a little locked door at the top of the staircase.

Despite the hardships and emotions of her risky peregrination, Silveria looked beautiful in her disheveled state: her blond hair was half unplaited and undone; her cheeks were flushed from exertion;

her bosom was rising and falling; and her eyes, brighter than usual, were ringed by the light purple with which fatigue had tinged the lids at the edge of her long, silken lashes.

Impatient and vexed by the obstacle in her way, Silveria pounded furiously on the door, using her pretty little hand, which was surprisingly strong, to deliver the most tremendous and resounding blows.

Nobody opened, and her impatience grew. She pounded again. Then she remembered the evocation and began to shout it.

"Come, Wizard, come—"

She didn't have time to finish it. All of a sudden the little door opened wide, and Silveria saw her poet standing there, filled with the same joy that she felt. Silveria shot a quick glance all around and recognized the castle room where Ricardo used to write and where she had visited him so many times. She then tried to repeat the evocation in jest, and began to say anew:

"Come, Wizard, come—"

But she couldn't finish it this time either. Ricardo sealed her lips with a prolonged kiss and wrapped her tightly in his arms so that she would not escape from him again. For a moment she gazed at him tenderly and afterwards closed her eyes as if in a swoon.

Birds, butterflies, flowers, stars, and fountains; the sun, spring with its finery, all the pomp, music, glory, and wealth in the world—she imagined that they were all being seen, heard, and enjoyed, and that they were immeasurably and infinitely better than in external reality, in the most intimate and secret part of her soul, which was sublimely and wonderfully enlightened on that occasion by the Wizard's supreme magic.

Silveria had found him, finally, favorably inclined and not opposed. And he, as a well-deserved reward for the altruistic undertaking that was tenaciously and valiantly realized, performed his most desirable and beatific miracles on Silveria and Ricardo's behalf.

We will not be astonished, then, and can even fall back on what has been related, to excuse Silveria and the poet for letting three hours pass before going to see the *Indiano* and his wife and relieving them of their anguish.

The contentment and satisfaction of both were indescribable when they saw their daughter safe and sound again, and also when they learned that, without having to go to the neighboring village or any other town, as the mother wished, but right in the middle of that distant solitude, Silveria had found a very handsome fiancé, one after her heart, one attuned to her temperament and to her amply demonstrated capabilities and aptitudes for all the lyrical and even for all the prosaic aspects of life.

I hope that all those who innocently and in good faith search for the Wizard find him to be as kindly as Silveria and Ricardo found him, and that they keep him in their company all their lives, as the two of them did.

Vienna, 1894

Benito Pérez Galdós (1843–1920)

A Canary Islander who went to Madrid in 1862 to study law, Galdós is universally considered the greatest Spanish novelist since Cervantes. He chronicled the span of the nineteenth century in Spain in five series of historical/fictional works called National Episodes *that range from the battle of Trafalgar to the times of Antonio Cánovas del Castillo, that is, from 1805 to the 1890s.*

*His contemporary novels are evocations of life in Madrid during the second half of the nineteenth century, and a number of them—*The Disinherited Woman [La desheredada] *(1881),* Fortunata and Jacinta *(1886–87), and* Angel Guerra *(1890–91)—truly merit comparison with the works of Balzac, Dickens, Thackeray, Eça de Queirós, Tolstoy, and Dostoevsky. The great theme of his novels, if we can label it as such, is the daily concerns, the daily cares, the daily comings and goings of his fictional creations, recurring characters mainly from the great middle class of Madrid and the myriad types who populate it.*

Galdós also wrote for the theater and achieved clangorous success with a few dramas that struck political or religious chords.

In all he wrote forty-six national episodes, thirty-four novels, twenty-four plays, and volumes of articles and miscellany, including tales of wonder about and for children, two of the most well-known of which are "The Mule and the Ox" (1876) and "The Princess and the Street Urchin" (1877).

Benito Pérez Galdós

"The Mule and the Ox"

(A Christmas Story)

I

THE poor little thing had stopped moaning. She turned her head, and, with sad eyes, stared up at the people standing around her bed. Little by little her breathing gave out and she died. Heaving a sigh, the child's guardian angel took wing and flew away.

The distraught mother could not believe so much misfortune, but Celinina's lovely face was turning yellow and diaphanous like wax. Her limbs grew cold and she became rigid and hard like the body of a doll. Then her mother, father, and nearest relatives were ushered from the bedroom as a number of women, friends as well as servants, busied themselves performing the last rites for the dead little girl.

They laid her out in an exquisite batiste dress whose skirt was as white and light as a cloud, and completely oversewn with laces and ruffles that made it look like foam. Then they slipped her feet in shoes, which were also white and whose soles scarcely showed signs of wear, and afterwards braided her sleek, dark chestnut hair, interweaving the glossy plaits with blue ribbons. They searched for real flowers, but were unable to find any because it was not the season, so they wove an attractive wreath with cloth flowers, selecting the prettiest and the ones that most looked like fresh roses brought from the garden.

A disagreeable man delivered a box, somewhat bigger than a violin case, that was adorned with blue silk and silver galloons and lined with white satin. Celinina's body was placed inside it, her head resting on a beautiful soft pillow so that she would not be in an unnatural position, and after she had been carefully accommodated in her funeral bed, they crossed her hands and tied them together with a ribbon, putting between them a bunch of white roses that had been so skillfully fashioned by the artisan that they actually appeared to be genuine.

The women then covered a table with ornate pieces of cloth, arranging it like an altar, on which the little casket was set. In short order they devised what looked like church canopies with rich white curtains that gracefully gathered on either side. From the other rooms in the house they brought a number of statues and images of saints that they methodically disposed on the "altar," as though forming a funeral court for the deceased angel. And immediately thereafter they lighted several dozen candles of the room's imposing candelabras, and their flames cast a sorrowful, flickering glow around Celinina's body. Finally, after repeatedly kissing the poor child's cold cheeks, they concluded their pious task.

II

The moans of men and woman came from the interior of the house. They were the mournful laments of parents who could not be convinced of the "little angels to heaven" aphorism that friends administer like a moral sedative in such agonizing moments. Those selfsame parents believed that the true and proper dwelling place of the "little angels" is Earth; nor could they subscribe to the theory that the death of a grown-up is more wrenching and disastrous than that of a child. They felt, mingled with their grief, the profound pity occasioned by the throes of a little one, and did not believe that any pain could surpass the anguish that was ravaging their insides.

A thousand memories and painful images knifed through them like razor-sharp daggers piercing their hearts. The mother continually heard Celinina's chatter, the delightful way that she would say things backwards and make the words of our language into amusing philological caricatures that flowed from her pretty mouth like the tenderest music that can touch a mother's heart. Nothing characterizes children like their locution, that genuine manner of expressing themselves and saying everything with an economy of letters, and that prehistoric grammar, akin to the first attempts at speech at the dawn of humanity, and their simple art of declension and conjugation that seems to be the innocent correction of languages regularized by usage. The vocabulary of a child of three, like Celinina, constitutes a family's real literary treasure. How could her mother forget the babbling little tongue that called a hat a "tat" and a chickpea a "pickpea?"

To make matters worse, the good woman saw everywhere the playthings that had gladdened Celinina's last days. And as they were the days before Christmas, scattered about the floor were clay turkeys with wire feet, a Saint Joseph with no hands, a manger with the infant Jesus like a little pink ball, and one of the Magi mounted on a splendid headless camel. What those poor figures had suffered in the last few days, dragged from one place to another, and twisted into different shapes, was known only by God, the mother, and the pure spirit that had flown to heaven.

The broken pieces were imbued, so to speak, with Celinina's soul, or decked out, as it were, in a very sad and singular light, which was her light. As she contemplated them, the poor mother trembled all over, pained and wounded in the most delicate and sensitive fibers of her being. What a strange union of things! How those pieces of clay wept! They seemed to be full of an intense sorrow, and so grief-stricken that the mere sight of them produced as much bitterness as the spectacle of the dying child herself had, when she looked at her parents with pleading eyes and beseeched them to take away that horrible pain from her burning forehead. For the mother the saddest thing in the world was a turkey that had lost its bill and its crest from frequent changes of posture, and still had its wire feet attached to clay.

III

But if the mother was bereaved, the father was even more deeply afflicted, because although both were mired in grief, in the latter it was compounded by the sharp pangs of remorse. We shall briefly relate this peculiar turn of events, calling attention to the fact that his response may strike some people as childish in the extreme, but we will remind those who believe such a thing that nothing occasions acts of childishness so much as pure pain, deep pain, the sort of pain that is unaffected by mundane concerns or the secondary distress of unsatisfied selfishness.

From the time that Celinina fell ill, she looked forward to the poetic holidays that fill children with joy—the Christmas holidays. Everybody knows how anxiously they await the arrival of these joyous days, how feverishly they long for presents and crèches, and how much they hope to eat and stuff themselves with turkey, marzipan, candied almonds, and nougats. Some of them even believe, naively, that they are capable of wolfing down all the edibles displayed at the Plaza Mayor and on adjacent streets.

During her spells of improvement Celinina never stopped talking about Christmastime. And since her cousins, who came to keep her company, were older and knew all about presents and crèches, the poor little girl grew more excited listening to them, and as her fantasy soared, her longing for sweets and toys became even more acute. When she was delirious, the fever having trapped her in its oven of torment, Celinina spoke continuously of the things that stirred her spirit, and it all had to do with beating drums, playing tom-toms, and singing Christmas carols. In the dark field surrounding her mind there were the *gobble, gobbles* of turkeys and the *peep, peeps* of chickens; mountains of nougats that reached the sky, forming a Mont Blanc of almonds; crèches full of lights that had at least fifty billion figures; bouquets of sweets; trees laden with as many toys as can be conceived by the most fertile Tyrolese imagination; the pond of Retiro Park* overflowing with almond soup; sea breams looking at cooks with glazed eyes; oranges that dropped from the sky, falling in fuller measure than raindrops on a stormy day; and a thousand other marvels beyond one's ken.

IV

Because Celinina was his only child, the father was beside himself with worry and anxiety. His business kept him away from the house, but he managed to look in often to see how his daughter was doing. The disease continued its course with treacherous swings, sometimes giving hope of a cure, other times taking it away.

The good man had sad forebodings. Celinina's bed, and her body in it racked with fever and pain, occupied his thoughts constantly. Mindful of what he might do to raise the child's spirits, every night when he came home he brought her a seasonal gift, always making it something different, but always dispensing with sweets of any kind. One day he brought her a flock of turkeys that looked so lifelike they only needed to gobble; another day he drew from his pockets half of the Holy Family; and the following one he produced a Saint Joseph with the manger and stable. Afterwards he presented her with some magnificent sheep led by splendid shepherds, and then he came up with some washerwomen doing laundry, and with a sausagemaker selling sausages, and a black wise man, followed by another with a white beard and a crown. To have something to bring, he even brought an old woman spanking a boy for not knowing his lesson.

Because of her cousins' chatter Celinina had become knowledgeable about what constituted a complete Nativity scene, so she knew that two principal figures were missing: the mule and the ox. She had no idea of the significance of said mule and ox, but watchful that everything be perfect, she asked her solicitous father time and time again for the pair of animals that had remained in Santa Cruz's shop.

He promised to bring them, and in his heart of hearts he firmly resolved not to return without both beasts, but that day, which was the 23rd, various matters and concerns piled up on him to such an extent that he did not have a moment's rest. On top of that, as luck would have it, he drew a prize in the lottery, and learned that he had won a lawsuit, and two good friends got in his way all morning long, so that . . . in short, he came home without the mule, but also without the ox.

Celinina was very disappointed when she saw that the only two jewels needed to complete her treasure were still missing. Her father wished to remedy the situation at once, but the girl had worsened considerably during the day. The doctor came, and as his words were not reassuring, nobody thought about oxen.

On the 24th the poor man decided not to step out of the house. For a brief spell Celinina experienced such evident relief that everybody nourished hopes, and, overjoyed, the father said: "I'm going for those two pieces right now."

But as a bird soaring skyward plunges swiftly when wounded, thus did Celinina plunge into the depths of a very intense fever. She convulsed, suffocating in the burning arms of the disease that was squeezing the life out of her. In the confusion of her delirium, and on the stormy wave of her thoughts, there floated, like the only object saved from a cataclysm, the obsession of an unsatisfied desire, that yearned-for mule and that longed-for ox that she ardently hoped to possess.

Her father left the house half mad and dashed through the streets, but in the middle of one of them he stopped and said: "Who can think about crèche pieces now?"

And running from one place to another, he climbed stairs, rang bells, and opened doors without pausing to rest, until he had gathered seven or eight doctors and taken them home with him. Celinina had to be saved.

V

But it was not God's will that the seven or eight (the exact number is not known for certain) disciples of Aesculapius should circumvent the sentence that he had pronounced, and Celinina's condition deteriorated with each passing hour; disheartened and burning up with fever, she struggled through indescribable anguish, like a butterfly that has been struck and trembles on the ground with broken wings. Her parents hovered over her with frantic anxiety, as if they wished, solely by virtue of eyeing her, to prolong their daughter's life, to arrest that rapid human disintegration, and with their breath restore the breath of the poor martyr who was fading away in a sigh.

Drums and tom-toms and the gay jingle of tambourines sounded in the street. Celinina opened her eyes, which had seemed closed forever, and looked up at her father; and with her expression alone, and a grave utterance that no longer resembled the languages of this world, she asked her father for what he had forgotten to bring her. Overwhelmed with grief, both parents tried to deceive her so that she would know some joy at that moment of supreme affliction. Offering her the turkeys, they said: "Look, sweetie, here they are—the mule and the ox."

But Celinina, even at death's door, had sufficient clarity of mind to know that the turkeys were nothing but turkeys, and refused them with a kindly gesture. Afterwards she kept her eyes riveted on her parents, and both hands on her head to show them where she felt the sharp pains. The rhythmic sound that is the last pulsation of life gradually grew more faint in her, and it finally fell silent, as a clock falls silent when its innards stop, and pretty Celinina was but a graceful shape, inert and cold like marble, white and transparent like the purified wax that burns on altars.

Can the father's remorse be understood now? In order to bring Celinina back to life he would have roamed the world over to collect all the oxen and all, absolutely all, the mules to be found. The thought of not having satisfied that innocent desire of hers was a sharp, icy sword that pierced his heart. In vain did he attempt to pull it out by reasoning with himself. But what good was reason if he was as much of a child then as the one who slept in the casket, lending, as he was, more importance to a toy than to all heavenly and earthly things?

VI

At length the sounds of despair in the house died away, as if grief, penetrating into the soul, which is its very own dwelling place, had closed the doors to the senses in order to be more alone and take pleasure in itself.

It was Christmas Eve, and if silence reigned supreme throughout that house so recently visited by death, in every other one, and outside in the streets of the city, there arose joyous sounds from crude musical instruments and the loud voices of children and adults singing about the coming of the Messiah. From the room in which the dead little girl lay, the pious women who kept her company heard, descending from the floor above, a terrible racket that disturbed them in their grief and devout prayers. Upstairs, numerous small children, along with an even greater number of big children and happy mamas and papas and jubilant aunts and uncles, were celebrating Christmas, ecstatic over the most delightful crèche imaginable, and a luxuriant tree that was illuminated by a thousand glittering oil lamps and had toys and sweets hanging from its branches.

What with all the din from up above, there were moments when it seemed that the ceiling shook, and that poor little Celinina shuddered in her blue casket, and that all the lights flickered, as if, in their own way, they wished to announce that they too were somewhat intoxicated. Of the three women who were keeping watch, two retired; only one remained, and she, feeling a great heaviness in her head, no doubt as a result of the fatigue generated by so long a vigil, slumped in her chair and fell asleep.

The lights continued to flicker and waver a great deal, despite the fact that no air entered the room. Anyone would believe that invisible wings were flapping about the space occupied by the altar. The lace on Celinina's dress also moved, and the petals of her cloth flowers proclaimed the stirring of a playful breeze or very soft hands. And at that very moment Celinina opened her black eyes.

They soon filled the room with anxious, eager glances that went from side to side and from top to bottom. Immediately afterwards she separated her hands, with no resistance from the ribbon that tied them together, and, closing both fists, she rubbed her eyes with her knuckles, as children normally do when they awake. Then she sat up quickly, effortlessly, and, looking at the ceiling, started laughing, but her laughter could only be seen, not heard. The only easily perceived sound was the noise of rapidly fluttering wings, as if all the world's doves were flying in and out of the deathbed room and grazing against the ceiling and walls with their feathers.

Celinina stood, extended her arms upward, and instantly sprouted short, white wings. Beating the air with them, she took flight and disappeared.

Everything remained the same: the burning candles that spilled copious streams of white wax over the socket rings; the images in their proper places, arms and legs unmoved, austere lips unparted; the woman placidly settled into a deep sleep that must have struck her as heavenly. Everything continued as before—except the blue casket, which now lay empty.

VII

What a marvelous celebration, this Christmas Eve at the home of Señor and Señora ——!

The deafening sounds of drums fill the room. Nobody can make the devilish children understand that they would enjoy themselves more by doing away with the infernal racket of those war instruments. So that no human ear will be in a functional state the following day, they add to the drum that invention from hell called a tom-tom, whose sound resembles Satan's growls. Completing the symphony is the tambourine, whose shrill pitch, like the screech of old pots and pans, grates on the calmest nerves. But, nevertheless, this discordant clamor with neither melody nor rhythm, more primitive than the music of savages, is merry on this most special of nights, and has a certain affinity with a celestial choir.

A crèche is not a work of art in the eyes of adults, but children see so much beauty in the figures, such a mystic expression in all their faces, and so much faithfulness in their dress, that they do not believe that a more perfect work has come from human hands, and they attribute this art to the peculiar industry of certain angels who have devoted themselves to making a living by working in clay. The cork entryway, imitating a Roman arch in ruins, is utterly charming, and the brook, represented by a small mirror with green spots that simulate aquatic plants and the moss of banks, seems to run the length of the table with a placid murmur. The bridge over which the shepherds pass is such that never has cardboard looked so much like stone, which is the reverse of what happens in many of the works of our modern engineers, who build stone bridges that seem to be made of cardboard. The mountain that occupies the center would be confused with a stretch of the Pyrenees, and its pretty little huts, smaller than the figures, and its trees, fashioned from tiny euonymus branches, appear more real than nature itself.

The plain is where one sees the loveliest details, the most characteristic figures: the washerwomen doing the wash in the brook; the turkey and chicken breeders tending their flocks; a civil guard leading two urchins under arrest; gentlemen riding in luxuriant coaches next to the camel of one of the Magi; and Perico the blind man playing his guitar in the midst of a group where shepherds who have returned from the stable are wandering about. A streetcar, just like the ones in the Salamanca district,* covers the length of the plain, and as it has two sets of rails and wheels it is continually running from east to west, to the great astonishment of the black king, who has no idea what that diabolical machine is.

In front of the stable there is a beautiful little square with a fishbowl in the center, and not far from it a boy hawking newspapers and two Madrid dandies dancing gracefully. An old woman selling doughnuts and another selling chestnuts on a street corner are the most amusing pieces in this marvelous clay village, and are also the ones that attract most of the children's attention. But what really makes all of them split their sides with laughter is a boy in tatters who holds a lottery ticket in one hand as he cleverly filches chestnuts from Aunt Lambrijas's basket with the other.

In short: the number one crèche in Madrid is the one in that home, one of the city's most illustrious, and it has brought together in its rooms the cutest and most well-behaved children for twenty streets around.

VIII

What about the tree? It's fashioned from oak and cedar, and the solicitous family friend who very painstakingly put it together declares that he never turned out a more finished and perfect piece of work. The number of presents hanging from its branches cannot be counted. According to the supposition of one little boy, their number exceeds the grains of sand in a sea. Sweets inside little cups of rippled paper; tangerines, which are the babes in arms of oranges; chestnuts wrapped in silver tissue; tiny boxes containing drops of therapeutic candy; various figurines on foot and on horseback—all of God's bounty, to be perfected later by Mahonesa or sold by Scropp, has been put on it by hands as generous as they are skillful. And such a profusion of multiwick oil lamps illuminated that tree of life that, according to the account of one four-year-old boy, there were more lights on it than stars in the sky.

The joy of this throng of children cannot be compared to any human feeling: it is the ineffable joy of celestial choirs in the presence of the Supreme Good and the Supreme Beauty. The abundance of satisfaction almost makes them restrained, and it's as if they were bewildered, in seraphic ecstasy, with their souls in their eyes, savoring beforehand what they are going to eat, and floating, like blessed angels, in the pure ether of sweet and delicious things, in the perfume of flowers and cinnamon, in the uncreated essence of play and desire.

IX

But all of a sudden the children heard a noise that did not come from them. They all glanced up at the ceiling, and, not seeing anything, looked around at one another, laughing. The sound grew louder, the sound of wings brushing against a wall and striking the ceiling. If they were blind, they would have believed that all the doves from all the dovecotes in the universe had flown into the room. But they saw nothing, absolutely nothing.

They did notice, though, and immediately thereafter, something inexplicable and phenomenal. All the figures of the crèche moved, all of them changed places without a sound. The streetcar climbed to the top of the mountain; the Magi stepped into the brook; the turkeys entered the stable without permission; and Saint Joseph came out of it thoroughly bewildered, as if wishing to know the cause of such confusion. And then numerous figures fell to the floor. If at first the movement occurred in a somewhat orderly manner, afterwards such chaos ensued that it seemed as though hundreds of thousands of intent hands were rummaging the crèche. It was a universal cataclysm in miniature. The mountain came tumbling down as its aged cement gave way; the brook changed course, and, expelling pieces of mirror from its channel, flooded the plain frightfully; houses sank their roofs in the sand; the stable shook as if it were under attack by fierce winds; and so many lights went out that it clouded over and the festive illuminations dimmed.

In the midst of the astonishment produced by such a phenomenon, some of the little ones were laughing wildly and others were crying. A superstitious old woman said to them:

"Don't you know who's turning things topsy-turvy? It's the dead children in heaven. On Christmas Eve God the Father lets them come down to play with the crèches."

It all came to an end, and once again they heard wings flapping, but this time in departure. Many of those who were present went to examine the destruction, and one man said:

"The table's caved in and all the figures have been upended or disturbed."

They began to pick up the figures and set them in order. After a careful recount and inspection of every piece they knew that something was awry. They searched carefully and then searched again, but to no avail. Two figures were missing: the mule and the ox.

X

Close to dawn the mischief makers were on their way to heaven, tickled pink, frolicking in the clouds, and there were millions and millions, all of them beautiful, pure, and divine, with short white wings beating faster than the swiftest birds on Earth. The flock that they formed was greater than anything that the eye can scan in visible space, and it concealed the moon and the stars, as when the firmament fills with clouds.

"Hurry up, everybody, let's get a move on, because it's almost daybreak," said one of them, "and Grandpa will scold us if we get back late. This year's crèches are worthless. They don't hold a candle to those of other times."

Celinina was flying with them, and as this was her first time in those altitudes she was a little bewildered.

"Come here," said one of her companions. "Give me your hand and you'll fly straighter. But . . . what've you got there?"

"They're fer me, fer me," replied Celinina, clutching two clay animals to her chest.

"Look here, girl, throw those figures away. It's very obvious that you're just now leaving Earth. You have to understand that although we have ever delightful and eternal games in Heaven, Grandpa sends us down to the world on Christmas Eve so that we can get into a little mischief with the crèches. They're also having a good time up there tonight, and I think they send us away because we upset them with all the noise we make. But if God the Father lets us go down, it's on the condition that we take nothing from the houses, and you've swiped that."

These powerful reasons did not register on Celinina, and squeezing the two animals more tightly, she replied: "Fer me, fer me."

"Look, you silly thing," added her companion, "if you don't listen you're going to get all of us in trouble. Fly back down and leave both pieces, because they're from Earth and belong on Earth. You can do it in a jiffy, silly. I'll wait for you on this cloud."

Celinina finally gave in, and, flying down, left her stolen goods on Earth.

XI

This is why the household saw that the hands of Celinina's beautiful body, what had been her visible persona, held two clay figurines of animals instead of a bunch of flowers. Neither the women who had kept watch over her nor Celinina's mother and father could explain it, but the pretty child, for whom everyone wept, went to her grave clutching the mule and the ox in her cold little hands.

December, 1876

Benito Pérez Galdós

"The Princess and the Street Urchin"

I

PACORRITO Migajas was a person of great note. He stood a little over three feet tall and had recently entered his seventh year. His skin was tanned and weather-beaten, and his wizened features made him look more like a dwarf than a child. He had lively black eyes with long, wirelike lashes that bespoke mischief. So ugly was his mouth that it scared people, and his cauliflower ears appeared to have been attached rather than grown. His elegant dress consisted of a shirt that was multicolored from grime, and trousers that were held up by a single suspender. In wintertime he wore a jacket that had belonged to his grandfather, a jacket that, after the sleeves had been cut off at the elbows, suited him to a tee as an overcoat. Around his neck he wrapped, after the manner of a coiled snake, a rag with pretensions to a scarf, and on his head he sported a cap that he had pinched at Madrid's flea market. He went without shoes, which he considered a big nuisance, and also without socks, because the stitching bothered him.

The family of Pacorrito Migajas could not have been more illustrious. His father, accused of attempting to break into a house by scaling a drain, had gone to Ceuta to recover his health but had died there. His mother, a very presentable woman who for many years had a chestnut stall in the Cava de San Miguel, had also fallen afoul of the law, and after numerous run-ins and squabbles with judges and notaries, she was shipped off to the prison in Alcalá. Pacorrito still had a sister, but, leaving her job at the tobacco factory, she decamped to Seville in amorous pursuit of an artillery corporal and never came back. So Migajas was alone in the world, with no family except himself, with no protection except God's, and with no guide except his own will.

248

II

But does the compassionate reader think that Pacorrito became frightened upon finding himself alone? Nothing of the sort. In his short life he had had an opportunity to take in the ups and downs of the world, as well as the false and deceitful ways of this miserable existence. Pumping himself up with energy, he confronted the situation like a hero. Fortunately, he was on good terms with a number of people of his own social condition and even with bearded men who seemed willing to protect him; and so, by virtue of mettle, with a push here and a shove there, he managed to cope with his sad state.

He sold matches, newspapers, and the occasional lottery ticket, which were three commercial enterprises that, when exploited intelligently, could assure him honest earnings. As a result, Pacorrito never wanted for enough money in his pocket to aid a cohort in a jam, or to treat his young lady friends.

He was not unduly concerned about domestic considerations or a landlord's demands. In summertime his palaces were the Prado Museum, and in wintertime the doorways of the Casa Panadería. A sober lad and a foe of mundane pomp, he contented himself with whatever nook he could find to spend the night. Like birds, he ate whatever he came across, and without ever fretting about his next meal, on account of the religious resignation that existed in his soul, and because of his instinctive faith in the mysterious assistance of Providence, which forsakes neither big people nor little people.

Perhaps the reader will believe that Migajas was happy. It seems natural that he would be. For if he had no family, he did enjoy the precious gift of freedom, and since his needs were few, he lived comfortably off his work, without owing anything to anyone, without having his sleep disturbed by worry or ambition. He was poor, but untroubled; his body was covered with threadbare clothes, but his spirit was filled with delicious peace. Nonetheless, Señor Migajas was not happy. Why not? Because he was in love—head over heels in love, as the saying goes.

Yes, ladies and gentlemen, that Pacorrito who was so small and so ugly and so poor and so alone was in love. It is an inexorable law of life: no one, whoever he or she may be, escapes this despotic yoke.

Our hero loved with dreamy idealism, free of all impure thought, and at times with a burning passion that caused frenzied ardor to course through his veins. His volcanic heart experienced sensations of all kinds for the object of his love—sometimes sweet and platonic ones like those of Petrarch, sometimes impulsive ones like those of Romeo.

And who had inspired Pacorrito with such a terrible passion? A lady who trailed velvet and silk dresses trimmed with eye-catching furs; a lady with blond hair that fell in ringlets on her alabaster neck; a lady who usually wore a gold pince-nez, and who sometimes sat at the piano for three days running.

III

Here, then, an account of who the celestial beauty was and how our hero made her acquaintance.

Pacorrito's field of commercial operations extended along half of one of the streets that open onto the Puerta del Sol, a very busy street with beautiful shops that by day display countless marvels of industry in their showcases and at night flood them with the brilliance of gaslight. The prettiest of these shops, which belongs to a German, is always full of lovely knickknacks that appeal to all age groups. It is the bazaar of children and adults alike. During Shrovetide it carries comical masks; for Holy Week, pious figures; at Christmas, crèches and trees weighed down with toys; and around New Year, magnificent items for presents.

Pacorrito's frenetic passion began when the German put a delightful collection of ladies in his showcase, ladies dressed in the kind of rich attire dreamed up by Parisian fantasy. Almost all of them were nearly two feet tall. Their faces were of fine, purified wax, and the carmine of fresh roses could not equal the blush of their chaste cheeks. Their still, blue glass eyes shone more brightly than human pupils. Their hair, of the softest crimped wool, could more properly be compared to sunbeams than to that of many distinguished ladies; and the strawberries of April, the cherries of May, and the coral of the deep seas looked ugly compared to their red lips.

The ladies were so judicious that they never moved from the spot where they were placed. Only the wooden hinges of their knees, shoulders, and elbows creaked when the German seated them at the piano or put spectacles on them so that they could look out on the street. Other than that, they caused no trouble and were never known to utter a word.

One of them—what a female!—stood out, for she was the tallest, the slimmest, the most beautiful, the most pleasant, the most elegant, and the most ladylike. She must have been a person of rank, judging by her grave, majestic manner and a certain protective air toward the others that suited her wonderfully.

"A great woman!" exclaimed Pacorrito the first time that he saw her. And for more than an hour he stood before the shopwindow contemplating such seductive beauty.

IV

Our Pacorrito found himself in that particular state of exaltation and delirium in which we see the heroes of romance novels. *His brain boiled; biting snakes coiled in his heart; his mind was a volcano; he wished for death; he abhorred life; he communed with himself nonstop; he gazed at the moon; he rose to seventh heaven;* and so on.

How many times night caught him unawares in melancholy ecstasy before the shopwindow, oblivious to everything, even to his own businesses and way of life! But the good Migajas had by no manner of means suffered a rebuff—I mean that to a certain extent he was reciprocated in his mad passion. Who can measure the intensity of a heart made of tow or sawdust? The world is full of mysteries. Science is vain and will never arrive at the gist of things. Good Lord, will it be possible someday to determine exactly the sphere of the inanimate? Where does the inanimate begin? Down with the pedants who stop in front of a stone or a cork and say to it: "You have no soul." God alone knows the true dimensions of that invisible limbo in which lies everything that does not love.

Pacorrito was quite certain of having struck a chord in the lady. She would look at him and, without moving or blinking or opening her mouth, tell him a thousand delightful things, now sweet as hope, now sad as the premonition of ill-starred events. These silent colloquies served to fan the flame that devoured the heart of our friend Migajas, and his daring mind conceived dramatic plans of seduction, abduction, and even matrimony.

One evening the infatuated suitor arrived punctually at the rendezvous. The lady was seated at the piano, her hands suspended over the keys, her divine face turned toward the street. She and the urchin locked eyes. Oh! How much idealism, how much passion in that exchange! Sighs followed sighs, endearments followed endearments, until an unforeseen event cut the thread of their sweet connection and with a single blow crushed the lovers' happiness. It was like those sudden catastrophes that wound hearts mortally, giving rise to suicides, tragedies, and other lamentable occurrences.

A hand from the shop reached into the showcase, grasped the lady by the waist, and carried her inside. Such an acute stab of pain came on the heels of Migajas's amazement that he wished to die on the spot. To see his beloved disappear as though some insatiable grave had swallowed her, and not be able to retain the life slipping away from him, and not be able to follow her even if it were to hell itself! The strength of a mere mortal could not cope with such misfortune! Migajas was about to collapse; he thought of suicide; he invoked God and the devil.

"They've sold her!" he murmured, numb with grief.

And he pulled his hair and scratched his face; and as he stamped his feet in desperation, his matches, his newspapers, and his lottery tickets fell to the ground. Mundane interests, you are not worth a sigh!

V

After he recovered from his violent emotion, Pacorrito looked toward the interior of the shop and saw several little girls and two or three adults talking with the German. One of the girls held the lady of his thoughts in her arms. He was tempted to dash inside, but did not, fearful that when they saw his outlandish appearance he would be given a beating or handed over to the police. Transfixed in the doorway, he reflected on the horrors of the white slave trade, and on the horrors of that abominable Teutonic establishment in which a few *duros* decided the fate of honorable creatures, subjecting them to the destructive ferocity of ill-bred children. Oh! How miserable human nature seemed to Pacorrito!

The people who had purchased the lady left the shop and got in a luxurious carriage. How the no-good so-and-sos were laughing! Even the smallest child, who was the most spoiled, took the liberty of pulling the hapless doll's arms, in spite of having for his exclusive enjoyment a variety of toys appropriate to his age. The grown-ups also seemed very satisfied with the acquisition.

While the footman was receiving his orders, Pacorrito, who was a man of bold and heroic decisions, conceived the idea of hanging onto the back of the carriage. And so he did, with the quadrumanous agility shown by urchins when they wish to take a carriage ride from one end of Madrid to the other.

Craning his neck to the right, he saw, sticking out of the door, one of the arms of the lady who had been sacrificed to filthy lucre.

That rigid arm and that rigid pink fist spoke forcefully to the imagination of Migajas, who, in the midst of the wheels' racket, heard these words:
"Save me, Pacorrito, save me!"

VI

At the portico of the great house where the carriage stopped, the urchin's illusions came to a swift end, because a servant told him that if he dirtied the courtyard with his muddy feet he would break his neck. In the face of this overpowering constraint, Migajas retreated, his heart filled with a burning desire for revenge.

His fiery temperament compelled him to go forward, to throw himself into the arms of fortune and into the darkness of the unforeseen. His soul adapted itself to noisy and dramatic adventures. So what did the little scamp do? He reached an agreement with the garbage collectors at the house where his beloved was in slavery, and by such means— which may not be poetic, but which show astuteness and a heart as big as the sky—Migajas slipped inside the palace.

How his heart pounded as he went up and entered the kitchen! The thought of being near *her* rattled him to such an extent that more than once his basket fell from his hands and spilled on the stairs. But in no way could he quench the burning thirst of his eyes, which longed to see the beautiful lady. He heard the distant squeals of children at play, but nothing else. The grand creature was nowhere to be seen.

The servants of the house, seeing that he was so little and so ugly, taunted him continually, but one of them, who was more compassion- ate, gave him sweets. One very cold morning the cook, out of pity or out of malice, gave him a drink of wine that was as bitter and fiery as the devil. The urchin felt a sweet warmth flood his body and burning fumes drift up to his head. His legs grew weak; his limp arms sagged with voluptuous abandon. From his chest came a playful laugh that rose to his lips like an endless stream, and Pacorrito chortled and held onto the wall so as not to fall.

A vigorous kick on the buttocks tempered somewhat his laughter, and with his hand on the part that hurt, Pacorrito left the kitchen. His mind was unhinged. He did not know where his steps were taking him. He ran, staggering and laughing again, stepping first on cold tiles, afterwards on smooth floorboards, and then on soft carpets.

All of a sudden his eyes fixed on an object that lay on the floor. Heavens above! Migajas let out a howl of pain and fell to his knees.

There, stretched out like a corpse, her clothes torn and in disarray, her alabaster forehead split, one of her arms broken, and her hair disheveled, was the lady of his thoughts. A pitiful, heartbreaking sight!

For a while our hero was unable to utter a word. His voice caught in his throat. He pressed that cold, inanimate body against his heart, covering it with burning kisses. The lady's eyes were open, and she gazed at her faithful admirer with melancholy tenderness. Despite her horrible injuries and the pitiful state of her body, the noble lady was alive. Pacorrito knew it by the singular light in her still, blue eyes, which emitted flashes of love and gratitude.

"My lady, who has mistreated you so?" he asked in an anguished, pathetic tone.

But anger quickly followed on the heels of his great distress, and Pacorrito resolved to avenge such flagrant evildoing.

Because he heard footsteps at that very moment, he took the charming lady in his arms and broke into a run to leave the house. He descended the stairs, crossed the courtyard, and flew out into the street. His mad dash was like the flight of the bird that, having stolen its grain, hears the hunter's shot, and, feeling itself unharmed, wants to put as much distance as possible between itself and the shotgun.

He ran down one, two, three, ten streets, until, believing that he had gone far enough, he took a rest and set the precious object of his senseless love on his knees.

VII

Night came, and Pacorrito noted with pleasure the soft shadows that enveloped the daring abduction and protected his chaste love. Carefully examining the injuries to his beloved's disfigured body, he determined that they were not serious, although you would be able to see her brain, if she had one, through the holes in her skull, and all of the tow of her heart was pouring out through various breaks. Her dress was in shreds, and part of her hair had been lost on a street somewhere during their swift flight. His spirit filled with sorrow upon realizing that he lacked the funds to get out of such a tight spot. Having quit his businesses, his pockets were empty, and a loved woman, especially if she is not in good health, generates an endless outlay. Migajas touched the part of his ragged clothes where he usually kept money, but did not feel a single coin.

Now, he thought, *now I'm going to need a house, a bed, no end*

*of doctors and surgeons, a dressmaker, a lot of food, a good fire . . .
and I have nothing.*

But since he was so exhausted, he laid his head over his idol's
body and fell asleep like an angel.

Then—oh marvel of marvels!—the lady gradually revived, and in
the end got up and showed Pacorrito her smiling countenance, her
noble forehead without a single injury, her slim figure without the
slightest break, her clean and whole dress, her curled and perfumed
hair, and her smart hat adorned with tiny flowers; in a word, she
appeared as perfect and as altogether beautiful as she had been when
the urchin first saw her in the shopwindow.

Oh! Migajas was dazzled, astounded, bewildered, speechless. He
got on his knees and worshiped the lady as one would a divinity. She
then took him by the hand, and in a clear voice, sweeter than the
song of a nightingale, said to him:

"Pacorrito, come. Follow me. I want to show you my gratitude and
the sublime love you have inspired in me. You have been constant,
loyal, generous, and heroic, because you rescued me from the clutches
of those vandals who were tormenting me. You deserve my heart and
my hand. Come, follow me and do not be foolish. And do not think
that you're inferior to me because you're wearing rags."

Migajas took in her dazzling elegance, her luxurious dress, and
said disconsolately:

"My lady, where can I go looking like this?"

The beautiful lady did not answer, but she did tug at Pacorrito
by the hand and whisk him off through a mysterious region of darkness.

VIII

At length the urchin saw an imposing, illuminated room filled with
precious objects whose shapes he could not distinguish initially. But
in a short while he began to make out a thousand different figures,
like the ones that peopled the shop where he had met his beloved.
What most attracted his attention was the sight of ladies in glittering
dresses coming forward to welcome them—all the ladies who had
accompanied the blond beauty in her showcase.

And the great lady responded to their greetings with a dignified
and ceremonious obeisance. She seemed to be of a higher station, like
that of a princess or queen or empress. Her royal dignity and self-
assured, but not haughty, mien showed her ascendancy over the others.

She immediately introduced Pacorrito, who became completely disconcerted and turned redder than a beet when the princess, taking his
hand, said:

"I present to you Señor don Pacorro de las Migajas, who has come
to honor us this evening."

The poor urchin's heart fell when he observed the boundless luxury
that reigned supreme there, comparing it as he did with his poverty,
his bare feet, his pants held up by one suspender, and his jacket cut
off at the elbows.

"I can read your thoughts," allowed the princess under her breath.
"Your attire is not the most appropriate for a celebration like the one
we're having this evening. To tell the truth, you are not presentable."

"Dear lady, my useless tailor . . . ," mumbled Pacorrito, thinking
that a fib would preserve his sense of decorum, "never finished these
clothes of mine."

"We will dress you here," said the noble lady.

The footmen in that strange mansion were very amusing little
monkeys. Tiny parrots, parakeets to be exact, as well as a number
of paper birds, acted as pages, and the paper ones never left their
lady's side.

The servants busied themselves at once with smartening up a bit
the good Migajas's shabby dress. Very attractive and gilded matchboxes
shaped like shoes soon appeared on his bare feet. They made him
a ruff from half of a red paper Chinese lantern, and a kind of little
pastoral hat adorned with pretty flowers from a wickerwork jardiniere.
Around his neck they hung, like decorations, the circular form of an
elegant kepi, a round matchbox that looked like a watch, and the glass
stopper of a small bottle of perfume. The paper birds had the felicitous
idea of strapping around his waist, in the manner of a sword or dagger,
a luxurious ivory paper cutter. With these and other ingenious occurrences to conceal his ragged clothes, the newspaper vendor looked so
handsome that he did not seem like the same person. When they stood
him in front of the mirror of a sewing box so that he could see himself,
he felt proud as a peacock. The boy positively dazzled.

IX

The dance began at once. Several canaries sang waltzes and habaneras
in their cages, and music boxes played by themselves, as did the

clarinets and cornets whose keys depressed unaided and with great skill. The violins also managed, in an odd way, to play their strings without manual assistance, and the trumpets blew one another. The music was a little discordant, but Migajas, in the exaltation of his spirit, found it enchanting.

There is no need to say that the princess danced with our hero. The other ladies had high-ranking military officers for partners, or sovereigns who left their horses at the door. Among the latter were such eminently interesting figures as Bismarck, the chancellor of Germany, Napoleon, and other great men. Migajas was bursting with pride.

It would be impossible to describe the emotions that he experienced as he swung into the dizzying spins of a waltz with his loved one in his arms. The princess's sweet breathing and her golden tresses gently caressed Pacorrito's face, tickling him and intoxicating him. A loving glance from the genteel lady or a soft moan of fatigue would only serve to drive him more mad.

At the height of the dance, the monkeys announced that dinner was served, and the ball broke up immediately. From that point on nobody thought about anything except eating, which gladdened the good Migajas's spirits, because, without prejudice to the spiritual nature of his love, he was famished.

X

The dining room was stately and the table magnificent, and the service and all the crockery pieces were of the best that has been made for dolls. A profusion of bouquets spread their perfume and displayed their colors in small vases, eggcups, and thimbles.

Pacorrito took the seat on the princess's right, and all the diners began to eat. The parakeets and paper birds waited on them as proficiently and as precisely as soldiers who maneuver in a parade on the orders of their general. The dishes, all of them uncooked or cold cuts, were exquisite. If the food did not displease Migajas at first, it soon began to produce some indigestion in him, even before having eaten like a horse. The banquet consisted of articles of marzipan, turkeys so small and birdlike they could be devoured in one mouthful, and tidbits of beef tenderloin and bream; a delectable entrée of hempseed and a birdseed pâté *à la canaria*, breadcrumb rissoles *à la perdigona*, and fricassee of pheasants' eyes in wild blackberry sauce; a moss salad, delicious candies, and fruits of all kinds, which the parakeets had harvested from a tapestry where they were embroidered, with the melons being like grapes and the grapes like lentils.

During the meal everybody chattered nonstop, except Pacorrito, who was timid and did not so much as utter a word. The presence of all those military men in uniform and gold braid bewildered him, and he was greatly surprised at seeing the talkative and playful side of those who had appeared so stiff and silent in the shopwindow, as if they were made of clay.

The one named Bismarck never stopped: he cracked jokes, he slapped the table with his hand, and he threw little bread balls at the princess. He swung his arms wildly, as though their hinges operated on a string and a hidden hand was pulling at it from under the table.

"I'm having a great time!" exclaimed the chancellor. "My dear princess, when you spend your life decorating a mantel in the midst of a clock, a bronze figure, and a begonia pot, these festivities rejuvenate you and cheer you up for the whole year."

"Oh, the ones whose only job is to decorate mantels and dressers are fortunate indeed!" exclaimed the lady in a melancholy tone. "They get bored, but they don't suffer as we do—those of us who live in continual torment, destined to be the playthings of little men. I cannot adequately describe to you, Chancellor Bismarck, how much we suffer when one person pulls our right arm and another our left, when this one cracks our heads and that one tears us apart, or drenches us, or slits us open to see what we have inside our bodies."

"I can imagine," said the chancellor, opening and closing his arms repeatedly.

"Oh, you poor things, you poor things!" exclaimed all at once the emperors, Espartero,* and other personages.

"And I'm not as unfortunate as most," added the lady, "for I have found a protector and friend in the brave and loyal Migajas, who was able to free me from my barbarous ordeal."

Pacorrito flushed a deep scarlet.

"Brave and loyal," repeated all the dolls at the same time, in a tone of admiration.

"Therefore," continued the princess, "tonight, when our Genius Creator permits us to gather to celebrate the first day of the year, I wanted to do him honor by bringing him with me and giving him my hand as his wife in sign of alliance and reconciliation between the lineage of dolls and compassionate, well-bred children."

XI

As the princess spoke, Bismarck was looking at Pacorrito with such a malicious and snide expression of mockery that our distinguished hero became angry. At the same instant the rascal of a chancellor fired a bread ball at him with such deadly aim that he nearly blinded Migajas. But as the latter was the prototype of circumspection, he prudently kept his own counsel and said not a word.

The princess gazed at him lovingly and gratefully.

"I'm having a great time!" Bismarck repeated, clapping his wooden hands. "Until the hour comes to go back alongside the clock and hear its incessant ticktock, let's enjoy ourselves, let's get drunk, let's be happy. If our gentleman friend Pacorrito wished to hawk his newspaper, it would give us a good laugh."

"Señor Migajas," said the princess, looking at him kindly, "did not come here to entertain us. That does not mean we couldn't enjoy hearing him hawk *La Correspondencia* and his matches, if he wishes to do so."

The urchin found this proposal so contrary to his dignity and decorum that he was deeply afflicted and did not know how to answer his beloved.

"Let him dance!" shouted the chancellor brazenly. "Let him dance on the table. And if he doesn't want to, I ask that his finery be taken from him, and that he be left in rags and barefoot, as he was when he arrived here."

Bismarck's demand made Migajas's blood boil. His rage prevented him from speaking a single word.

"Do not be cruel, my dear chancellor," said the lady, smiling. "As to the rest, I hope to rid the good Migajas of his fury."

General laughter greeted these words, and what a sight it was to see all the dolls, and the most celebrated generals and emperors in the world, simultaneously clubbing one another on the head like Guignol puppets.

"Let him dance! Let him hawk *La Correspondencia!*" they all clamored.

Migajas felt his legs go weak. The notion of dignity was so strong in him that he would die before suffering the humiliation that they wished to visit upon him. He was going to respond when the malicious chancellor took a long, thin straw, apparently from a workbasket, wetted the end with saliva, and stuck it in Pacorrito's ear so quickly that our hero did not notice the coarse familiarity until he had smarted under the nervous jolt generated by such tomfoolery.

Blind with anger, he put his hand to his belt and brandished his paper cutter. The ladies started shouting and the princess fainted. But this did not placate the fierce Migajas; on the contrary, he became more irate and attacked his insolent foes, raining blows left and right and cracking heads with impunity. You could hear yells and curses and threats. Even the parakeets squawked, and the paper birds moved their tails as a sign of panic.

A few moments later nobody made fun of the ill-tempered Migajas. All the emperors had ended up without noses, and the chancellor went around the floor retrieving his two arms and two legs (a strange case that defies explanation). But little by little, with saliva and a certain skill, they mended all the damage, inasmuch as dolls enjoyed the advantages of self-repair. The princess, who had recovered from her faint with the aid of smelling salts that her pages brought to her in a hazelnut shell, called the street urchin, and, leading him to her boudoir, spoke to him alone as follows:

XII

"My illustrious Migajas, what you have just done, far from lessening my love for you, increases it, because you have demonstrated your indomitable courage by triumphing easily over that mob of buffoonish dolls, the worst group of beings that I know. And so, moved by my tender love for you, I now solemnly propose that you become my husband without delay."

Pacorrito fell to his knees.

"Once we're married," the lady continued, "every one of those little emperors and chancellors will respect you and revere you as they do me myself, because you need to know that I am the queen of all those who exist in that part of the world. And my titles are not usurped, but transmitted by the divine law of dolls that was established by the Supreme Genius who created us and governs us."

"My lady, my dear lady," Migajas said, or tried to say, "my happiness is so great that I am unable to express it."

"Very well," the lady responded with majesty, "since you wish to be my husband, and, consequently, prince and lord of these doll kingdoms, I must inform you that in order to do so you have to renounce your human personality."

"I do not understand what Your Highness means."

"You belong to the human race. I do not. Our natures being different, we cannot unite. It is essential that you exchange yours for mine, which you can do easily by an act of will. Answer me, then. Pacorrito Migajas, son of man, do you wish to be a doll?"

The peculiarity of this question held the street urchin in suspense for a moment or two.

"And what does it mean to be a doll?" he finally asked.

"To be like me. Our nature may be more perfect than human nature. To outward appearances, we lack life, but within ourselves we have it in abundance. To the imperfect senses of man, we lack movement, emotion, and speech, but such is not the case. *You* see how we move, feel, and talk. Our lot is not, in truth, very gratifying at present, because we serve as the playthings of the children of your race, and even of the grown-ups, but in return for this disadvantage, we are eternal."

"Eternal?"

"Yes, we live eternally. If those cruel children break us, we are reborn of our destruction and begin life anew, perpetually describing a dark circle from the shop to the hands of the children, and from the hands of the children to the Tyrolese factory, and from the factory to the shop, forever and ever."

"Forever and ever!" repeated Migajas, entranced.

"We go through some very difficult times, to be sure," the lady added, "but on the other hand, we do not know death, and our Genius Creator allows us to gather on certain holidays to celebrate the glories of our race, as we are doing this evening. We cannot evade any of the laws of our nature, nor can we pass into the world of humans, despite the fact that humans are permitted to pass into ours and become full-fledged dolls."

"How extraordinary!" exclaimed Migajas, struck with amazement.

"Now you know all the particulars to be initiated into a doll's life. Our principles are very simple. Consider them carefully and answer my question: Do you wish to be a doll?"

The princess had the imperious manner of a priestess of old, which captivated Pacorrito all the more.

"I wish to be a doll," declared the street urchin with aplomb.

And the princess at once traced some diabolical signs in the air, in the process uttering strange words that for all Pacorrito knew could have been Latin, Chinese, or Chaldean, but which surely were Tyrolese. Afterwards the lady wrapped the brave Migajas in her arms and said to him:

"You are now my husband. I have the power to perform a marriage, just as I have the authority to welcome neophytes into our great Law. My beloved prince, blessed may you be forever and ever."

The entire court of figures entered all of a sudden, singing· with the music of canaries and nightingales: "Forever and ever."

XIII

They strolled through the salons as couples. Migajas gave his arm to his consort.

"It's a pity," said the latter, "that our hours of pleasure are so brief. Soon we shall have to return to our posts."

His Most Serene Highness experienced, from the moment of his transformation, odd sensations. The strangest one was having completely lost the sense of taste and the notion of food. All that he had eaten stayed in him as though his stomach were a basket or a box, and he had put in it a thousand indigestible cardboard dishes that had no nourishment, no weight, no substance, no taste.

Furthermore, he was no longer master of his movements and had to walk in a difficult rhythm. He noticed an overall hardness in his body, as though he had turned into bone, wood, or clay. When he touched or tapped himself, it made a sound like porcelain. Even his clothes were hard, as hard as his body.

When he was finally alone with his dear wife and squeezed her in his arms, he did not feel any divine or human pleasure, only the jarring perception of two cold, hard bodies. He kissed her cheeks and found them frozen. In vain did his spirit, thirsty for enjoyable sensations, call out to nature in a frenzy. Nature in him now was the stuff of crockery. He felt his heart beat like the mechanism of a clock. His thoughts survived, but all the rest was unfeeling matter.

The princess looked very content.

"What's wrong, my love?" she asked Pacorrito, seeing his distressful expression.

"I'm supremely bored," he replied.

"You'll get accustomed to it. Oh, what delightful times! But if you kept this up, we wouldn't be able to live."

"Your Highness calls this delightful?" asked Migajas. "Good heavens! What coldness, what hardness, what emptiness, what stiffness!"

"There are still some human elements left in you, as well as the defect of man's corrupt senses. Pacorrito, control your outbursts or with your bad example you'll turn the entire doll world topsy-turvy."

"Life! Life, blood, warmth, and skin!" shouted Migajas in despair while gesturing like a madcap. "What's happening inside me?"

The princess embraced him and, kissing him with her red wax lips, exclaimed: "You're mine, forever and ever!"

At that very moment they heard a great disturbance and numerous voices saying: "It's time, it's time!"

A bell began to peal and the stroke of twelve rang in the New Year. All of a sudden everything disappeared from Pacorrito's eyes: princess, palace, dolls, and emperors. He was alone.

XIV

He was alone and in profound darkness.

He tried to scream and had no voice. He tried to move and could not. He was a stone figure.

He waited, filled with anguish. Day finally broke, and Pacorrito saw his former self, but all of him was in one color, and apparently all of him was of one material: his face, his arms, his hair, and even the newspapers that he held in his hand.

"There's no doubt about it," he said, crying inwardly. "I'm just like a stone."

Pacorrito then realized that in front of him there was a huge sheet of glass with inverted letters on it, and that to one side of him stood a multitude of figures and objets d'art.

"I'm in the shopwindow! How dreadful!"

A clerk grasped him carefully by the hand, and, after dusting him, returned him to the same spot.

His Most Serene Highness saw that on the pedestal where he stood there was a card with this figure: 240 *reales.*

"Good heavens! I'm worth a fortune. Well, that's some consolation at least."

And people stopped on the outside of the glass to look at the amusing yellow clay sculpture of a boy selling newspapers and matches. They all praised the artist's skill, and they all laughed at Migajas's features and ordinary figure, while the former street urchin, in the depths of his unfeeling clay, exclaimed over and over and in anguish:

"A doll! A doll, forever and ever!"

January, 1879

Leopoldo Alas, Clarín (1852-1901)

Author of one of his country's greatest novels, La Regenta *(1884-85), Clarín—almost always referred to by this pseudonym—also wrote some of the most incisive literary criticism of his time, and in so doing he earned the respect and admiration of some and the enmity and hostility of others. Although he lived in the provincial capital of Oviedo nearly all his life, he knew the literati who resided in Madrid. Conversant as he was with the writings of his contemporaries, in and out of Spain, he became one of the first Spaniards to recognize the genius of Galdós and to champion his works.*

Clarín has also been recognized in another field, that of the short novel. Pipá *(1882),* The Two Boxes *[Las dos cajas] (1883),* Doña Berta *(1891), undoubtedly one of the most lyrical yet poignant pieces of fiction written in the nineteenth century, and* The Lord *[El señor] (1892) attest to his special ability to explore the human psyche on several planes, to be tender without being maudlin, to be idealistic without being simplistic, to be religious without being dogmatic, to be, in a word, profound.*

His short stories exhibit these very same qualities, along with humor, satire, honesty, intellectualism, indignation, and passion. And a sense of wonder, for when it comes to one witnessing one's own funeral there are several legends, examples of fantastic tales in nineteenth-century Spanish literature, with which he was surely familiar. "My Funeral" appeared in 1883 and "Socrates' Rooster" in 1896.

Leopoldo Alas, Clarín

"My Funeral"

Discourse of a Madman

ONE night I spent much more time than I should have playing chess with my friend Roque Tuyo* at the San Benito Café. When I left to go home the street lamps were out, except for the pilot burners. It was springtime, with June approaching. It was also warm, and the spirit more than the body was refreshed by the pleasant murmur of water that ran freely from hydrants, forming rivulets on the sidewalks. I arrived home with my feet wet, and the dampness and my head, which was killing me, could have done me a great deal of harm, like, for instance, driving me mad. Between the chess and the moisture I was already suffering considerably. Anyway, the cops, asleep on street corners, their arms folded and leaning against the carriage entrances of various mansions, looked like black rooks. So much so that when I passed by San Ginés* and one of them yielded the sidewalk to me, instead of saying "Thank you," I blurted out "Castle," and continued on my way. Upon arriving at my house, I saw that the balcony of my bedroom was open and that from it came the kind of light generated by thick candles with four wicks. I gave the three prescribed knocks on the door. A throaty voice, like that of a person half asleep, asked:

"Who is it?"

"The black king!" I replied, and nobody let me in. "Check!" I shouted three times in the space of one minute, and still nobody let me in.

I summoned the night watchman, who was unlocking doors on both sides of the street, going from square to square with every step.

"My good man," I said to him when he was at the remove of a pawn. "Not even if you were a knight! You have some way of capturing!"

"'Knight'? 'Capturing'? Don't talk nonsense, and keep the noise down, because there's a dead man laid out on the fourth floor."

"A victim of the dampness!" I exclaimed, filled with compassion, and with my feet soaked.

"Yes, sir, of the dampness, but some people wonder if he died of a drunken spree. Because he did have his vices, although he tipped well. In any event, the missus'll find consolation, seeing as she's a looker and still young, and what's now conducted in darkness and goes against justice can be done in the light of day and in keeping with the law."

"And what do you know, you gossip?"

"Don't call me names, señorito. I'm the night watchman and up till now my lips have been sealed, but now that he's gone . . . I'm coming!" shouted that Pyrenean bear, and off he ambled to unlock another door.

A servant came down to let me in. It was Perico, my faithful Perico.

"You took your sweet time, you idiot!"

"Sh! Don't shout. The master has died."

"Whose master?"

"My master."

"Of what?"

"Of a cerebral hemorrhage, I believe. His feet got wet after a game of chess with Señor Roque, and, naturally, it was what Don Clemente said to my mistress: 'Don't worry. One of these days your brute of a husband will drop from sight, dying like a beast, and on account of getting his feet soaked after racking his horns."

"He must have said 'racking his brains.' The expression is racking his brains.

"No, sir, he said 'horns.'"

"Well, he must have been joking. Anyway, getting down to brass tacks. If your master has died, then who am I?"

"Who are you? The man who's going to lay him out. Don Clemente said that he would send you around at this time to avoid talk. Come up, come up."

I went up. In the middle of my bedroom there was a bed surrounded by large single-wick candles, as the guests' coffins are in *Lucretia Borgia*.* The balcony was open. Stretched out on the bed was a body. I looked at it. Sure enough, it was me. I had on a shirt and socks, but no shorts. I started dressing, I mean, laying myself out. I took my black frock coat, the one I wore for the first time at the rally at Price's Circus, when Martos said what he did about "traitors like Sagasta" and the deceased Mata spoke about the Danaides' waterpots.* And I never did learn what waterpots they were! In any event, I wanted to begin changing my socks, because the dampness was bothering me a great deal, and besides, I wanted to be clean going to the cemetery.

Impossible! They were stuck to my skin. Those socks were like the tunic of someone I don't remember, except that they didn't burn, they soaked.* That sensation of moisture sometimes produced cold and sometimes warmth. Occasionally I imagined that I felt my feet on the very nape of my neck and that my ears were shooting stars. In the end, I dressed in mourning, as befits a dead person going to his best friend's funeral. One of the wax candles twisted and drops of burning liquid began to drip onto my nose. Perico—who was there alone, because the man who had laid me out had disappeared—Perico was asleep a short distance away in a chair. He awoke and saw the destruction that the hot wax was wreaking on my face; he tried to straighten the large candle without standing up, but his arm did not reach the holder . . . and, with a yawn, he fell back into a peaceful sleep. The cat came in, jumped up on my bed, and, curling around my legs, made himself comfortable. And we spent the night like that.

At dawn the cold in my feet became more intense. I dreamed that one of them was the Mississippi and the other a very long river in northern Asia whose name I don't recall. What torment I suffered on account of not remembering the name of that foot of mine! When the light of day, coming in through the cracks, mixed with the yellowish light of the candles, Perico awoke; he opened his mouth, yawned in Galician, and, taking out a green innkeeper's purse, started counting money on the deathbed. A black horsefly settled on my wax-covered nose. Perico glanced absentmindedly at the insect as he counted on his fingers, but he made no attempt to deliver me from that nuisance. My wife came in around seven o'clock. She wore black, like those comic actors who get dressed in mourning beforehand when something sad has to happen in the third act. My wife's face was pale, and sorrowful, but the expression of grief on it seemed more like a sign of bad humor than anything else. Those wrinkles and contortions of pain appeared to be bound by an invisible cord. And so they were! Willpower dominated the muscles and held them captive. In the presence of my wife I felt the extraordinary faculties of my conscience as a dead man; my mind communicated directly with the minds of others. I saw through the body into the very depths of the soul. I hadn't managed to see that miraculous aptitude before because Perico was my only company, and Perico did not have a mind in which I could read a thing. "Leave," said my wife to the servant, after which she knelt at my feet and stayed with me by herself. All of a sudden her face grew calm and you could see signs of sleep, but none of grief. And she prayed mentally as follows:

Our father (the other one's certainly taking his time) *who art in heaven* (do you suppose there is another life and that this dead husband of mine is watching me from up there?), *hallowed* (I'll make it an inexpensive mourning period because I don't want to spend a lot of money on black clothes) *be thy name; thy kingdom come* (the funeral's going to cost me a fortune if the members of his political party don't take it upon themselves to pay for it), *thy will be done* (and if I do marry the other one, my wishes take precedence, and I won't put up with insults or jokes) *on earth as it is in heaven* (can this dead idiot be in purgatory already?).

At eight o'clock another person arrived, Clemente Cerrojos, member of the party's central committee from the Latina district. Cerrojos had been a political associate and personal friend of mine, although I didn't think he was as involved in my affairs as he evidently was. I used to play chess with him, but when I realized that he cheated and surreptitiously moved his pieces, I broke off with him, as a chess partner, and went to the café in search of a more noble opponent. Clemente spent every evening at my house keeping my wife company. He was dressed in the manner of shopkeepers' etiquette, which consisted of a long and full black frock coat cut from a plain, shiny fabric, and trousers, vest, and tie, also black. Clemente Cerrojos was cross-eyed in the right eye, and the pupil almost always shone without moving, expressionless, as if a tiny knob was fixed there, a knob like the ones that decorate trunks and doors. My wife didn't raise her head. Cerrojos sat down on the deathbed, making it creak from head to foot. For five minutes they didn't say a word. But, oh, I read their minds, the monsters! Suddenly my wife thought about how awful and criminal it would be to embrace that man or to let herself be embraced there, in front of my presumed corpse. Cerrojos thought the same thing. And both ardently wished to do so. It wasn't love that lured them, but the pleasure of enjoying, with impunity, a great crime, delightful because it was so horrendous. *If he dared to, I wouldn't resist,* thought she, trembling. *If she made a move, I wouldn't be far behind,* said he to himself. She coughed, smoothed her black skirt, and exposed her foot as far as the ankle. He touched her shoulder with his knee. I felt the fire of sacrilegious adultery pass from the one to the other, through their clothes. Clemente was already leaning toward my widow, and she, without seeing him, felt him getting close. I couldn't move, but he thought that I had. He looked at my eyes, open like windows without wood sashes, and took several steps back. Then he approached me and closed the "windows" with which my poor corpse was threatening him.* And then people arrived.

They carried the casket down to the vestibule and left me there next to the door, one of whose leaves was closed. Part of the casket, the foot of it, got wet, as a fine rain fell. Always the dampness! I saw— that is, I felt through the supernatural means at my disposal—the party of mourners coming down. They were all dressed in black, in out-of-style frock coats. Every member of the district committee was there, along with numerous party faithful, the ones who show up only when money is collected for a fellow adherent who's suffered a disaster and the subscription lists are published. Among the group was my bartender, who more than likely wished to shed a tear or two, and indulge in a wistful thought or two, in memory of the deceased, but his ill-fitted frock coat had become tangled between his legs and his tie was itching him and suffocating him, and as a result he didn't think about me for a single moment. The party of mourners gathered together, I was placed in the hearse, and people started getting into carriages. There were two discrete factions, one of which was to be the family grouping, but as I had no relatives, it consisted of my close friends and house intimates, and was headed by Clemente Cerrojos, who had Roque Tuyo on his right and my landlord on his left, the very landlord who would come around to see if we were damaging his property. The other faction was political, and smack in the middle of it was Don Mateo Gómez, an honorable, upright man who professed the dogma of "My friends are my party cohorts." And he swore that Madoz* had appropriated this famous saying from him: "I'll follow my party even when it errs." One of Don Mateo's claims to fame was that not one of his fellow adherents had died without his accompanying him to the cemetery. Don Mateo held me in esteem, but the truth be told, as we made our way to what he intended to call, in the oration that fate had charged him with, the "final resting place," he was turning all the shades of red. Something or other was stuck in his craw, and he rued the day that I was born and even more the day that I died. I had gotten inside Don Mateo's head from the hearse thanks to the double vision that I spoke about earlier. The good patrician—there's no point in lying—had memorized his speech: it was more or less just like the funeral oration, published in the newspapers, for a certain fellow adherent that had been delivered by a celebrated orator of our party. But good old Gómez had forgotten more than half, much more than half, of his not very well learned speech, which put him on the spot. While his two companions very calmly discussed the ups and downs of the grain market, in which both were deeply involved, Don Mateo attempted in vain to reconstruct the collapsed edifice of his oration. He finally became convinced that it would be necessary for him to improvise, because he could no longer expect anything from memory. "For some ideas to occur to me," he thought, "the best thing would be to sincerely regret, with all my heart, the death of Ronzuelos (my last name)." And he tried to be moved, but in vain; despite his sorrowful-looking face, he didn't really give two hoots about the death of (Don Agapito) Ronzuelos, that is, *my* death.

"It's a loss, a veritable loss," he said out loud so that the others would help him to lament my disappearance from, as Pérez Escrich* says, "the great book of the living." "A great loss!" he repeated.

"Yes, but the grain was spoiled, so let's be grateful that it could still be sold," said one of his two cohorts.

"What do you mean, 'sold?'" said Don Mateo. "Ronzuelos was incapable. He was . . . as honest as they come . . . that's it, as honest as they come."

"But who's talking about Ronzuelos, my good man? We're talking about the grain sold by Pérez Pinto—"

"Well, I'm talking about the deceased."

"Ah, yes. He was a character."

"Exactly, a character, which is what we need in this country without—"

"Without characters," his interlocutor finished for him

We arrived at the cemetery, and for the first time the mourners remembered me. The political party that Don Mateo followed even in its erring ways gathered around the casket. There came a moment of silence that I won't call solemn because it wasn't. All those present were waiting for Gómez's speech with malicious curiosity.

"He's inept, and we're going to see that now," several people said.

"He doesn't know how to talk, but he's an energetic man."

"Which is what we need," observed another person.

"Less talk and more action is what the country needs."

"Right! Right! Right!" many of them exclaimed.

"Riiight!" the word echoed in the distance.

"Señores," Don Mateo began, after coughing twice and unbuttoning and buttoning a glove. "Señores, another champion has fallen as though struck by lightning (he didn't know that I had been done in by dampness) in progress's struggle with obscurantism. A model citizen, husband, and liberal, the great civic virtue of consecution shone among his virtues like a superior astral body. A man of uncommon probity, his heart was an open book. A model citizen, husband, and liberal—"

All of a sudden Don Mateo remembered that he had already said this. He shook like a leaf and thought that memory and all ideas were sinking into a darker hole than the grave that was going to swallow me, and in that moment he envied me and would have changed places with the dead man. The cemetery began to spin, the mausoleums were dancing, and the ground was caving in. Lying there in full view of everyone, I had to make a great effort not to laugh and to maintain the gravity befitting a corpse in such a funereal ceremony. The silence of graves reigned once again. Don Mateo sought the elusive word while his listeners waited quietly, with a hush that had the impact of an outburst of boos. The only sounds came from the sputtering of the candles and the whistling of air through the branches of the cypress trees. As he attempted to regain his train of thought, Don Mateo cursed his fate, cursed the deceased, the party, and the disgusting craze for talking, which leads to nothing, because what is sorely lacking is action. "What good has a life of sacrifice done me on the altars or on the wings (Don Mateo had never known whether one says wings or altars in this context) on the wings of freedom," he mused, "if, because I'm no Cicero, I now find myself the butt of ridicule in the eyes of many who are less consequent and less patriotic than I?" He was finally able to pick up what he called the thread of his discourse and proceeded:

"Ah, Señores—Ronzuelos, Agapito Ronzuelos, was a martyr of the idea (of the dampness, my dear man, of the dampness), of the sacred idea, of the pure idea, of the idea of progress! He was not a man of words, I mean he was not an orator, because in this unfortunate country what there is more than enough of is orators and what's needed is character, action, and much consecution."

There was a murmur of approval, and Don Mateo took advantage of it to conclude his speech. The cortege broke up. A little was then said about me in order to criticize the funeral oration of the effective head of the committee.

"The truth is," said one of the mourners, striking a match on the lid of my casket, "the fact is that Don Mateo only came out with a few platitudes."

"That's right," said another. "The usual trite remarks. As to the rest, this poor Ronzuelos was a good person and nothing more. What character was he going to have?"

"Or consecution?"

"What he was, was a great chess player."

"That's a matter of opinion," a third person chimed in. "He won because he cheated. He kept pieces in his pocket."

The one who said this was Roque Tuyo, my rival, the scoundrel who castled after having moved the king!

I couldn't contain myself.

"You lie!" I shouted, jumping out of the casket.

But I didn't see anybody. All the mourners had vanished. Night was beginning to fall, and the moon appeared behind the cemetery walls. The cypresses bent their pointed crowns with a melancholy back-and-forth movement while the wind moaned through their branches, as it did shortly before, when Don Mateo interrupted himself. A grave digger came.

"What're you doing there?" he asked me, a little afraid.

"I'm the deceased," I replied. "Yes, the deceased. Don't be frightened. Listen, I'm renting that niche. I'll pay you so that I can live in it better than if it were occupied by a dead man. I don't want to return to the city of the living. My wife, Perico, Clemente, the party, Don Mateo and . . . especially Roque Tuyo disgust me."

The grave digger went along with everything. We agreed that the cemetery would be my inn, and the niche my bedroom. But, oh, the grave digger was a man too! He sold me out. The following day they came in search of me—Clemente, Perico, my wife, and a delegation from the very bosom of the party, with Don Mateo at its head and at its foot. I resisted as much as I could, defending myself with a femur, but I was outnumbered. They seized me, dressed me in a white straightjacket, like a white pawn, put me in a black compartment, like a square, and here I am, without anybody moving me, threatened by a knight who's not capturing me once and for all and is only toying with me. And with my feet soaking wet, as though I were rice.

Leopoldo Alas, Clarín

"Socrates' Rooster"

CRITO, after closing his master's mouth and eyes, left the other disciples around the corpse and withdrew from the prison, prepared to carry out as soon as possible the last commission that Socrates had given him, perhaps jokingly, but one that he took literally on the chance that the master was indeed serious. As he lay dying, Socrates had uncovered his face, which was concealed to hide from his disciples the sad and ignoble spectacle of the throes of death, and had said what were his last words:

"Crito, we owe a cock to Asclepius. Do not forget to pay this debt." And he said no more.

For Crito that commission was sacred. He did not wish to analyze, he did not wish to examine whether it was more likely that Socrates had only wanted to make a joke, a somewhat ironic one perhaps, or whether it was a question of the master's last will, the master's last wish. Had not Socrates always been, despite Anytus and Meletus's slander, respectful of the popular cult, the official religion? It is true that he ascribed to the myths (which Crito did not label as such, of course) a very sublime and ideal philosophical, symbolical character, but through poetic and transcendental paraphrases he demonstrated his respect for the faith of the Greeks, the positive religion, the cult of the state. And this became manifest in a beautiful episode of his last discourse (for Crito noticed that at times Socrates, in spite of his method of questions and answers, forgot his interlocutors and spoke at great length and in a very flowery manner).

He had described the wonders of the next world with topographic details that conformed more to traditional imagination than to rigorous dialectics and austere philosophy.

And Socrates had not said that he did not believe all of it, but neither did he affirm the reality of what he had described with the stubborn certainty of a fanatic. This, however, was not cause for surprise

274

in someone who, even with respect to his own ideas, like the ones he had set forth to defend the immortality of the soul, recognized, while renouncing illusions and pride, the metaphysical possibility that things might not be as he imagined them. In fine, Crito did not believe that he was impugning the method or the master's conduct by looking for a rooster as soon as possible in order to offer it to the god of medicine.

As if Providence were in the know, no sooner had Crito gone one hundred paces from Socrates' prison than he saw, on top of a wall, in a kind of small, isolated square, a striking rooster with splendid plumage. He had just sprung from a garden to the ridge of that wall, and was getting ready to jump down to the street. He was a rooster on the run, a rooster emancipating himself from miserable servitude.

Crito guessed the bird's intent and waited for him to jump into the small square in order to give chase and catch him. The disciple had gotten it into his head (because man, when he begins to compromise with religious ideas and feelings that he does not find rational, does not stop until he comes up against the most puerile superstition) that the rooster in question, and no other, was the one that Asclepius— that is, Aesculapius—wanted to be sacrificed to him. And so he readily attributed the coincidence of the encounter to the will of the gods.

Apparently the rooster did not share this view, because as soon as he noticed that a man was chasing him he began to run, flapping his wings and crowing quietly, no doubt highly annoyed.

The biped was well-acquainted with the man giving chase, as he had seen him a number of times in the garden, endlessly debating love, eloquence, beauty, etc., etc., while he, the rooster, was seducing a hundred hens in five minutes time, without so much philosophy.

What a situation, thought the rooster as he ran and made ready to fly, which he could do, if the danger increased, *what a situation when these learned men, whom I detest, insist—against all natural laws, laws that they ought to know—on having me for one of their own. It would be a fine kettle of fish if, after escaping the unbearable servitude in which Gorgias* kept me, I fell immediately into the clutches of this poor devil, a middling thinker and much less amusing than my chatterbox of a master.*

The rooster continued running and the philosopher continued giving chase. When the latter was about to lay hands on the former, the rooster flapped his wings, and, flying and leaping in one motion, landed, with the supreme effort induced by panic, on top of the head of a statue of none other than Athena.*

"Oh, you irreverent rooster!" shouted the philosopher, now an inquisitorial fanatic, and pardon the anachronism. And silencing with a pseudo-pious sophism the shouts of the honorable, natural conscience that was saying to him, "Do not steal that rooster," he thought: *Now, on account of your sacrilege, you really do deserve death. You shall be mine, you shall be a sacrifice.*

And the philosopher stood on tiptoe, stretched as far as he could, and jumped up, not very high and looking ridiculous, repeatedly. But it was all in vain.

"Oh, you fake, idealist philosopher!" said the rooster in a Greek worthy of Gorgias himself. "Don't bother. You won't fly even as far as a rooster. What? You're amazed that I can talk? Don't you know me? I'm the rooster from Gorgias' poultry pen. I know you. You're a shadow. The shadow of a dead man. That's the fate of disciples who outlive their masters. They're left here, like ghosts, to frighten children. The inspired dreamer dies, and left behind are his unimaginative disciples, who make of the poetic ideality of the sublime seer one more cause for fear, one more sadness for the world, a superstition that turns to stone."

"Silence, rooster! In the name of the Idea of your species, nature commands you to be quiet."

"I speak and you cackle about the Idea. Listen, I speak without permission from the Idea of my species and because of my ability as an individual. From having heard so much said about rhetoric, that is, the art of speaking for speaking's sake, I've learned a thing or two about the craft."

"And you repay your master by fleeing from his side, by abandoning his house and denying his authority."

"Gorgias is as crazy as you are, albeit more pleasant. Nobody can live alongside such a man. He proves everything, which perplexes and tires people. The person who *demonstrates* all of life leaves it hollow. To know the why of it all is to end up with the geometry of *every*thing and without the substance of *any*thing. Reducing the world to an equation is reducing it to absurdity. Look, why don't you leave, because I can be saying things like this for seventy days and seventy nights. Remember that I'm the rooster of Gorgias the Sophist."

"All right then, because you are a sophist, because you are sacrilegious, and because Zeus wills it, you are going to die. Give yourself up!"

"In a pig's eye! The second-rate idealist who can lay a hand on me has yet to be born. But what's behind this? What cruelty is this? Why are you chasing me?"

"Because Socrates, just before he died, asked me to sacrifice a rooster to Asclepius in thanksgiving for the true health being given to him—liberation, through death, from all ills."

"Socrates said all that?"

"No, he said that we owed a cock to Asclepius."

"So you imagined the rest?"

"And what other meaning can those words have?"

"The most benign one. The one that does not entail blood or errors. To kill me in order to please a god, in whom Socrates did not believe, is to offend Socrates, to insult the true gods . . . and to do me—for I do indeed exist, and am innocent—immeasurable harm, as we know neither all the grief nor all the prejudice that there can be in mysterious death."

"Well, Socrates and Zeus want you to be sacrificed."

"Consider that Socrates spoke with irony, with the serene and bileless irony of genius. His great soul could, without danger, amuse itself with the sublime game of imagining that reason and popular fantasies are harmonious. Socrates, and all creators of a new spiritual life, speak through symbols, and they're rhetoricians when, familiar with the mystery and respectful of what is ineffable in it, they give it poetic forms. The divine love of the absolute touches its soul in this way. But, consider how austere, laconic, and detached of all useless imagery their maxims and moral precepts are when they leave off this sublime game and give lessons to the world."

"Rooster of Gorgias, be silent and die."

"Unworthy disciple, off with you and *you* be silent. Be silent forever. You're unworthy of those of your ilk. All alike. Disciples of genius, deaf and blind witnesses to the sublime soliloquy of a superior conscience, through his illusion and the one you share, you believe that you can immortalize the perfume of his soul when you embalm his doctrine with drugs and prescriptions. You make a mummy of his corpse in order to have an idol. You petrify the idea and use subtle thought like a knife that makes blood flow. Yes, you are the symbol of sad sectarian humanity. From the last words of a saint and a sage you draw as the first consequence the blood of a rooster. If Socrates had been born to confirm the superstitions of his people, he would not have died for the reason that he did, nor would he have been the saint of philosophy. Socrates did not believe in Asclepius, nor was he capable of killing a fly, and much less a rooster, simply to humor the common people."

"I stand by his words. Give yourself up."

Crito picked up a stone, aimed it at the rooster's head, and blood issued from his comb.

Gorgias's rooster lost consciousness, and as he fell he sang out:

"Cock-a-doodle-doo! Destiny be served. The will of imbeciles be done."

And the rooster's blood trickled along the jasper forehead of Pallas Athena.

Notes

Page references to this volume precede each note.

74   *Itálica:* An ancient city in Roman Spain; near present-day Seville.

96   *Maricastaña:* A proverbial character in Spanish lore who symbolizes antiquity.

97   *Charcot* (Jean Martin, 1825–93): French neuropathologist.

99   *cellars . ·. . Prast:* A well-known, and much patronized, imported foods store.

101   *Desdemona's . . . salice:* From *Othello,* Giuseppe Verdi's opera in four acts, first produced on 5 February 1887 at La Scala, Milan.

102   *Battle . . . Economus:* In which the Roman consul Regulus won a decisive victory in the first of the Punic Wars.

108   *Montagut:* A place-name in Catalonia, northeast Spain.

119   *Segre River:* It originates in France and flows south through Catalonia.

134   *Gil Gil:* While it can happen that a Spaniard will have identical surnames, it is unusual for the given name to be the same as the family name. Perhaps Alarcón is suggesting that Gil, as the reader will soon see, had no legitimate last name inasmuch as Juan Gil was not his biological father.

·139   *Espronceda:* José de Espronceda (1808–42), the greatest of Spanish romantic poets. The reference is to his vision of death in canto 1 of his poem "Devil World."

142   *La Granja [San Ildefonso]:* Palace built by Philip V in Segovia, in imitation of the one in Versailles. It is famous for its gardens and fountains.

142   *Philip V* (1683–1746): Duke of Anjou, the first of the Bourbon line to occupy the Spanish throne.

145   *Louis I* (1707–24): Philip V's son by his first wife, María Luisa of Savoy. Louis became king at his father's abdication in 1724, but died a few months later of smallpox.

145   *False . . . dear:* (King) Charles I of Spain and Naples and (Emperor) Charles V of Germany, who renounced the throne of Spain in 1556 in favor of his son Philip II and retired to the monastery of Yuste in Extremadura (west-central Spain).

146–47 *Your . . . fable/I . . . other:* Possibly a reference to Aesop's "The Dog and His Shadow," in which a dog walking across a bridge with a piece of meat in his jaws sees his image in the water and, believing it is another piece, opens his mouth to retrieve it, drops what he has, and ends up with nothing.

170   *Pygmalion . . . lips:* Pygmalion carved an ivory statue of a maiden and fell in love with it. In response to his prayers, Aphrodite brought it to life as Galatea.

170   *Garcilaso de la Vega* (1503–36): Spanish lyric poet of the Golden Age.

239   *Retiro Park:* An enormous public park in the heart of Madrid with numerous walks, fountains, a rose garden, a crystal palace, an artificial lake, zoo, and statuary.

244   *Salamanca district:* Built by José de Salamanca y Mayol (1806–83), Spanish banker, lawyer, and politician who made a fortune in the railroad business.

258   *Espartero* (Baldomero, 1793–1879): Army general and politician who espoused the cause of Queen Isabel II and fought against the Carlists (the supporters of her father's brother).

266   *Roque . . . Café:* Much of this story is told in terms related to chess. *Roque* is the Spanish word for *rook.* In the original it is *Roque tuyo,* i.e., "your rook."

266   *San Ginés:* Which tells us that the action takes place in Madrid; San Ginés is a church on Calle del Arenal, not far from the Plaza Mayor.

267   *Lucretia Borgia:* Drama (1833) by Victor Hugo in which five coffins illuminated by large candles are prepared for guests that Lucretia poisons in act 3.

267   *Danaides' water pots:* The fifty daughters of Danaus, forty-nine of whom were punished in Hades by being condemned to refill leaking water pots forever for having murdered their husbands.

268   *tunic . . . soaked:* To reawaken Heracles' love for her, Deianeira gave him a shirt soaked in a drug and the blood of Nessus (a centaur who had tried to rape her), but as soon as the shirt touched his skin, a burning sensation ate his flesh away, and he sought death on a funeral pyre. Leopoldo Alas, *Cuentos,* ed. Angeles Ezama, 61.

269   *closed . . . him:* The surname Cerrojos—*cerrar:* to close; *ojo:* eyes—represents at this moment a play on words, since Cerrojos closes his "windows," that is, his eyes.

270   *Madoz* (Pascual, 1806–70): Spanish politician.

271   *Pérez Escrich* (Enrique, 1829–97): Popular Spanish dramatist and author of serial novels.

275   *Gorgias* (485–380 B.C.): Greek philosopher and Sophist, that is, one who taught "the art of persuasion."

275   *Athena:* Pallas Athena, whom the Greeks worshiped as the goddess of war, wisdom, and fertility.

Select Bibliography

EDITIONS USED FOR THE TRANSLATIONS
(IN ORDER OF APPEARANCE)

- Caballero, Fernán [Cecilia Böhl de Faber]. "Los deseos" [The wishes], "La niña de los tres maridos" [The girl with three husbands], and "Bella-flor" [Lovely-Flower]. In vol. 5 (CXL) of *Obras*. Madrid: Biblioteca de Autores Españoles, 1961.
- Trueba, Antonio de. "Las aventuras de un sastre" [The adventures of a tailor] and "El yerno del rey" [The king's son-in-law]." In *Cuentos y cantares*. Edición de Alfonso M. Escudero. Madrid: Aguilar, 1959.
- Hartzenbusch, Juan Eugenio. "La hermosura por castigo" [Beauty as Punishment], A comparative reading of two sources. (1) *Obras escogidas, I*. Leipzig: F. A. Brockhaus, 1863; (2) *Cuentistas españoles del siglo XIX*. Edición de Federico Carlos Sáinz de Robles. Madrid: Aguilar, 1962.
- Coloma, Luis, SJ. "Pájaro verde" [Green bird] and "Ratón Pérez" [Pérez the Mouse]. In *Obras completas*, vol. 6: *Lecturas recreativas: Cuentos para niños, V*. Quinta edición definitiva. Madrid: Editorial Razón y Fe, 1956.
- Bécquer, Gustavo Adolfo. "Creed en Dios" [Believe in God] and "La cruz del diablo" [The devil's cross]. In *Leyendas, apólogos y otros relatos*. Edición de Rubén Benítez. Barcelona: Editorial Labor, 1974.
- Alarcón, Pedro Antonio de. "El amigo de la muerte" [Death's friend]. In *Narraciones inverosímiles*. Madrid: Librería General Victoriano Suárez, 1943.
- Valera, Juan. "El pájaro verde" [The green bird] and "El hechicero" [The wizard]. In *El caballero del Azor y otros cuentos*. Selección y prólogo, Carmen Bravo-Villasante. Madrid: Mondadori España, S.A., 1988.
- Pérez Galdós, Benito. "La mula y el buey" [The mule and the ox]" and "La princesa y el granuja" [The princess and the street urchin]. In *Torquemada en la hoguera*. Madrid: Viuda e Hijos de Tello, 1898.
- Alas, Leopoldo, "Clarín." "Mi entierro" [My funeral] and "El gallo de Sócrates" [Socrates' rooster]. In *Cuentos*. Edición de Angeles Ezama. Estudio preliminar de Gonzalo Sobejano. Barcelona: Crítica, Biblioteca Clásica, 1997.

Secondary Sources for the Nine Authors

Alarcón, Pedro Antonio de. *Historia de mis libros*. In *Obras*. Madrid: Sucesores de Rivadeneira, 1909.

Amores García, Montserrat. "Moraleja, moralina y reflexión ética en las adaptaciones de cuentos folclóricos del siglo XIX." *Revista Hispánica Moderna* 53 (2000): 293–303.

Anderson Imbert, Enrique. *El cuento español*. Buenos Aires: Editorial Columbia, 1959.

Baquero Goyanes, Mariano. *El cuento español en el siglo XIX*. Madrid: Consejo Superior de Investigaciones Científicas, 1949.

Balseiro, José A. *Novelistas españoles modernos*. New York: Las Américas, 1963. (Luis Coloma, pp. 334–52.)

Becerro de Bengoa, Ricardo, Fermín Herrán, José María de Arteche, Emiliano de Olano, José María de Lizana, F. Miguel y Badía, Pablo de Alzola, y Juan Ernesto Delmas. *Biblioteca Bascongada*. Tomo I: *En honor de Trueba*. Bilbao: Müller y Zavaleta, 1896.

Benítez, Rubén. Introduction to *Pequeñeces*, by Luis Coloma. Madrid: Cátedra, 1982.

———. Introduction to *Legends and Letters*, by Gustavo Adolfo Bécquer. Translated by Robert M. Fedorchek. Lewisburg, Pa.: Bucknell University Press, 1995.

Berenguer Carisomo, Arturo. *La prosa de Bécquer*. Buenos Aires: Hachette, 1947.

Bravo-Villasante, Carmen. *Biografía de don Juan Valera*. Barcelona: Editorial Aedos, 1959.

Brown, Rica. *Bécquer*. Barcelona: Editorial Aedos, 1963.

Castro Calvo, José María. Introduction to *Obras de Fernán Caballero*. Vol. 1 (CXXXVI). Madrid: Biblioteca de Autores Españoles, 1961.

Cavallo, Agatha. "The Use of Folklore in the Works of Fernán Caballero." Master's thesis, The University of Chicago, 1925.

Cernuda, Luis. "Bécquer y el poema en prosa español." In vol. 2 of *Poesía y literatura*. Barcelona: Seix-Barral, 1964.

Charnon-Deutsch, Lou. *The Nineteenth-Century Spanish Story*. London: Tamesis, 1985.

———. Introduction to *Death and the Doctor: Three Nineteenth-Century Spanish Tales*. Translated by Robert M. Fedorchek. Lewisburg, Pa.: Bucknell University Press, 1997.

Coloma, Luis. *Recuerdos de Fernán Caballero*. In vol. 17 of *Obras completas*. 3d edition. Madrid: Editorial Razón y Fe, 1949.

———. *Relieves y crítica*. In vol. 19 of *Obras completas*. 2d edition. Madrid: Editorial Razón y Fe, 1950. (Págs. 33–50, Cartas de Fernán Caballero.)

DeCoster, Cyrus. *Bibliografía de Juan Valera.* Madrid: Consejo Superior de Investigaciones Científicas, 1970.

———. *Juan Valera.* Boston: Twayne Publishers, 1974.

———. *Pedro Antonio de Alarcón.* Boston: Twayne Publishers, 1979.

Escudero, Alfonso M. Introduction to *Cuentos y cantares,* by Antonio de Trueba. Madrid: Aguilar, 1959.

Ezama, Angeles. Prologue and notes to *Leopoldo Alas, Cuentos.* Barcelona: Crítica, Biblioteca Clásica, 1997.

Ferrer del Río, Antonio. Biography of Juan Eugenio Hartzenbusch in vol. 1 of *Obras Escogidas.* Leipzig: F. A. Brockhaus, 1863.

Flynn, Gerard. *Luis Coloma.* Boston: Twayne Publishers, 1987.

García Viñó, Manuel. *Mundo y trasmundo de las leyendas de Bécquer.* Madrid: Gredos, 1970.

Geddes, J., Jr. Introduction to *La coja y el encogido,* by Juan Eugenio Hartzenbusch. New York: Henry Holt and Company, 1911.

González Blanco, Andrés. *Antonio de Trueba: Su vida y sus obras.* Bilbao: Librería del Villar, 1914.

Herrero, Javier. *Fernán Caballero: Un nuevo planteamiento.* Madrid: Editorial Gredos, 1963.

Iranzo, Carmen. *Juan Eugenio Hartzenbusch.* Boston: Twayne Publishers, 1978.

King, Edmund. *Gustavo Adolfo Bécquer: From Painter to Poet.* Mexico: Editorial Porrua, 1953.

Klibbe, Lawrence. *Fernán Caballero.* New York: Twayne Publishers, 1973.

Kronik, John W. Introduction to *Ten Tales,* by Leopoldo Alas. Translated by Robert M. Fedorchek. Lewisburg, Pa.: Bucknell University Press, 2000.

Martínez Ruiz, José (Azorín). *Andando y pensando.* Madrid: Editorial Páez, 1929.

Miller, Stephen. Introduction to *The Nun and Other Stories,* by Pedro Antonio de Alarcón. Translated by Robert M. Fedorchek. Lewisburg, Pa.: Bucknell University Press, 1999.

Montesinos, José F. *Pedro Antonio de Alarcón.* Zaragoza: Editorial Librería General, 1950.

———. *Introducción a una historia de la novela en España en el siglo XIX.* Madrid: Editorial Castalia, 1955.

———. *Valera o la ficción libre.* Madrid: Gredos, 1957.

———. *Costumbrismo y novela.* 2d edition. Madrid: Editorial Castalia, 1960.

———. *Fernán Caballero. Ensayo de justificación.* México: El Colegio de México, 1961.

———. *Galdós.* Vol. 1. Madrid: Editorial Castalia, 1968.

Montesinos, Rafael. *Bécquer: Biografía e imagen.* Barcelona: Editorial RM, 1977.

Ocano, Armando. *Alarcón.* Madrid: EPESA, 1970.

Oleza, Juan. "Don Juan Valera: Entre el diálogo filosófico y el cuento maravilloso." In *Juan Valera: Creación y crítica*. Actas del VIII Congreso de Literatura Española Contemporánea, Universidad de Málaga, 15, 16, 17 y 18 de noviembre de 1994. Málaga: Publicaciones del Congreso de Literatura Española Contemporánea, 1995.

Pardo Bazán, Emilia. *Obras*. Madrid: Manuel de la Revilla, 1883.

Pardo Canalis, Enrique. *Pedro Antonio de Alarcón*. Madrid: Compañía Bibliográfica Española, 1965.

Ríos, Laura de los. *Los cuentos de Clarín: Proyección de una vida*. Madrid: Revista de Occidente, 1965.

———. Introduction to *La comendadora, El clavo, y otros cuentos*, by Pedro Antonio de Alarcón. Madrid: Cátedra, 1975.

Royo Latorre, María Dolores. Introduction to *Los relatos*, by Pedro Antonio de Alarcón. Salamanca: Universidad de Extremadura, 1994.

Sebold, Russell. *Bécquer en sus narraciones fantásticas*. Madrid: Taurus, 1989.

Shaw, Donald L. *A Literary History of Spain: The Nineteenth Century*. London: Ernest Benn, 1972.

Smith, Alan E. *Los cuentos inverosímiles de Galdós en el contexto de su obra*. Barcelona: Editorial Anthropos, 1992.

———. Introduction to *Benito Pérez Galdós: Cuentos fantásticos*. Madrid: Cátedra, 1996.

Sobejano, Gonzalo. *Clarín en su obra ejemplar*. Madrid: Editorial Castalia, 1985. (Chap. 3, pp. 77–114.)

———. Preliminary study in *Leopoldo Alas, Cuentos*. Barcelona: Crítica, Biblioteca Clásica, 1997.

Van Horne, John. Introduction to *Short Stories by Antonio de Trueba*. Chicago: B. H. Sanborn & Co., 1922. ("La imitación," "Querer es poder," "La mujer del arquitecto," "Crispín y Crispiniano," "El maestro de hacer cucharas.")

Williams, Stanley T. "Washington Irving and Fernán Caballero." *Journal of English and Germanic Philology* 29 (1930): 352–66.

GENERAL FOLKLORE

Aarne, Antti and Stith Thompson. *The Types of the Folktale: A Classification and Bibliography*. Helsinki: Suomalainen Tiedeakatemia, 1961.

Anderson, Graham. *Fairy Tales in the Ancient World*. London: Routledge, 2000.

[The] Arabian Nights. Translated by Husain Haddawy. New York: W. W. Norton and Co., 1990.

[The] Arabian Nights II. Translated by Husain Haddawy. New York: W. W. Norton and Co., 1995.

Bacchilega, Cristina. *Postmodern Fairy Tales: Gender and Narrative Strategies*. Philadelphia: University of Pennsylvania Press, 1997.

Bacchilega, Cristina, and Danielle M. Roemer, eds. *Angela Carter and the*

Literary Märchen. Special Issue of *Marvels & Tales: Journal of Fairy-Tale Studies* 12, no. 1 (1998).

Bettelheim, Bruno. *The Uses of Enchantment: The Meaning and Importance of Fairy Tales.* New York: Alfred A. Knopf, 1976.

Blecher, Lone Thygesen, and George Blecher, eds. and trans. *Swedish Folktales and Legends.* Translated by Lone Thygesen Blecher and George Blecher. The Pantheon Fairy Tale and Folklore Library. New York: Pantheon Books, 1993. (The introduction and "Godfather Death," pp. 309–12.)

Boggs, Ralph Steele. *Index of Spanish Folktales.* Helsinki: Suomalainen Tiedeakatemia/Academia Scientarum Fenica, 1930.

Bottigheimer, Ruth B., ed. *Fairy Tales and Society: Illusion, Allusion, and Paradigm.* Philadelphia: University of Pennsylvania Press, 1986.

————. *Grimms' Bad Girls and Bold Boys: The Moral and Social Vision of the Tales.* New Haven: Yale University Press, 1987.

Busk, Rachel Harriette, ed. "Starving John the Doctor." In *Patrañas or Spanish Stories, Legendary and Traditional.* London: Griffith and Farran, 1870.

Campbell, Joseph. *The Hero with a Thousand Faces.* Princeton: Princeton University Press, 1949.

Carter, Angela. *The Bloody Chamber.* London and New York: Penguin, 1981.

————. *Fireworks: Nine Stories in Various Disguises.* New York: Harper & Row, 1981.

————. *Saints and Strangers.* New York: Penguin, 1987.

————. *Burning Your Boats: Collected Short Stories.* New York: Henry Holt, 1995.

————, ed. *The Virago Book of Fairy Tales.* London: Virago, 1990.

————. *The Second Virago Book of Fairy Tales.* London: Virago, 1992.

Christiansen, Reidar Thoralf. *Studies in Irish and Scandinavian Folktales.* Copenhagen: Rosenkilde and Bagger, 1959.

Cooper, J. C. *Fairy Tales: Allegories of the Inner Life.* Wellington, U.K.: Aquarian Press, 1983.

Darnton, Robert. *The Great Cat Massacre and Other Episodes in French Cultural History.* New York: Basic Books, 1984.

Delarue, Paul. "Les contes merveilleux de Perrault et la tradition populaire." *Bulletin folklorique d'île-de-France* 14 (1953): 511–17.

Dorson, Richard M., ed. *Folklore and Folklife: An Introduction.* Chicago: University of Chicago Press, 1972.

Downey, Gerard, and Gerard Stockman. "Death and the Doctor: A Gaelic Folktale from Tyrone." *Ulster Folklife* 38 (1912): 54–59.

Dundes, Alan, ed. *The Study of Folklore.* Englewood Cliffs, N.J.: Prentice-Hall, 1965.

————. *Interpreting Folklore.* Bloomington: Indiana University Press, 1980.

Franz, Marie-Louise von. *An Introduction to the Interpretation of Fairy Tales.* New York: Spring, 1970.

Friedlander, Judith. "Pacts with the Devil: Stories Told by an Indian Woman from Mexico." *New York Folklore* 16, nos. 1–2 (1990): 25–42.

Fromm, Erich. *The Forgotten Language: An Introduction to the Understanding of Dreams, Fairy Tales, and Myths.* New York: Rinehart, 1951.

Grimm, Jacob, and Wilhelm Grimm. *Grimms' Fairy Tales: Complete Edition.* Translated by Margaret Hunt and [revised by] James Stern. Introduction by Padraic Colum. Commentary by Joseph Campbell. The Pantheon Fairy Tale and Folklore Library. New York: Pantheon Books, 1972.

———. *The Complete Fairy Tales of the Brothers Grimm.* Translated by Jack Zipes. New York: Bantam Books, 1987.

Haase, Donald. "Gold into Straw: Fairy Tale Movies for Children and the Culture Industry." *The Lion and the Unicorn* 12, no. 2 (1988): 193–207.

———. "Feminist Fairy-Tale Scholarship: A Critical Survey and Bibliography." *Marvels & Tales: Journal of Fairy-Tale Studies* 14, no. 1 (2000): 15–63. (Includes eighteen pages of a very extensive bibliography.)

Hagen, Rolf. "Perraults Märchen und die Brüder Grimm." *Zeitschrift für Deutsche Philologie* 74 (1955): 392–410.

Heuscher, Julius E. *A Psychiatric Study of Fairy Tales: Their Origin, Meaning and Usefulness.* Rev. ed. Springfield, Mass.: Charles C. Thomas, 1974.

Jones, Steven Swann. *The Fairy Tale: The Magic Mirror of the Imagination.* New York: Twayne, 1995.

Llano Roza de Ampudia, Aurelio de, ed. "El médico y la muerte." In *Cuentos asturianos recogidos de la tradición oral,* 69–70. Madrid: Rafael Caro Raggio Mendizábal, 1925.

Lüthi, Max. *The European Folktale: Form and Nature.* Translated by John D. Niles. Bloomington: Indiana University Press, 1986.

———. *The Fairytale as Art Form and Portrait of Man.* Translated by Jon Erickson. Bloomington: Indiana University Press, 1987.

McGlathery, James M., ed. *The Brothers Grimm and Folktale.* Urbana: University of Illinois Press, 1991. (Fourteen essays by well-known Grimms scholars like Ruth B. Bottigheimer, Linda Dégh, Alan Dundes, Gonthier-Louis Fink, Betsy Hearne, Wolfgang Mieder, and others.)

Murphy, G. Ronald. *The Owl, the Raven, and the Dove: The Religious Meaning of the Grimms' Magic Fairy Tales.* New York: Oxford University Press, 2000.

Perrault, Charles. *Perrault's Complete Fairy Tales.* Translated by A. E. Johnson et al. New York: Dodd, Mead, 1961.

Propp, Vladimir. *Morphology of the Folktale.* Translated by Laurence Scott. 2d rev. ed. Austin: University of Texas Press, 1968.

———. *Theory and History of Folklore.* Minneapolis: University of Minnesota Press, 1984.

Review of Contemporary Fiction 14, no. 3 (1994). Special Angela Carter [and Tadeusz Knowicki] issue.

Risco, Antonio. *Literatura y fantasía.* Madrid: Taurus, 1982.

———. *Literatura fantástica de lengua española.* Madrid: Taurus, 1987.

Roemer, Danielle M., and Cristina Bacchilega, eds. *Angela Carter and the Fairy Tale.* Detroit, Mich.: Wayne State University Press, 2000. (The book form, with an introduction by the editors, of the special issue of *Marvels & Tales: Journal of Fairy-Tales Studies* 12, no. 1 [1998].)

Rowe, Karen E. "Feminism and Fairy Tales." *Women's Studies: An Interdisciplinary Journal* 6 (1979): 237–57.

Silver, Carole G. *Strange and Secret Peoples: Fairies and Victorian Consciousness.* New York: Oxford University Press, 1999.

Tatar, Maria. *Off with Their Heads! Fairy Tales and the Culture of Childhood.* Princeton: Princeton University Press, 1992.

Thompson, Stith. *Motif Index of Folk-Literature.* Helsinki: Suomalainen Tiedeakatemia/Academia Scientiarum Fenica, 1932-36.

———. *The Folktale.* New York: Holt, Rinehart & Winston, 1946.

———. *Motif Index of Folk Literature.* Bloomington: Indiana University Press, 1955.

———. *Motif-Index of Folk Literature: A Classification of Narrative Elements in Folktale, Ballads, Myths, Fables, Mediaeval Romances, Exempla, Jest Books, and Local Legends.* 2d ed. 6 vols. Folklore Fellows' Communications, 106–11. Copenhagen: Rosenkilde and Bagger, 1955–58.

———, ed. *One Hundred Favorite Folktales.* Bloomington: Indiana University Press, 1968.

Todorov, Tzvetan. *Introduction à la littérature fantastique.* Paris: Editions du Seuil, 1970.

Untermeyer, Louis, and Byrna Untermeyer, eds. *The Complete Household Tales of Jakob and Wilhelm Grimm.* 2 vols. New York: Heritage, 1962.

Vidal de Battini, Berta Elena. *Cuentos y leyendas populares de la Argentina.* 9 vols. Buenos Aires: Ediciones Culturales Argentinas, 1980–84.

Waelti-Walters, Jennifer. *Fairy Tales and the Female Imagination.* Montreal: Eden, 1982.

Warner, Marina. *From the Beast to the Blonde: On Fairy Tales and Their Tellers.* New York: Farrar, Straus, and Giroux, 1995.

———, ed. Introduction to *Wonder Tales: Six French Stories of Enchantment.* Translated by Gilbert Adair et al. New York: Farrar, Straus, and Giroux, 1996. (Contains: Marie-Catherine d'Aulnoy, "The White Cat"; Marie-Jeanne L'Héritier de Villandon, "The Subtle Princess"; Henriette-Julie de Murat, "Bearskin"; Charles Perrault and François-Timoléon de Choisy, "The Counterfeit Marquise"; Henriette-Julie de Murat, "Starlight"; and Marie-Catherine d'Aulnoy, "The Great Green Worm.")

Yolen, Jane, ed. *Favorite Folktales from Around the World.* New York: Pantheon Books, 1986.

Zipes, Jack. *Breaking the Magic Spell: Radical Theories of Folk and Fairy Tales.* Austin: University of Texas Press, 1979.

———. *Fairy Tales and the Art of Subversion: The Classical Genre and the Process of Civilization.* New York: Wildman, 1983.

———. *Fairy Tale as Myth/Myth as Fairy Tale*. Lexington: University Press of Kentucky, 1994.

———. *Happily Ever After: Fairy Tales, Children, and the Culture Industry*. New York: Routledge, 1997.

———. *When Dreams Came True: Classical Fairy Tales and Their Tradition*. New York and London: Routledge, 1999.

———, ed. *Spells of Enchantment: The Wondrous Fairy Tales of Western Culture*. New York: Viking, 1991.

———. *The Oxford Companion to Fairy Tales*. Oxford and New York: Oxford University Press, 2000. (An altogether outstanding resource volume, this *Companion* contains a very useful introduction ["Towards a Definition of the Literary Fairy Tale"] by Zipes, a plot summary of the major tales, minibiographies of writers, artists, and illustrators, and survey articles on countries, as well as such related topics as music, art, film, cartoons, etc. It provides, in addition, a thirty-page bibliography of fairy-tale studies, a survey of classical and contemporary collections, and a list of specialist journals.)

———, *The Great Fairy Tale Tradition: From Straparola and Basile to the Brothers Grimm*. Selected and translated by Jack Zipes. New York: W. W. Norton, 2001. (See especially his essay, "Cross-Cultural Connections and the Contamination of the Classical Fairy Tale," pp. 845–69.)